A CONSPIRACY OF ANGELS

BOOKS BY **FRANK ROSS**

A CONSPIRACY OF ANGELS   1987

THE SHINING DAY   1981

THE 65TH TAPE   1979

SLEEPING DOGS   1978

DEAD RUNNER   1977

A CONSPIRACY OF ANGELS

Frank Ross

ATHENEUM   1987   NEW YORK

Library of Congress Cataloging-in-Publication Data

Ross, Frank, 1938–
    A conspiracy of angels.

    I. Title.
PR6068.O8187C6   1987   823'.914   86–47695
ISBN 0–689–11853–8

Published simultaneously in Canada by Collier Macmillan Canada, Inc.
Manufactured by Fairchild Graphics, Fairfield, Pennsylvania
Designed by Kathleen Carey
First Edition

FOR MY DEAREST LOUISE—

*With love and gratitude
and never-say-good-bye.*

BOOK **ONE**

Let a man accept his destiny,
No pity and no tears.

EURIPIDES

ONE

The city lay dead on a funeral pyre of neon: first the river running blue-black, snaily slow, left to right, then a cluster of flashing towers hurling commercial fire at a sky the color of apricot jam. No movement to speak of on the far bank except for the weave and pulse of headlights, and from the shallow graves of the streets no more than the muted snore of suppressed exhausts, but over here, on the near side . . .

The watcher ruled a toy Armageddon. From the eighth floor of the Intercontinental Hotel he held the city in the palm of his hand. Figuratively speaking. Armageddon. The image appealed to his growing sense of importance, and to savor it properly, he put down his binoculars and dabbed a handkerchief to his eyes. Perfect night for it, he thought. "Perfect night for it," he murmured to reassure himself.

The camera operator jerked his head up irritably. "Too much light iss," he snapped tartly, but then he was German, a purist, local labor. More to the point, he was a victim of the decadent American habit of paying according to results, so this whole evening could yet turn out to be a waste of time and effort: no film, no paycheck. Still fretting, he stepped around the camera and stuck his head out the window.

Directly below, on a floodlit slab of concrete wedged between the Untermainkai and the river, a swirl of roller skaters cruised the Nizza rink with the single-minded fluidity of a watch movement, their pace locked to a sedate orchestral version of "Can't Buy Me Love." In the room they could hear the music quite plainly, the faint familiarity of it rising through the open window on a hot breath of traffic blast and people hum, as sad over that distance as a child's sobbing, a lost sound. The window was open to give the camera maneuvering space if necessary and also because the German had a thing about the image-distorting properties of modern glass, but open or shut, it would have been just as hot; Frankfurt was in the grip of a spring heat wave; the city was an inferno.

The cameraman returned to his mark, bent once more to clarify an already perfect focus, and hissed through his teeth at the gauzy fuzz created by fifty different light sources bombarding the atmosphere between camera and target area. Floodlights, streetlights, headlights, neon—and all of it filtered through that God-cursed lacework of chain-link fence around the rink. What was he supposed to do—work miracles?

"Ten-thirteen," the watcher intoned comfortably. He'd had a tall stool sent up from the bar to give him added height. "See him yet?"

"No!"

The watcher cleared his throat and began to sing softly in a light, not unpleasing tenor. "Can't buy me lu-huhu-huv, Can't buy me luh-huv, Can't buy me—" Then the cameraman broke in with a violent "Here!" and in a flak burst of German as good as a declaration of war: "Stand still, you bastard, or I'll kill you dead!" He chuckled, a dry little chuckle, to show it was just the tension.

"Where is he? Where!" The watcher swung his glasses left and right in panic. "Where, dammit?"

"The rink, on the outside. From the left end, five posts."

"Got him! Okay, great. Now don't lose him, you hear? Hold that baby real tight for papa."

But the cameraman had cut him out of his life, cut out everyone, everything but the small, hunched figure in the shapeless, colorless raincoat: the star of the evening, ladies and gentlemen, now pacing in nervous circles around the peppermint stage of the viewing screen.

4

The German let go a short, sharp chuckle. Payment according to results, eh? So here results iss.

The tune sliced deep into Larry Bartell's subconscious, and before he knew it, he was weeping. Real tears; hot, coruscating, life-shortening tears.

It was happening a lot lately. No warning, no reason he could ever pin down precisely at the time; just some half-assed association of time and place popping up out of the old cold memory cupboard and—bang!—the tears flowed. Ridiculous. Brain wrack, Mr. Bartell, sir—you copy? You dig? Blown fuses, cerebral disconnection. A dying shame, old man.

At times there was only one way to shake off the monkey on your back, and that was to walk away from it, so he stomped over to the rink fence and glared at the skaters as if it were their fault. He could hate the skaters on sight. Hate the freaked-out kids with their Mohawk haircuts and clothes you wouldn't believe. Hate the teenyboppers in microminis and the fags in leather and lace. Hate the bank clerks plugged into Walkmans that short-circuited the brain, and the mid-forties fanatics who thought they'd found the back door to eternal life. He hated them all, hated their pathetic posturing and their bromide self-delusion. The whole damn world was drowning in self-delusion.

You hear what I'm thinking! he shouted in his head. You're dead, you crazy pricks—you're all dead!

But he didn't shout because the tears were talking. Because the drink or two he'd taken awhile back had blunted his tongue. Because he had a fugitive's fear of bright light. And because he was presently out of his mind with hope and scared witless for the fine, soft skin of his vulnerable neck.

"Can't buy me lu-huhu-huv, Can't buy me lu-huv, Can't buy me—"

Who was he crying for anyway? Lydia? The kids? The man he was, boy he had been . . . ?

Don't answer that! Any of it!

5

He turned his back on the skaters and faced the Main, though there was precious little comfort there for a man in his condition. River of no return, you could say. One more river to cross. A small, neat German train chuckled by on the Hafenbahn and disappeared under the Untermainbrücke, its taillights winking. What's the Morse for s-u-c-k-e-r? he wondered, watching them go. What happens if the kid says no? What happens if he stays away? What happens . . .

Out in the stream a tug throbbed throatily against the tide, stringing three loaded lighters in its wake, and he recalled a line from Miko's creed: "The Germans never sleep." Verse One, Chapter One of Holy Writ. On land, on sea, or in the air—right, Miko?—the German antiterrorist branch never shuts both eyes at once. Every shadow a cop, every stone an eye. Miko knew.

If the kid didn't come soon . . .

He would do what, for crying out loud? Walk away? Run? Lead a pure and blameless life till death did him part asunder?

He pulled the raincoat more tightly about him because heat was life, even in a heat wave, and found himself wishing again that he'd made time to shave, get a haircut, primp and preen a little, shape up, because appearances were conclusive, fact of life; with inside straights like Todd Hales, probably all-conclusive. You are what you wear. What you seem. What you can persuade an unforgiving world to believe. Sure—and wishing you looked some other way was the same as wishing you were someone else, someplace else, some planet else, some easy-living fat cat with a wife to fetch and carry for, kids to feed, and quids pro quo, milord of the Harvard campus, a caged somebody feted and fawned on; and that road led to Basketville, baby. Right, Miko? That road was yesterday.

"Can't buy me lu-huhu-huv, Can't buy me—"

Can't buy me yesterday either.

He looked at his watch, the one Miko had bought him last month in Geneva to replace the one he'd hocked to buy booze. Time: 10:16. Will he, won't he, will he, won't he . . .

He needed a woman; that was hang-up number one, the root of the problem. What he needed was a toothsome lay. Medicinal. But first a drink because without a couple of slugs beforehand he couldn't deliver; the sacred flame was on miser heat these days. "Dying is a farce," he informed the river loudly, safe under the loudspeakers' boom. "Dying is a farce and socially disadvantageous." Or as Nietzsche—another unsleeping German—might have put it, "The dying are better off dead."

Right. Better dead than dying. No question. And wasn't that what he'd read in the jovial eye of the Zurich witch doctor the day he delivered the glad tidings? "Cirrhosis off ze liffer, Herr Bartell. Also, you a naarsty bleedt off ze stomach hef. Ent enlaaarched veintz at ze endt off ze oesophagus. Zerefore, bloodt you vomit. Iss logical, no?"

Iss logical, yes, and thank you, Doc, for a truly wonderful diagnosis. You win the coconut and the big cigar.

He peered anxiously into the shifting dark-light, but still no human shape obtruded. He's watching me, he thought, the way I'd be watching him: from the shadows across the Hafenbahn tracks, or the far side of the rink, or up there by the Untermainbrücke, with glasses. Make 'em wait, make 'em sweat: first rule of the game. Instinctively he moved back to the fence, to the swirl of human activity and light and sound. Sure, the kid would watch. But what else would he do?

He tried to recollect something comforting about Todd Hales, anything at all that gave him human scale, but after all these years there was no subtle shading left, not a glimmer; just the vital statistics. Six feet five, 215 pounds, mostly muscle; a running back for Notre Dame who made all-American; two years at Harvard to clinch his master's. (In what? Couldn't recall, but probably political history because he'd been assigned to Vin Thurmond's clutches, which meant Langley had owned him even then.) Blond boy, blue eyes. Should have been a—

"Don't turn around." The voice spoke from behind, very distinctly but with great gentleness. "Just relax. Hands up on the wire as if you're watching the nice people. Now."

Shock kills. From somewhere Larry Bartell found the presence of mind to obey. "Right! Fine! Got you! No problem!" Voice cracking.

A hand touched his shoulder from very high up and ran lightly down his right chest and side, up his leg into his crotch, down the left leg, up the left side; turned him slowly around. "You mind opening the coat?" Todd Hales towered over him, the colossus of cliché, flesh made mountain. Belted raincoat, silk scarf, dark suit.

"Hey, Todd. It's good to—"

Bad moment for social intimacies. Hales took a step back. "Now the jacket. Wide. Wider. Good, hold it there." He had the longest arm Larry had ever seen. Its hand dipped into Larry's inner pocket, came up with the French passport, flicked it open, flicked it shut, replaced it, dropped down to flush the side pockets. "Pull the pants up. From your *shoes*. I need to see your socks. Okay. Good."

Satisfied, he stepped back another pace and squinted into the mist of lights over Larry's head as if he had an arrangement with the Almighty. Then he turned Larry around to face the rink, presumably to get a better look at his face.

"We alone, Mr. Bartell?" His voice had rather less passion in it than a computer-generated phone message, but enormous depth.

"I am if you are." Larry flashed the famous grin; they used to say his grin was irresistible, but it seemed to have lost its power to charm. "Come on, kid, you've been watching me ten, fifteen minutes already."

Hales gazed down at him blank-faced. "I asked if you were alone, sir." The sir was terrifying in its impersonality.

"Yes, I'm alone."

"That's good." He edged a yard to his right and glanced back quickly toward the hotel. Watcher, Larry guessed, heart banging; he's got a static post back there, a minder. With a rifle? A camera? Probably both. "This is the deal, Mr. Bartell," Hales

8

was saying. "Give me any reason for thinking this is a trap and I'll kill you, understand?" He displayed something black and angular in a hand bigger than a baseball mitt.

"No trap," Larry said eagerly. "Believe me."

At which point the pains came on: hot knives skewering up from the liver, the bowels, the gut. Dying pains. His face contorted, and he sucked air hard, deep, but Hales was concentrating on one thing at a time. His face, at no stage of his development a revealing window on the soul, had acquired the wooden inscrutability of the legalized hood; his eyes, a discouraging acrylic flatness.

"I'll give you five minutes, Mr. Bartell. You say it in five or you don't say it. Agreed?"

Larry swallowed pain in monstrous doses. "Fine with me. Sure. Whatever you say."

"So what's this all about, Mr. Bartell? How'd you find me?"

"I—" The pain reached his chest, and for a moment he could feel it fingering his heart. "I saw you leaving the hotel last night. With the Arab. Recognized him, recognized you."

"You were in the hotel?"

"Outside. In a car, outside."

"Doing what, Mr. Bartell?"

"Waiting."

"For whom?"

The pain nearly doubled him over, bent him in the middle, exploded there in red mist and agony.

"You ill, Mr. Bartell?" There was no trace of concern in the question, only the mechanical curiosity cops and spies set store by: name address age sex alive/dead. As he asked it, Hales's blue eyes swept the area like a lighthouse beam. Give me any reason for thinking this is a trap . . .

"I said, are you ill?"

"Nothing. Really. Look—"

"You're in pain. What kind of pain?"

Larry swallowed a lot of air at a single gulp. "Liver. I have this—" He nearly fell. Knives! Ten times worse than yesterday; a thousand times worse than last week. "Look, I don't have *time* for this. I'm—"

Hales came forward very fast, sniffed his breath, swung away again, cute as a dancer, all on his toes. "You had treatment?"

A needle in the liver, Miko. They stick a needle in your liver and munch-munch suck-suck at your life's meat. Miko, are you listening to me? They do that, and then they tell you, "My, oh, my, Herr Bartell, you're bleeding inside; inside your stomach, Herr Bartell. Come back next week, and we'll tell you when to book the hearse."

The final immobilizing pain ripped open his belly, and as the eruption began, he tried to duck it. He could do that occasionally, think around it, outrun it emotionally, but it was too fast for him this time. The music boiled up around him and the dazzle from the rink sent his eyes climbing up into his skull for deliverance. Can't buy me yesterday, Miko. Can't buy me a ticket home. As he fell, giant hands caught him, swung him up, and dumped him full length on a bench at the far end of the fence. But Larry Bartell, dead or dying, had his own way with pain: You don't sit *on* it, you sit *around* it, buster, and not for a second, not for a racing heartbeat, do you black out. In the presence of Hales or Miko or the Holy Ghost. He push-pulled himself into a half-sitting position, head in his hands, while his breath screeched over his larynx and his bones turned to jelly.

Stars wheeled in mighty courses in his head. The skaters were back with the Beatles, "Michelle."

"Todd?"

"Still here, Mr. Bartell. Can you talk?"

"I'm okay. It comes and goes. Nothing, believe me." Don't say *believe me!*

"You said you were waiting. I asked for whom."

"Contact. Somebody here in Frankfurt."

"Name?"

"In good time! Christ, man, give me *time!*"

"All right. So why ask me out here?" His hand touched the pocket with the gun in it, slipped inside.

"I—" When it came to it, the words had a special banality all their own. "I want to come home."

The boy's huge head canted right, owllike. "Home?"

"Home. I want to go back."

"You!"

"Me."

Hales suppressed a look of acute disbelief. "You mean you want a pardon? Amnesty?"

"I just want to come home. They can do what the hell they like."

"Why now?"

Larry took a deep breath, then let it out without using it. "Because"—he raised his head, squinted up to where Hales was—"because the pain in my gut is—"

"That's not a reason, Mr. Bartell."

"Because I'm *dying*, goddammit! Because I don't have any more *time!*"

"I see. So what am I supposed to do about it?"

"You'll think of something."

"Name it."

Larry's eyes flooded with tears as the pain came back again, scalpeling back: up into the stomach wall, the liver, the lungs. "You were Vin Thurmond's boy at Harvard, Langley material. Now you're carrying bags for Arab oil ministers in Frankfurt. For chrissake, Todd, you're Company."

"Is that why you wrote me the note? Got me here?"

"Why else?"

"Then you wasted your time, Mr. Bartell. I'm not Company."

"You are! You were—"

"I'm in private security, Mr. Bartell."

"But you were—"

"And now I'm in private security."

A finger as broad as Larry's wrist slipped under Larry's chin and tipped his head back. "But—you listening to me, Mr. Bartell?—maybe I can arrange something. Is that what you want? At certain levels, in certain situations, I can make a connect." His voice was low-pitched, smooth, sleepy sibilants; so sleepy Larry's head fell off Hales's big fat finger, got top-heavy and fell. The big hand caught it instantly. "You hear me, Mr. Bartell? What do you say?"

Larry shook his head and tried to make the words come, chewed at them, rolled them around his salt mine of a mouth. "Garfield!" He spit it out, sobbed it out, choked on it.

"Is that *Garfield?*"

"Garfield!"

"First name? Address? Garfield who?"

From a billion miles behind him Larry heard the crescendo roar of massed wheels in formation. "Lucas. Lucas H. Garfield. State Department. Reach him. Get someone to—"

"And tell him what?" Hales's face came down to his and hung there, an inch away, like a satellite moon.

"That I want to"—Hopeless! The world is deaf!—"to come home."

"And why would he care? Supposing he doesn't care."

"*Tell* him!" Larry wept, the tears like molten lead, hot and heavy, stinging his eyes, burning his cheeks. "Tell him, tell the girl. He'll know. He'll *care!*"

"Girl? What girl?" Hales's head still hovered, filling the sky. "She have a name?"

"Garfield." No more, no more.

"And if Garfield says no, what then, Mr. Bartell?" Mister mister mister.

"He won't. He'll know. I'll have goods to trade. Names, places, connections. Tell him. Tell Garfield."

"And what am I supposed to do—take you to him? Take you back to the hotel and—"

"No! No." Too many emotions crowded in at once, hysteria uppermost. "Tell him, he'll know."

"And how does he reach you?" Hales's voice purred up from the bottom of a very deep and lonely well, as sonorous as God's. "How does he get to tell you yes or no, Mr. Bartell?"

"The girl. Tell him go talk to the girl. He'll—"

A new wave of pain swept through him: a blanket of pain so complete, so intense, so soon after the last, that he let it sweep the last barricades of resistance aside. No stopping it. The hot knives turned in his gut one more time, and he let go. Let go.

Then the pain took him for a long, long ride down to the creepy, painless dark, and soon he felt nothing at all but free.

Cool, loose, and free.

TWO

Luke Garfield was reading when he heard the rowboat coming: a faint splash of oars three hundred yards or so away, unmistakable. For a moment the hairs stood erect on the backs of his hands. Here it comes, he thought. Maybe.

He glanced at the wheelhouse chronometer—2:03—and registered the fact that it was dead low water out there, though the state of the tide could have no possible bearing on his living or dying. Fleetingly the question Who goes rowing for pleasure at two in the morning off Mount Desert Island, Maine? flew into his mind unbidden and flew out just as quickly because it was not only rhetorical but academic. For antique spies who love life there can be only one answer to a question like that: Fear the worst!

Especially at two in the morning.

He switched off the reading light, closed his book, slipped it tidily into the rack between Adlard Coles's *Heavy Weather Sailing* and Heaton's *Singlehanders*. No harm in leaving things shipshape if they have to be left. He stood up, pulled a knitted black wool cap over his beacon of white hair, and waited for his pulse to steady. Die economically, die clean, he thought mawkishly. Whose motto was that?

When the final crisis came—*if* it came, if this were it—there'd be little enough he could do to defend himself; he'd always known that. There'd be no running away. First, because he was unarmed. Second, because he was alone. Third, the clincher, because he was older than old, and though tough durable resilient resourceful shrewd—all the macho vanities—he would be no match for a skilled young killer. And that's who they'd send someday, should it please them, God forbid. They, in this labored instance, being any one of several thousand enemies he'd made in a long and distinguished career.

He grasped the afterhatch rail and heaved himself silently up and out, dropped to his knees in the cockpit well, raised the flap on the binnacle locker, took out the glasses. Nice and slow, no noise. Now, who goes there, this still, flat night? Friend or foe?

Well, would it matter so much one way or the other? he mused, keeping the conversation alive in his head. After all, some of his best enemies were friends, weren't they? Honestly? And the best enemies of all were family: children of the intelligence family, men he'd lived and plotted with for the better part of a drawn-out lifetime, men he'd hounded for nearly a generation during his reign as chairman of the National Security Advisory Committee (the Cleaners, as presidential insiders knew it). And yes, hounded was the right word. You pursue a man over his principles, hound him for his weaknesses. His brief had been to monitor the infernal urges of the American intelligence community—a laudable aim in theory, even noble— but what it had meant in practice was needling ambitious fools till they broke; rooting out corruption, featherbedding, privateering, internecine warfare, treachery, and all the other petty sins of the flesh; exacting toll from the culprits; cracking knuckles till they bled.

Some people believed that Lucas H. Garfield had brought the CIA to its knees and its supporters to the brink of impotence in his day. Certainly he'd harried the cowboys of the trade, raked up their dirt, displayed the evidence, pronounced banishments, buried the facts, cleaned stables, made himself a positive pain in the stern gland to a whole generation of secret savants, many of whom, having survived his punishments, had no doubt been restored to office, full of bile and a passion to get even. And why not? It was in the nature of the trade. Forgiveness lay within heaven's gift, not Langley's. Amen.

Trouble was—he poked his head cautiously over the cockpit coaming—they had him on toast here, friend and foe alike. Lucas Haines Garfield, White House myrmidon, reduced now to Luke Garfield, senior citizen, God help him—an antique nobody ten months into the padded cell of retirement, a superannuated schoolboy playing yachtsman as he'd always dreamed he would someday, beating Down East under all plain sail in a fifty-foot gaff-rigged cutter that was older than he by sixty or more caulk-seamed summers. Built to outlast eternity, he'd assured Polly, iroko on oak, flexibility on strength, can't beat it.

Pity he hadn't been built to the same specifications, she'd said with a sniff.

Sound woman, Polly. Sensible. Recognized lunacy in the male when she saw it.

He quartered the inlet with the glasses, keeping the mizzen tabernacle and the falls between him and the approaching boat. No moon tonight, no wind: well chosen. But the oars splashed again, and he saw the flash of foam. Caught a crab, whoever he was. Or fouled the bottom. Not a local man, then, or he'd have known better than to run in close under the point. There were shallows in there under the pine fringe, a rock-strewn minefield ready to rip your bottom out if you took it too fast at low water. So, not a boatman either, and—his ears caught a new sound—muffled oars and rowlocks. Priceless, the way landsmen thought you could stop noise from traveling over water. Yes, there he was again, making for deeper water, all arms. The boat itself was low-cut, narrow, more an exercise rig than a work boat, a skiff with outrider rowlocks. So what was he planning, this amateur? To circle *The Duchess* and look for a way in? He'd tie up on the port side, then, when he saw the rope ladder slung from the midships chain plate.

Right.

He felt for the boat hook rack; fingered a stout oak stave and rejected it; plucked a newfangled aluminum one from the snap clamps and unscrewed the rubber plug at its handling end. He hefted it for feel. It didn't *look* much like a rifle barrel, admittedly, but in the pitch-dark, at two in the morning, pressed to your temple as you came over the side, it might sure as hell feel like one. Heaven help him, it was the best he could do.

The skiff came perilously close on the starboard quarter, turned in the nick of time, and yawed wildly as the rower shipped oars and stood up. *The Duchess* stirred unhappily to her anchor as a pair of inexperienced hands grabbed her toe rail, but the freeboard was far too high for a man to climb aboard unboosted, too high even for a very tall man to get a look on deck—and this man was very tall indeed. He handed himself along the hull to the bows, encountered the anchor chain, and wobbled under its fall to the port side. All this Garfield followed in his mind's eye as he flattened out on the wheelhouse roof forward of the hatch, the boat hook extended barrel first, his heart beating drums in his head. He heard the skiff slip-slap down to midships, where *The Duchess*'s tumble home bulged so extravagantly she might have been carrying twins. Then the slats of the ladder clicked, wood on wood, and Garfield heard the voice in his head say quite distinctly, "Easy, son; have a care."

A hand appeared over the toe rail and felt around, fastened on a deck cleat, and lashed the painter. Another hand followed. Black, this one. Gloved. A head rose cautiously, also black, a swarm of curls. A face. A fanged mustache.

Garfield pressed the open end of the boat hook against the

curly head and said softly, "One more step, my friend, and I'll blow your brain back to Martha's Vineyard." He felt a visceral shock jar up the pole to his hand, and switched on the flashlight. The beam struck the intruder full in the face, and in his shock he flinched wildly and almost fell.

"Luke, for crying out loud, will you *can* that! Please!" bawled Alfred Goldman.

Before they went below, Garfield restored the rubber plug to the pole and snapped it back in its retaining clamp.

"A *boat hook*?" Goldman said incredulously.

"Not loaded," Garfield assured him.

Only the talk was loaded.

It went around and around like the fatal bullet in an unresolved game of Russian roulette while both men tensed for the bang.

Goldman's tension was the product of shock. Garfield's grew out of resentment. Plain resentment.

On deck, in the starlit dark, Goldman had struck him as pretty much the man he'd known: a rangy ascetic, a lean tower with curls, a Tatar horseman a long way from the steppes. And there was comfort in that. But the moment they went below, the saloon lights revealed discrepancies, small worry points of taste and scale that caught Garfield off-balance. He wasn't prepared for them. The famous curls, for instance, a Washington landmark, were now aggressively longer, fuller, cut to an unmistakably Afro style. Goldman's mustache grew to his jawline and gave him a baleful Arab cast (presumably deliberate, presumably good for business). His clothes were sober enough and no doubt vastly expensive but in small ways shrieked of exotic chic. And he *glittered*: two heavy gold rings; a gold identification bracelet; a gold coiled snake amulet; gold shoe buckles; a fine gold chain around the knot of his tie. And the scarlet handkerchief tucked nonchalantly into his sleeve was a howling affectation by any standard of American dress.

Fred Goldman gave off the shallow glister of opportunism, the flash vulgarity new money brings, no matter how well you handle it.

So—resentment. It hurt. And to make it worse, Garfield felt responsible. Fred Goldman had been his man, after all, his creation. In the late sixties he'd plucked him from a promising niche in army intelligence and made him his right hand. Fred had been an original: incisive, tough, cool—and correspondingly honest—a puritan in many ways but a fighter, too, all the qualities Garfield aspired to in his successor. What he couldn't have foreseen was that Fred was also fatally flawed, as saints are flawed. When the time came to fight the last battle, Fred opted for martyrdom, turned the other cheek. A lot of things were responsible, of course, not least the catastrophe of America's defeat in Southeast Asia, when the Cleaners were sucked into the vortex along with every other government agency. Expediency and justification became the overnight godheads, "the good of the people" the handy cure-all. The Cleaners were instructed to avert their eyes from certain glaring anomalies in the conduct of American undercover activities at home and abroad; they were ordered to bend with the wind, look on the bright side, count their blessings. Garfield's response had been to carry on the fight behind closed doors, to take them all on: Langley, State, Defense, the Pentagon, the president. Goldman's was to watch and wait and finally to wash his hands of the whole sad carnival. Principle, he said, as if he'd invented it, and went back to teaching literature at Stanford.

So it came as a shock to hear that he'd slipped back into harness—private harness, this time: 1979, a good year for decisions. The shock waves of world terrorism were registering crisis levels on the Richter scale just then; every businessman in the free world worth kidnapping was braying for protection; individuals, corporations, and governments were giving new impetus to the whole notion of security. And Fred had cashed in on it; he'd put together a protection agency of international scope and potency. Word had it that he was now well on the way to his tenth million.

Which for quite other reasons also hurt, as all sellouts hurt, for in the board rooms of commercial security what-you-know runs a long second to who-you-know, and Fred's cachet was that he knew everybody. That had been Garfield's personal bequest to him, and in the old days Fred would have been the first to admit that such bequests are privileged and not for sale. But then, in the old days Fred had worn his style on the *inside*.

The longer he sat, the less Goldman seemed inclined to want to get to the point. His talk rambled through old times, old faces, old ghosts and went on from there to wallow in that brand of locker room prattle Polly defined as verbal silence. The clock showed 2:30 when Garfield decided it had gone on long enough. He topped up his protégé's whiskey.

"What do you say we take it for granted you're not out here for the fishing, Fred?"

Goldman flashed his Tatar's grin, brilliant white teeth, annoyingly regular. "Polly said to duck," he reported, answering the unasked question, and lit one of his elegant black cigarillos for courage.

"You saw her or called her?"

"Saw. I dropped by the house tonight."

"How was she?"

"Beautiful as ever. Guarded. Protective."

"She tell you where I was?"

"Cruising, she said. Try Connecticut or Maine." The teeth displayed again to show he forgave her. "Said you wouldn't thank me for reminding you there's a world out there."

"Did she now? So how'd you find me?"

"I didn't. I called Woods Hole and told the coast guard to find you. Pin you down, give me a fix—whatever they do." He waited for a return of service, but Garfield let it pass. *Told* them, did he?

"I see. Well, why don't you go ahead and put us both out of our misery, Fred?"

Goldman dipped his cigarillo in salute. "Have a message for you, Luke. From Larry Bartell."

He was a good storyteller, professional. Garfield had forgotten how professional. His style was intimate and relaxed, his pace nicely judged to seduce his audience, yet had the words been written down, they would have scanned as clinically as a lab report. Garfield heard him out in silence and, at the end, hooked his oldest, blackest briar from the rack, filled it with a rich black shag he normally reserved for long night watches at sea, and set a match to it in ponderous slow motion.

Had his wife been there to watch this display, she would at once have read the signs of excitement—a blankness about the eyes, a cultivated sluggishness of manner, an air of acute un-interest—but Goldman's insights into his mentor's personality had never gone that deep, and he took time off to study his impeccably polished shoe.

"So." Garfield let go a lot of smoke and watched it skid along the polished mahogany of the tabletop. "Larry Bartell, eh?"

"The Harvard messiah," Goldman confirmed.

"You sure it's my name he took in vain?"

"Lucas H. Garfield, State Department. Tell him I want to come home. Say—"

"Goods to trade. Names, places, connections—yes, so you said."

"And you'd know how to reach him," Goldman added with heavy emphasis.

"Yes, so you said."

Garfield closed his eyes and in the privacy of his skull reconstructed an image of Larry Bartell from old photographs and half-forgotten television pictures. A small man, very bouncy—Lord, how they'd hated his bounce! Bright brown eyes, infinitely intelligent, constantly amused, and frequently contemptuous of what they saw. Lots of color in his dress—pinks, mauves, lilacs,

greens, blues. His detractors had taken it for homosexual display. (Dear God, what would they make of the current crop of
androids?) And his voice, of course; no way could one forget
the voice: soft clear lucid cruel, the inciter *par excellence.* He
looked up again and met Goldman's gaze in midstream.

"Mind if I ask how come *you're* delivering this message, Fred?
Hardly your speed, is it, messenger boy?"

"Todd Hales is one of my people, didn't I mention that? He
works for me. Based in the Paris office."

"A Paris office? Well, now, that's very impressive, Fred. And
convenient."

"How do you mean, convenient?"

"Well, what would you call it? I mean, here's our friend
Larry Bartell, not noticeably a creature of the social center,
comes out of the German dark and bumps into a fellow he knew
at Harvard. But not just any fellow. This one works for you, my
oldest, closest working colleague—"

"Ex-colleague," Goldman objected sharply.

"Ex. And whose name trembles on Larry's lips? Mine, would
you believe? Tell Garfield, he says. And who better to pass the
message down the line?" He appeared to be mesmerized
momentarily by a colored print of a barkentine in a hexagonal
frame. "Convenient, Fred, that's all."

"It happens."

"So I hear. All right, tell me about Hales. How long has he
been with you?"

"A little over a year. Say fifteen months."

"And before that he was with the Company. Bartell got that
right, did he?"

"Ten years with Langley, yes. And good, Luke. One of the
best."

"Naturally," Garfield said primly, and wondered not for the
first time how many other good Company men fed at Goldman's trough and how extensive their operations were and what
they did to earn their keep aside from nursemaiding itinerant

21

Arabs. The line of speculation depressed him more than he could say; he abandoned it. "Let's run over the sequence again. You say Hales picked up his client in the Gulf on Monday afternoon."

"And flew him to Frankfurt."

"And that night Bartell saw the two of them leaving the Inter-Continental."

"Right. They'd just checked in. They had to stop by the local consulate to pick up some papers."

"And what exactly was this Arab doing in Frankfurt?"

Goldman shifted his lanky frame uncomfortably in the green leather seat. "Luke, this is confidential."

"Cross my heart and hope to die."

"The guy was over to talk oil contracts with the West Germans. Ostensibly."

"But in fact—"

"The two countries have—let's say mutual problems in the terrorist area. You know what I mean."

"I can guess. So Bartell couldn't have read anything about the visit in the papers, seen something on TV?"

"No way."

"Yet within minutes of their touching down old Larry picks up the phone—"

"Writes a note, Luke." Goldman cut in anxiously. "Checked with the front desk, left a note Tuesday midday. 'Meet me ten-fifteen at the Nizza rink.' That kind of note."

"And brave Hales to the dark tower came. Left his client—"

"Under protection!" Goldman eased his conscience by refilling his glass from the lead crystal decanter. "He considered the possibilities, called in reinforcements, a camera team—"

"Conveniently on tap."

"—and did what he had to do."

"Out of curiosity?"

Goldman swirled the drink in his glass with unnecessary verve. "It was his job to go. His duty to the client."

"Well, of course. The client flies in to talk terrorism, and who's out there waiting in the dark but a genuine terrorist? Or so we're led to believe." Garfield sighed. "I suppose it didn't occur to Hales to call the police. There's a warrant out for Bartell in West Germany, isn't there?"

"Invite the cops in and you get the media, Luke, you know that. The client was buying secrecy. We had a contract."

"Sacred."

Goldman shrugged off the insult. "Body watch, protection, surveillance: Hales had an obligation to go out there and meet the guy."

"His old Harvard buddy. A college reunion."

"They weren't buddies."

"No." Garfield grinned balefully around the pipestem. "But he was a good Company man, Hales; must have had Larry's curriculum vitae at his fingertips. There can't be many ex-Company men who don't."

"He knew, sure."

"Yet at the end of the day he's learned nothing beyond the fact that Bartell's running a French passport. Wonderful!"

"I explained that. Bartell passed out on him twice. First time he humped him to a bench. Second time he got him as far as the parking lot next to the hotel."

"Where he left him?"

"What was he supposed to do—drag him in there? He went inside to get one of his team down and—"

"Don't tell me. Larry had a miraculous recovery and tiptoed off into the night."

"It was *minutes*, Luke. From start to finish less than five minutes."

As if in confirmation, the saloon clock chinged the three-quarter hour.

Garfield felt *The Duchess* swing suddenly as an unfriendly breeze picked her up and ran her off to starboard. Backing westerly, the weather report had promised. Force four to five.

23

"So—" He pumped life into the tobacco with new vigor. "Hales called you, and you did what?"

"Well—" Goldman did theatrical things with his long, open hands. "I took it to Langley, Luke, the way you would. Ran the film, told the story."

"For which they were eternally grateful."

"You tell me."

"And after mulling it over, they sent you to me. Now why should they do that, Fred, any theories?"

"He *asked* for you. Bartell asked for you personally. Not me, not Langley, *you*. Lucas H. Garfield. Tell him." He paused. "Tell Garfield, tell the girl."

"Ah, now I'd forgotten her. The girl. He didn't mention *what* girl. You have any ideas?"

"Don't play games with me, Luke, it's too goddamn late in the day."

Garfield chuckled. "Come, Fred, where's your sense of humor? Your sense of the ridiculous? All right, so what's the verdict down there in Fairfax County? Where do the institutions stand on prodigal sons this month? Does Larry get to come home or doesn't he?"

Once again Goldman found it impossible to sit at ease on Garfield's green leather. "In principle, yes. Subject to conditions."

"Names, places, connections."

"Right. A comprehensive debriefing. No locked closets, no Bartell-type bullshit. If he accepts that, they'll talk amnesty."

"If he lives that long."

"Sure."

"If you can get him back here."

"If *you* can, yes."

Garfield shook his head in wonder. "Is he worth all this?"

"Maybe. I don't know."

"Is that why Langley prefers not to be involved?"

"Well, Luke." Goldman squirmed anxiously this way, that

way and as a final outlet for his discomfort resorted again to the decanter. "They see this as a private affair, between you and Bartell. Initially. He's asking you as a private citizen—responsible public figure, diplomat, so forth—to make contact and discuss his case. That's all. An overture, man to man, in the hope you can act as intermediary. Exploratory."

"You put it so well, Fred. And when we've explored?"

Goldman attempted a brave grin. "You're an independent cuss, Luke. You're the type who likes to handle things your own way. Privately."

Garfield reached up to a porthole over his head and pushed it open; the smoke haze in the saloon took flight in a rush.

"Privately discuss and privately do, is that it? Privately spirit him out of Europe—provided Mother Russia doesn't object. Privately spirit him home. What do they mean by exploratory?"

"Oh, setting it up. Getting him out."

"While Langley sits and watches. Well, I can see the logic in that. What about resources: money, manpower, services?"

"No manpower, no services. Funding on a personal basis. You pay your way; you claim later. They don't want the federal services involved, Luke, at any stage, here or overseas. And stay away from diplomats; embassies are out. No embassies, no media, no official European contact."

Garfield nodded, his eyes on a distant inner star. "And how do they see it, as a proposition? In the realm of practical politics?"

"I'm just the messenger boy, Luke." Goldman grinned.

"Uh-huh." He was quiet for a moment. "Tell me, Fred, did anyone down there stop to ask what happens if I say no?"

Goldman considered the question on its merits. He shook his head. "No, I don't believe anyone did."

"Ah." Garfield got up and tapped the barometer. "Then what can I say?"

25

THREE

Garfield's kingdom—or, more accurately, his wife's—straddled a rocky promontory jutting into Long Island Sound. In winter, murderous northeasterlies clawed it to the bone. In summer, shrill westerlies tore the stunted trees to shreds. But in spring, ah, now, in spring the gods called a halt to the wanton havoc, switched on the sun and garlanded the buttery hills with wild flowers, carpets of wild flowers.

Lucas Garfield approved of spring. His wife, Polly, lived for it.

Their home was by no means a dream house—unless the dream was a bad one Alfred Hitchcock had had while reading Daphne du Maurier—but what saved it was its position, poised up there at the summit of the headland. On either side of it the sea had cut deep inlets where scimitars of pebble beach curved close in under seventy-foot cliffs so that at any time of day or night, whatever the weather or state of the tide, the shush and boom of the surf were always there to remind everyone in the house of how tenuous man's lease was on the land.

Lucas Garfield loved the house. Polly Garfield loved her husband. The equation made life at Cooper's Reach supportable.

It had taken Garfield a full day to obtain a mooring for *The Duchess* on the mainland at Blue Hill, and much taxing of the patience, plus a second day spent unshipping batteries and gas bottles, shedding and bagging sails, pumping out bilges, cleaning up, stowing, and generally snugging down—a host of jobs he'd had no intention of dealing with till the season's end, late September or so, God and the Gulf Stream willing. However, there was no doubt in his mind that Larry Bartell represented some kind of personal responsibility, though in what moral direction he was presently unable to say; in any event, he had to be dealt with, and it couldn't be done from his beloved wheelhouse. So be it.

On the third day he reached home, greeted his life's partner with a vague embrace and a preoccupied peck on the cheek, and entombed himself in what he was pleased to call his reading room. The nineteenth-century roughneck who had built the house had created a hideaway room, a sort of unpriestly priest-hole, on the seaward end of the living room and had concealed it behind a hinged bookcase. A playroom for previous owners' children, probably, but for Garfield a unique storehouse for the more private papers of his public career. He had installed shelving and file cabinets in the eight-by-ten space and a small table, and there he withdrew within ten minutes of arriving home to update his recollections of Laurens Tadeuz Bartell, né Eisenstern.

(Now why should he have remembered that tidbit?)

Leaving the bookcase wide open as a concession to Polly, Garfield pulled the Bartell file. A slim one; not that that implied any lack of substance. Quite the contrary. Many of the files he'd gathered in this room against all known laws and civil processes were preshrunk, starch-reduced versions of the bulky ones compiled by the Cleaners and added to over the years until they became too fat to handle on anything bigger than microfilm. But in Garfield's experience very little of the information intelligence agencies considered it essential to file ever repaid its keep, and besides, he had a memory like a NASA computer. All it required to function smoothly was basic input: Punch a key in his brain, and out it came, neatly paged in sequential order, just as he'd punched it in a year, a decade, a quarter century ago. It was a knack he had. Useful. Nothing to boast about.

Laurens Tadeuz Bartell, né Eisenstern.

Protestant family, the Bartells, and here was a yellowed page from *Fortune*, dated April 1933, in praise of it. Virginia hunting-and-fishing fraternity, big on college endowments and the politics of isolation, short on government aid programs to the needy. Hated Roosevelt but surprisingly voted Democrat; supported John Nance Garner to a man (the women didn't count,

of course). Garfield turned to a *Time* clipping. Fought tooth
and nail to keep America out of World War II, then pitched in
when the Japanese bombed Pearl and gave three sons—of five;
two daughters—to the cause. Vast holdings in steel, chemicals,
oil. In the peace Thurlan Bartell III took control of the family
octopus and reached out into Costa Rica, the Caribbean, Brazil;
bought into the world's fourth-largest tanker fleet, the second-
largest sugar corporation, the third-largest gold mine in South
Africa. So on and so on.

By no stretch of the imagination a family in urgent need of
a Laurens Tadeuz Eisenstern to improve the bloodlines. But
that's who it got. That was the trick. "Call me Larry Bartell,"
he'd said with a grin (he had a disarming grin, Larry; reduced
women to their baser urges). "Call me Larry Bartell," he invited
the newspapermen when he brought his child bride home from
Mexico City that year. (The classic elopement, of course.
Thurlan Bartell would have rejected Larry as a son-in-law if
he'd come wrapped in Japan's world trade surplus, so they'd
eloped.) "Call me Larry Bartell," the beautiful boy announced
with that cynic's caged sneer he'd perfected. "Who needs a
name like Eisenstern when you can be a Bartell?" He took her
name, his lovely Lydia's name, the thief. Grand larceny of the
person. Thurlan Bartell, sensible man, had tried to wrest his
daughter and his name back through the courts—underage,
Mexican nuptials, this and that—but the girl fought him every
inch of the way, and in the end he gave up in that special
frustration only adoring fathers know. Two children subsequently born to the union, a girl and a boy, now in their
teens; Bartells both by birth and birthright, heaven help them.

So what had Larry brought to the marriage?

A myth, what else? Himself. Even then he was a myth. Little
Larry Eisenstern, born Cleveland, Ohio, May 26, 1932; Jewish
baker's son, baker's grandson, no previous recorded genius strain.
An infant prodigy as ever was. Graduated high school at the age
of ten, American grandmaster in chess at fourteen. Took three

degree courses at Harvard simultaneously and at the age of eighteen streaked home with honors in all three. Appointed an associate professor of social history at Harvard in 1963—with tenure yet. (God, how the faculty must have loved him.)

Without warning, a plate descended on the clipping under Garfield's nose: diet rye bread, diet cream cheese, sliced tomato, lettuce.

He looked up. "What's this?"

"Did you eat breakfast?" Polly demanded, standing over him.

"No."

"Lunch?"

"I didn't have time."

"Eat!"

He ate but shoved the plate aside so he could read, too.

Polly drew up a chair from the living room and sat down and began to do things with three balls of wool and a short plastic needle that came out looking like striped knitting but wasn't knitting. "Who's that?" She nodded at the clipping. She could do whatever she was doing without looking at it, a constant source of wonder to Garfield.

"Larry Bartell," he grunted.

"The Harvard boy?" She glanced over his shoulder.

"Boy of fifty-odd, to be exact."

She eyed him squarely, the impulse to laugh only just held in check. "That's what I said—what about him?"

"He wants to come home."

"Has he been away?"

He glared at her and went back to his reading.

In May 1967 the *New York Times* asked Larry Bartell—in what it coyly described as a front-line interview—how he came to be leading the anti-Vietnam War lobby from the rear: a mischievous question, as were most questions aimed at him by the press, though at the time not inappropriate. He replied, "I model myself on Lyndon Johnson. Where the jungle is thickest

I send in the bombers; where it thins out I send in the troops. Like Lyndon, I figure, why get hurt when you can stand on the sidelines and cheer?"

There were times when it seemed that perfecting this brand of self-inflicted irony was his life's work, and he practiced it with such flair that in the course of the sixties he was, in succession, burned in effigy by the Ku Klux Klan, beaten up by the Knights Templars of the John Birch Society, and—mystifyingly —nominated a public enemy of the people by both the Communist party of the United States and the Daughters of the American Revolution. He also enraged to apoplexy that great slab of public indifference known commonly as "ordinary America" and suffered a scourge of hate mail rare even among southern liberal reformers. But hate was Larry's lifeline, and he clung to it. He became a poet and tract hack in the service of the golden weed, served as an archdeacon of flower power ("Everything is Beautiful in its own way"), and even took up the guitar, at which he became accomplished in a matter of weeks. Having slipstreamed behind Martin Luther King's lunch counter campaign of the early sixties, he engineered a sensational television confrontation with Stokely Carmichael after the assassination and announced the initiation of his own War on War—WOW, of course; only Larry Bartell could have hoped to win mileage out of such an acronym. He took a ride for a while on Eugene McCarthy's gravy train, then switched tickets to George McGovern. In politics as in marriage, he had an appetite for other people's names.

"Last thing he ever wanted was office," Garfield growled into his glass of milk.

"The last thing *you* ever wanted was office," Polly said lightly, catching his eye. "You could have been attorney general."

"Rubbish."

"Drink your milk," she said, clinching the argument.

According once again to the *Times*, Larry "was everywhere to be seen and nowhere to be found when the action got heavy" that sticky summer afternoon in Washington when the people

marched on Nixon. But when the president made his final tear-
ful farewell and stepped aboard the helicopter into temporary
banishment, the third talking head from the left watching him
on a monitor in the studio was Laurens Tadeuz Eisenstern
Bartell. "This country," Larry had said, flashing his famous
come-and-kill-me-you-bastards grin, "this country has just cut
out its putrefying heart. But since it's the only heart America's
got, you can bet it'll be beating back there any minute,
whumpata-whumpata. So will Richard Milhous Nixon."

A prophet, too.

Though one without honor in his own land. Even among his
own kind. Two things led to Larry's undoing, and typical of
him, they both were clichés of unreasonableness. Having ridden
WOW into the ground to very little effect, he embraced the
long-running fugitives of Students Against the War still holding
out against the FBI—draft dodgers and flag burners, most of
them, kids who had electrified the late sixties and early seventies
by turning to urban terrorism. A particularly heavy-handed
Harvard commencement address delivered by a Vietnam general
gave him his opening. He wrote for the *Village Voice* a piece
entitled "Vermin on the Mount." It began with the immortal
line "Blessed are the bombers, for they shall be called peace-
makers. . . ."

But the final, truly unbeatable card Larry Bartell played in
his own downfall was the International People Power conference at Cambridge, Massachusetts, in June 1973. How he managed to arrange it at all with the FBI steaming open his mail
and listening to his phone calls Garfield was still at a loss to
explain, but over a period of six months he found the means
somehow to construct what amounted to a political time bomb.
It was bound to blow up in his face; he must have known that.

It was afterward held to be remarkable that every one of the
conference's foreign "delegates" had legally applied for and was
freely granted a U.S. visa—remarkable, that is, until it was
established that none of them had applied individually to attend
the conference but had entered the country as members of

31

various good will groups: golfers and nutritionists, grain nego-
tiators and Christadelphians, beekeepers and bankers—one
delegate to each group. The delegates, of course, proved to be
highly vocal professional activists from the hairier "democracies"
of totalitarian Europe, Africa, and the Orient. The *Boston
Globe* described their open-air deliberations as "a standing insult
to constitutional democracy" and Larry himself as "a mincing,
predatory Pan, the devil we thought we knew revealed as a
sardonic orchestrator of man's passion for self-destruction." The
conference ended dramatically in its tenth day, when the FBI
dropped in on a so-called Midnight Think-In, a mass poetry,
pot, and sex orgy involving several hundred students from nearby
campuses. Larry was arrested on drugs and morals charges and
bailed out on Lydia's surety of a hundred thousand dollars.
Two days later he crossed into Canada and flew to Europe. His
wife followed a month later.

The rest of Garfield's file was a catalog of Larry's wanderings
—or what bureau and Company analysts judged at the time to be
his search for a new homeland. Between 1973 and 1978 he was
spotted variously in Israel, Lebanon, Egypt (where his daughter
was born), Turkey, Holland, France, and Spain (his son's birth-
place), but he always contrived to move on before an extradi-
tion request could be processed. Then, in February 1978, he
settled in Amsterdam and petitioned the Dutch government for
what he called "moral sanctuary." Immediately the Justice Department swooped in for the kill, brandishing writs and charges
and righteous indignation. The case went to court at The Hague
and ran for eighteen memorable days. Larry won his freedom
by the simple expedient of reading a selection of his newspaper
clippings aloud from the box. He offered, as a natural parallel
to his own predicament, Christ's persecution by the Pharisees.
It brought the house down.

After this pyrrhic victory he seemed to find no degree of anti-
Americanism too disagreeable to espouse. An extensive docu-
ment defining the scope of CIA recruitment among foreign
students in American universities appeared under his name in

the French Communist newspaper *L'Humanité* and was subsequently syndicated worldwide. He published a "hit list" of U.S. Defense Department facilities in Western Europe, which still served as the bible of antimissile protestors. In 1979 he launched his own revolutionary news sheet, *Open Door*, but Amsterdam proved to be infertile soil for English-language hand-pressed weeklies, and it went broke.

At which point his private world began to come apart at the seams. Lydia left him and made a ghastly mess of smuggling herself and the children back to America. Getting wind of the "escape," Larry tried to snatch the kids back at Schiphol Airport, only to be foiled by a flying wedge of unidentified muscle. His flat-footed, gaping surprise was captured by a strategically placed photographer, and the pictures had their day in court when Lydia sued for divorce. To celebrate this humiliation as only he knew how, Larry got himself arrested by the Dutch narcotics bureau and jailed for six months for "occasioning the use of drugs in minors," a charge he vociferously denied all the way to the paddy wagon. On release, he eluded press and FBI alike and slipped into West Germany. There he joined a community of student squatters in Hamburg, honed them to a fine edge of social aggressiveness, was caught leading an assault on a demolition site (from behind, of course), and bounced by the German immigration police.

Whether the KGB actually recruited him at this point or simply rode to the rescue of a soul already theirs, no one could be sure, but on the afternoon of August 12, 1980, Larry Bartell was photographed walking into the Geneva headquarters of the Council for Ethnic Freedoms on the arm of a known Soviet hood. The house functioned as a low-grade mail drop for KGB operatives in Switzerland running diplomatic or UN cover; the hood was an elderly has-been with third secretary status in the embassy at Basel. In other words, the whole exercise had about it the stale stench of poverty. As a result, the FBI overseas dogwatch team responsible for taking the pictures that day put Larry Bartell on a back burner and in due course dropped him.

The bureau handed the file to Langley. Langley graciously noted. As far as all parties were concerned, Larry Bartell had found his level at last. He'd gone to join his soulmates.

And there the visible trail went cold. Dead cold.

Another president came and went, and the CIA shed its skin in the hand-over, then shed another and shortly a third. Yesterday's bright young computer brains were dismissed overnight as shifty and unreliable dilettantes, and men Garfield had last known as fresh-faced OSS adventurers in wartime London reappeared in Washington, plump and balding and saggy-eyed, to run Langley as it *should* be run, then promptly lost favor and were replaced by more of the same. When yet another change of tenant assailed the White House, Langley responded with more convulsions of policy and personnel. Priorities changed; targets were refocused; accountants moved into the intelligence business and began paring, slicing, whittling away. No cause was deemed so sacred that it couldn't be re-budgeted.

And somewhere in the midst of all this Larry Bartell disappeared through a crack in the landscape. When Garfield had vacated his desk at State a year ago, the pretty pictures taken in August 1980 were still on record as the final sighting, but the interpretation of what he was doing had changed. Larry was back in student radicalism, sure enough, but this time undeniably for Moscow: organizing structures—mainly in Europe—writing pamphlets, distributing handbooks on the urban martial arts, running instruction courses on education and cell control. The Italians turned him up first; a raid on a Red Brigades hideout in Milan revealed a stack of literature with Larry's name on it, translations of his commentaries in *L'Humanité* and the underground press mostly, photocopied in Prague and run off ad nauseam. Later the French found a cache of booklets on guerrilla warfare at a château near Nîmes and identified Larry as the "German visitor" who had brought them there. (Larry spoke German fluently, as he spoke French, Spanish, Italian, Arabic, and Russian; as fluently—for all Garfield knew—as he spoke the

Indian sign language.) In swift succession the Dutch tied him into the anti-cruise-missile movement, the Belgians into Flemish nationalism, the West Germans into their rambunctious environment lobby, and the Spaniards into Basque separatism, all without actually setting official eyes on him.

Larry, the all-purpose Don Quixote, the invisible man. Contagious as Asian flu and twice as elusive.

Garfield pushed the file aside and chewed his lip.

"Stop chewing your lip," Polly ordered without looking up.

"I don't get it," he said vacantly.

"You don't have to get it, just stop it." Her fingers flashed, flick-flick, flick-flick, and a woolen arm grew below the needle, white band, green band, black.

"I mean Larry."

"Why *Larry*? I didn't know you were on a first-name basis." She leaned across him again and studied the picture; Larry and friend entering the Council for Ethnic Freedoms in Geneva. "Hmm." She tapped the boy with her needle. "Maybe you're right. He *is* a Larry. Handsome. Kind of debonair."

"You have a short memory. He's a traitor, an agitator, a pain in the—*Professor* Bartell. There's a price on his head."

Polly resumed her work—flick-flick, flick-flick. "He's still handsome. What color eyes?"

Garfield consulted the rap sheet. "Hazel. Hair brown, prematurely gray. That was in 1973, by the way. Skin tone dark; height five-nine; weight a hundred forty pounds."

"See his smile?" Polly jabbed with her needle. "Was he under arrest there?"

"I suppose you could call it that. Why?"

"Well, just look at him. He's so *sad*. All that bravura, they can't touch me, and inside he's bleeding to death."

"Known as poetic justice I believe. Well, as a matter of fact, you're right. He is bleeding inside. Cirrhosis of the liver."

"Oh." Hand to mouth, arrow to the heart. Poor Polly.

"I repeat, I don't get it." Garfield sifted again through the sheaf of clippings, but they had nothing more to offer him.

35

"What don't you get?"

"Why we should have anything to do with him. On any grounds. He's a dead man, for all practical purposes. Dying."

She stopped working, very angry. "*Because* he's dying. Isn't that what makes us different from them? Because we care about people. Because he has children. Because he's at his wits' end. Because—"

"Rubbish! Whether you like it or not, he doesn't happen to be the fugitive with a heart of gold. On the evidence he's a petty thief, a huckster, a random killer of innocent bystanders." He swept aside the clippings. "At best he's a bag carrier for Dzerzhinsky Square. Little bags. He runs errands for the KGB directorates—*if* that. They peddle him around the European campuses because an American sniping at America rates more publicity than a comrade doing it. He keeps elements of the radical left on the boil. Maybe. He acts as go-between for student guerrilla groups. Probably. He writes pamphlets and vaguely seditious books, most of them milder than anything you'll find advertised in the *Village Voice*."

"So?"

"So who needs him here? And why? We have no reason to forgive him. And no reason to think he knows anything we don't."

"Another reason then."

"Good answer. But it would need to be a damn fine reason at that. Get him back here and he's trouble. We can't admit him without arraigning him—not legally, not openly. So it has to be in secret: false names, false passports, FBI surveillance around the clock. For the privilege of allowing an enemy of the people, so called, to die peacefully on American soil. Go ahead, convince me it's reasonable. Better still, tell me those people down in Washington are sentimentalists. Brock Stafford, for instance. Good old Brock. You think he's a Larry lover?"

"I doubt it," she said with a sigh.

"Or Davis Lang? Or that other Texas red-neck over at

Langley. You ever thought of Ralph Kramer as the voice of sweet forgiveness?"

"You've forgotten the president," she said acidly.

"Oh, no, I haven't, not by a mile. My friend the president." The image settled in his mind like an early frost. "Those guys eat Larry Bartells for breakfast. But they want him home. They've said—"

"Exactly! They've *said*. They've decided, past tense." Polly triumphant: game, set, and match.

Garfield flopped back in his chair. "I know, you're right. That's what I mean: I don't get it."

He slipped into bed a few minutes short of four in the morning, feeling larger than life size and rather more fulfilled than he had in months. Pure displacement therapy, of course—he wasn't so deluded he couldn't see that—but the feeling was no less satisfying. When it came right down to it, all a man needed to be halfway happy was employment. Employment brought with it the wonderful tonic of daily renewal. And renewal—

Renewal? Wasn't that what *retirement* was supposed to bring? He punched the pillow hard and turned over, dismayed by the perception.

Truth was, he'd retired out of simple guilt, because Polly's depressions had stripped him of the illusion that they still had time on their side. "You'll die in harness," she'd been telling him for years—a woman's joke, not intended to amuse; not intended to sting either, but true all the same—and what she'd meant, bless her, was "*I'll* die in your harness," a *cri de coeur* he'd woken up to in the nick of time. He'd resigned. (Not that they hadn't been happy to see him go: the White House had been shoving for months. He was old stock, implacable, nobody's ally.) So he'd grasped old age by the horns, sold up in Georgetown, and withdrawn as planned to the house on the Sound, where for several months they'd walked around each other on tiptoe, waiting for the sky to fall. At length Polly had

37

called the meeting to order. "Look," she said one evening, "what are we trying to prove? I love you, you love me, and the show should run for years. So why am I breaking out in a nervous rash because you're around the house all day? And why do you jump three feet in the air every time I ask if you want another cup of coffee?"

Remedies, she said. "We may be one, but we're also two. Let's act like it. Go play with your toys before it's too late, and leave me to play with mine."

Her toys were the garden, her easel, her books and music, her friends.

His were *The Duchess* and the sea.

In Garfield's book the best part of a boy's life was that part he'd never lived but wished he had, so he became a boy again, and for the first time in his crusted experience, wealthy beyond his needs, embittered—if the truth be known—against his worst expectations yet hopeful beyond his right to hope, he'd put the two ends of his life span together and retreated into his oldest boyhood dream, a life of messing about at sea. The house on Long Island Sound became the crucible for an experiment in real and sustained marriage; the boat, a magic nostrum for turning back the clock. A royal flush in any man's language. Or was it?

On the house side of it, and Polly, and two-as-one-but-separate—yes, that worked fine.

The other?

Well, now, how do you quantify a dream? How do you measure its quality? Physically he'd grown as hard as any young recruit just out of boot camp. Calluses cushioned the palms of his hands, and he was burned the color of Williamsburg brick. But he hadn't recaptured his boyhood, nor had he found a way of forgetting the real past or of putting an end to the nightmares that came screaming up out of it every now and then. And for sure there was no way of escaping the present. In fact, paradoxically . . .

Each day he tuned in to the VHF bands for coastal weather

reports, and each day the ether spewed out at him the banal brutalities of his recent trade: assassinations; coups d'état; kidnappings; insurgencies; border clashes; defections; terrorist bombings; lies; counterlies. And each day his reactions were twofold and curious. The first reaction was despair. Half a century of his life devoted to skulduggery and deceit in a cause he'd judged to be honorable, and he had changed nothing by so much as a jot. The second reaction was simple unalloyed envy. The world's chaos roused in him an insatiable longing to be part of it; to control, to direct, to manipulate, to change.

To be recalled to the field of play, however temporarily, however shady the circumstances, at this moment in his life struck Lucas Garfield as a form of divine intervention. It was not a summons to be ignored, put it that way.

For most of the evening he had sat in the reading room poring over his form book, a compendium of names and brief biographies of men and women in all walks of life who at one time or another had been drawn into his operational net, often unwillingly. And from his private files and the biographies and the host of unanswered questions swirling around in his head, he had assembled an outline proposition—a very personal statement of what he saw as the logical probabilities lying ahead of him—and, to set alongside it as a companion, he penned an initial approach, which he thought of as a kind of road map into the deep undergrowth of the case, if not exactly one that led out the other side. His initial approach called for five basic steps, each of which he would have to take in the most visible way—that is, right out there in the open with the sun at his back, no cover, no supporting fire.

And his objectives?

Made the head swirl all over again to think of the scale of his vanity.

Objective one: to ascertain why Washington should be prepared to forgive Larry Bartell. (Nothing to it; all he had to do was to look into the president's mind and read it without alerting him.)

Objective two: to ascertain if Bartell's appeal for sanctuary was genuine.

Objective three: to ascertain if *Washington* thought it was genuine (and, if not, why it was still prepared to welcome him home).

Objective four: to protect Larry against Washington and Washington against Larry and himself against the two of them if, as he considered likely, either or both were playing games invisible to the naked eye.

And that was all. That was really all he had to prove. Except...

Oh, yes. Objective five: to ascertain if Lucas Haines Garfield was still the man he thought he was or the old fogy society insisted on making him.

Objective five was the cruncher.

FOUR

Like Frankfurt, Geneva was having a heat wave.

Larry Bartell took the airport bus to the *gare routière* and stashed his valise at the left luggage counter. He thought seriously, and for as long as it took to dismiss the idea, of cashing in his Deutsche marks—the rate against the Swiss franc had improved since he left—but he knew Miko would blow his stack if he did, and this was no time to start falling out with Miko over things that didn't matter. Besides, the lines at the cash window were lousy with skiers—it was the tail-end of the Easter season—and too many of them were Americans, his least favorite nationality when floating between engagements. So cool it, Larry, he told himself. Stay loose and pray. Just ease it over the edge, no sudden moves.

He hadn't felt a twinge of pain in two days.

He pulled on his cord cap, adjusted his new Porsche sunglasses, and drifted down through the buses parked in the square, feeling good. The colors were dazzling: volcanic reds in contramotion, blazing greens and yellows, lots of white, and khaki was in again this year, a sure sign of war psychosis; all these shades not in the leaves of the trees or the hues of earth, sky, and water but in the clashing smashing vibrancy of the ski suits. He passed two girls burned berry brown—pink and white two-piece, sun gold zip suit—and gave each of them that upward waggle of the jaw that in its day had called to a thousand maids across the primeval swamps of Boston, Mass. And walked on. They giggled the way kids do when their chemistry takes seriously something their minds can't, and the old Adam rose in him again, for at least the space of a bus width. Time: 12:02.

On either side of the square stood a coffee shop, one good, one not so good, and he toyed with the idea—the way you do when you're killing time, nothing serious—of walking in and ordering a slice of chocolate cake lopsided with thick, fresh cream and wolfing it down in a minute flat. Or better—he had reached the end of the square where the buses curl around, coming and going—how about *that*? Across the street, the word *Bar* flashed in polished brass from the side entrance of the Beau Rivage. A few couples were sitting out on the little terrace overlooking the lake, and it was hot there because the men had slipped off their jackets. Come on, Larry, how about it? he taunted the drinking man who lived in his liver. A slug of something deadening. He thought of Miko, of Miko eavesdropping on this conversation with himself, and grinned. "If you want drink at all, absolutely, you drink at home, Lerry, not those swank hotels by the lake, unnerstand me?" Miko's rule. "We all know the type you meet that kind of places." Actually Larry didn't know, but he was ready to take Miko's word for it because Miko was deep. And no doubt about it, so was Geneva. The only people who could really afford to live here were people who didn't belong: diplomats; actors; swindlers; deposed dictators; pop singers; spies. *La crème de la crème.* And Larry Bartell.

For if he could be said to live anywhere on a permanent

basis, Larry Bartell lived here, too—if you could call it living—though few of the people who didn't belong belonged here less than he. He had a tiny apartment up in the old town, a *box*, a padded nest wedged between a tobacco warehouse that looked like a church and a church that looked like a warehouse, where on warm spring evenings one window brought him the rich nuances of Virginia, Turkey, and Havana, while the other admitted the benisons of Holy Rome. Occasionally, in his recent past, Larry had added a little hash to this bouquet, and on a good night, a night when Miko called off the dogs and threw him a bonus—a bottle of Chivas Regal, a girl from the residency—he'd feel as close to heaven up there on the fifth floor as he'd ever felt anywhere in his whole lousy life. But, then, those were also the nights that ended with his getting crazed, stupid drunk and weeping over remembrances of times past. Weeping for Lydia. Weeping for the kids. Weeping for . . .

Miko didn't like him hanging around Geneva any more than he had to.

He turned the corner. The waterspout rose from the lake, white and still as candlewax in the warm air, and Larry stopped to take it all in: the sweep of the bridge and the awkward jumble of ancient-and-modern climbing the stubby hill to the old town; the gardens on the far shore burning with scarlet hydrangeas; the swans, the anchored lake steamers; the impression the whole scene gave you of having dropped off a thirties postcard. The cool, quiet, moneyed Swiss, clinging to their valleys and the fine old virtues of thrift and isolation. Don't knock it, friends. It's the past, and it works.

Right turn again, the fourth side of the block. Now 12:09.

Miko was a tiger for timing; he could forgive anything but unpunctuality. "To time be true," he would admonish, waving a finger in your face. "Time, Lerry. To time be true." Twelve minutes past the hour was his rule. Larry glanced across at the American Express travel bureau where Miko sometimes lurked among the vacation brochures to watch him perform on occasions like these—check-in sessions, where Larry ambled nice and easy while Miko and the tripehounds swept his trail front and back. But Miko wasn't in there today, meaning he was in the church, the English church right next to the bus station. Miko actually went to services there on occasional Sundays, not because he was religious or because he was English; he simply liked to be around Englishmen—the kind, anyway, you found in church on a Sunday in Geneva. It was a hobby of his, he said. Given the choice, he'd have asked to be born English. "Why not? Is good enough for God, is good enough for Miko Schellenberg." For a man who loved England to death and spoke with impeccable fluency in other tongues, Miko's English was a little wayward, though he insisted this was a virtue, the most English thing about him. He was an inspired amateur, he said, not a professional. "Dental mechanics is professionals." Someday, Larry promised himself, he would get to the core of Miko Schellenberg, understand him, sort the wheat from the chiffchaff.

And then again, maybe he wouldn't live that long.

Miko wasn't in the church anyway. The doors were padlocked; heaven was out to lunch. It was 12:12 exactly. Where—

"You have a light, sir?"

The accent was University of Leningrad-American as spoken on the overseas service of Radio Moscow, except that Rostov lent it a genuine touch of Madison Avenue. Rostov had been with Aeroflot in New York for three years and had a mouthful of flat A's to prove it. He dressed with Saks and Sulka, very tasteful; you could have mistaken him for an American anywhere on the moon. His tan Burberry was worn in the approved Bogart fashion, collar up and unbuttoned, belt tied, and his lightly tanned boyish face said everything there was to be said in favor of a balanced diet and plenty of sleep. Rostov was a ladies' man, Miko said, and had a distressing habit of beating up on his conquests. Larry thumbed his Dupont, and the Russian bent to light his cigarette: Marlboro, of course.

"Thank you." He nodded, almost a bow, and Larry was reminded painfully of Todd Hales. Same type, same die-for-nothing mentality. Big, hard, soulless. He was carrying the *Herald Trib* rolled around the *Financial Times* and touched this baton to his clipped flaxen hair in a wry salute to show how genuinely grateful he was. "Obliged, sir." He took a step away, then came back again for the reprise. "Er, you live here by any chance?"

"Just passing through," Larry said, bored by it. Why couldn't they just clear his tail and pick him up instead of putting him through all this crap? Where was Miko?

"I was recommended a restaurant. The Mövenpick in the rue du Cendrier." Rostov flashed his detachable smile. "Do you happen to know it?"

Larry loved to catch them off base. "Never heard of it," he rapped. The sidewalks were thick with people, streams of office girls making for the lakeside and the self-service diners. What the hell was wrong? Miko had never missed a check-in, not in five-plus years. Quick as a flash the pain started up in his liver.

Rostov pointed with his rolled papers at the rue du Cendrier just across the street. "It's down there. Maybe I should try it anyway before the rush starts."

"That's right," said Larry. "Maybe you should."

"See you," the Russian said easily, and crossed against the light.

Larry ordered a mushroom omelet for his ulcer and a bottle of white Neuchâtel for his nerves. Rostov ate to achieve a perfect harmony of mind and body and called for chopped tomato salad and cold sliced breast of chicken, no dressing, no disfiguring additives. He drank orange juice with a milk chaser.

"What do they feed you at home?" Larry asked.

The boy had Miko's sense of humor. "Small children, sir." He grinned.

"No kidding."

They ate in silence for half an hour.

The tables were very small and bolted to the floor, and the seats very hard. The general idea was to keep the clientele turning over at speed, and the waiters achieved this by coming by at regular intervals to frown if you stopped eating.

"Where's the old man?" Larry asked casually after a while. The wine came in a dinky little carafe, and every time he filled his glass Rostov stared at him as if he were drinking the Politburo's blood.

"Oh, I think he's around. You know, busy-busy."

"Too busy to come say hello?"

Rostov shoveled a forkful of lettuce into his mouth and chewed it the regulation thirty-six times before replying, with a foxy angling of the head, "Speak as you find, don't they say?"

"Yeah. They do."

Had he been tailed? Had Miko put a tail on him in Frankfurt? The pain in his lower abdomen was beginning to threaten his sanity. Rostov was watching him closely, mouth crunch-crunching its way to health and strength, one brow raised in unspoken comment, exactly the way Todd Hales had watched him that night at the Nizza rink. It's God's curse on the human race, Larry thought. He makes hoods in matched pairs and distributes them equally, one to Moscow, one to Washington, call this one Rostov, call that one Hales, mix and match. Known in the lab as the balance of nature.

At the table on his right a mountain of flesh in Sherwood green was lecturing a mild-mannered clerk on the perils of the second Löwenbräu before lunch. On his left an American matron regaled her husband with the staggering fact that in Switzerland you can walk into a jewelry store and the stuff isn't even locked up. Having rehearsed garbled scenarios of what he would do in a situation where Miko found him wanting and shipped the crushers in, Larry dismissed both couples as possible allies in a crisis.

Rostov folded his napkin neatly and looked askance at Larry's plate. "You don't like the way they cooked the omelet?" he asked politely.

"Why? Is it worrying you to death?"

"A friend said you were ill, that's all." Rostov's eyes were the kind that pursued you in bad dreams: black at the centers, gray-white edged again with black, then more white. "He's worried about your health, I think," he added delicately.

"So worried he's not here."

"Later maybe."

"Only maybe? You don't know for sure?" It was ridiculous, childish. The eyes told him so.

"I'm not his keeper," Rostov said amiably. "I'm not his confidant."

"What are you then exactly?"

The Russian stood up. He draped the folded trench coat over his shoulder with one hand and tossed a hundred-franc note on the table with the other. "See you, pal." He tapped his yellow forelock again with the rolled newspapers, then stopped, looked back. "Oh, by the way, that book you asked about. I saw it a while back at Naville's. You know? The bookshop in the square? Paperback section, in the corner, to the left as you face the cash desk, know where I mean? *The Tears of Autumn* you said, right? Charles McCarry?"

"That's right," Larry said mechanically, and picked up the banknote before the waiter did.

He took his time because Miko operated strictly according to Hoyle. It was already twenty past the hour, and if Miko gave you no set time, he expected you to float patiently and openly, returning every twelve minutes past the hour to check the appointed rendezvous. In Switzerland he might keep you cruising like this for hours at a time while he sat and walked your tail, crossing and recrossing it till he was sure you were carrying no excess baggage. Outside Switzerland, on the rare occasions he set foot outside, the process could go on for days. In Stockholm, once, he'd kept Larry on the hop for a whole week; he was practically a basket case at the end of it.

But Naville et Cie. was a second home to Laurens Tadeuz Bartell, and Miko knew it. Nominating it as a rendezvous was an act of charity. Larry took a long slow ramble around the block, repeating the noon performance, then cut through the buses in the square and entered the shop. An assistant recognized him and smiled. The cashier waved from her cubicle. The manager spotted him and, book-laden, came over to shake him by the hand. They exchanged pleasantries. The heat wave. The collapse of the dollar. The war in Lebanon. Terrorism. Graham Greene's latest. A limited edition of Witold Rodzinski's *A History of China*. Steadman Jones's study of class relationships in Victorian England. The copy Larry ordered had come in weeks ago; would he like it now? And guess who was in the store last month? Robert Ludlum. Not a bit like his jacket photograph.

Larry glanced at the clock—3:10—and pretended to browse, working slowly into the corner: M for McCarry. He pulled the book, *The Tears of Autumn*, and riffled through it quickly. Nothing inside. Damn! Resentment, anger, frustration, disappointment—all those things—but mostly pain. He was about to move on when a very small hand reached past him and lifted the book alongside the one he'd taken.

"Is inspirational for a title, you think, Lerry?" Miko turned the book over in his spotless silver-gray gloves, a second copy of the McCarry book. And before Larry could say a word: "Why you think Western writers so innerested in the East, hey, Lerry?"

"Maybe because it's a long way away," Larry said, the pulse racing in his throat. He looked around furtively. "Anything wrong, Miko?"

"I think you joke a liddle," Miko said, unheeding. "You know what I think? I think in the West we have the logic, absolutely, and in the East they have the answers. Hey?"

"Miko?" Larry now found it impossible to keep his hands still.

"*The Tears of Autumn*, huh? Is about Vietnam?"

"Miko, look—"

"You know a big truth about that place, Lerry?" His little gloves caressed the book's cover. "You people drop a million

47

tons of bombs on that place; maybe two, three million. So why the insects still living there? Why the flies still flying, the ants still crawling?"

"Classic lesson of history," Larry said shakily, eyes swiveling till it hurt. "Nothing changes nothing."

"Here." Miko plucked the book from Larry's hands and substituted the other. "I buy you the book. I make you a gift of the book, Lerry, okay? You read it, you tell me how it go. Is good, maybe I read it sometime." He moved on, selected another book at random.

Larry followed. "All I want to say, Miko, is—"

The old man had a way of looking up at him sometimes— sharply, almost shocked—as if they'd never met before, and sometimes he did it so well you could almost believe him. Sheer personality. There was nothing else to Miko but brain and personality; nothing you could take seriously anyway. Physically he was a joke. Five feet tall in built-up heels, and so chic it hurt. Today he was wearing his royal equerry silver-gray, *le tout ensemble* gray—suit, tie, shoes, coat, rolled umbrella, gloves, bowler hat. His carnation was pink-speckled-white, and his hair a cap of black patent leather that smelled like a truckload of freesias.

"Miko?" An edge of desperation crept into the appeal, and to explain it away, Larry clutched his gut.

"Again?" Miko, blank-faced.

"Getting worse."

Miko Schellenberg had one blue eye and one brown and that mild thyroid imbalance which sets the eyes at an angle outward so that you're never quite sure which one to look at. To the best of Larry's knowledge he was on the downhill side of seventy-five, though the best knowledge anyone had of Miko was almost certainly fictive; no doubt even Miko had forgotten who and what he really was, if he'd ever known. When he first courted Larry, he'd handed him the standard biography as a gift between friends: born in Hanover, sired by an eminent lawyer and named for his Czech uncle Miroslav; thus Miko, his mother's pet name. Later he let Larry into the *real* secret: born in St. Petersburg to a Russian banker and his German mistress, an operatic soprano; subsequently reared in Vienna, Florence, and London. But Miko was constantly confiding in men he didn't trust, and among other secrets he'd dropped in Larry's ear were that he'd been schooled in Paris, had taken a degree in economics at Bonn, studied banking in New York, played tennis for France, fought for the Germans in Hitler's War, switched to the Allies, and retired to pursue charitable works. The only certainty Larry was in any position to vouch for was that Miko existed. That and the fact that he ran the Soviet machine in Switzerland. Not to mention probably the entire Russian destabilizing effort in Western Europe.

Miko's trade was fooling most of the people most of the time in the interests of Soviet political preeminence, and he did it well, his first and toughest target having been himself.

There was a brief commercial break at this point while Stegelmann, Miko's bodyguard in chief, strolled through the stationery department, a short, broad anvil of a man in a black homburg. He selected a copy of the *Frankfurter Allgemeine Zeitung* and paid for it at the cash desk. As he went out again, he took one hand in the other as if pulling on a glove and held up four fingers.

"Was bad this time? In Frankfurt was bad, eh, Lerry?" Miko's concern was never either patently genuine or disingenuous; if Larry had a criticism, it was that no man alive could switch genuine emotions faster.

He shrugged. "You know what I've got down there, Miko. It's *bad*. What do I have to do, spell it out in blood?"

"I think nerves is your problem, Lerry." Miko actually twinkled; chuckle-chuckle, his little game. "First is the ulcer. Okay, I send you Dr. Roesch and you go in the clinic in Vevey and we make you better. But Dr. Roesch say no more booze, Lerry—he say that, okay? But you sneak a liddle here, a liddle there and is bad again in a month, in *weeks*, Lerry. Same the liver, huh? Same thing all over. No booze, Lerry. Dr. Roesch say any booze and you kill yourself dead, no question. A couple days later—boom!—Lerry's drunk on the floor. Nerves, Lerry. All people drink for is nerves."

The manager staggered by under a mountain of books, made signs with his head that the Steadman Jones awaited Larry on his desk, and directed a wary smirk at Miko.

"What do you expect—nerves!" Larry whispered desperately. "You send Rostov after me today to make me feel good?"

"You don't like Rostov?" Miko preened his left lapel.

"He gives me the fucking creeps."

Miko nodded sagely. "Is nerves, Lerry. Believe me what I tell you, okay? So, this pain. I send you again Dr. Roesch up in Vevey. You go to the clinic in Vevey couple weeks; have tests, Lerry, sleep a liddle, eat careful. You want I arrange that?"

It was the last thing on earth Larry Bartell wanted at that moment, but he made the appropriate noises.

Miko propped one elbow in his hand and cupped his chin. A mist filmed the blue eye; the brown one stared off into space. "You know something, Lerry? You get my age and is nothing but pain. Pain in the body, pain in the heart. Old age, Lerry. Sooner or later you get old. Okay." He reached up and very gently flicked a speck of dust from Larry's shoulder. "The thing is, Lerry, the best rule, is never brood. You unnerstand brood?"

"Look, Miko, all I need is to go home and sleep. I just want to—"

"Is bad, this brooding. Bad for the heart, bad for the brain, Lerry. A man get to be full of pain, and he think maybe he's dying. He think to himself, Time I got my life straightened out good, empty my soul, repent my sins." The blue eye fixed on him unwaveringly. "You haven't wrote no letters to your wife, have you, Lerry? Your kids? Nothing like that? Set-the-record-straight-type letters?"

Larry felt as if every part of him were collapsing at once, from his face down, a final, total, unconditional surrender to forces beyond his control, but somehow he summoned up a faint bark of disdain, jabbed his hands on his hips, and demanded, "And what do you suggest I say to them, Miko? Ever give a thought to what I could *say*? 'Sorry, gang.' Is that what I'd say? 'So sorry for fucking up your each and every—' "

Miko took him by the arm and squeezed it warningly: *too loud.*

Larry steadied. "No!" he whispered angrily. "I didn't wrote no letters to my family." It was pathetic the way he tried to punish Miko through his creaking grammar.

But the little man didn't seem to have noticed. He held on to Larry with both hands. "Now you listen, Lerry, you listen good. We make you fine all over again, is what we do—me and Dr. Roesch." A twinkle of sheer mischief curled up one corner of his mouth and touched the brown eye. "Maybe I get Stegelmann help, and everybody help. Even Rostov, okay, Lerry?"

"Great, Miko. Thanks. But for a day or so I'd—"

"Get Lerry good and well, no more pains. We take you in the clinic moment you get back."

"Back?" He had to hold his chest, hold the heart in. "Back from where?"

"First I have need you take a liddle trip down in Paris for me. Three, four days, no more."

"Miko, I can't!"

Mustn't. Daren't. The point of contact is here in Switzerland, Miko. If Garfield comes through, it'll be *here*.

"Miko, listen. I'm *ill*. Am I getting through to you? I'm—" He felt the manager's gaze on him, wary, uncertain, and turned his back on him. "I'm bringing up *blood*, Miko. I get blackouts, I get dizzy, I hallucinate. I forget things. I'm no use to you like this, goddamnit. I don't know what I'm doing half the time. Christ, in Frankfurt—" He cut himself off so fast he choked. God help him, he was on the point of telling Miko how he had blacked out beside the skating rink. I yield! I yield! Take me!

But there was no arguing with Miko.

"Is vacation, Lerry, you hear what I say? I send you on liddle vacation in Paris. You go there, you take a liddle something for friend of mine, you sleep, you read"—he tapped the paperback in Larry's hand—"you come back, tell me how it end. Maybe I read sometime."

"Wait a minute. Look, Miko, why don't you send Rostov, what do you say? Why don't you—"

Miko hooked a gold half hunter out of an inner pocket. "You have one hour and a half, Lerry. Your plane is five-thirty, tickets and cash at airport. Use your French passport, unnerstand me?"

"But what *for*, Miko? Why do I have to go to Paris?"

Miko paused in the act of withdrawing. Neither eye had Larry in perfect focus, but both thought they were looking at him. "You take the book I just buy you, Lerry, okay? Take the book. You get in Paris, Orly, someone tell you who and where. Carry your book. They see, they know who you are, absolutely." He contemplated this, eyes on his feet, then nodded firmly several times. "Good. Good. I go now, Lerry." And raised his neat little bowler and strutted out the way Stegelmann had come in.

Larry started after him—why? what do you have in mind, Larry? an appeal against sentence?—but stopped in mid-stride at the top of the ramp leading down into the greeting card room. Miko was already out of reach; he was climbing into his car, one of those stretch limousines the Germans make for funerals and state occasions. Stegelmann was riding shotgun. The driver wore maroon.

There was no sign of Rostov.

FIVE

Garfield called Nick Montero from New York, and Nick was waiting for him at Dulles with an armor-plated Lincoln Continental.

"I don't need an armor-plated Lincoln," he protested.

"I don't got no other kind," Nick said proudly.

"I just need a car and a driver. Anything."

"You think I'd let you ride around in anything?"

Nick was rail thin and downright ugly, but at any speed over thirty no man alive was more at home behind the wheel of a car. He had been Garfield's personal driver for twenty-eight largely uncomplaining years.

"I might be here for several days," Garfield warned him, eyeing the great black slug of the Lincoln with some trepidation. "You can't afford that much time. And I'm not sure I can afford you."

"What's to afford?" Nick swung up the solitary valise and put it to bed in the carpet-lined trunk. "Listen, did I tell you I got me fifteen of these tanks now? Fif-*teen!*" He slapped the car affectionately.

"Seems everybody I know is in private security these days," Garfield reflected out loud. Inside the car he had the sensation of sitting in his coffin.

"There's a fortune in it," Nick agreed, belting up. "It's a question of status, mostly, my way of thinking. Rich guys, politicians, diplomats, Arabs, that kind—they all wanna be bulletproof these days, know what I mean? They like people to think they're such big shots some guy's dying to blow 'em away every minute of the day. Good for the image, good for me. I'm first choice with State, Defense, Justice, and the White House appointments office. Six hundred bucks a day per vehicle plus extras."

"That's a lot of worry," Garfield said, thinking again of Fred Goldman.

"Worry? Who's worrying? I got Lyn running the office—you remember Lyn? A kid when you seen her last—and Joe's running the garage. Who needs me anymore? Like Spencer Tracy said that time, life is a terminal disease, right? Cash in while you can." He pulled out onto the parkway.

"If you say so."

"Sure I say so. I always said so. Where we going?"

The Liberty Tower overlooked Rock Creek Cemetery, one of

those glistening glass and concrete phalluses Washington whites cling to against their better judgment in an otherwise all-black sea of urban decay. Its upper half was lost in morning smog-mist, and the amputation left the bottom half curiously characterless; it could have been a morgue or a laundry or an institution for the insane. In any event, without Nick Montero, Garfield would have penetrated no farther than the concrete triune, *Inspiration with Holes*, in the front lobby, for in its way the Liberty Tower was also in the private security business and a bitterly hostile environment for unaccredited strangers. Luckily it was also a favored dormitory for foreign diplomats, and as a chauffeur to the bulletproofed great, Nick was in and out of there all the time. He was known. Even so, it took fifteen minutes and three sub rosa telephone calls to God knew whom before the chief security officer cleared Garfield to ride under escort to the tenth floor. The guard rang the bell for him.

A boy answered it, a boy by Garfield's standards: a tall, thin, pale houseplant of a kid who could have been eighteen or twenty-eight but not much more. Garfield's height and girth were apparently too much for him at first, for he flinched behind the security chain; but the sight of the guard evidently came as a morale booster, and with an apologetic jerk of the head he uncoupled the hardware.

"Mr.?" Garfield gave it a question mark.

"John Sayer. Didn't they say downstairs?" For a moment he glanced worriedly at the guard. "Didn't they tell you anything downstairs?" He was dark, liberally hairy on the backs of his hands and forearms. A pair of tortoise-shell glasses hung at his chest from a cord around his neck, and when he saw Garfield's eyes on them, he touched them protectively. "I don't know why anyone didn't . . ." he started to say, but the guard saluted and walked back to the elevator. "Why can't people just say?"

Garfield smiled encouragingly. "My fault probably. My name's Goodrum, John Goodrum. Is Mrs. Bartell in?"

"Sayer!" The boy colored. "Her name's *Sayer*! Jesus, didn't they say *anything* downstairs?" He pulled Garfield in and slammed the door. "I'm sorry, it's a hell of a mess in here. The kids are on Easter vacation. Driving me nuts."

Halfway down the rosewood-paneled hallway he stopped. "You want to see the kids?" His right eye was the bad one, a roamer.

"Well . . ."

"You might as well. Lydia's not here." He opened a door and shoved his narrow shoulders into the gap. "Hey, you two, say hello to—" He looked back at Garfield. "Sorry, I forgot your name."

"Goodrum."

"Mr. Goodrum, friend of your mom's."

Garfield looked in. The children were Larry-scale pocket editions of the real thing: young-old, small-boned, curly-haired, distressingly ugly in the way that ducklings are ugly but with half the appeal; not a shadow of emotion on their flat, almost identical Pekingese faces.

"Good morning," Garfield said, acutely embarrassed by their stares.

They made no response.

"So say hello, you dummies!" Sayer flared.

"Hello."

They said it in unison, as if that were the arrangement, and, having released the word, relapsed again into plastic immobility. They had been reading, perhaps pretending to read, a volume each of the *Encyclopaedia Britannica*, and the books lay open on their knees; but at either end of the room, roughly on a line with their overstuffed chairs, two globular white television sets, his and hers, showed pictures without sound, a cartoon cat chasing a cartoon mouse through a junkyard, Clint Eastwood shooting Italian Mexicans with blank-faced indifference.

Sayer's hands were balling. "What do you use for manners, you slobs? Come on, on your feet! The man's talking to—"

"No, please." Garfield backed out. "They're reading. Let it be."

"They're not reading." Sayer's stretched triangle of a face

colored again. "I said they couldn't go out, so they're sulking." He turned on them angrily. "You're supposed to be grown up! Mature! Christ Almighty!" He slammed the door on them. "Little bastards! Kathryn looks like Larry and thinks like Lydia; Seth looks like Lydia and thinks like Larry. If that's eugenics, you can keep it. You want to step in here?"

The living room was high-ceilinged, long, and airy, and Garfield silently wagered good money that Lydia's hand had designed it. The furniture was of stripped pine, smoked glass, and pale cream leather. Huge unframed pictures of the chuck-it-and-see school hung on walls of a blinding sandy yellow. The statuary was baldly bad and mainly in roughcast bronze. As in the children's room, the seating was airport modern and fat; something Japanese and tinkly spun from the ceiling. At the end of the room a wall of sliding glass gave onto a terrace of Spanish tile and a misty, panoramic view of Rock Creek Cemetery, a consummation devoutly to be wished by anyone intent on suicide.

"One thing money can still buy is bad taste, right?" Sayer waved around him. "She was into interior design. Design!" He threw himself into a chair. "Flop, why don't you?"

Garfield lowered his bulk with rather more care. "You said she's not here. Does that mean—"

"You family or something?"

"Just a friend."

"Of her father's?" The reaction came whipcrack fast.

"Well, no. We haven't met. Yet." Garfield paused. "You said she isn't here."

The boy's face reddened again. "That's right. She left. Walked out. Retired from the fray." He glared down at his large feet. "She left the kids on deposit and went out into the world to make something of herself. Ha!"

"I don't understand."

"Welcome to the club." John Sayer threw a swatch of dark hair off his face with a defensive flick of the head. "Role reversal; I stay home and play mother."

"What about your job?"

"This *is* my job." He said it with his jaw out as if he expected an argument.

"But your career. Surely—"

"Systems analyst. I was with Brooke-Davis out on the Beltway. Aerospace consultants. I flew a computer."

"And you gave that up to—"

"It gave me up. Don't you read the papers? The *Washington Post* ran a story about me and Lydia getting married—last Christmas, sixteen months after the event. Shock, horror, scandal: 'Larry Bartell's ex weds in secret' kinda crap."

"What did that have to do with your losing your job?"

"Oh, nothing, nothing at all." He was too naïve a soul by far to carry irony with any flair. "They just said, 'Hey, look, fella, we're government contractors, right? We work for secret people, right? Secret people don't dig the Larry Bartells of this world, right? So blow.' " He swung a sudden ridiculously girlish uppercut at the air.

"And that's why Lydia left?"

The clothes hanger shoulders rose around the cab door ears and fell again. "Do women ever need reasons? Jesus! You know what?" He looked up brightly, his eyes suspiciously red. "I even *knew* it was going to happen. From the beginning I knew. Larry's track record, Lydia's hang-up about him, the kids blowing hot one minute, cold the next. 'We don't *need* a new father' —that kinda shit, all that stuff, I knew it."

Garfield waited.

"But what you think is—you think, we can work it out. Like the song, right? The whole deal's crazy, but we'll work it out. Her forty-two years old, me twenty-six: impossible, but what the hell, *life's* impossible."

"But she left you," Garfield whispered. They might have been in church.

"Two days after the *Post* broke that goddamned story, maybe three, I can't remember."

"No speeches? No discussion? She just up and left?"

"She came home this particular day—I don't know; afternoon,

57

late, Saturday afternoon—and starts going on about how she has to *realize* herself. You like that? *Realize* herself. Couldn't look me in the eye. Had to be herself for a change, she said, instead of three or four other people. Bullshit!"

"How so?"

"How *so!*" He was pretty light on mimicry, too. "I'll tell you how so. Because she had a bag already packed, that's why. Because the kids knew she was going, that's why. Because she said she'd gotten this job, just dropped into her lap, thirty-five thousand a year and extras. Come *on!*"

"You're a little ahead of me, John." Garfield used the given name gently. "What job?"

"With Stellatronics Industries. Executive assistant to the president, lying bitch."

"Why should she lie?"

"Because a job that big you'd have to work for for months. Because they'd grill you sunny side up and over lightly ten times a day and talk to everyone you'd ever met or written to or bought from. Because Stellatronics is high-tech, the highest. Missile systems, satellite navigation, NASA, air force, navy, top secret stuff. I mean, Christ, I said to her, 'You think I was born yesterday?' She had to have worked for that goddamn job for months, and her old man pulling strings all the way."

Garfield managed somehow to hold down his elation. "You lose a job because of Larry Bartell and Lydia gains one? Doesn't seem very logical."

"Thurlan Bartell doesn't deal in logic. He deals in influence. So does his daughter. Logic sucks."

"Then what does it mean, in your opinion?"

The boy propped his chin in his hands and stared sightlessly at the floor. "Object of the exercise was to get her away from me, that's all. Out of the marriage."

"Leaving her children behind? On deposit?"

"Why not? They know what's going on."

"But you don't? Exactly, I mean. Has she asked for a divorce?"

"She will."

"Have you tried talking to her? Have you called her at Stella-tronics, for instance?"

Sayer shrugged again and stretched his long, pointed face till the cheeks hollowed. "I get as far as the fifteenth assistant secretary down the line and she says, 'Sorry, Lydia's in confer-ence,' or 'out to lunch,' or whatever. In with the president."

"Who's he?" Garfield asked casually, knowing. Knowing.

"He's called Tyler Bloomfield. Friend of her father's, nat-urally. You know him?"

"I've heard of him. A scientist, isn't he?"

"Science, technology, business, politics, the works."

"And Lydia." Garfield wanted it over suddenly, out of the way. "Where does she live? With her father?"

"I don't know."

"But surely she sees the children. There must be some arrange-ment for her to—"

Sayer couldn't meet his gaze. "A guy comes. This gorilla comes over Saturday mornings early, picks up the kids for the weekend. Brings them home Sunday night. Her lover maybe. I didn't ask for his credentials."

"He have a name?"

John Sayer looked up finally. "His name's McKinnon," he said hoarsely. "That's all I know. The kids call him Uncle Roy."

Outside, the sun was shining. So was Nick Montero's face. "Where to?" he demanded, a man with secrets to tell.

"Sixteenth Street."

"The Gold Coast?" Nick swung in and started the engine. "Who you got your sights on this time? The queen of Sheba?"

Garfield's heart sank, but for old times' sake, old Nick's sake, he met the joke head-on. A smart-ass grin, a wink, a tweak of the tie. "You mind driving the car, sonny," he retorted with phony hauteur.

"Well, I'll be damned!" Nick gave a cockcrow of delight and pulled out into traffic.

They had this long-running gag, a quarter of a century long-

59

running, in which Nick pretended that Luke Garfield was the preeminent stallion of the Washington inner circle and Garfield pretended it was true. How or why they'd confected this calumny—and for whose amusement other than Nick's—Garfield had no idea, but it had run too long to be quashed now. Trouble was, it had passed through so many stages of unedifying ritual that Garfield was half disposed to think Nick actually believed it. The truth was—Garfield mused moodily—that real friendship was impossible without intellectual equality. The rest is concession. As Larry Bartell had no doubt discovered with Lydia. As Lydia had probably found with poor John Sayer. *Poor* John Sayer?

"Did you pick up anything back there?" he asked sharply.

"Lydia's old man owns the apartment. Thurlan J. Bartell *theee* Third. Owns fifty percent of the stock in the building, too. Used to live there hisself one time—kinda peed-a-tair for when he was in town from Vahginnyah"—Nick gave it the required southern diphthong—"then Lydia comes home with the kids— you know, skipping out from that husband of hers back in Europe—and she moves in."

"The old man here often?"

"Not since Lydia married the joker he ain't—this Sayer guy."

"They don't get along?"

"Far as the old man's concerned, he don't know him, ain't met him, and won't. Raised hell when Lydia married him, tried to get the kids away from her, that kinda deal. Then they kissed and made up—him and Lydia, I mean, not Sayer."

"Leaving the boy out in the cold," Garfield muttered, half to himself.

"I wouldn't say that exactly." Nick was enjoying the role of informer. "He's a dummy, that kid, general opinion of the staff and flunkies. But a smart dummy. He picks up a thousand bucks cash from Papa every month; every fourth Friday, regular as clockwork, that chief security grunt there takes him a envelope. Salary for minding the kids. And Sayer don't pay for nothing up there. Papa takes care of everything. Food, entertainment, booze, car, gas—you name it. There's a checking account, no plastic."

"I'd have said that entitled the old man to visiting rights, then, Sayer or no Sayer, wouldn't you? How does he get to see the children?"

Nick pulled up at a red light and glanced over his shoulder. "They go visiting for a weekend in Vahginnyah once a month."

"And he's happy with that?"

"Seems to be. At least he gets to keep tabs on the kids."

"Once a month?"

"He's got other ways." Nick's left eye flickered perceptibly. "I, er, I had to slip the security grunt a coupla hundred," he said delicately.

"All right. Remind me later. Go on?"

Nick tapped the side of his unlovely nose. "The old man's had that apartment bugged since the day Lydia and the kid got married. Even the bathroom. Nothing goes on up there he don't know about. Some guy works for him goes up twice a week to change the tapes on the bug deck."

Garfield closed his eyes in a commendable bid to hold on to his temper. "Well, thank you very much, Nick," he said tightly. "Thank you very much indeed."

"What could I do?" Nick appealed, easing away from the lights. "You'd been up there twenty minutes when this came up. Anything you were gonna say you'd already come right out with, so—"

Garfield sighed. "All right, all right. What else?"

"The chief grunt—that's the guy in the lobby—he takes home four hundred a month for looking in on the apartment whenever the kids are home. He looks in three times a day and last thing at night and calls this answering service of Bartell's to say everything's okay."

Garfield contemplated this revelation for a while. "Nick, if you were in Thurlan Bartell's shoes, would you rent out your grandchildren to somebody you couldn't stand the sight of?"

"Not this side of paradise," Nick said with relish.

"Nor would I. Nor I'm sure—" He was about to say "would he—from choice" but stopped himself. What *choice*? How much choice were any of them really free to exercise? A multimillionaire martinet pays a fortune for the privilege of seeing his grandchildren once a month. A twenty-four-year-old husband plays *Hausfrau* because overnight his wife decides to *realize* herself. A mother deeply attached to her children leaves them on deposit five days a week. "Maybe I'm just out of touch," Garfield murmured. "Maybe this is happening to families all over the country. Even the rich."

"There ain't no rich like there used to be," Nick replied. "Believe me, I know; I haul 'em around all the time. Nowadays the rich are just poor people with money."

Garfield smiled frostily. "What did your friend have to say about the mother?"

"Lydia?" Nick lifted a hand from the wheel and made a swooping downward movement, thumb first. "On Lydia, baby, money don't buy. I offered the guy another coupla hundred, but he went deaf. No way."

"Did he mention someone called McKinnon? Roy McKinnon? Comes on weekends to take the children to their mother."

"The heavyweight that'd be. Yeah, he mentioned him. Every weekend he comes and goes. I asked the grunt if he thought there was anything going on between him and Lydia—you know, hanky-panky—but he went cold on me."

Roy McKinnon. Tyler Bloomfield. Straws in the wind. Garfield turned the key in the appropriate memory bank, and out they came, exactly as he'd fed them in.

McKinnon, Roy James Albert; Silver Star, Korea, 1950; CIA selection course, 1952; inducted 1953. Field service in paramilitary category Iran, Egypt, Vietnam, Laos, Vietnam again, Cambodia, Japan, Vietnam a third time; European theater activities based in Paris. Langley back room boy, 1978. No data beyond '78. Age: middle fifties.

Bloomfield, Tyler Hallet: Yale class of '38; wartime submarine commander, later Annapolis instructor; entered the CIA's Remington compound at San Diego for three-year course in advanced electronics (missiles), 1968; co-opted to Langley's Board of Advisement, 1972; appointed presidential consultant on military uses of outer space, 1974; resigned government service to join the multinational conglomerate North American-Stafford, 1976.

North American-Stafford being the industrial and financial base from which Alden Healey ("Brock") Stafford subsequently launched himself into the political stratosphere, first as secretary of commerce, then as special counselor, and for the past twenty-odd months as national security adviser to the president.

Convenient. Garfield spoke it aloud, unconsciously.

"What?" Nick leaned back, eyes on the road.

"Nothing."

Nothing but everything. Well, now, which of the several propositions could he entertain? On which side of a two-way mirror do you stand to observe the truth (provided there is one)? The easy answer, even the logical one, was that Langley was in the process of making a complex approach to Larry Bartell—via Brock Stafford via Roy McKinnon via Tyler Bloomfield via Lydia Sayer via Thurlan J. Bartell III—though why it should be interested and why this vast chain of man- and woman-power should be judged necessary was beyond Garfield's comprehension. Still, an approach to Larry to cross over was a bare possibility; Langley had psyched itself into far more unlikely dream states in its time. But why? The same old sticking point. What was Larry worth on the hoof? On past performance, very much less than the thousand a month Thurlan J. was paying John Sayer. Far, far less than the heartache, the dislocation, and the self-denial of Lydia and her children. In fact, looked at the other way around, Larry was actually worth nothing at all; he was offering himself for free, wasn't he? He *wanted* to come home; he'd said so out there in the Frankfurt dark not ten days ago. Wonderful coincidence.

"Nick"—he broke in on himself—"did your man mention reading a story about Sayer in the *Washington Post*? Around Christmas?"

"Hey, you saw that? The one that took the lid off of the marriage—yeah, I read that. I suddenly remembered when I was talking to the security stiff. He said they had this reporter and photographer staked out in front of the building for over a week, just sitting there waiting. Said he had to sneak Lydia and the kids in and out through the boiler room in back. Yeah, he mentioned that."

"Did he talk to the reporter?"

"Tried to talk sense, yeah. But all he got was the usual bullshit: It was their job and all that. 'You have a public responsibility to tell me what you know,' she says to him, this reporter; she's a woman, see. I mean, where'd they get off talking crap like that, these people? Anyway, he sticks his gut in her face and says to move on or he'll break her feet off at the shoulder, official. So they take a picture of him doing it, and she says, 'See how you like it with your ugly mug all over the front page, schmuck,' and he says—"

"Any theories about how the story got out?"

"Hey, now that was funny. I mean, the stiff thought it was funny the way it turned out afterward." Nick turned onto Sixteenth Street. "When they cornered Lydia and Sayer that day, took the pictures in the supermarket and stuff, Lydia came home bawling her eyes out, big scene. She was telling the stiff on the desk all about it and he was thinking maybe he should call old Thurlan J. when, what do you know, the old man comes on the line hisself; he's calling the stiff. Wants to know every detail, who did what, who said what."

Garfield cut in on him. "That's the place. See it? Copper-colored building on the right." He pointed ahead over Nick's shoulder.

"Got you."

"So what was funny about that?" Garfield asked, his concentration broken.

"Because, like the stiff said, how'd the old man get to know so quick? Nobody'd told him yet. Lydia hadn't; she was standing right there having hysterics. So the stiff gave her the phone, and she told her papa how it was."

A cold shudder of comprehension ran along Garfield's spine. "Perhaps the reporter called him for a quote," he suggested. "They do that."

"There wasn't no quote from him in the story. The stiff said there was just a line in it said 'Lydia's father, Mr. Thurlan J. et cetera, was not available for comment.' You know, like they say in these stories."

"And what did the, er, stiff conclude from that?"

Nick pulled over to the curb and checked his wing mirrors thoroughly. Satisfied, he switched off the engine and addressed Garfield through the rearview mirror. "Just it was funny, that's all. Maybe somebody who saw what happened at the supermarket phoned him and tipped him off. Maybe that."

"Yes, that's probably what happened," Garfield said.

And maybe pigs can fly, he thought, levering himself out onto the sidewalk. If anyone tipped off the *Post*, it was Papa, directly or indirectly. That was the logic of it, wasn't it? The way the finger pointed? Certainly it was. Had to be.

A nice little electric shock to throw the girl off balance. And when it was over, the crying done, the damage done, the story in print . . . "It's time you got out of that apartment. Out of that damned marriage. It's time you *realized* yourself, girl." Yes, that would be Papa Thurlan's role: the far-sighted pragmatist, the prescriber of revolutionary cures.

"Get out and *do* something. Stand on your own feet. Be yourself. Try it. Just give it a trial for a month or so; I'll see the kids are taken care of. Now, listen, there's a good friend of mine, Tyler Bloomfield . . ."

The only thing wrong with the scenario was that he couldn't for the life of him think of a justification for any of it.

65

SIX

The building was a copper-colored box of glass and stucco with
two very Caucasian gods holding up the porte-cochere, a nude
god with a beard and a nude god without, each with a hand on
his hip in an attitude of unmistakable come-on. Sixteenth Street
is the vena cava of black middle-class Washington, and it occurred to Garfield in passing that the statuary was meant to
convey a message of some ethnic significance. But then everything in Washington is meant to have ethnic significance and
messages are a dime a dozen. He took the elevator to the third
floor.

The office was at the very end of a long corridor and seemed
to be the only one not to have changed hands in recent weeks.
The plate on the door was old-fashioned brass and highly
polished, but a rash of cards and scribbled notes, most of them
timeworn, peppered the paintwork around it. "Don't forget
EHO Del—Thurs," said one. "Dave on China High—call," said
another. A Señor Alph. Berenguela of Buenos Aires had left his
card, and so had Dr. Fritz Münche, jnlst, of *Die Welt*, and
Carl Rodriguez-Mahon of the Commonwealth Secretariat—
"New York 5th Oct to 27th, Sherry Netherland." Under the
brass plate was pasted a strip of glossy paper bearing the legend
"Prisoners of Conscience, Inc. is a self-supporting nonprofit-
making body relying on the good will and generosity of the
public for its survival. Remember this, please, when you leave."

Oh, yes, he thought, you'll do.

The outer office was unmanned, and the telephone answering
machine switched to automatic. The inner door was ajar, and he
pushed it wide. She had her back to him and turned quickly, her
hair sweeping the air like a scythe, her dark eyes wide for a
moment with the fear that isn't quite fear but apprehension
tinged with anger. When she saw him, she made a brief O of
recognition—a soft mouth, too big to be beautiful. Then she
smiled and the room teemed with sunlight.

"*Oh, no,* I don't be*lieve* it! Luke?"

She came at him with a huge old file box clutched in front of her, and they laughed when he tried to embrace her and couldn't. Backing away, looking for somewhere to put it down, she realized there wasn't a table, desk, or chair in the room that wasn't already stacked high with debris, and with a loud "oh, dammit!" she dropped it on the floor and threw herself into his arms.

Her hair was black and satin-soft and fragrant as honeysuckle, and as it blanketed his face for a moment, he sent up the old man's traditional prayer, "Oh, Lord, make me twenty-five again, if only for the next ten seconds." He released her and was touched to see tears in her eyes. Pretty as a—

"You look pretty as a picture," he said.

"And you're an old *ham*." She threw her arms around his neck and blotted the tears on his shirt. "Why do I always *cry?*" she wailed. "Once every three months if I'm lucky—four this time—and all I do is . . . *bawl*." She snatched the handkerchief out of his breast pocket and dabbed her eyes, big, black, helpless eyes, a cosmic phenomenon, he'd always thought, black islands of utter desolation set in a sea of total serenity. Polly, who was immune to the charms of most members of her sex, thought that C.J. was in every single minor particular the picture she'd always carried in her mind's eye of Mary Magdalene, and while that might have been overdramatizing things a bit, Garfield knew what she meant.

They cleared a couple of chairs and sat face-to-face holding hands. Che Guevara watched benevolently from a poster over her head. Allende from another. She smiled at him. "I bet you weren't just passing through. I bet—"

"You're right. You're always right."

She pressed his hands together in hers. "You come only when you want something. Am I right?"

"Polly sends her love."

"Is she here!"

"Not yet. Maybe later."

"Sidetracking me again, you old—"

"Fox?"

"Wolf! Coming in here taking advantage of a kid half your age."

"*Half* my age?"

The smile deserted her, the appetite for banter, too. She stared into his face. "I miss Polly so much," she said softly. "I can't tell you. I miss you both."

"We miss you," he grunted, embarrassed, and tried to remember when he'd last given a moment's thought to her. Months.

She looked thinner, more vulnerable, a small girl, five-two in her black pumps, frail under the sweep of hair and a white ruffled blouse with a collar that overflowed her shoulders. C.J. Poole, Candida Jesfa Poole, born Pulewska, secretary-general of Prisoners of Conscience, Inc. and quite half Luke Garfield's age, closer to forty than she deserved to be. And Poole because she'd learned her lessons in lifemanship early: Even political prisoners at the extremity of despair had had reservations about accepting help from a radical Polish Jew, so she'd changed her name.

She put on a show of brightening up. "Three guesses why you came this time. Larry, Larry, and, er, Larry."

He shrugged. Maybe he colored a little; it felt like it. "You're too good for me. Old Larry."

"Well, this is how it is, Mr. Moonshine." She hooked a thumb over her shoulder at a framed collage of yellowing press clippings on the wall behind her desk. "That's the only Larry I know, Luke Garfield. History, that's all he is to me."

"You were still campaigning for the restitution of his passport last year," he reminded her gently.

"That was principle." She let his hands fall, folded hers primly in her lap. "The passport was principle. Larry, too, I guess, in a way. The government was out to get him for years, you know that. He was out of step, out of sync. When they do that in Russia or Latin America"—she couldn't look at him—"we're the first to scream foul!"

"And you're a honey-tongued dreamer. Let me remind you,

Larry Bartell was arrested on drugs and morals charges. By his own admission he was legally and morally responsible for what happened. That's why he skipped the country. That's why they took away his passport. He didn't cotton to the idea of jail. It didn't fit his image."

She shook her head, fast and firmly at first, then with less confidence. She smiled. "Will you tell me why we always go through this? You know what you know, and I know what I think. We're not going to change. Are we?"

"No. But maybe he's changing."

He told her then, talked directly into that sea of serenity and watched the black eyes deepen and deepen until he found her distress unbearable and reached again for her hand. When he finished, she got up and walked to the desk.

"I ought to make you coffee or something," she said distractedly.

"And I ought to buy you lunch." He jumped up too fast and received a jab of exquisite pain through his right shoulder. "Aaaah!" He clapped his hand to it.

She turned on him. "Now that's what you get for sleeping on boats," she said triumphantly. "Polly wrote and told me. All through that damp—"

"I know what Polly wrote you," he growled. "And she's wrong. It's just cramp."

She said the sunshine was too rare to waste, so they compromised and went to stare at old Abe Lincoln while Nick Montero withdrew to a place he knew where they made the finest liverwurst sandwiches in the universe. When he came back, they spread a plaid rug on the grass and ate like real people.

Garfield was oppressively aware of the loom of the White House through the trees across the Ellipse; it was newly painted and glowed in the bright sunshine like the architectural white elephant it was fast becoming. The first time he ever saw her, he remembered, was from the White House. She was ramrodding a demonstration outside the gates. Students Against the War, circa 1967. Placards, endless chanting, a coffin labeled "America's future." In those days the only political prisoners she had on her mind were American draft dodgers wilting away in durance vile over the Canadian border, but that was before Larry Bartell found her and gave her the world. Larry had set up Prisoners of Conscience, Inc. in 1968 and given it a genuinely international stance (if "genuine" was a word one could use in connection with Larry Bartell). Unfortunately for C.J., it became apparent early on that all of POC's chosen targets were pro-American— Britain, France, West Germany, Italy, Turkey, South Africa, the South American states—for Larry, as he was happy to tell anyone at any time, was uncompromisingly pro dissident: pro IRA, pro Red Brigades, pro Baader-Meinhof, pro the African National Congress, pro PLO, pro the Cuban left, and anti practically everything else you cared to name, including the presidency. Wherein lay his charisma, of course. The kids loved him.

C.J. found him irresistible. Garfield suspected they'd shared more than ideology for a while because in the summer of '69 POC's headquarters was shunted abruptly from Cambridge, Massachusetts, to Washington, and C.J. with it. Perhaps Lydia's eagle eye had fallen on her; who could say? In any event, at a stroke she sacrificed her education, her love, and her future— and, to top off the debacle, broke her unfortunate mother's heart. *Ideals*. And of course, she'd hardly turned her back before Larry was sidling off to plumb deeper, more satisfying concepts. POC was shoved onto a back burner, and C.J. was left to cope. When Larry ran for Europe four years later, she was left holding a very explosive baby indeed, a squalling brat owing eight months' rent and about to be busted by the FBI's antiterrorist squad.

Garfield moved in just in time. "Bought in," as the jargon has it.

It would have been madness not to. First, because of C.J. herself. She was just twenty-three years old, a college dropout, an idealist with more star dust in her eyes than vision, and five years of solid activism behind her—far too good a prospect to waste. Secondly, the machine she'd created was truly remarkable, in spite of Larry. POC had become the student clearing house of world suppression, a collection of faces, names, causes, sympathizers. Hundreds of thousands of men and women under arrest for their political beliefs were minutely logged in POC's files, and—infinitely more important—alongside them, all neatly filed and cross-indexed, were the pressure groups actively campaigning for their release, many of them banned organizations and several with established terrorist connections. As a monitor of radical activism around the world, POC was potentially a gold mine, and Garfield was quick to see it.

Rightly or wrongly—wrongly from the emotional standpoint —he'd made the harnessing of Prisoners of Conscience, Inc. his personal project, and arguably it couldn't have been handled any other way. First, he'd courted C.J. Using his permanent cover as an assistant undersecretary at State, he had played on the girl's loneliness—and to some extent her urgent need of a father figure—and slowly gained her confidence. He'd introduced her to Polly—for which his wife had only recently forgiven him— and eventually to the softer fringe of his social circle. C.J., in time, had yielded. The rest was easy. He had encouraged her to develop her existing clientele and broaden her political base— the personal touch, fatherlike, not the shadowy recommendations of a Washington mandarin. He funded the initial relaunch through Langley and arranged for annual grants-in-aid to be pumped in under the guise of individual and corporate donations. POC, Inc. rose again from the ashes. As far as he knew, it was still serving a useful purpose, including the purpose C.J. thought it was serving.

After the picnic he sent Nick back to the car and took C.J. for a stroll by the Reflecting Pool. She knew something was coming; he could feel the tension in her.

They strolled for a while without speaking. Then he said, squeezing her arm, "Do I have to say it? Help me?"

"Define help."

"He's got cirrhosis of the liver. It's bad."

She leaned into him, stumbled, pushed him away. "I told you, Luke, he's history. It was his choice, not mine, and now he's—"

"Now he's dying, and his choices are virtually nil."

She took his arm again. "You can get treatment for—"

"He's had treatment." He tried another tack. "Look, I didn't ask for this, I'm just the pig in the middle. I'm here because Larry put me here. 'Tell Garfield to go talk to the girl.' Not the president, not State, *you*. That's what he said. Now how do you suppose he got my name?"

"I don't know. How should I know?" She dropped his arm abruptly.

"Out of a fortune cookie, you think?"

"I'm not his keeper."

"No, you're his good right arm. You're his shield, the lifeline he only has to reach out to. Always there. When everyone else gave up on him—his wife, his kids—there was good old C.J. Poole, rallying 'round." He tried to gauge from her expression what she was thinking, but nothing showed, so he went for the jugular. "And you still haven't given up on him, have you? You're in touch with him. Have been for years."

Her gaze was unwavering, rock steady. "Am I?"

"You bet you are. He doesn't know me from Adam; he just knows my *name*. And he knows it because you told him. Because you wrote him about this old buzzard who helped fix up Prisoners of Conscience and put it back on the road. You probably mentioned I was something special over at State. And why not? Nothing harmful in that, no disloyalty intended; you meant it as a compliment. Gratitude. Besides"—he got an armlock on her and clamped his fist around her hand—"Larry'd want to know that kind of stuff, wouldn't he? Stuck over there in Europe, wherever, starved for news."

He knew that all he had to do was to keep on talking, that in the end her patience would snap, and probably her temper, too. He was right. She pulled up beside him very suddenly indeed, wrenched her hand and arm free, and planted herself in front of him.

"Why don't you damn well take up residence in my brain and be done with it?" she flashed. "I swore to him on my life, on my mother's life—"

"Your mother's dead."

"—that I wouldn't breathe a word to a living soul. I mean, I *promised* him, no matter how bad things were on his side or mine."

"Great! Then I guess we'll just have to let him die."

She shoved him, side on, two-handed; there was no weight to her, no strength. He said kindly, "Old men are worse than kids: long on temper, short on memory. Sorry."

C.J. Poole nodded wearily. "What did you have in mind?"

"A couple of weeks of your time. Maybe less."

"That's impossible. Luke, you know as well as I do I can't leave POC for two weeks. Gracie's a secretary, not an administrator, and—"

"Suppose I offer you Harry Warner as a stand-in."

"Warner of Amnesty? That Warner? You couldn't. He wouldn't come."

"He's standing by. You just have to pick up the phone." He trapped her hand again. "Two weeks, C.J. Two weeks."

They were back at old Abe again. C.J. looked up at his graven calm and made that open-palmed gesture of the hand that means, what do you *do* with someone like this? Abraham Lincoln had no views on the subject.

She sighed. "All right, what do I have to do?"

Garfield spotted Nick's black limo cruising by on the avenue. He urged her toward it. "I want to make contact with him," he said easily. "You write to him where?"

"Luke, please, I—"

"Where?"

"It's in Montreux. Switzerland. Luke, I swore to him—"

"After that, I'd like you to go to Europe and bring him home."

"Home!"

Garfield slipped an arm around her shoulders and hugged her close. "He needs someone he can trust, honey. His good right arm. Who else would I send?"

SEVEN

Larry Bartell had been born too late for Paris. By the time he got there the glory had died, a victim of self-inflicted wounds.

The Paris of the French kings, the Paris of Haussmann, even the Paris of Hemingway's "moveable feast"—all that was so much travel poster hype. What Larry walked into all wide-eyed and hopeful that first time was a third-rate honky-tonk, a traffic-sodden clip joint where madmen were free to roam the streets in high-powered murder weapons and the price of everything tripled if you had an American accent. Since then it had merely deteriorated.

He hated it.

Because of its infernal nerve-shattering noise. Because of its stultifying vanity. Because of its dirt. Because of its passionate hypocrisy. He hated the snack bars and the fast-food shops and the hamburger joints pustulating down through the boulevards into ancient streets where real food had once been a religion. He hated the kids with their massed motorbikes on Saturday nights and their swaggering brutality. He hated the yellow-eyed faces of the foreign muggers in the Champs-Élysées (he'd been mugged twice himself—once outside Fouquet's, for Christ's sake!). He hated the police—oh, *boy*, how he hated the police— and from his gut he hated the CRS riot cops, a couple of whom had jumped the sidewalk behind him on a motorbike one night and belted him stupid with a nightstick for being "in evidence" on the boulevard Saint-Germain after midnight.

But mostly he hated Paris for what Miko in his old-fashioned way called *le milieu*, which in this instance meant the psychos of the French radical left, Larry's playmates from time to time and, under various flags, his friends of convenience. The truth was he couldn't trust them, nor they him. They resented outside interference, even Miko's. They were sly. They drank, smoked, sniffed, mainlined, ate, and screwed around to excess. They were a polyglot bunch of mental masturbators whose philosophy stopped short at the point where they blew society to smithereens. Someday he was going to ask Miko what the fuck he was doing rolling in their goddamned gutter.

For the moment, though, he was late, and that posed other problems. The five-thirty flight had left Geneva at eight-thirty, thanks to a strike by Air France cabin staff, and when it finally tucked into the stack over Paris, passengers were informed they would be landing at Charles de Gaulle, gateway to the new Europe, not at Orly, as advertised. At Orly there was a strike of Air France baggage handlers.

No one was paging him at Charles de Gaulle; no one lay in wait at the end of the shiny Plexiglas exit tube, no welcoming hand to tip the cool hello, not even a long-haired literate to wide-eye his copy of *The Tears of Autumn*. He hung around for as long as his nerves would stand it, then hopped an airport bus to the Porte Maillot terminus and took refuge in a bar across the street from La Défense to consider his next move. He had two in mind. One—obligatory—was to call Miko's cutout number and reconnect the Paris pickup. The other—personal—was to call Mena in Montreux and find out if Garfield had made his move yet. The dilemma it took a second Pernod to resolve was which one to call first.

Frankly it was a bad year for calling Switzerland from Paris, particularly at a quiet hour of the evening. The French treasury police had recently acquired yet another list of French citizens holding numbered accounts in Swiss banks, and the acrimony between the two governments was at its height. Who could say how many snoops were manning the public exchanges? Who knew how many paid spies there were in the swollen ranks of the phone service?

But as Garfield had already observed, Larry Bartell's range of choice was limited. He took a cab to an all-night PTT phone center behind the Arc and dialed Mena direct.

"Who this is?"

Mena had developed a hag's voice for answering the phone and, under Larry's instruction, learned never to volunteer her name or number. Mena was Iranian—or Persian, as she preferred —and to hear her tell it, the ayatollah was personally combing Europe to find her. Her husband, a banker, had been among the first fifteen hundred to die in front of the firing squads when Khomeini declared his paradise on earth, and Mena had taken the hint. No slouch when it came to underwriting her bread and water, she had ducked the funeral and skipped to Geneva on a diplomatic passport, carrying in her skirt her life's savings—or their kilo equivalent in high-grade heroin. Mena was tall the way Larry liked them, fruitfully bosomed, and sexually provident once he'd shaken out the myriad hang-ups. She was also a very rich woman indeed, so rich that the greater part of her waking hours was given over to disproving it. She subsisted in a rented apartment the size of an ice cube tray on a hilltop behind Montreux, shopped once a week to limit visibility, avoided all forms of social contact, and lived in constant terror of Allah's wrath. Larry had bumped into her two years ago and charmed her stupid. She loved him to distraction and beyond, and in one sense at least he loved her back, for Mena was one of only three people on earth Miko didn't know about (please, God) and his one precious unquestioning link to the outside world.

"Who this is?"

"This is he whose voice is thunder, baby," he said, and she gave a little sob, which was not so much wild joy at the sound of his voice, he judged, as relief at its not being the grand imam's.

"Daaarling! Oh, daaarling!"

"This is an open line, Mena. You know what I'm saying? I'm calling from Paris. Now listen, baby, was there anything in the mail for me in the last day or two?"

She was weeping. They never met without Mena's spilling tears on him. "Oh, my daaarling, daaarling one! I so miss—"

"Yeah, Mena, sure, me, too. Now listen to me, will you? I have seconds, that's all. Is there anything for me?"

For a woman who had swayed through Geneva customs with nine and a half kilos of dreamdust slung from her hips, Mena had surprisingly little emotional control. She was having a small *crise de coeur* at the other end. Larry swore under his breath and glanced quickly around him. Only two of the booths in the big room were occupied, both by Frenchmen yelling at the tops of their voices.

"Sugar, listen. Honey?" He dropped his voice to a whisper. "Beloved?" Shit for it, any port in a storm. "Beloved?"

"Oh, my dearest one, my—"

"Listen, Mena, I promise. Tomorrow, early, without fail, I'm going to call you again, and we'll talk. You know what I'm saying—*talk*? Only right now, *please*, just tell me if there's anything for me, will you? Mena?"

"Oh, daarling!" A wrenching sigh. "Wait, I get it." The phone went down with a crack, and he heard her cross the room, heard the ting-tong as she delved among the brass gongs and figurines on the sideboard. "Daaarling?"

"What have you got?"

"A letter."

"Mailed where?"

"Not mailed. Was delivered by person. In hand. Two hours ago, maybe three. Larry?"

He would have fallen down if the phone hadn't been there to support him. "Hand-delivered? To the apartment? By whom?"

"A man. Swiss-Italian. A man in—what you call?—leather clothing. Mmm, a round hat, metal—a helmet."

"A biker? Guy on a motorbike?" He didn't hear the answer to that. "What's on the envelope? Come on, woman, what does it say?"

"I reading, daaarling, I reading now. Address is to me, but same as always on the bottom, 'Urgentest,' then the numbers 'three-ten-sixteen.' "

Larry let his breath go in a torrent. Jesus! All present and correct. The lousiest code in the world—3/10/16 or, alphabetically, CJP for Poole—but no code in the world could hide you once they had your number, so the simpler the better. "Open it, Mena. Come on, quick."

He heard her nail slicing into the bond.

"What does it say?"

"Is typing, not hand. No signature, no date. Saying, 'Your request reached me. The answer is provisionally yes. But no further moves will be considered until I hear from you personally. In the interests of speed and security I am dictating this for dispatch by hand from Lugano. Call me day or night on'—" Mena broke off. "Here is a number now, daaarling. Many numbers. Do you want I—"

A Washington number, he noted, writing it down. "Mena, listen. You burn that letter, now, you got that? And the envelope. Burn it now."

"Oh, daaarling, when you come home? When you—"

"You're the soul of my soul, Mena." Sometimes he could even believe it himself, though not right now. "I'll call you tomorrow, honey. Burn the letter. Burn it now."

He hung up, ripped the sheet off the notepad and the next half dozen sheets as well in case of print-through, then folded the top sheet into a long, thin spike and fed it into the scroll of his belt. After that he was so wrung out he had to take a walk along the avenue Wagram and around the block.

It rained.

Larry Bartell had to pump up his courage for a solid half hour before he could bring himself to call Miko's cutout number in Geneva. At first he decided not to. Play a long shot, why not? What could they do about it? Then the pains started, and his confidence dropped like a brick. Worst thing he could do at that point was to arouse Miko's always simmering suspicions. It didn't take much after all. There was a system for cutout calls, and grievous punishments for not observing every last detail of time and method. So . . .

Back at the PTT center he dialed, the number scribbled on his airline ticket. The tone zipped six times, and Larry hung up. He dialed again, let it ring four times, and hung up again. On the third call Stegelmann picked up on the second ring and said he was the Council for Ethnic Freedoms, duty officer. Larry blurted the recognition code, "Sorry, wrong number. I was calling the home of Señor Marron," and waited to be switched into the recording equipment. He simply wasn't prepared for what happened next.

"Lerry?"

He was alone in the phone center at that moment, except for the blond *grandmère* behind the bulletproof glass and the real one swabbing the floor, so his terror enjoyed a privacy it didn't deserve. He tried to get out the word *Miko?* but it stuck in his throat. Miko! Impossible. For twenty-five years Miko Schellenberg had studiously resisted the seductions of the telephone. Some old painful memory, no doubt, a bug he'd fallen foul of, but one of his fetishes, a known hate. He'd told Larry so many times: an abomination, such things. "How you expect a thing so easily raped remain loyal, absolutely?" So you never heard his voice at a distance. Stegelmann's yes, occasionally Rostov's, now and then one of the crushers he employed as matching bookends. But Miko? It would be easier to get Gorbachev on his bathroom extension at home.

"Lerry? Is you?"

"Of course it's me." How the hell he ever got it out he'd never know. "How's the weather your end, Miko?" Big joke, but he had to win time for recovery: nerves, ulcer, liver, heart, all on the boil. I am no longer the sum total of my parts, Miko; I am some parts of my total, none of them whole.

"Lerry, you okay down there?" To Miko, anywhere out of Geneva was down.

79

"Sure I'm okay. Why shouldn't I be? There was a strike, that's all. We put down at Charles de Gaulle and—"

"Strikes! Lerry, you can' trust nobody these days do a liddle service proper. You tired, eh? You have pain down there. You want get home quick. I unnerstan. Where you talking?"

Where he talking? The initial panic subsided, but it left behind a residual throb of despair, an actual noise, like the plates of his skull rubbing together. Why Miko? What did he know, for Christ's sake? What had he guessed?

Miko answering a phone!

"A phone booth, Miko. A public phone."

"Where?"

"At the Arc. A PTT center behind the Arc. I thought I'd—" But he stopped because Miko had cupped a hand over the mouthpiece. If you don't use a phone much, you don't know what it means to be cut short that way. Miko's voice, muffled, followed by Stegelmann's: Miko, Stegelmann, Miko—

"Lerry, sorry. Sorry, Lerry."

Larry cut in before he lost the initiative. "Miko, I'm bleeding again, inside. You hear what I'm saying? I blacked out on the plane. In the airport bus. I can't hold out much longer, Miko. I don't think I can even make it to—"

"Lerry, you listen now, eh? You stay there, right there. You siddown and wait and a friend come. A few minutes is all, fifteen, twenny minutes, no more, then food and drink and a warm bed. Lerry. And I tell you what. You there, Lerry?"

"Miko, I—"

"I get Dr. Roesch call a good man in Paris, what you say? A specialist, okay?"

Oh, great—a specialist. "Miko, you mind telling me what the fuck I'm doing here? Who I'm supposed to—"

"Right there you siddown, okay? Okay, Lerry?"

"Okay, Miko."

Miko hung up first. He was not built to move at speed, small and agile though he was, but the click of that receiver going down embodied all the kinetic energy of a starting gun. Miko was the master of understatement, but there was nothing understated about his power to act. Larry strode back to the desk and asked the electric blonde if he could make another call, please, but on another phone, if madame didn't mind, the last one had been jammed with static. Crazy, but somehow he'd feel better talking to Garfield on a phone that wasn't tainted with Miko.

He dialed, got a busy signal, tried again. The line gave out weird bleeps, then a high tone. He cursed the French and their goddamned phone system and tried again, carefully breaking the number into its component groups, international code, area code, local exchange, a long delay between each group. He glanced at his watch. Four minutes since Miko had said a *friend* was on the way. The friend who'd failed to make the pickup at Orly? Another friend?

For the second time in minutes Larry's natural defenses let him down. A voice, a woman's voice, said nervously, "Hello, this is Larry's place, can I help you?" and his world swung on its axis. "I said this is Larry's place," the voice repeated. "Is there anything I can do?"

A zillion years ago the same voice had said, "I don't mind as long as we can talk once a day on the phone. Do you think that's stupid?"

A zillion years ago she'd said, "I don't think of love as an obligation—like, nobody's obliged to breathe, right? Nobody's obliged to think. Nobody's obliged to feel."

A zillion years ago he remembered screaming at Lydia, "What do you mean, *affair*? What's an affair? She's a student, isn't she? I *teach* students. What am I supposed to do—go down on my knees and apologize for every piece of rape bait I give the time of day to?"

He turned to check that the blonde wasn't watching him, but he couldn't see her for the tears.

"Is that you . . . kid?" he got out finally.

"Larry?" Another hand went over another mouthpiece; he guessed she was crying, too. For one million dollars, Mr. Bartell, what does the continent of Europe have in common with the United States? We weep, Mr. Interlocutor, we weep.

"Larry? Are you all right?"

He lit up the irresistible grin. "You really want to know, I'm bawling my eyes out. Christ, it's good to hear your voice."

"Me, too. It's been so—" The bass rumble of a man's voice interrupted. She went on: "I'm being asked, is your position secure or do you have to move on?"

"Insecure. I have to get out of here. Listen—"

"He says—"

The phone was plucked out of her hand, and the no-nonsense bass said curtly, "There's no time for this. You have to move?"

"Is this—"

"You asked for me, you got me. Now you'll do exactly as I tell you, agreed?"

"I was only saying—"

"Yes or no?"

"Okay! Yes, all right, you're in charge!" Larry yelled. Tears dry fast in a cold climate.

"Good. This is the position. The official word is yes, as I said in my note. Yes with conditions. Are you free to travel? Any pressing restrictions?"

"Pressing restrictions! Christ, what is this? You think I'm down here on vacation?" Eight minutes since Miko promised help. "I'm not free. I've got things on my back. People. I have to get out of here, out of the area."

"What area?"

"Paris, public phone behind the Arc."

"You have to be anyplace special in the next twenty-four hours? You have any commitments, a program?"

"Yeah, I have commitments," he snarled down the line. "I'm committed to an early funeral. I'm being picked up in five or six minutes."

"Very well. Do you know the place d'Italie?"

"I know it."

"Take a cab there. A little street east of it called rue Saint-

Auban. There's a converted church halfway along, a hospice. It's run by a priest called Father John Lattimore. He knows me; he'll give you somewhere to sleep. It might be the floor, but it'll be safe."

"Okay, but when—"

"I'll have a courier on the Concorde flight from Washington tomorrow morning. Could you make a rendezvous tomorrow evening, say, ten-fifteen?"

Rendezvous. Larry closed his eyes. Would she remember? Would she sell him out? How was it, in the feminist age, with women you'd kicked when they were down? He sighed. "Yeah, okay, sure. Where?"

"Somewhere out of the way. Be on the corner of the rue Taiti at ten tomorrow night. That's up in the Twelfth between the rue de Picpus and the boulevard de Picpus. The metro runs on the surface out there, along the boulevard. Walk east, got that? Toward the Bel Air metro station."

"And then what?"

"You'll be met."

"Oh, really. Well, now, isn't that nice?" Four minutes left. "I just hand myself over to the first stranger who comes along. Here I am, America, take me."

"Not exactly," Garfield said. "You'll recognize her."

"Her?"

"You don't imagine I'd send anyone else, do you?"

Larry hung up because he couldn't hold back the sob that came up from somewhere deep inside and engulfed him like a wave. He wiped his eyes on his sleeve, turned to head for the desk, pulled out some notes and began counting them, then—

They stood in the open door, two of them, though not exactly one of Miko's matched pairs. The tall, thin one wore a suit of mortician's black and a black raincoat. The other wore a flat cap, shoulder-length hair and a cavalier beard, a blue work jacket and jeans, a red checked shirt and yellow boots: drifter chic. The drifter was leaning in the doorframe as though weary after a long chase, but his smile was intact and fixed, as if someone had nailed it there. He said in French, "We missed you, pal," and nodded at the copy of *The Tears of Autumn* sprouting from Larry's jacket pocket. "And you remembered the book. You see that, Émile? He remembered."

"Vivre libre ou mourir!"

The drifter brought his gloved hand down—splat—on a scuttling cockroach. He displayed the remains, first for Émile, then for Larry, a brownish jam spread on the huge powdery cushion of his palm. *"Tu compris ça, copain?"* he asked, smearing the mess on Larry's sleeve.

"Compris what exactly?" Larry asked, watching him do it.

"Vivre libre ou mourir. It's a—how you say—phrase, yes?" He tipped his cap up on his strawberry-colored hair. "In English it say, 'Live free or die.' *C'est vrai,* Émile?"

Émile had nothing to contribute to the debate.

"I see. Live free or die." Larry stretched the skeletal grin on his mouth till it hurt. "And that's significant, is it? Something you learned in reform school?"

"Significant?"

"Never mind."

The drifter's glove clamped menacingly on Larry's arm. "What means *significant?*"

Larry said quickly, *"Important. En français on dit important."*

"Ah, oui." He grinned broadly and lay back in his rickety chair, thumbs hooked in his belt. "In the war was significant. When we fight the Nazis. 'Live free or die' was motto of *la résistance.*" He lapsed into French again. "They used to write it on walls. On trees. Sometimes they'd sneak out at night and paint it on the side of a German tank." He took a wing of his yellow mustache in the curl of his tongue and worked it into his mouth. "That was really living, I bet. Live free or die." He kicked Larry playfully under the table. "That significant for you, *copain?* If you can't live free, why live. *C'est vrai?*" The thought creased him up.

"Yeah," said Larry. *"C'est vrai* all right."

He was numb. All over numb. No sensation anywhere except the sensation of flesh melting on his bones. In the car the drifter had held Larry's hand the whole time, talking incessantly the way psychos do when they're tripping out on the razor's edge. At one point he'd started to massage the hand with his thumb, not hard, not to cause pain, but sexually, the way you do it with a girl; Larry had tried to pull free, but it was like trying to shake off a thumbscrew. From there on in he was lost, done for. With psychos there's a clearly defined point of no return; once beyond it, you're theirs, body and soul.

"In America you also say, 'Live free or die,' *copain?"*

"In America we say, 'The dying are better off dead,' " said Larry.

"Exactement! Bon! Chouette!"

The *patron,* a small, bald, greasy man with an outsize French gut hanging over his belt, came with their order. He shifted a Gauloise from the right side of his mouth to the left and banged down the plates as if they were hot: *"Deux boeuf en croûte, poulet rôti."* He unloaded a basket of bread from his tray and three glasses of red wine and three paper napkins the size of postage stamps. *"C'est tout?"* he demanded sharply. In a certain category of French industrial bistro, the question "Is that all?" is a challenge.

"Go screw," the drifter told him merrily, and picked up a chicken leg streaming with garlic sauce. He wore ancient yellow work gloves, soiled and holey, and didn't take them off to eat. He hooked his head at the *patron* as he stalked back to his kitchen, "Fucking Jew-boy." He grinned. And with feigned interest: "You Jew-boy, *copain?"*

"Is this Miko's idea?" Larry asked. It was a stupid question, stupid for all sorts of reasons—not the least of which being that they wouldn't know Miko from John the Baptist—but you have to say something, have to stay in there pitching.

"Miko? Do we know a Miko, Émile?"

Émile not only didn't talk but didn't eat either: He sat

85

watching his companion maul the chicken leg with the fixed expression of a fox at an egg-laying ceremony.

"Where do we go from here?" Larry pressed, trying for an opening.

"We tuck you up quiet for the night, *copain. Tranquil*, eh, Émile?"

Tranquil.

Larry began to shake and couldn't stop. It started in his legs and moved up, juddering along his spine, radiating out through his arms to his hands till, in self-defense, he had to sit on them. The drifter glanced at him in a proprietorial way and motioned with the chicken leg.

"Eat up, *copain*. Long night, long way to go, need your strength."

"I'm not hungry."

The drifter stopped eating, the food bulging in his cheeks. "You don't—" He turned his head and spit a stream of mulched chicken at the floor. "You don't like it? I pay for this, *copain*. Out of my pocket. I *pay* for it!" He glared at Émile. "He say, fuck my—*comment est-ce qu'on dit, hospitalité?*"

Émile shrugged.

Larry said, "I'm just saying I'm ill and I don't care to—"

"You *eat* now! *Compris? Eat!*"

Larry took one hand from under his haunches, broke the piecrust with a fork, and shoved some of it in his mouth.

"*Merci*," the psycho said gravely. "*Il faut manger. C'est bien, non?*"

"*Très agréable.*"

"*Vraiment.*"

It would have helped to know where he was. Not much, but some. They had driven for perhaps ten minutes when they left the Arc, but he'd been too preoccupied with the drifter to notice in what direction. By the time he started taking note, they'd arrived. All he could remember of the street outside was that it was badly lit and flanked with parked cars. At the end of the street three or four towers of sprinkled light stood close together, and he'd put these down as workers' flats, the face-less, soulless subsidized housing beloved of the Communist councillors of Paris. He thought it might be Aubervilliers, but only because of the poverty, it could just as well be Fresnes or Pantin. Not that it mattered. He wasn't going anywhere. The bistro was in a basement, and he had about as much hope of running up the steps to the street as he had of scaling the north face of the Eiger.

Careful to avoid the drifter's eye, he checked the mirror.

The café was filling up fast. A factory whistle had sounded around eleven-thirty, and the first half dozen customers trooped in not long after that, middle-aged men in orange coveralls with coats thrown over their shoulders against the rain and the sudden chill. More followed within minutes, and now there was a rush. All fifteen tables were full, and the *patron* was distributing folding chairs from a stack by the stinking toilet. Fifteen minutes to midnight. Larry had his back to them, but in a mirror on the wall behind the drifter's head he could see everything. The talk was loud and relieved, last weekend's foot-ball and a big strike at Peugeot. The drink was white wine, served with carafes of water and bowls of sugar to preserve its strength when you diluted it. Another gang arrived, all wearing the same orange coveralls, and there were raucous shouts of welcome as they trooped in: *"Oho, les héros!"* *"Allons-y!"* *"Comme ils sont beaux!"* *"Hé, chou-chou!"* The newcomers took stools at the bar and banged on it loudly shouting, *"Patron! Patron!"* as if he weren't there. Someone leaned over and switched on the radio, and for a moment there was Schubert, a snatch of the Trout Quintet, cool as a mountain brook, but a howl of protest went up immediately, and the twiddler quickly found Europe One. The room filled with an adenoidal cockney rendition of "Drink and Drugs and Rock 'n Roll."

The drifter was shouting to make himself heard. "Émile, you'd better go check the car, yes?"

Émile got up without a word and walked out. The *patron* watched him go, then switched his stare to the drifter, who beamed beatifically and raised his cap an inch and made a little bow. "*Viens, viens!*" he ordered Larry, and they went on eating. For a while the drifter was content to deal with his food; then he sat back and glanced at his watch and glared around. He brought his tattered gloves together in a slow handclap over his head till the *patron* deigned to notice him, then raised an imaginary glass to his mouth. The *patron* brought two fines on a tray, and the drifter drank both, one after the other, a gulp at a time; he burped with great satisfaction and fell back in his seat, the lunatic grin still nailed firmly in place.

"That Émile," he said conversationally, nodding toward the door. "You tell him, 'Go do this, go do that,' and before he's gone ten meters, he can't remember what you said. You heard me. 'Go check the car,' I said. So where is he?" He stood up and leaned across the table, took the back of Larry's neck in the sticky palm of his glove, and, before Larry could move, kissed him hard on the mouth. "You be a good boy now. I'll go find that fool and bring him back." He caught another barbed stare from the *patron* and with a flourish produced a folded note from his breast pocket and dropped it on the table. "He thinks we're trying to crook him," he told Larry with a wink. "Jew-boy! I won't be a minute. Keep an eye on my bag, okay?"

Larry watched his retreating back in the mirror, the way you watch people in dreams levitate or walk under trains, the same feeling of total helplessness pervading, of being set in concrete, paralyzed, cursed, violated, unable to move. The *patron* came up on his shoulder and grabbed the banknote. "*Terminé?*" he demanded. Larry nodded. He even got as far as shuffling word groups into coherent patterns—Look, these men want to kill me/I need help/Tell someone/Call the police/No, don't call the police/They mustn't see me talking to you—but before he could get his script straight, the man turned away and went back behind the bar. Not that he would have helped anyway.

Outside! Larry thought. Now! Come on, run! Chance it! But running was a physical impossibility, and chance was a fine thing on a good day.

Keep an eye on my bag, okay?

There'd be a gun in the bag. Had to be, he wasn't wearing one. Or had they some other method in mind? Like drowning. A river, a park lake, a pond, a bath, a hand basin—Jesus Christ, you could drown a man in a wet sponge! Or a hit and run with the car? A knife? A hammer? An ice pick? A steel spike through the heart? A garotte? A—

"No!" he shouted in his head, except this time it got out, very loud.

Momentarily the talk behind him ceased, and thirty-odd pairs of eyes fastened on him curiously. He dragged his own eyes down from the mirror. Anyone else, anyone with two cents' worth of guts, would reach for that bag right now, take out the gun, slip it in his pocket, and when the time came . . . Or was that why they'd left him alone with it? They could be standing outside right now, just waiting for him to do something prick stupid like that. And the moment his hand touched the bag . . .

He stood up very abruptly, and back came the eyes, hordes of them. He faced them and found the *patron*. Jerked his thumb at the toilet and began to walk.

What was he doing? What are you doing, Bartell? Where do you think you're going?

The door screamed as he opened it and groaned when he pushed it shut. The stench was dizzying. The urinal overflowed the floor. Webs of graffiti covered the walls. The hot tap had been wrenched bodily from the washbowl. The toilet was choked with old newspapers.

But there was a window.

High. Dimpled glass, caked with dirt, a brass handle. Larry stretched up but couldn't reach the handle. Sobbing with effort, he climbed up on the washbowl, steadied himself, yanked

89

the handle hard—and nearly broke his wrist. It was stuck solid. Holy God, spare me at least this. A handle that moves. A fucking window that opens. He looked back frantically over his shoulder. A jimmy, that's all he needed, a rod, a staff, a lever. Give me a fulcrum, and I'll move the world. But there were no handy jimmies or rods or staves; nothing he could use to force the handle or break the thick glass. In rage and frustration he pressed his forehead to the glass and pounded it with his fists and—screamed?

Or perhaps the scream came later. A millisecond later, when the bomb exploded.

EIGHT

Garfield settled back in the leather throne behind the desk. "What did you expect?" he asked gruffly, sorry for her.

C.J. Poole lay in a near-fetal ball on the couch across the room. She fluttered a fan of fingers at him in self-defense but wouldn't turn around. "What do we ever expect? The same, no change. He had such a beautiful voice once."

"I never noticed. You sure it's him?"

"I think so. Pretty sure."

"You'd better be better than pretty sure or you don't go. Are you taking this in? If for one minute you think there's a chance it's not him—"

"It's him! I'm going!"

"Listen again."

Garfield tapped the rewind key, and the speakers hissed back at him from all four corners of the big room. Quadraphonic confession, good for the suppressed ego. Or so his friend Art assured him. Art was the owner of the palatial establishment in which he was presently making himself comfortable. Art was professor emeritus in the Department of Booby Bashing at

Georgetown (his coinage), as well as father confessor to half the befuddled psyches on Capitol Hill, so Art should know. Conveniently Art was also happily conventioning with other eminent booby quacks in Antibes, so Garfield had commandeered the place. The sixth-floor corner suite in the Watergate complex suited him very well.

He set a match to a new fill of tobacco and swiveled the chair to the window. Outside, lances of pale evening sunshine were drilling the cloud layer, spraying the city with fool's gold; a mile or so away it was raining steadily. Lightning flashed; thunder rolled. The tape thunked home and began to replay itself behind him: C.J.'s voice saying, "Hello, this is Larry's place, can I help you?"—her idea—and the pause, and the nervous repeat, and finally, Larry hiccuping with emotion, "Is that you . . . kid?" And their tears colliding, mingling. Garfield glanced over to see how she was taking it, but she hadn't moved.

Was it real, her weeping, his? Art had a theory that all extreme emotion was in some part theatrical, a conscious attempt to reduce the opposition by an exhibition of frailty. Guilt conversion, he called it. A woman's prerogative, he said, but infinitely more lethal psychologically when wielded by a man. Did C.J. know that? Believe it?   •

"—bawling my eyes out," Larry mourned through quadraphonic tears. His throat lining had gone, Garfield decided, which was what C.J. had meant by different. He's different somehow. No, not different, girl, just terminating.

He swung back to the window. It had been at Art's desk that he had composed the note to Larry Bartell and dictated it to another old ally, Enzo Barra of the Overland Trust Bank in Lugano, for immediate delivery by dispatch rider to the address in Montreux, no questions asked. The fact that Bartell had responded within hours was now the only cause Garfield had for concern. An old spy's concern. Things were moving far too fast, far too smoothly, for his liking; in a mind as densely booby-trapped with professional suspicions as his, speed and smoothness reeked of either stage management or beginner's luck, and the interest payable on both was frequently twice the expected dividend.

"Yeah, I have commitments," Larry was rasping in his pain of a voice. "I'm committed to an early funeral."

Wisecracker. Wiseacre. That's how his generation would remember him—*if* they remembered him. The fastest lip on the eastern seaboard. In Larry's golden age to be hip was everything, a whole lot smarter than being wise. To be Larry was to be hip; to agree with him was to be right; to know him was to be in. An entire industry had grown up around his notoriety, and at times it seemed that all his energies were devoted to fueling it. Breakfast with Larry. Spin along with Larry. Late-night Larry. "And on the show tonight, ladies and gentlemen, a barrel of brain and beeyutiful bullshit; from the left, Norman Mailer, Andy Warhol, Lenny Bruce, and the voice of treason himself, Pro-fessor Larry Bartell . . ." Nowadays they'd be lost for words to describe him. Once you've accepted the solecism *superstar* to describe a tennis player or a banjo strummer there is really nothing left.

The walkie-talkie on the desk behind him gave out a sudden thaaarp! of accusation. Garfield grabbed it in a rush and pressed the Morse button twice. He looked down to the exit road below; Nick raised a hand in salute and went back to polishing the gleaming black carapace of the Lincoln. More farce. All clear, Nick was reporting. Still here, Garfield was replying. Nick had insisted on standing guard just like old times—against what? whom? low-flying Russians? closed vans marked "Secret Service"? the Seventh Cavalry at the charge?—and nothing Garfield could say would dissuade him, so they'd dug out his emergency communications kit, and here they were, the two of them, blowing raspberies at each other every fifteen minutes.

"Oh, really. Well, now, isn't that nice?" Larry Bartell from the loudspeakers, a long way off his old form.

Farce, all of it. But farce with a purpose. Garfield snapped new life into his dead pipe. This playlet Langley was walking him through, this pretense of trust in a trusted son, this parody of private enterprise: Did they imagine he was so feeble-minded he'd forgotten how it was done?

They'd been on his heels since Goldman came rowing out to *The Duchess* that night: on his heels, in his house, on his phone, and as far as possible in his head, because the higher calculus of body watching is anticipation, the gift of—call it predestination. Without seeing them, without even sensing their presence —because they were good at their work—he'd known they were there. In singles and in pairs, in cars and trucks and delivery vans, around him on the plane, slipstreaming in his wake every step of the way, shaking down poor John Sayer when he left him that morning, turning over Prisoners of Conscience, Inc. (not that it should have been necessary, being theirs in all but name), staring up at Abe Lincoln, running the computer's eye over C.J. Poole, relocating her physical connection with Bartell at Cambridge; checking in, taking note, reliving old issues, fielding bland supplementaries from some deskbound logistics king at Langley.

Curious thing, though, he felt no pain, no agitation. He'd been used before, after all, and rightly; it was a spy's business to be used. And there was comfort in that, because when C.J. went looking for Larry Bartell in Paris, the hounds would be loping at her heels, too.

The tape ran out. C.J. called out from across the room, "It *is* him." And as Garfield swung the chair to meet her eye: "Definitely."

"You're sure?"

"What do I have to do—swear on the Bible?"

"No, just consider the consequences of being wrong."

"I have. It's Larry."

Garfield nodded, because he knew it, too.

"And you mean it about flying me out tomorrow?"

"Can you?"

"I guess so." She was braiding a strand of hair in her fingers, already several thousand miles, and possibly a lifetime away from the Watergate.

Garfield said gently, "You can still back out, C.J. You won't win any medals for going, and you certainly won't lose face for staying home."

"I didn't ask for medals, did I?" Her attempt at a sweet-sour smile was pathetically underrehearsed.

"All right. So what else is worrying you? Something is."

Again the twisted smile. "I was just wondering what to wear," she said archly. "A girl ought to look the part, don't you think?"

Which got him thinking on quite another tack.

Outside, a sky of towering storm cloud draped velvet night on the city. Inside, the room had shrunk to a pyramid of white light poised over the visitor's spiky crew cut.

"So what do we have?" Garfield settled back in the leather throne.

Brad Cotten fished a single sheet of folded foolscap from an inner pocket and glanced cautiously right, left, and behind before opening it out and setting it on the low table beside him. He hooked on a pair of heavy horn-rims bound at one corner with Scotch tape.

"Stellatronics Industries, Inc." He read for a moment, shook his head. "Nothing much I can tell you about the company you can't read in the *Wall Street Journal*. Seventy percent government contract work—NASA, air force, navy: missile guidance systems, ground-to-air triggering mechanisms and controls, plus the usual CIA research they don't talk about in the balance sheets. In the marketplace the stock is blue-chip. They were into home computers ahead of the field and out ahead of the field. They've launched two satellite communicators, and a third goes up next month. There's talk about cornering the satellite TV market in Europe. Also electron microscopy, cable TV, body scanners, facsimile transmission of—"

"I get the picture," Garfield interrupted impatiently. "They're solvent. Tell me about Bloomfield."

"Businesswise, the cat's spats. Sound scientist, brilliant manager, first-class politician. Knows everybody, loves the press. High on social consciousness, big on conservation." To show how much he was enjoying the recitative, Cotten cracked his knuckles one at a time in a snappy rat-a-tat-tat. He was a short, overweight man with a drinker's engorged nose and the slept-in look of the bachelor workaholic. A longtime White House press corps hack for a small midwestern daily, Cotten had had the bright idea ten years earlier of launching a weekly buzz sheet-cum-directory catering to the capital's lobbying industry. The gamble had paid off. As a chronicler and keyhole watcher to Washington's body politic he was unsurpassed. His middle name, of course, was Irony.

"He walks in beauty as the night. Nothing to hide." Garfield said dryly.

"Not a thing. He's squeaky clean."

"Loved and respected by friend and foe alike."

"You've been reading the script," Cotten accused him, covering his notes.

"What kind of private life does he have?"

"Not the kind you mean. Married thirty-six years, beautiful wife, dutiful children, three grandchildren. Last word in domestic cuddle-up. No Commies in the family woodwork, no junkies, dropouts, bankrupts, jerks, or ax murderers. Also a practicing Catholic; goes to church every Sunday wherever he happens to be in the world. Gives generously: twenty cents on the dollar to charity. *Every* dollar."

"Oh, Susanna."

"Yeah, I thought you'd like it." Cotten gazed over his horn-rims. "I hate to say this, man of my experience, but we might just be dealing here with the sole survivor of an extinct species, ever think of that? The honest American tycoon."

"Yes, I've thought about it. Now tell me why we're not."

Cotten glanced down again at his notes but found no inspiration there for what he had to say. He temporized instead. "You know me, Luke. I'm a facts man, always have been. Opinion is cheap; facts are sacred."

"But for the time being you'd prefer to veer off into a little shrewd speculation."

"I didn't say that." He took hold of the lobe of his left ear and worried it mercilessly. "Only thing I can lay on Bloomfield is association."

"No man is an island, Brad. We choose our own associations. Get to it."

"Okay. You said to check out the Brooke-Davis setup on the Beltway."

"And?"

Brad Cotten gave his ear another mangling. "Associations. You start with Sayer, and you end up with Bloomfield. You start with anyone in this scenario, and you end up with Bloomfield. And after Bloomfield—"

"Let's start with Brooke-Davis, shall we? Who are they?"

"Aerospace consultants, like you said. Founder-members of the Beltway Bandits."

Garfield made a note on the pad in his lap—*bandits*—and enshrined the word in a pair of crossed cutlasses.

Washington shorthand.

It was the rooted belief of all Washington bureaucrats that anyone not subsisting on a government paycheck *must*, by implication, be a crook and a hustler. Why else would any sane person choose to work in a town that was half slum, half museum? This blanket insinuation was aimed widely: at the ninety thousand employees of the potboiling lobbying industry, for instance; at the forty thousand-odd lawyers lickspittling away on K Street; at the two and a half thousand jackass journalists cluttering up the place, and the myriad other whores, pickpockets, and commercial chauvinists who fed off the fat of the fat of government. But more particularly, it was aimed at the community of independent consultants out on Route 495, the Washington Beltway.

The Beltway Bandits: the titled rich of the private sector.

For the most part the bandits were small, highly skilled agencies peddling one specific discipline—a whole pantheon of exotic expertise ranging from fish farming to nuclear power station design—and since they survived almost exclusively on government contracts, a certain bustling competitiveness marked their business style. They hustled. They fawned. They bought and sold. And needless to say, their expertise came at a high premium: The Bandits were prime targets for cost-cutting congressional committees, and every president since Kennedy had vowed to cut them down to size. But shrinkage was against Beltway policy. In one decade the Bandits' share of the budget had soared from five billion dollars a year to nearer ten billion. It was still rising. Garfield was not alone in regarding them as an undeclared burden on the taxpayer.

"So." He put down his pen. "John Sayer was a Bandit, was he? How'd the rest of his story check out?"

"All the way, with variations." Cotten consulted his notes again. "Caltech, Bachelor of Science. Two years with Texas Instruments, then dropped out of sight—found the competition a little heavy. Moved up and down Silicon Valley for another year and a half, met Lydia Bartell, and after that everything was just peachy. He joined Brooke-Davis right after they got married. Systems analyst, not bright but not a dummy either. The word is he'll be fine as soon as he grows up. Around Christmas the story broke in the *Post* about his tying up with Larry Bartell's ex and—whammo!—Brooke-Davis handed him his hat. The Pentagon said to get rid of him, or else." Cotten looked up. "This have anything to do with Larry Bartell, Luke?"

"Why should it?"

"Oh, just asking." Cotten gave him his I'll-believe-anything look and returned to his notes. "All right. Brooke-Davis is big money—NASA contracts, air force, navy, CIA. That tell you anything?"

"Same category as Stellatronics."

"Same organization." Cotten stared fixedly over his horn-rims.

97

"Stellatronics bought Brooke-Davis fourteen months ago. And what do you think?"

"You're at the wheel."

"Brooke-Davis spent last year buying out eleven other agencies on the Beltway. Guy who did the buying was their senior partner, Fred Anhalt. Fred came to Brooke-Davis from guess where?"

"Stellatronics?"

"Right. And where'd he move from six months before that? After twenty years of unbroken service?"

"I can't imagine."

"The Bartell Corporation. Coincidence?"

"Is it?"

"Wait. You want to guess the board of directors Bloomfield joined a few months back?"

"Tell me."

"The Bartell Corporation. And you want to guess who's a corporate stockholder in Stellatronics?"

"The Bartell Corporation?"

"There you go." Cotten wore the shark's preprandial smirk. "You begin to see what I mean by association. Around and around and back every time. Okay, now we get down to cases. Stellatronics, as you know, is a subsidiary of North American-Stafford." To relieve his inner tensions, Cotten removed his glasses and blew loudly on the lenses. "North American-Stafford is your classic industrial colossus. Oil, chemicals, shipping, electronics, armaments, agriculture, bauxite, coal, et cetera and so forth. The Stafford family empire." He glared at Garfield severely, as if he'd challenged his manhood. "With which, of course, the Honorable Brock Stafford has for the moment no personal or corporate link, real or imagined, diddly-dah. Under the Carter ruling he—"

"Was obliged on taking office to divulge and divest all business interests likely to occasion a—"

"Okay. But we have another association here, don't we? Who joined Stafford in '76 as his number one right-hand man?

Tyler Bloomfield. Who moved over to Stellatronics when Stafford went into government that first time? Tyler Bloomfield."

"What are you trying to impute? Corruption?"

"Now that'd be some joke, wouldn't it?" Cotten almost forgot himself and grinned. "A man gives up the presidency of the eighth-biggest multinational on earth, shakes off a conservative two and a half billion dollars' worth of personal holdings, then goes into government to make a few bucks in kickbacks. Oh, sure."

"Then what?" Garfield pressed.

"Then nothing I can put my finger on." Brad Cotten sighed. "Like I said, it's all association. You start with Bloomfield, and everything else makes a wide turn and comes right back to him. I mean"—he plucked off the horn-rims and waved them at Garfield—"you *could* say Bloomfield fired Sayer the same week he hired Sayer's wife, right? Indirectly. Because as boss of Stellatronics he's also boss of Brooke-Davis. Then you have to ask yourself why? And then you recall he's on the board of the Bartell Corporation, which owns stock in Stellatronics, so maybe he was doing Thurlan Bartell a favor. And beyond that you have Thurlan Bartell paying John Sayer to look after Lydia's kids. Why? And when you think you've reached the end of that particular line, you come up with somebody called Roy McKinnon."

Garfield stiffened.

"Now here's a guy lives right next door to Lydia Bartell in Georgetown but isn't playing around with her. Here's a guy who picks up her kids on weekends and most other times follows her around like some kinda bodyguard. Here's a guy appeared out of nowhere five, six months ago and walks into a sinecure paying thirty-five thousand bucks a year and expenses. That's Roy McKinnon. The guy who employs him is Tyler Bloomfield, okay? Who employs Lydia. Whose old man pays John Sayer to look after the kids. Who're picked up every weekend by Roy McKinnon. Who works for Tyler Bloomfield."

"Is that all?" Garfield asked impassively.

"Not everything, no. To answer your question, I don't think we're talking about corruption here, exactly—corrupt anything—but we're sure as hell talking about more than coincidence. I picked up something else." He folded the sheet of notes and stuffed it into his pocket. "The talk on the Beltway in the last few months is all about poaching."

"Of what?"

"Business. What else do they care about? Contracts are going to people they didn't go to before."

"So?"

But Brad Cotten wasn't to be hurried. "Listen. A study of U.S. aid spending in the Horn of Africa switched from a long-standing Beltway agency to a Johnny-come-lately. A check on the cost-effectiveness of refugee relief in Thailand; a survey of the computer market in Europe; a feasibility study on water desalination in Iraq—all these deals arranged behind the scenes, no public tendering, taken out of established agencies, given to new ones."

"That's bad?"

"Not necessarily. I wouldn't know. But goddamn coincidental, seeing how every one of those contracts went to an agency in the Brooke-Davis group. You'll notice they're all overseas-oriented, okay?" He examined his nails at some length. "Your average Beltway Bandit is no slouch, Luke. People start in snatching the bread from his kids' mouths, and he's liable to check with other guys in the same boat, add two and two, dig around a little. These Bandits are insiders. They've picked up some very interesting material.'"

"Such as?"

"You know the first thing Ralph Kramer said the day he took over at Langley? He said he expected the CIA to be as cost-effective as any other department of government. That's why he set to and cut it to the bone, right? Two thousand bodies get shown the door overnight—out!—and more to come. It was one of the president's campaign pledges, remember? An end to invisible government, diddly-dah."

Garfield frowned. "You're casting a pretty wide net here, aren't you?"

"I'm a guy who likes wide nets," Cotten drawled wickedly. "Gimme time. Okay. Also, like these guys on the Beltway, I remember things I read in the papers. I remember, for instance, how Ralph Kramer was just a cop in Austin twenty years ago. I remember how Brock Stafford made a corporation lawyer out of him, made a place for him in North American-Stafford. I remember another employee of Stafford's, too, an ex-university swell name of Davis Lang, and I remember how the three of them worked their tails off that year to get the good governor into the White House. The Texas Arrangers the papers called them, remember? No smoke without fire."

"And that's your point?"

"My point is this," Brad Cotten went on, unabashed. "Where'd those two thousand CIA bodies go after Kramer chucked them out of Langley?" And before Garfield could interrupt his flow: "The guys on the Beltway think they know where. They're working for the Brooke-Davis group: first-class brains with first-class frames, all ex-Company. In the last year Brooke-Davis *tripled* its work force. A little scouting around, and I bet you'll find Stellatronics took on another three or four hundred, and North American-Stafford and the Bartell group the rest. Now, I'm not pretending I can even guess what's going on, Luke, but I know this. Of those three Texas Arrangers, Brock Stafford is now national security adviser, Lang runs the White House, and Kramer heads up the CIA. Three corners of a triumvirate, Luke, the central predisposition of which happens to be the security of the nation. I'd say the chances are they're still arranging, wouldn't you?"

It was enough. More than enough. Garfield came around the desk, and Cotten rose to meet him.

"Look, Brad"—Garfield threw an arm across his shoulders and urged him toward the door—"let's not get carried away now, shall we? I'm more than happy with your readout on Bloomfield. I'm obliged. I appreciate it. But I don't need fairy tales at bedtime to make me feel better, thanks very much. Security of the nation!"

"You don't buy it?" Cotten looked crestfallen.

Garfield admonished him lightly. "An old hand like you falling for stuff like that. The conspiracy theory went out with Nixon, didn't it?"

Cotten looked up at him and shook his head in wonder. "And they say the devil has all the best tunes." He sighed. "Okay, Luke. Have it your way."

At the door he gave Garfield another measuring look and squashed his hat on the back of his head. "This having nothing to do with Larry Bartell," he said pointedly, "I guess you wouldn't be interested in a buzz I picked up."

"What buzz?"

"You changing your mind?"

"Spit it out, Brad. What buzz?"

"That one of the New York networks is making a TV documentary about old Larry."

Garfield eyed him narrowly. "And?"

"Isn't that enough?"

"Which network?"

Cotten grinned broadly. "Go see Don Sherwood. Go visit with your fat friend on the Hill and ask him." He held out a piece of tightly folded notepaper. "Ask him what he's got going with a guy called Clayton Waldren. You might find it interesting." He flicked the brim of his hat and winked. "Not that you're interested in old Larry, though, right?"

"Keep this to yourself, Brad?"

Cotten stepped into the corridor, looked back. "Why, sure, Luke. Vow of silence. For at least a week."

For more than half an hour after Cotten had left, Luke Garfield sat slumped at the desk, contemplating the island of light thrown by the reading lamp. At his back, Washington twinkled and flashed in its world-famous impression of Sodom and Gomorrah, but Garfield had no eye for it, and no ear. For the moment, the circle of light held far more immediacy for him, it encompassed the only true world.

He felt a million years old, immovable as Mount Rushmore; he nearly slept.

Coming out of it, he unclipped his fat old Waterman and with due ceremony unscrewed the top. Slowly he drew an arc on the green blotter, then gave it an arrowhead, then drew another and another until he had a circle of arrows, going nowhere. He labeled the arrows—Larry, Lydia, Sayer, Goldman, Bloomfield, Thurlan, and TA (for Texas Arrangers, whom he now thought of as an institution: Stafford/Lang/Kramer)—and glared at them for inspiration, but they had nothing to say. Switching targets, he wrote underneath, "A night in Frankfurt, neat coincidences all in a row." Head on one side, he examined this for a long time, then added, "What came first: Lydia's job at Stellatronics or a ploy to bring Larry home?" Under this again, urgently now, he wrote, "What connection between Larry and a shake-up on the Washington Beltway?," then firmly, with a flourish, "None." For a while he allowed his eyes to glaze over; then with a grunt he added a question mark to the word *None*.

He thought of something else and scribbled very quickly, "TV documentary—why?" But at this point his pen went off into a dream sequence of its own and drew a tree bending in the wind, leaves blowing from it in artistic flurries, falling to earth as a series of dots in a whirligig pattern that became a name: Don Sherwood. Taking command again, Garfield added a note: "Call DS A.M. for appmnt."

Privately extricate Larry Bartell from Europe? Privately? All right, so a measure of discretion in a case like this did no harm, but if privacy were the essential factor, why tempt Providence by saturating the background with official legmen? Watchers, snoopers, heel tappers. Unless—his pipe had gone out; once again he snapped a match to it—unless none of them was strictly, demonstrably official. How great a stretch of the imagination would it take, for instance, to think of them as employees of—well, the Bartell Corporation, Stellatronics, Brooke-Davis? CIA material usefully privatized, as Brad Cotten had suggested. Even—and why not?—employees of that other superior operator in the private sector Mr. Alfred Goldman. Now there was a thought. There was a very nasty, unwholesome thought—

"Luke?"

She was standing in the shadows by the far door, in pajamas, blue cotton, with, if you please, a nuclear disarmament logo on the pocket. She was rubbing her eyes on the back of her hand. She looked about nine years old.

"Luke?" She was also half-asleep, he gauged.

He got to his feet and pointed a commanding finger, more than a little shocked that he'd been caught woolgathering. "You get back to bed right now, woman. Now!"

"I have to—I mean, there's something I want to tell you."

"Tell me when you're back in bed. *Off!*" He swept the blotter into the top drawer of the desk and locked it, then followed her out. He stood at the bedroom door as she scrambled back between the sheets. "I'm listening," he growled. "You're supposed to be getting a good night's sleep."

"It's about Larry."

His skin crawled. Premonition?

"I said I'm listening."

"Luke, I don't know what to say. I'm sorry. I meant to tell you right after he called, but, well—oh, God." Her head bowed, and an avalanche of black hair hid her face.

"Feel free to get to the point anytime you like," he snapped. "Come on, C.J., cut it out."

"Ooooh!" She swept the hair aside. In the half dark only the high points of forehead, cheekbones, and nose registered the outline of her face. "It's about the rendezvous, the one you told him about, in the rue Taiti tomorrow night."

"Well?"

"He won't keep it."

Garfield felt the iceman come; slowly, up through the veins.

"Oh, won't he?" he said lightly. "Why not?" He couldn't trust himself to say more.

"Because—oh, Luke!—because he knows I won't go there."

"Well, that's very interesting. You care to tell me why?"

She hesitated again. He heard the nervous click-clicking of the long, shaped ends of her nails as they interlocked, over and over. "Because there's already a rendezvous for Paris. It was in his first letter, right at the beginning, 1980, I think, September, about then. He said someday he might need someone to turn to, if things went bad on him, he'd need a fallback, and there was only me." Garfield felt her eyes search his face for distress signals. "He said there wasn't anyone else in the world he could trust, Luke."

"And you believed him?"

"I—I guess I wanted to believe him."

Arrangements, she said; Larry had made provision against the evil day when fate might try to chop him off at the knees. To offset that eventuality, he had selected six European cities where they could meet if ever he had to run for it. One was Paris; the others were London, Rome, Copenhagen, Amsterdam, and Dublin; she'd know where he was because he'd call POC collect from a public phone. The Paris rendezvous was to be at the corner of the rue Saint-Jacques and the boulevard Saint-Germain at twelve minutes past the hour in any hour between nine o'clock and noon on days of even date from the moment of notification. A walk past, Larry called it: She would walk, and he would watch. Maybe he'd watch through a morning before he tapped her, maybe a whole week, whatever was necessary to make a secure connection, but meanwhile, no matter what happened, the rendezvous points were to be considered fixed and nonnegotiable. It was their only guarantee of safety.

Their safety, Garfield noted. The year of writing was 1980, and already he was planning *their* security. He put his finger on the anomaly. "Tomorrow's not an even date," he said bleakly.

"No." She hung her head.

"So you were planning to roam around Paris for twenty-four hours without telling me." He stepped further into the room, halted at the end of the bed. "How did you think I was going to react to that? Or didn't you think I'd notice?"

"I didn't think it would make any difference. Not at first. Oh, Luke."

See how he twists, see how he turns, Garfield thought. The flyblown has-been. He let out his breath slowly; he had no intention of losing his temper at this stage. "So he'll keep his own rendezvous, if he keeps any."

"Yes."

"*Will* he keep any? You think he'll really be there day after tomorrow?"

Her shoulders rose and fell. Maybe, maybe not. He couldn't have put it better himself.

"So he won't hide out at the hospice overnight either." He wanted to rant and rage, to break things—preferably Bartell's neck—to curse and pound the walls.

"He won't trust anyone," she whispered.

"Do you still want to go? You think there's any point in going?"

She looked up quickly. "Yes."

"Why?" Justify my actions, he was saying. Make them morally creditable.

But she dropped her head. No answer.

"And if I said I was calling the whole thing off?" he asked sharply.

"I'd go anyway. It's my right. You can't stop me."

He saw the funny side of it then and grinned in the dark. What was the chess term for an unavoidable move? Larry would know, of course. Larry, the flyblown has-been of record. Larry, the chess master, the *grand*master. Curious how everyone overlooked that part of him. So long ago perhaps. Old history. As a boy of fourteen, little Larry Eisenstern had electrified the American chess scene with his mass challenges: Larry versus fifty or sixty adult opponents at a time. Larry *über Alles*. Unbeatable. His genius, they said, lay in shaping and controlling the other man's game. In raising false hopes and laying false trails. In gulling an opponent so completely, he ended up slitting his own throat. Young Larry, they said, had honed to perfection the science of psychological warfare. Learned to throw a man off guard, off his food; learned how to play on his nerves, ruin his sleep, destroy his confidence.

But of course, that was the *young* Larry . . .

"Go back to sleep." Garfield bent forward, took her hand in his, touched it to his lips.

"I can go?" She was holding her breath.

"How can I stop you?" he said.

An hour later Garfield took the service stairs to the ground floor and went out the back way, avoiding the glitterati thronging the lobby. Outside, limousines of vast capacity were disgorging Washington's finest, but Garfield had no eye for them. At the end of the driveway, a young black cop in a streaming cape and cap guard stood swatting his palm with a nightstick, staring keenly at everyone but the middle-aged man approaching on foot. However, as Garfield crossed the street, the boy raised his nightstick in a high arc over his head, and that was too much. It could have been cramp, of course, a perfectly innocent aid to circulation on a cold, damp night. But Garfield was a million years old and knew better.

Personally he had no objection to being followed and made no attempt either to deceive or to identify his tail. He strolled for fifteen minutes at a leisurely pace, enjoying the air, such as it was, enjoying the freedom, such as it was, until at length he found what he was looking for. It was an all-night pharmacy, not that its line of business was of any interest to him. What mattered was that the public phone was installed in an old-fashioned closed-in booth at the far end of the store. He went in. The night clerk, a frail and aged black seated on a stool behind a bulletproof glass screen, welcomed him by reaching instinctively for something just out of sight. Sure, he said, visibly relieved at the request, call anywhere you want, didn't make him no richer, didn't make him no poorer.

Garfield called Polly first and kept it light and in the process confirmed what he'd already taken for granted: that they'd tapped his home phone. That giveaway cut-in was always too late. He asked her to come down to Washington and wondered what his listeners would make of that.

Then he called Paris collect. It was after midnight there, but the subscriber was wide-awake. Behind his coldly furious *"Oui!"* Garfield heard a woman's voice, very close, pitched high, pitched at heaven. "Ah, *non, c'est insupportable! Ah, chéri, chéri, chéri . . .*"

"Good evening, Joss," Garfield said pleasantly. "I'm not interrupting anything, am I?"

NINE

Larry Bartell woke to a dull, watery roar, and that part of his brain not already residing in his feet put a name to it.

Niagara Falls.

At this a large part of him gave up the ghost. Rocks, he thought. Over the top in a barrel. Flip. Plunge. Over and over. Smash. Minced Bartell on the rocks.

Ha!

You'll die laughing, you will, his father said gravely, walking very gingerly on the water nearby. You'll go to the devil laughing, boy. His father wore a yarmulke and prayer shawl.

And if not Niagara Falls, the sea. Surf seething, snoring, pouring. And if not the surf, a stream. A trout stream. And if not a—

He went back to sleep for a while and had a small enlightening dream. He watched Larry Bartell climb unsteadily onto a washbasin and take the brass handle of a window in his hand

and with a mighty heave—aaaagh! Agony! Bastard! Help! *Scream?*

S-c-r-e-a-m. Rachmaninoff's variations on a scream by Bartellini. Monstrous thunderclaps in the tympani section, a cloudburst of flying discords.

He came to again, and the water was still roaring. The back of his head felt cold. So did his arms and his spine and the backs of his legs. He could smell urine. He could taste blood. He could hear water. He could see—nothing. On his chest sat the weight of ages, the weight of years, the weight of unconscionable unplumbed sin. Except that when he *mooooved*— like this, like that—it moved. Move, schmuck. *Move!* He wriggled—ouch!—swayed, heaved. The weight rolled from him —plap!—and turned slowly on the bosom of the deep, and as it turned, a face swam silkily past his own, a face without a top to it and hollowed-out eyeholes, the mouth wide as if straining for the highest of all impossible high notes. Aha, he thought, and heard it scrape and slop away into the doomful black.

"*Non, c'est pas possible.*" The voice came from above, a voice in the sky.

"*Mais nécessaire, non? On a besoin d'un—*" But what they needed was lost in a general thumping and banging and hissing and crackling from up there. *Up?*

Twenty feet or so above him there was a hole of light in a black sky. Heads moved in it, and foreshortened bodies, shiny black anthropoids with shiny gold Martian heads, and men in black helmets and white helmets, and behind them smoke and a great light, smoke rising and falling, and through the smoke distant trumpet calls, a lot of them, coming and going—wee-wah wee-wah wee-wah—and these unlocked his mind at last. Klaxons. Fire. Police. Ambulance.

The rest came back to him in perfect chiaroscuro, like a series of hand-painted lantern slides, click-clack. The toilet door had come across the room at him with the first crack of thunder, flattening him to the window; then the blast had grabbed him from behind and sucked him out and down. But . . . Where the toilet floor had been there was now a hole, a hole in the earth that was now the sky. He took his face in his hands to hold his head together. Work it out, Larry. You were sitting at the back of the room, a table at the back of the room with those two creeps, agreed? Agreed. Except now there's a hole in the world where the table should be, and you're at the bottom of the hole. Half the joint is a hole. No floor for yards, right around the spot where you were sitting with Émile and the drifter, where the drifter's bag—

Keep an eye on my bag, okay?

Oh, no, he groaned, getting it all at once. Oh, Christ, Miko, no . . .

He'd fallen into a sewer. In Paris they have sewers. You can do the tour. Years ago, when the world was young, Larry had done the tour up in the Eighth. He was lying in water, face up, a river of water, a river of —don't think about it.

Somehow he got upright and propped his bones against the curving wall. They lacked cohesion, the bones, had a tendency to spread like a busted deck chair; but they functioned—just.

From the wall he could see more of the bistro up there—or what was left of the bistro up there. The zinc bar—a big slab of it anyway—was embedded in the ceiling, and gay little wisps and tags of orange cloth hung from it, all lifting gently in the breeze like funerary flags. The bistro no longer had a front, it seemed, because the wind blew free; he could hear it.

Move, he thought, and shoved off in any old direction. Clop-clop-clop, he went in the ankle-deep water. *Quiet!* Changing gears, he moved like a cross-country skier, dragging his feet; that was better—till he fell over the body. It hadn't floated far; got snagged up on a little mudbank. He could see its face by the light from the bistro. Mouth wide, still going for that high note. Maybe he saved my life, Larry thought, disengaging his foot from the corpse's armpit.

Throw up or move!

Somewhere in Paris tonight, he thought, pressing on—Stay

awake, Larry, you hear me? listen to the story, there's a good boy—somewhere in Paris there's one guy in orange coveralls who decided to give the bistro a miss tonight. There's always one. Every disaster you ever read about. And right now he's calling his wife on the phone and telling her kindly to step down off the walls because he's *alive*, Josette, *c'était un véritable miracle*. It was raining, he'd tell her, so he decided to stay at the factory. Or he was short of dough. Or his liver was acting up again. Anyway he'd stayed behind and now he's alive. Till Yahweh calls him home. This year, next year, sometime, never . . .

Luck, they'd call it. Fate.

Whatever limits us is fate, he thought. Emerson? Emerson.

The last of the light from the bistro died, and to celebrate, he walked slap into a projecting wall, an arch. The impact rocked him on his heels, and what with the snaggy tug of running water, he had to sidestep quickly to keep his balance. The third step took him over the edge and a long way down. First he hit water, then masonry, hard: shoulder, head, hip, knee, ankle, in that order. The water was more than knee-deep here and one hell of a lot faster. He choked up the liter or two he'd swallowed going under. Ka-bah! Ka-bah! His coughing boomed along the cavern like cannon fire. A much broader thoroughfare this one, wider, higher. Also slimier underfoot. It took him a good three minutes to learn to stand upright and another three to find the wall, like walking on butter an inch thick. He set off again, schussing along, ski style, keeping time by singing in his head.

Schlep down, schlep do-own, that lonesome ro-had, before—

He lost his footing somewhere and went windmilling down again, but instead of going under this time, he sprawled on a raised ledge, a narrow sidewalk running along the right-hand wall. After a minute or two he dragged his sodden legs up to join the sodden rest of him, got a grip on the wall, and summoned up the strength to stand. Whew! On, on, Sir Lerry—through shit and derision to the green fields beyond! And watch your step, okay? This is my best suit.

Die laughing. . . . Go to the devil laughing. . . .

At about this point the watch Miko bought him in Geneva—a *Jap* watch, the goddamn cheapskate! a Jap watch in *Geneva!*—gave out the double bleep that marked the hour. Larry figured this for midnight in the general scheme of things and thought no more about it. Till—bee-beep—it sounded a second time about ten minutes later. He called this midnight, too, on the ground that he must have misheard the first alarm. But then it beeped a third time, and he concluded that certain lacunae were intruding into his time scale. Aeons later he actually woke up in the middle of one of these lapses, a kind of state of grace. He was standing upright, not even leaning on the wall, sleeping. And if not asleep . . .

He seemed to be climbing now. Keep walking. *Keeeep* walking.

He thought a lot about C.J., but her image was several lifetimes out of date, and besides, her face kept turning into Lydia's, so he concentrated on Seth and Kathryn for a spell, and that nearly brought on a heart attack. He saw their infant faces eyeless, the tops of their heads missing, their rosebud mouths stretched wide for the highest of high notes, and he bawled silently: *Enough!* At least he hoped it was silent.

He might have killed himself on that narrow brick road if Miko hadn't come to warn him.

Miko, of all people. "Hey, Lerry," old Miko whispered over his shoulder, little Miko all in gray, "Lerry, you don' notice nothing different here?"

Larry pulled up short. What do you mean—*different?*

He snapped out of it very fast then. The first thing he noticed was that the water was whooshing a lot farther away than it should be. The second thing was that he was some distance *above* it. Third, the sidewalk was sloping *up*, by God, like a hill. Fourth, he had both hands plastered to his lower right abdomen, and he could feel—for the very first time *feel*—his liver, like a slug of ebony when he pressed it, smooth and hard and slippery as ebony.

And fifth, he could hear the swish-swash-swish of boots in the tunnel ahead and see the skippety-blip of torches.

Oh, no. Oh, please God, no. Not now.

Freeze, you cluck, *freeze.*

They were almost on him, a mumble jumble of voices echoing and reechoing off the ancient walls and the swish-swash-swish of boots coming nearer. The brickword blushed from black to gray to mid-brown to honey and slowly changed shape. Where Larry stood the narrow sidewalk fell away fifteen or twenty feet to the sewer floor and, above him, rose twenty feet more to a narrow exit chimney studded with iron climbing rings. Jacob's ladder. Don't let them look up, he prayed. Don't. *Please.* Rooted to the brickwork, he watched the men come around a slight bend. He counted five of them—no, six; one trailing—six squeaky goliaths in waders and shapeless oilskins and miners' headlamps. They passed right under his feet, swish-swash-swish-swash, the light of their lamps enclosing him for a moment, then leaving him in peace. They sloshed on out of sight, but he let them go a long, long way before he dared move again, so far away he couldn't hear their splashing anymore.

He climbed the hill to the exit ladder.

It wasn't very high, no more than ten or twelve feet, but he seemed to spend a lifetime on it, mostly on the topmost rungs, heaving and straining at the goddamn manhole cover. Trouble was he had no beef in him, no strength, no grip, and when it came to putting his shoulder to that solid cast-iron discus—a hundred pounds if it was an ounce—he lost all rudimentary contact between body and brain. Finally he hit lucky and nudged the plate just right, at one side, and in a great rush skewered his trunk up through the slit till he sat in the street, in the cool, cool air of the world, with the plate trapping him across the thighs, unable to move it another inch. He must have dozed because when he came around again it was getting light, and the light scared the holy shit out of him. He kicked free and staggered into the nearest alley and out the other end into a square. It was a small tree-lined square, cobbled, the Paris of the brochures, and at his feet a widish street opened out and ran for half a mile to a kind of Roman senate house. And towering over it, a mile high in the green-gray dawn, the domes of Sacré-Coeur gleamed pink and naked at the summit of Montmartre.

Show-off! Goddamn show-off! He was wheezing. Choking. Bleeding. Wet. Weeping.

In the place du Tertre he found a public phone booth that wasn't vandalized and blew a whole ten-franc piece on a five-second local call, the last coin he had in the world. Happiboy was asleep, of course, but he said he'd come fetch him.

Larry stood well back under the trees in the middle of the square, trees immortalized by Renoir and Utrillo and Dufy, and hugged the sodden rags about him to stop his shivering. His teeth chattered. His bones quaked. His head ached. His mouth bled. His body cried out. Yet on the inside he burned. On the inside he laughed.

Oh, God, you made it.

You done made it *home*, you creakin' old mother!

Happiboy drove with both windows open and the plastic sunroof full back, but a wind tunnel of morning air was no solution to Larry Bartell's problem. The bouquet of him—of ripe Parisian effluvia—filled every corner of the neat little Deux Chevaux.

"Never get rid of this fucken stink," Happiboy grumbled, head stuck out in the tearing air.

"You think I crawled under Paris on my hands and knees for the fun of it?"

"Your private hang-ups are your own affair. Look, Larry—"

"And if you can't remember the name on the goddamn passport, just zip your lip, buster, you mind?"

Happiboy raised a fine little hand on a wiry little arm and petitioned heaven. "It's four-thirty in the fucken morning,

Jesus," he said despairingly. "What does he expect—J. K. fucken Galbraith?"

He was small and lithe and curly gray like Larry, though ten years younger and a whole lot fitter. Fitness was one of Happiboy's things. Fitness of the mind to inhabit the body. Fitness of the body to house the mind. Great. Alvin Hapgood Straker, soldier of misfortune, Larry's most enduring private recruit and still unlisted—please, God—in Miko's directory of European contacts. A nice middle-class American boy, ex-University of Houston, ex-teacher, ex-exemplary son of the 101st Airborne in its hottest, greenest hour.

Ex-junkie, ex-con, ex-bum.

Larry had scraped Happiboy off the floor at a peace movement soirée on the Left Bank three years ago. Built him up, set him in motion, enrolled him in a course on Oriental philosophy at the Sorbonne. Within a year he was pushing quality hash and occasional coke to his classmates and in two years held sole distribution rights to all the disparate campuses of the University of Paris. An organizer, Happiboy. An opportunist. Wrinkle for wrinkle, he was also the oldest, most decorated Vietnam vet in the city, a distinction which did him no harm socially in certain sublime American expatriate circles in the Latin Quarter. Also, for reasons close to Larry's interests, he was currently a cadet disciple of the Lord Muhammad and a prince of the Paris environment lobby, though religion, political or otherwise, was not his bag.

Generally speaking, gratitude was Happiboy's only registered brain malfunction. Gratitude to Larry Bartell. He held true to Larry as Sancho Panza had held true to the Man of La Mancha, and for pretty much the same hopelessly confused reasons.

One day they'd work out what they owed each other, Happiboy frequently told himself. Account for it.

"What was it you heard on the radio?" Larry asked, still shuddering with cold.

"Said someone blew up a Jew joint in the Nineteenth. A bomb."

"Jew joint?"

"Jewish workers' bistro—they hang out there in the breaks from a factory down the street. Petrochemical plant."

"Do they say who did it?"

Happiboy threw him a withering glance. "It happened four hours ago, dink. They're still scraping the clientele off the walls." He turned away sharply as the stench got to him again. "What's your version?"

Larry told him, minus certain excisions to keep his mind easy and his back to the wall, but at the end of it Happiboy merely shrugged. He was beyond surprise. After the second Tet, he said, no one had the right to be surprised by anything man did to man.

"You know who they play with, those two dinks of yours?" he asked. "*Action Directe?* The Trots? PLO? I could maybe identify them somehow. We got ourselves one hell of a selection of Jewfuckers in this town."

Larry shook his head, and Alvin H. Straker took the hint without rancor. With Larry, some areas were closed, even to careful drivers. He wouldn't ask again. Guaranteed.

They parked in a walled courtyard off the rue Saint-Jacques and took the back streets to Happiboy's apartment on the quai Saint-Michel. Traffic was already clogging the boulevard Saint-Germain, and by the river the cacophony was total, like a continuous organ note. Larry cringed. Once upon a time, he thought bitterly, they'd had an institution called *dawn* in this town. A regular thing, used to steal downriver like a silver-fingered ghost, parting the Seine mists, touching spires, towers, cupolas, domes; raising Notre-Dame ten feet above the ground; spilling across the face of the quai d'Orsay like smoke. All in silence, except for the bird song. In those days a garret on the quai Saint-Michel with views across the river to the Île de la Cité rated among the most desirable addresses in Paris. A private box in the theater of the real. But that was long ago, as long ago as the war, Miko said, before the city fathers turned the quays of the Left Bank into a four-lane speedway. Larry looked up as they came to the house, a segment of a once-grand row, its plaster now cracked and peeling, burned black with gas and diesel fumes, its paint chipped, windows cracked and coated. In the inner courtyard the walls had been laid back to the brickwork in patches by rising damp and resonance.

It was no better inside till they reached Happiboy's haven on the fifth floor. Then even the last flight of stairs was carpeted. "You get out of that crap," Happiboy ordered. "I'll rustle up some chow." But first he filled a tub and laced it with Badedas till the foam overflowed onto the floor. Larry immersed himself and let the heat enter his bones, his vital organs, his soul, and wallowed in the dizzying luxury of it, and finally slept. Happiboy woke him with a plate of fried eggs and charred bacon, and there was an interlude while Larry pretended to eat the stuff. When the performance was over and he was sipping his coffee, Happiboy lit up.

"I just caught the news on the BBC World Service. They're carrying a line on your farewell party last night. Seven killed outright, sixteen critical, nine serious, five under observation. The owner's dead. But his wife made it. She was in back, in the kitchen. You see her?"

Something in the phrasing made Larry look up sharply. "No, I didn't. Why?"

"The pigs are looking for three men. One wearing a suit and raincoat, thin, dark, about thirty. Another taller, heavier, fair, long hair, a beard, kinda hippie, blue jeans, an a red checked shirt. The third about your age, your build, your type."

Larry groaned.

"You'd better keep your head down for a day or so," Happiboy said. "Wanna stay here?"

"They'd put you away for a thousand years."

"If you won't tell, I won't."

Larry closed his eyes and leaned back on the sponge-filled neck pad. Warm water squeegeed out and massaged his scalp. "I could sleep for a week," he groaned. "Ten weeks."

"Long as you like. There's a bed if you want. Plenty of chow. Clothes. I'm burning that stuff of yours, by the way. Anything else you need?" The straight line of his mouth puckered. "Piece a tail?"

"All I need is this, man." Larry resettled his neck. "Hey, listen, maybe there is something. A favor. Big favor." He kept his eyes shut because to look up into that all-suspecting, all-forgiving face was to teeter on the brink of self-annihilation. The guy's lost already, he argued sensibly in the back of his head. Be practical. He's been around; he knows the score. Sticking his neck out is his hobby, his choice, like feeding shit to bored housewives and half-assed students.

He opened his eyes and saw exactly what he expected to see. As far as Happiboy could be said ever to smile, he was smiling.

"What's the word, bro?" He swung his Spanish boots up onto the rim of the bath.

Larry tried the old infectious grin for encouragement. "I have to be somewhere for a coupla hours, H. Without being there." He swallowed a mouthful of scalding coffee.

"You mean an alibi?"

"Kind of."

"You want me to fill in for you," Happiboy said slowly as if he were instructing a child in class. He turned to look at himself in the mirror, measured what he saw there against the face in the bath. "They don't know you, I hope."

"No chance."

A dozen questions sprang simultaneously into Happiboy's flinty face, but he gave expression to only one, characteristically the practical one. "Where do you have to be? Someplace here in Paris?"

"You go to see a priest, American priest name of Father John Lattimore. Runs some kind of hospice up behind the place d'Italie. You go there."

118

"The Hospice of Our Lady? Rue Saint-Auban?" Happiboy's face was stone.

"You know it?"

"It's a freak-out pen for junkies. You want *me* to hole up *there?*"

The note of incredulity was carefully underplayed, so Larry just as carefully ignored it. "For a few hours, man, what's the difference? Four or five hours. Say till noon."

"Say till noon," Happiboy repeated dully.

"You tell the priest Luke Garfield sent you. Luke Garfield talked to you on the phone from Washington last night and told you, 'Go see Father John and ask for a bed for the night.' Well, it was a long night and you got sidetracked, but now you're asking. Luke Garfield. Remember the name."

"And that's all?"

"That's all."

"Suppose this Garfield checks up while I'm there? Is there a chance he'd do that?"

"You tell the priest you won't talk to anyone on the phone, period."

"And after that?"

"After that"—Larry Bartell slid luxuriously under the steaming water till it lapped his mouth—"after that, pardner, you bury my heart at Wounded Knee, hear? If you can find it."

He found this extremely funny. Laughed till he choked, Happiboy told old Hervé several hours later. It was a little frenzied, that laughter, a classic emotional response to tension, though, considering the state he was in, hardly surprising. But then that was Larry all over, frankly—an emotional response to tension. Personified. Up one minute, down the next.

Personally the joke about Wounded Knee—if it *was* a joke—passed Happiboy on the blind side.

Very little else was allowed to pass him on the blind side that morning. It started out cute and got progressively clever.

But there was no question in his mind that Larry was sleeping when he left. That was the mystery. The guy was out on his feet, he told Hervé, so exhausted Happiboy had to hip-carry him from the bathroom and dump him on the bed. Hadn't the strength to crawl. Which didn't exactly square with the situation Happiboy found when he got back a little after three o'clock, admittedly—and, yes, being two hours late didn't help —but what the hell, was he his brother's keeper? Besides, he'd had one hell of a morning.

Man! That *dump*!

He'd checked in at the hospice around five-thirty and for openers endured a breakfast of gray slop doled out by a quartet of hundred-year-old nuns. At first he argued with them—he had no appetite for breakfast; he never *ate* breakfast; he was a friend, not a lost soul, a friend of a friend—but godliness is one hell of a virtue to tackle on its home ground at five-thirty of a Paris morning, and Happiboy proved no match for a quartet of hundred-year-old nuns. He joined the human debris at the festive board and amened along with the rest of them for what he was about to receive. Father John, they told him, was in church: he liked to pray at this hour for strength to combat the day.

Happiboy sympathized with him.

After breakfast, in spite of his protests and to his eternal shame, they made him strip and take a cold bath; then his hair was searched for lice by a youth with suppurating acne. A younger nun—eighty-five if she were a day, a real stunner, needed a shave—asked him nicely if he was a practicing homosexual. Not that they held it against him or anything, she said; it was just a precaution, the AIDS scare. If he was gay and it bothered him to admit it, he could give a false name; most people did anyway.

In due course Father John came by on his rounds, and Happiboy's heart sank like a stone at the sight of him. He was a very big man, round-shouldered as big men often are after middle age, and knobbly, red-faced. He carried a lot of white hair, a lot of sweat, a lot of dandruff, and his technique with the fallen was that of a long-suffering uncle winning over a spoiled brat, a cheery, chafing innocence that involved much wiggling of the hairy brows and reassuring winks. Love is the Way, he told Happiboy several times in a tobacco-stained Irish descant. He didn't mention Garfield after the initial "Ah, Luke," but in deference to his old friend's request showed Happiboy to an empty dormitory on the second floor and watched him settle down on a camp bed in one corner. The room was tall and whitewashed and broken on one side by eight windows, all of them wide open to let out the night smell. In the street below, a casual market had just struck up trade, and the noise from it was soon deafening.

But it was merely the prelude to the masterwork, and Happiboy knew it. The best was yet to come.

It came around seven o'clock.

The recital started with a low moan from the floor above, just one: first violin sounding the key, F major. Seconds later another moan joined it, slightly lower in pitch but more insistent; then several more came in all at once, wildly discordant like trumpets in a Stan Kenton arrangement. Knowing what was coming, Happiboy got his head under the blankets, but it didn't help much. The first scream sliced through the walls bright as cold steel, followed quickly by another. Then a third, a fourth. The rest was solid choral work, and it went on for four hours, not a concerted screaming—these throats were anything but together—and not constant either in volume or pitch, but continuous, the way a baby's wailing is continuous when it tries to grab attention; and Happiboy remembered that cold turkey was mostly a state of conscious unbeing and that to impose a sense of being on yourself, you had to fight and scream and claw because without pain you were nothing. In his own private and special hell a few years back, they'd found him singing hymns while he beat time on the walls till his hands broke. I'm *here*! he'd sung (screamed). I *live*! Coming out of sedation in the cold light of morning on the cold turkey farm was like dying from lack of air, like waking up six feet under the ground. I'm here! I live!

By eleven-thirty he'd taken as much as he could take. He crept downstairs and got as far as the back door when he met Father John coming in. "Aha, leaving already?" The priest laughed. What in the length and breadth of his sainted world there was to laugh at Happiboy couldn't guess, but laugh he did. He was always laughing. He slung a meaty arm across Happiboy's shoulders and turned him right around again. "Ah, the curative powers of the young! Miraculous so 'tis. You'll stay for lunch, I hope, Larry." By this time they were back inside and the good father was soul-deep into a lecture on poor misguided pushers who in their ignorance wrought havoc upon the human race, and shortly after, they came to the third-floor corridor, where Happiboy was permitted to spy through jalousie windows in solid oak doors while the animals inside blew their minds.

Nothing, but *nothing*, passed him on the blind side that morning.

When he escaped finally a little before noon, he was feeling pretty awful. It didn't occur to him to watch his back, and, if he had, it's doubtful he would have spotted his tail. She was just another middle-aged housewife. He took the metro to Jussieu and changed for Odéon, and was about to change again for Saint-Michel when he felt the top of his head coming off. He charged up into bright sunlight—hard white light, everything white, one of those brassy, overhung Paris days, the sidewalks jammed, the cafés, too. He cut down to the rue Galande, where —merciful charity—Celestine Mornet received him with joy and gratitude. Big, beautiful, bulbous Celestine. She made him a soufflé afterward, which accounted for his lateness. A cheese soufflé, *pour encourager l'autre.*

Replete, returned to life and something approaching sanity, he walked around the block onto the quay and up to the apartment.

To find Larry Bartell dying in an ocean of blood.

TEN

Happiboy's reactions were quick and unemotional, a soldier's reactions. He felt for a throat pulse, found one—weak—confirmed the corpse was breathing freely, then took off down the stairs three at a time. Old Hervé lived just around the corner, and Happiboy was lucky to find him in, luckier still to find him only mildly stoned. The old man's accustomed rate for house calls of a conspicuously sensitive nature was five hundred crisp new ones, cash in hand before he'd move a step, but for a responsible client like Mr. Strah-keer, and taking into account the fullness of the hour, the heat, and the— Happiboy dragged him bodily through the midafternoon crowds on the quay, shoved him up four flights of stairs, and heaved him, still protesting, into the bedroom. Hervé came to rest, panting and blowing. Bent over the bed, touched Larry's throat. Stared. Sniffed.

"Wine!" he gasped, fighting for breath. "*Wine!*" He planted two hundred pounds of blown flesh on the bed. "The *salaud* is bleeding *wine!*" He picked up a half-empty bottle from the floor—one of four Happiboy had overlooked in his haste—and sniffed it. "A Beaune?" He read the label. "A '78 Beaune. Three and a half bottles of Beaune in one drunken *swill?*"

"He's dying, you fat-assed fag!" Happiboy roared from the door.

"Dying? Pah! He's drunk!"

Feeling criminally abused, Happiboy came to the bed and took a look for himself. Larry had an ulcer, he pointed out defensively. Maybe it had bled. Look, wasn't that blood? There, in the corner of his mouth. You telling me *that's* fucken Beaune?

So Hervé got to work.

The neighborhood gossip was that back in the Dark Ages, at the height of his social and professional prominence, Hervé had had his license revoked for misconduct. He'd sliced up a Very Important Patient the wrong way during a Very Expensive

Operation, and when the hospital checked him out, he couldn't tell north from south, shit from ambergris. Stoned. Stupefied. Since then he'd waxed fat on socially sensitive house calls and fashionable abortions. On the Left Bank Hervé was universally mistrusted and mocked; problem was, in certain highly delicate situations there was no one else to turn to.

"Come, lamebrain—water. Clean water, warm. And towels." Hervé's pudgy, far from clean hands kneaded Larry all over, punching and thumping, screwing the stethoscope into his bony crags. Together they bathed him, and together they stripped the wine-sodden, blood-tinged bed linen. Happiboy produced clean sheets, clean pillowcases, clean blankets. "Is he your guest?" Hervé asked, looking around for clues.

"Fuck off," Happiboy said shortly.

For five hundred francs a crack the bare minimum is no-hear no-see no-speak.

Hervé got his act together. He placed both hands on the swollen belly and almost immediately made the discovery Larry himself had made not twelve hours earlier. "Aaaah." The liver swayed under his touch; solid, smooth, hard.

"What is it?"

"You knew your friend was an alcoholic?"

"I knew he took a drink now and then, yeah."

"A drink now and then!" Hervé petitioned heaven, eyes rolling. "You people! Ask no questions, hear no lies."

"Cut the shit, Hervé. What's wrong with him?"

The old man stuck a shovel-ended finger in his ear and pawed at the jungle of white hairs. "What's wrong is he's drunk. If you wish my professional opinion—"

"Not if it's gonna cost another five hundred, I don't."

"Oh, bof!" Hervé chuckled. Americans! "In my opinion your friend is suffering from cirrhosis of the liver."

"Bad?"

The plump hands rose and fell. "Fatally bad."

In Nam, Happiboy had seen WIAs by the truckload and had learned to read the signs: nearly dead is dead. In death, stripped to the vital fundament, a man is neither fat nor thin, neither ugly nor handsome, white nor black, weak nor strong. In death—to Alvin H. Straker's embattled eye—the human form took on the contours and texture of discolored meat. And that was how Larry Bartell quite suddenly looked to him now. Discolored meat awaiting the body bag. His eyes were half-open and glazed, unseeing. His mouth gaped, revealing a spastic tongue. His breathing was so shallow you couldn't hear it, and his bones poked through the canopy of flesh like the ribs of a broken umbrella. The only part of him that moved was his belly, and it pulsed in one special place like a small engine—throb-throb, throb-throb—as if it were functioning as a surrogate for all the other organs. He was bruised all over, rainbow shades, pink and yellow and blue and purple, but the belly was sickly white, the gross, distended white of a woodland toadstool.

Discolored meat. Why hadn't he noticed before?

Hervé had gone back to thumping and pressing him, sounding the bony back and chest with his stethoscope, peeling the body off the sheet when he needed to as though it had no weight, but quite suddenly he stopped and folded the instrument back into his bag. "This is pointless," he said.

"Pointles for you or pointless for him?"

"For both. Alcoholic cirrhosis. I can't help him, he can't help himself."

"What about a hospital?" It was a test question; Happiboy didn't really want to get involved that deep.

"No hospitals. I'm sorry, my friend, but if you want hospitals, you must arrange them yourself. One of my little rules: no hospitals."

"A clinic then—a private clinic?"

"Ah, now." For a moment Hervé's face softened. Arithmetical progressions of a five-hundred-franc fee mounted and multiplied dizzily in his mind's eye. "Yes, actually I do happen to know of such a place. In the Auvergne. Beautiful country. Exquisite." He smiled, already there.

"They can cure him?"

"Cure!" Hervé turned the word in on itself. "My dear boy, there's no *cure* involved. I repeat, treatment is pointless." His plump little hands made a soulful marriage in the air. "I said fatally bad, and I *mean* fatally bad. Look at him." He swiveled around to get a better view of his patient. "Cirrhosis is a long road, hm? Long. In this man's case, the first stage—shall we say, the retrievable stage—is many, many months past. Anorexia, morning sickness, general malaise, obesity"—here he prodded Larry's pulsing toadstool of a belly—"enlargement of the liver—all this is history. Your friend is at the end of the second stage, now, the *critical* stage. The body has given him fair warning: severe vomiting; diarrhea; anorexia; jaundice; intense pain. Now he's hemorrhaging inside." He scraped at the blood around Larry's mouth with a furrowed, yellow fingernail. "Here, you see? He vomits blood. Hemorrhaging." He pulled down the scalloped skin under Bartell's right eye. "He dies, *voilà*. By his own hand. A form of suicide. Alcohol *arouses* the condition, so he drinks to kill the pain the alcohol arouses. Cause and effect."

"So what am I supposed to do?"

"Lock up your wine as a first priority. Let him sleep. Then get rid of him. Send him home if he has a home."

"And that's it? No way of easing the pain?"

"Oh, one can make him comfortable, of course. Dull the pain. Prolong his life a few days more, a few weeks. In the clinic, now—ah, well, they would give him proteins, vitamin B complex, folic acid. Tranquilizers to suppress the craving for alcohol. A needle biopsy to determine the severity of the alcohol's effect, so on." He lifted the surviving half bottle of Beaune from the floor, tested its nose, sipped delicately, nodded to himself, took a swig. "But the exercise would be vastly expensive, my friend, and wholly futile. Death is death. Man must die." He took another swallow. "Hmm, this is very good."

"But can't you do something for him? Short-term. Drugs or something?"

"*Or* something?" Hervé glared at him, outraged. "Or *some-*

thing? No, m'sieu, not me. Oh, no." He took another long pull at the bottle and smacked his lips. "You know, this is really very good indeed. I compliment you." He squinted at the label. "Do you buy from the *négociant* or the château?"

Alvin Straker held on to his cool by an effort of will too great to measure. His instinct was to hammer this ball of French shit till he screamed for mercy, then hammer him some more, rend him limb from limb and scatter his brains; but that was his normal instinct, a quotidian state of mind; he'd been feeling like that about most people since the second Tet, and five months in a vet's hospital had done nothing whatever to change his state of mind.

"The château," he said absently.

"Then perhaps you'll let me have the address, hm? Now it's late. I must be going."

The Frenchman got to his feet a trifle unsteadily. Grabbed the bed for support. Adjusted his jacket of soiled cream linen. Patted the five strands of lank gray hair stretched across his scalp. Hoisted his voluminous pants. Freed his crotch.

Happiboy took up his station in the doorway, arms folded to keep his hands out of temptation's way. "He'll need drugs, Hervé," he said calmly. His voice was very low, very reasonable. "Whatever he can handle, whatever kills the pain. Maybe a shot."

"Of course." Hervé scrabbled nervously in his bag, conscious suddenly of a new tension between them. "Give him these." He produced two vials of blue and white capsules and a bottle of white pills. "Follow the dosage on the label; not more, not less." He swept his battered Panama off the bedpost and jammed it on his head. "But I warn you, without complete rest, without proper medical attention—" He was suddenly, quite exceptionally angry: Failed doctors, like failed priests, carry the full weight of their inadequacy to the grave. "Can you make him rest? Stop his drinking? Tell me—can you?"

"No more than I can stop the fucken world," Happiboy whispered.

127

"*Et voilà!*" Hervé beamed, a small victory. "Now you're being sensible."

Larry saw it all. Heard it all.

Heard it through the misty dawn that used to grace the Seine. Saw it through the southernmost aspect of his eyes. When they stopped talking, he felt a needle go in and prepared himself for sleep, but surprisingly sleep didn't come. A state of weightlessness, but not a loss of consciousness.

He watched shadows swim across the room like fish in an aquarium, some of them speckled with lacy light where the sun fell through the curtains, and from time to time the windows sang at him as the traffic thundered by outside: soprano from the shivering glass; tenor from the frames. The light faded and the long day died, and in the dark he found a superhuman rationality. He was master of his ship, captain of his soul. A surgeon, too.

Mustering all his powers of concentration, he sent his brain sliding down the magic beanstalk of his nervous system on a deep and meaningful exploration. Aha, now then, here he was, midgetlike, at the base of a giant lung, his left lung—feel it?—a vast cathedral of howling winds and stertorous organ notes soaring way, way up into the cavernous dark, and he switched on a flashlight he was carrying and passed it over a fan-vaulted ceiling and arches and columns and hanging tapestries of malodorous tissue. "Get this cleaned up," he told Happiboy sharply, and took a narrow and uncharted sewer down to the stomach. Oh, this is the place all right, he thought, looking around. This is the harvest home of pain. Splashing toward the ulcer on the far lower wall, he felt the heat emanating from it a good hundred yards away, a million kilowatts of tortured energy, and he had to turn away because it was too much for him, much too much, the heat and the vicious red glow of it.

Happiboy was waiting for him at the door to the liver. He knew he would be; it was just the sort of fool trick he'd pull. "Look, Larry, do yourself a favor, what do you say? Don't go in there, huh?" They all said that. Don't think about it, don't worry about it, too late, too late. But he went in on tiptoe, and it lay there in a glass case, royal purple in color and diamond hard; whumpata-whumpata, smooth, tactile, a beautiful, evil thing. Larry walked around it several times to familiarize himself with its defects, though it seemed to him absurd that anything so beautiful could have defects. He still thought so when he came out. Locking the door behind him, he said to Miko, "They must mean some other liver, Miko. That's the best liver I ever saw."

Paddling down the wide thoroughfare to the heart, Happiboy called out to him again. "Larry? Hey, Larry!"

And Larry sighed wearily because there was so much left to do. "What is it?" he answered. "Can't you leave me alone down here for five minutes?"

"Dumbhead old dink," Happiboy said. "I turn my back on you for five minutes and you're stoned clear out of your mind."

"What's he talking about?" Larry asked Miko.

"You wanna watch TV?" Happiboy whispered.

This was obviously a dream. I've strayed into a dream and nothing's making sense, he thought, irritated. Better snap out of it. Get back to the heart later. "What?" he said.

"Larry? Can you hear me? I said, do you wanna watch TV?" Happiboy again.

"What?"

"Larry? They played pictures of the bombing on the early news. I taped it for you. Wanna see it?"

Through half-closed eyes Larry could make out gold filigree, columns and arches and fan vaulting. Over it hung Happiboy, faint in the dark, but yes, definitely Happiboy. The gold filigree was the bedstead. The dark was the dark. Larry felt no pain anywhere.

"Okay," he said. "You want me to get up?"

Happiboy backed off at once, alarmed, hands raised, palms outward. "Hey, now, bro, relax. No sweat. Don't talk. Go back to sleep, okay?"

"What do you mean, sleep?" Larry said indignantly. "Wheel it in. If you want to show me something, wheel the damn thing in."

But Happiboy continued to back away and closed the door without a sound. As if he hadn't heard. As if he hadn't heard a word.

"How'd you like that guy?" Larry snapped crossly.

"Americans," Miko said, right behind him.

The night rolled over him again. At its far edge, too far away at first to be more than a rumor, a blade of light sub-tended. Larry watched it grow and continue to grow and expand and rise and open like a flower until it straddled the horizon, and when the blade of light pierced his brain—an hour later, two, maybe three—Happiboy stood in the middle of it, his hand resting on the door. "Hey, skipper!" he whispered. "You awake? Hey!"

Skipper. Military jargon. An acceptable intimacy between the inhibited.

"Hey, Larry, you hear me?"

"I hear you." He noted a difference this time, a big difference. He could hear the sound of his own voice.

Happiboy bent over him in the blade of light, a white grin slicing his flinty face. "Hey, man, how you doing?" he whispered. He sounded pleased.

For no good reason he could think of, Larry's eyes filled with tears.

Happiboy planted the tray on the chair and pulled the chair close to the bed.

"I didn't know if coffee was bad for you or what," he said. "What do you think?"

"Who knows?" Larry took the mug. "If I ate and drank what was good for me, I might still be alive." The coffee was good. Black. The stimulant worked on him like an electric charge. "You wouldn't have a blast of cognac or something handy, would you?"

"No booze. Official." Happiboy looked grim.

"I see."

"You'd better, bro, because I mean it."

"Sure you do. You're gonna spend the rest of my life chasing my ass in case I sneak a drink. Good luck to you. Who's Hervé anyway?"

"A quack. Lives around the corner." Happiboy had trouble with the muscles of his face but finally got them to crack a death's-head grin. "Hervé says you're on the way out, bro. Cirrhosis of the liver, alcoholism, anorexia, jaundice, diarrhea, gastrointestinal hemorrhage. Any of that new to you?"

Larry poured a lot more of the hot black liquid down his internal pathways. "I admit I'm a little worried about my complexion," he said dryly.

"You had treatment?"

"Plenty."

"Wanna tell me about it?"

"Nope."

Straker consulted the square toe of his Spanish boot. "Any last-minute requests?"

"Sure. I'd like to live another fifty years. Arrange it for me."

"No problem. I know just the guy. John Lattimore. Great connections."

Larry felt obliged to grin. "Touché. How'd that scene play?"

"Don't even ask."

"Who is he?"

"Irishman with dandruff. Big guy, about sixty-five. Winks a lot, digs you in the ribs. Says love is the Way."

"Wonderful. Remind me to make a note in my will."

"Who's Luke Garfield?"

"Don't even ask." Larry raised his mug in salute and drank deeply.

He was beginning to feel stronger. Not physically, of course, he couldn't expect that—to be able to move at all later on would be a miracle, one foot in front of the other—but already he sensed a flowing back of confidence, of intellectual strength.

Yes, he could actually lie there half-dead and believe that. He was back on top of things, exposed but secure, in a curiously detached way even impregnable, the way he'd felt a million times as a kid when an opponent—usually someone three or four times his age—responded unexpectedly to a conventional opening gambit. Aha, he'd think, cute, and his overdrive would cut in, the certain knowledge that he couldn't lose. Intellectual impregnability. Little Larry Eisenstern, boy wizard of American chess, unbeatable. (God, was that the last time he'd felt secure? As long ago as that?)

Happiboy was studying him impassively. "You wanna see that stuff I taped off the news?"

"Why not?"

A TV had been set up in readiness on a wheeled cart at one side of the bed. "I missed the first few shots getting plugged in," Happiboy said apologetically, and switched on.

The sequence opened with violent movement, a combined pan and zoom that made Larry's stomach roll. Then the camera's eye steadied on a large brown stain splashed across a yellow wall. He took awhile to register it as blood on whitewash; the SECAM color was strident, or perhaps it was the tape.

". . . cowardly attack now all too familiar to the citizens of Paris," crackled the voice-over.

The action cut to firemen in oilskins, Larry's golden helmets in the sky, wading through rubble and decapitated tables and smashed chairs.

". . . widely known that the café is Jewish-owned and a haunt of Jewish workers in the area. However, a number of men injured in the explosion were non-Jews, including four Moroccans."

"What does that make it—*more* cowardly or *less*?" Larry inquired sweetly.

". . . regularity. Twenty or thirty men ate there at the same hour every night before going home at the end of the first night shift."

More zoom shots of brown bloodstains and a long pan across

132

what had been the end wall of the bistro. It appeared to have imploded across the bar, smashing it to matchwood, yet the zinc bar top, confounding the laws of physics, had blown straight up. There was a shot of it embedded in the ceiling, the funerary flags of orange cloth still nodding and sighing in the breeze. No part of it was as Larry remembered.

". . . unofficially estimates the device to have contained between fifteen and twenty kilos of high explosive. Nothing less could have achieved such total devastation, he said. The motive, therefore . . ."

The camera cut to the street outside, to a pandemonium of wailing police cars, ambulances, riot-squad minibuses, a half dozen fire trucks. TV floodlights glared popeyed out of the dark, exploding like star shells where they encountered rain spots on the camera lens. Hoses trailed like gorged worms across the pavement; the remains of a plate glass window glittered in the gutter; a ragged poster for Yves Rocher perfumes fluttered from a projecting roofbeam. And corraled behind barricades at either end of the street, the great French public hunched against the drizzle in coats and hats and nightwear. Someone waved at the camera: Look—it's me!

". . . Chief Inspector Baudin of the Bomb Squad." The reporter nudged a grizzled man in a white raincoat into position. A floodlight came on full in his face, and he shied away, arm up, momentarily blinded. "Chief Inspector, why such a big bomb? Fifteen to twenty kilos—"

The cop, Larry thought, could have walked straight out of Simenon. He was tall and bowed and very gaunt, the gray functionary of French legend. He eyed the reporter as if he'd just pissed in his pants. "The device was designed to kill," he said shortly. "Antipersonnel, not antiproperty. They had no interest in making political gestures, these people. The intention was mass slaughter. To kill human beings. Jews."

"It was specifically anti-Semitic, Chief Inspector? You're convinced?"

"Set off a bomb in a place like this any hour of the night or

133

day and you'll kill a Jew. The attackers knew that." The police-man's anger was cold, calculatingly professional, all the more passionate for being restrained. Tomorrow he'd get it in the neck from the politicians.

"Was there any warning? A phone call?"

"None."

"Can you say at this stage who might be responsible?"

Again the look of weary disgust. "No."

"But you have a description of three men you suspect—"

"Not suspect." The policeman cut in harshly. "Three men I wish to interview. Mme. Monte, the proprietor's widow, saw three men leave the bistro minutes before the explosion. They sat together at a corner table and left one at a time. They were strangers here. The last of the three left a bag under his chair, a leather valise—"

"Like a doctor's bag, that sort?"

"Yes."

"Big enough to hold twenty kilos of—"

"Which may have contained explosive. And equally well may not. I'd like those men to come forward and tell me what they know."

"Oh, sure," Happiboy whispered.

"But meanwhile, you're circulating their descriptions to—"

"I'm proceeding with my investigation in the usual way," the cop snapped, and turned away. End of interview.

The voice-over rattled on. ". . . photo kit likenesses of the three men from descriptions given by Mme. Monte. Anyone recognizing these men, particularly anyone who saw them entering or leaving the bistro last night . . ."

Three Cro-Magnon heads flashed up on the screen, all in a row, and at the sight of them Larry let go a nervous laugh— one note, very high. Fantastic! Two were clean-shaven. He guessed he was meant to be the one in the middle with the marceled hair, and Émile the scowl on the right. No doubt whatever, though, about the face on the left. Mme. Monte, bless her, had fixed the drifter in every fine particular: shoulder-length hair, cavalier beard, flat cap—all the way down to that permanent see-through smirk of his. He was actually shown smiling, a beautiful, wide, white, psychopathic leer.

"Which one are you?"

"One in the middle, I think."

"Ah. No sweat then."

"No. No sweat."

No sweat as long as you discount old Miko, Larry thought, easing back on the pillows. No sweat as long as you pin up in the forefront of your tiny but still extant mind that Miko Schellenberg—sweet, lovable, bumbling, book-loving old Miko—has just cut a swath through the human race as an excuse for obliterating one little life. Larry Bartell's one little life.

The screen filled with a shot of a Mercedes gliding through the gates of the Élysée Palace, then went blank. Happiboy switched off. "That's all," he said.

"That's plenty."

"More coffee?"

"Thanks."

Happiboy poured. Larry watched the long, narrow muscles of his forearm flex and tighten under the weight of the pot. Small, lean, hard, trusting Happiboy. Inside and out. Loyal. Uncomplaining. "The meeting's open to questions from the floor, man," Larry said as casually as he could.

"Uh-huh."

Happiboy replaced the pot without meeting Larry's eye. Standing up, he carefully rearranged jugs, spoons, bowls, plates, mug, and pot on the tray as if his life depended on the exactness of the geometry, then carried it through to the kitchen. Larry heard him unload it, heard him flush the coffeepot under a tap, flush the sink to clear the grounds, wash and dry his own mug, replace the crockery in a cupboard, the spoons in a drawer, clatter-clatter, all at a snail's pace. A long silence followed, perhaps five minutes, before Happiboy sauntered in again, as devoid of expression as when he left. He was rolling a joint, not—as was his custom—in his fingers, one-handed, the vet's easy dexterity, but in a roller, a sure sign of insecurity. He dropped onto the bed and wedged a boot under the mattress to take his weight. He lit the joint with too much ceremony and inhaled deeply, held it down for a half minute, sighed it out. "Here you go, bro." He passed the joint to Larry, and for several minutes they smoked in silence.

"Question," he said at length, so abruptly Larry's nerves jumped.

"Shoot."

"Those two dinks were hired to ice you up there last night, right?"

"You make it sound like—"

"They were or they weren't?"

"I guess so."

Happiboy laid the butt to rest in an ashtray but couldn't seem to take his eyes off it. "They pick you up at the Arc. They drive you across town. They *feed* you. Then they walk out."

In the silence Larry heard his heart triphammering in his head. "So?"

"So after they left, why didn't *you* leave?" Happiboy's gaze fixed on a point one-tenth of an inch below Larry's eyes.

"Because"—he fought down the urge to shout—"because I had the sense to realize they were waiting outside, that's why."

"Where they'd have iced you anyway. Bullet, knife, blackjack, hit and run."

"That's right."

Happiboy's gaze dropped. He glared at the ashtray again. "So why go to the trouble of setting you up in that bistro in the first place?"

Let me tell you the story of my life sometime, Larry thought hopelessly. How can I explain Miko when I can't explain myself? He said, "Because that was the order from upstairs, H. The preferred line of action, you dig? They had priorities. It's what they were told to do."

"You're that big?" This time Happiboy's eyes actually met

his. The curiosity in them was genuine and tinged with more than a little admiration.

"Big?"

"You know what I mean, come on. *Big*. A potential embarrassment. Dangerous. They killed seven guys and maimed twenty more to get to you, for Christ's sake. They packed enough goddamn bang-bang in that bag to put half Paris on the moon. And you were sitting on top of it. Jesus, man, what did you steal? They were all set to cream you to *nothing*."

"Don't draw pictures on my account," Larry said.

"Well, on my acount then." A shadow crossed Happiboy's face and took with it—it seemed to Larry—a good deal of the phony self-possession he'd miraculously acquired in the kitchen. Robbed of the mask, he looked ridiculously young; by any standards, including his own, hopelessly out of his depth. "Listen," he said urgently, "I need to get this straight in my mind. Those two dinks had a contract to waste you, but not the easy way. Not a bullet in the brain or a knife in the back; not a straight kill; not any way that left an identifiable corpse behind."

"They didn't confide in me," Larry said tartly. "You'd be surprised how little we had in common." His legs had gone to sleep all of a sudden. No feeling in them. He prodded his thigh. Wake up. Wake up!

Happiboy moved on. "Okay. But we get an essential twist in the logic around here, don't we? They could have blown you away anywhere, no problem. Drive out of Paris, say, find a quarry, some lonely spot, tie you down, stick that bomb up your ass—bang! All over. So why didn't they?"

Larry said nothing. The story of my life, he thought. My life and Miko's.

But Happiboy had his own answers, hot and ready to serve. "It was too simple. Too simple, therefore too complicated. Safety in numbers. Hit thirty to get one." He looked up. "Hey, now that's cool, Larry. That's really fucken cosmic. Bury one big un under thirty little uns. You dig?"

"It's your scenario."

"Bullshit! You know and I know." Happiboy gazed raptly at the palm of his hand and with his index finger traced the fine lines of life and death, marriage and happiness, up and down, left and right, as if the key to human fallibility lay there on some convenient crossroads of the soul. "They put that bang-bang so close in under your ass there'd be nothing left. No trace: who you were, what you were. And who's to point the finger afterward? It was a Jew joint; this is the logic, right? Just another regrettable anti-Semitic outrage, probably retribution for something that happened in Israel or Lebanon last week or a hundred years ago, or—who knows with the kinda fucken freaks we got around here nowadays? Oh, boy, oh, boy. Your friends are real cute, Larry. Right here in Paris there's a thousand certified goons'd give their souls to waste a bunch of Jews overnight, you know that? Sure, you know it. Because most of 'em are clients of yours, guys you do business with, guys I do business with—one big happy, screwed-up family. Extreme right, extreme left, radical center, liberal revanchist, militant Catholic, Pan Arab, Palestinian homeland, lunatic Libyan, breakaway PLO, Shi'ite Muslim—take your pick, we got 'em! Not forgetting the permutations. An IRA hit team doing a one-off blowaway for Quaddafi. Or the Red Brigades pulling one out of the hat for the Corsican nationalists. Or Yugoslav separatists playing an away game for the Basques. Or Baader-Meinhof reciprocating for *Action Directe*. Or vice versa. Sure, you know all the orchestrations, Larry. You wrote 'em."

Larry found himself looking into a pair of grossly enlarged pupils and a very white face. He couldn't remember ever seeing Happiboy so transparently moved. He said pacifyingly, "All right. That's how it works, H. Congratulations," and slipped a hand back under the bedclothes and ran his fingers along the ridge of his right thigh. Still nothing there. No sensation. From the bottom of his rib cage to the soles of his feet, nothing. Oh, God, he thought, not paralysis. Anything but paralysis.

Happiboy was now leaning down the bed at him, his small, neat gray head craning out on his skinny neck, shadows where his eyes should be, shadows thrown by the bedside lamp. The darkened eyeholes narrowed and grew deep black lesions at the corners, and Larry guessed he was at least four or five joints to the good already. "Larry?" He sounded perplexed. "Larry, tell me something. What reason'd they have for blowing you away?"

It was no great decision when you actually got right down to it. *Tell him*, the commanding half of Larry's mind said, and the motion was passed unanimously.

"I'm going home, H," he said. A lump bobbed into his throat; tears sprang, rolled, flooded, fell. "I'm going *home*."

"Home? To America?" Happiboy's astonishment was no less than Todd Hales's had been.

"Home."

"*You?*"

"Me."

"You're kidding!"

"On the level, H. I swear."

Below the sheets, no pain, no feeling, no functioning parts.

Happiboy seemed unable to cope with the revelation sitting down. He got to his feet, draped himself over the end of the bed. "You think they're gonna take you back just like that? Come on in, Larry, old pal, welcome home?"

"All fixed." Larry sniffed up an avalanche of mucus.

"When?"

"Next day or so." If I live that long. If I have the strength of mind and body to run, walk, crawl.

He pinched frantically at the wasted flesh of his thigh, but there was no response. A side effect of the sedative? Of the wine? He couldn't remember even *drinking* the goddamned wine. Couldn't remember getting up, looting cupboards, carting it back—four bottles! And least of all could he remember pouring it down his throat, over himself, over the bed, oceans of it. Not another drop—I swear on my father's grave. *Please,* grant me one more week of life. A month only. Is that so much to ask?

Happiboy gazed at him through a russet fog, a great truth dawning. "So that's why they wanted you gone. You're going back over. You're selling out."

"I'm going home."

"Without something to sell? Without collateral?" Happiboy pointed at him down the bed, a rusty forefinger. "Okay, so how do you plan on getting out? Don't tell me those friends of yours in Geneva are gonna wave you off on the next jumbo. You crazy or something?"

"I'll need help." Larry wiped his eyes on the sheet. "A little help."

"A *little*! I've got one pair of hands, man. One *neck*."

"There'll be someone else. Someone I trust."

"And who the fuck is he?" Happiboy rapped, straightening up. And Larry registered a curious fact from a long way off: that Happiboy was profoundly shocked and deeply hurt at the suggestion that there might be anyone else alive in whom Larry Bartell was prepared to invest his trust, that he resented the implication of alternative friendship, and why hadn't he been *told*, dammit!

"She," Larry said. "It's a girl—a woman."

"*She!*" Happiboy's resentment came liberally dosed with sarcasm. "You think after what happened last night some *chick's* gonna—"

"She'll need all the help she can get. All you can give her. H, listen to me. No, wait a minute, please—listen."

ELEVEN

She should have gone in hours before, but walls pose threats, and she wasn't up to dealing with threats just yet.

"Per'aps mam'selle wood prefair ze lounge," the terrace

waiter had tempted her awhile back, his old face blue with cold under the courtyard lights, but the lounge, though big and bright and warm, was also crowded—she could hear the babble of voices—and people posed threats, too. "No, thanks," she said, flashing him a smile to last him the rest of his life, "I'm fine actually, great, wonderful, fantastic."

He thought she was mad. There was a fair chance he was right.

In the interests of self-possession and comfort in the field, C.J. Poole had downed four large brandies in something less than two hours, the first to settle a revolutionary stomach—jet-lagged from the Concorde—the others to ward off the bitter cold. And lay the ghosts. She was having a lot of trouble with ghosts tonight. Rémy Martin was a great spirit medium, taken neat, she'd decided after much thought and conjecture, sitting out there in the Paris cold under a gulf stream of stars and a waxing moon. By contrast, the hotel was a living tomb. Only Garfield could have found it. Only Garfield would have wished it on her.

It lay in a hushed courtyard behind the Faubourg Saint-Honoré, and you came into it from the street through a door in a pair of huge old wooden gates: first a whitewashed tunnel filled to the brim with spring flowers; next a yard of ancient stones with a lily-clad fishpond, a wishing well, and a screen of whispering willows; then a terrace gay with white and gold parasols and the hotel rising all around like a castle in the air. Probably the last word in security.

When she first came out after dinner, she thought she'd flushed a watcher: a thin boy in a blue linen suit, American-looking, dark, trying hard not to look her way, and—incongruous —hiding behind a pair of sunglasses with deep wraparound frames. They were alone on the terrace, except for the waiter, and as it got progressively colder, the boy actually began to shiver. C.J. had felt—God!—such *power*. She'd ordered another cognac to celebrate and raise a fire inside and sat and stared at him for an hour, savoring his stiff-necked discomfort. Oh, it was so *good*.

Then an elderly American woman came in from the faubourg and led the boy away. "David, I'm sorry, the traffic was terrible. Why didn't you ask someone to take you in?"

The accents of the Midwest, the concern of a mother. The boy was blind.

On the strength of this small jolt to the morale C.J. Poole called for her fourth double, and on the broad shoulders of M. Rémy Martin, the ghosts swarmed out of the shadows to greet her, armies of them, her father in the lead, though, to be fair, her father was a pretty frail kind of ghost as ghosts go, having no face that she could remember or voice or peculiarity or trick of movement to set him apart from other ghosts. A lost soul. Her only surviving image of him, in fact, was of a gray cliff towering over her at bedtime, a kind of saddle-soapy smell to his clothes and deep splits in his knuckles that winked down at her like Chinese eyes. The splits were caused by the heat in the foundry where he worked—or so her mother had said—and the heat of the foundry had killed him when C.J. was three. Yes, a genuinely lost soul, her papa. After the funeral they'd moved to New York and a cold-water walk-up on Mulberry Street, to nightlong choruses of Italian heat, a succession of stepfathers who never quite stayed the course, and a greater succession of bums and drunks and unpaid tradesmen who for ten minutes' worth of her mother's pale passion behind the kitchen boiler were prepared to be nice to the kid and pet her and stroke her glossy hair and occasionally, when her mother's back was turned, slip their hands up her dress.

"Concentrate on realities," Garfield had said to her on the way to the airport in Washington that morning. "You know Larry—he doesn't rate truth a virtue. In his book it's a negotiable asset. So don't listen to what he says. Judge him on performance. Judge him on reality."

Reality! B-rother! Did he think he could tell *her* about reality?

Reality had been the principal mourner at her papa's funeral. Reality had stolen her innocence at the age of three and her maidenhead at fourteen. Reality, for your information and guidance, Mr. Undersecretary of State, is a father without a face, a lover without a body; it's Prisoners of Conscience instead of kids, principles instead of stretch marks. Reality is Larry Bartell carving out your future, doctoring your past, and leaving you flat.

"So what's it supposed to be—some kind of moral imperative?" Larry on the subject of reality. "It's a *word*, kid, a word we made up to fit a commodity we don't dig."

It was the year they'd had a little local difficulty about her running Prisoners of Conscience, Inc. About a *Polack Jew* running Prisoners of Conscience, Inc. He'd come down to D.C. to explain. "I don't believe you," she'd said, shocked when he told her. "I *can't*. You're joking. You must be." No joke, he'd said; the third world didn't go for it. At that stage POC had badly needed third world sponsors, and in Africa and the Mideast and Asia, Jew meant Israeli, it was as simple as that. Suspicion, Larry had explained; the world was up to here in strategic suspicions, political, religious, racial, economic, sexist; you name it, they're there. So why not accommodate them? Bend a little. "If you believe POC is a good thing, worthy of your time, be what they want you to be. The fairy godmother is a WASP. Okay, be one. What do you care?" Only a complete bastard could argue with the conviction of a saint.

So he had changed her name legally. Nothing to it, a painless experience. "No worse than a dye job," he'd said, flicking her hair. "No worse than a nose job," tweaking her nose. "You wanna nose job, kid?" In show business, he said, they did it all the time.

Oh, yes, Larry was all for change. Change for the sake of it. Change for the pleasure it gave him. Change for the chaos it trailed in its wake. "For one thing, it confuses the media," he would tell you at the drop of a metaphor, "which is the sacred and patriotic duty of all right-thinking Americans. And for another it refreshes the id. Never neglect the id, kid." At the height of his notoriety it was nothing for Larry Bartell to switch an entire political commitment overnight—or a creed, a philosophy, a loyalty, a personal friendship. "Sorry, kid," he'd say, slicing you off at the knees with a grin of radiant sympathy, "you know how it is," and down you'd go like a good soldier, another victim of heat in the foundry.

Who was he anyway?

A clown. A traitor. And a stranger, too, now, according to Garfield: older, grayer, sicker, dying. A shell. Emptier. But then he'd always been a shell. Something tropical. A dapper, bumptious tropical blaze of color. Dark brown hair tinged emotively with gray (boy, how he'd hated the thought of growing old, of leaving the young behind). Fine, expressive hands. The feet of a small boy. The eyes of a satanic spaniel. A grin that lit up half the world (his half, of course). All a shell. And currently the ghost of a shell, a decaying, old crock of twenty going on fifty-five, who at any moment—

Sorry, kid, you know how it is.

She stood up too quickly. Her chair went over backward, and the remains of her fifth cognac swilled across the white tablecloth. "Oh, God!" She gulped and in mindless panic fled—through the French windows to the dining room, into the lobby, the hounds of hell at her heels. The waiter caught up with her at the elevator and made her sign for the five double ghost chasers, but she had no idea what she scribbled on the stub, no idea at all. In the elevator, alone, she closed her eyes for a moment and grew dizzy. Blundering out of it, fumbling at the door in her almighty hurry to get in, she missed the vital fact that her key did not turn in the lock, that the door opened at her touch, that a veil of Turkish tobacco smoke stained the air. She slammed the door behind her and fell back on it in the dark, praying for the room to settle. But it was still spinning when a voice said from the bed, "Look, I realize this is a bit thick . . ."

When she opened her mouth to scream, nothing came out. For a Technicolor second or two her brain ran a high-speed *Son et Lumière*, then blew all its fuses at once. She blacked out.

. . .

She came to on the bed. Fully clothed, shoes and all. Numb.

"Drink this," he said.

"What is it?"

"Brandy."

"Oh, no!" She fell back on the pillow, her stomach in her throat and rising (*something* rising).

"You're sure?"

"I'm *sure!*"

"Well, waste not, want not. You mind if I, er—"

"Please yourself."

"Cheers then."

I'm dreaming this, she thought.

He had switched on a pinkish lamp across the room, a rather dim pinkish lamp, and its light informed only his margins; the middle parts remained in silhouette. Much later, when she saw him clearly for the first time in the light of day, his features came as no surprise to her, as if she'd designed them herself to a long-cherished private recipe. At the time she half saw, half visualized a long face, very smooth, good bones, tanned, short light brown hair. A strong face, faintly puzzled; a serious face, faintly amused; a capable face in need of mothering. Young-old. All these impressions stemming from the depth and timbre of his voice, she realized afterward, from his voice and his manner, his way of moving, of holding himself. English, of course. Top-drawer. What her mother would have called "old money."

"Terribly sorry about the thing," he drawled over his shoulder. He was rinsing the glass under a tap.

"Thing?"

"Scaring the life out of you like that. I drifted off, I'm afraid. On the bed. Been waiting for you up here since a quarter to eight. Thought you were there for the duration."

"Why?" she asked tonelessly. Her head was spinning.

"Why what?"

"Waiting. Why were you waiting?"

"You mean Garfield didn't mention it?"

Thank you, Mr. Undersecretary, she thought, and felt a surge in her throat and blurted wildly, "I have to go to the bathroom quick. Quick!"

It was a comfort to find someone who thought fast on his feet.

Afterward he massaged her shoulders, her neck, and her face. He didn't ask; he just did it. Beautifully. Small, economical movements, no creepy sexual undertones, pure rhythm. For ten minutes or more she floated between the reeling bed and seventh heaven, and when he finally let up, she was able to focus sufficiently to take more of him in. He was about a mile high and slim. Polished shoes, the type with laces and toecaps. A gold chain strung across his vest. A tie with stripes. Somehow she knew instinctively that he wore his collars starched and carried a cane; that he was on good terms with dogs, horseflesh, sporting guns, and fine wines and wore a Burberry when it rained. Officer and gentleman—the part of him that showed, anyhow. Curiously, in spite of the circumstances, she had no fear of him, a fact that would have worried Garfield on principle and amused Larry no end. The fact was, C.J. Poole had no defense against natural authority. It disarmed her. Up to a point.

"Why didn't Garfield tell me?" she snapped. "He's too damned secretive."

She could tell right away he didn't care for the word *damned* or for the strident tone of her voice. He became very cool, very distant. "Just looking out for your welfare, I'm sure. Nothing sinister. Good man, Luke, you want my opinion."

"I don't."

"No, of course." He palmed a gold cigarette case from an inner pocket like a conjurer warming up a difficult audience, snapped it open, proffered it. She shook her head and looked for an engraving, but there wasn't one. "Mind if I do?" he asked politely.

"As a matter of fact, I do. I'm opposed to smoking." Supercilious cow!

"Oh, well. Free country," he murmured vaguely, and put the

trick away before moving on to the next: the gold half hunter at the end of his watch chain. "Nearly midnight. D'you feel up to traveling? I don't want to rush you or anything, but—"

"Traveling?" She came up off the pillow. "Travel where?"

He was on his feet again, yards of him, his shadow running up one wall, across the ceiling and down the next like an outsize collapsible beach chair. "Not far. Car's back there in the Boétie." He waved a nonchalant thumb in the general direction of the South Pole. "Don't bring too much. A coat's a good idea; perhaps a change of clothes for the morning. Make-up, toothbrush, so forth. Nothing too bulky. You can buy what you need later. You have a hatbox or something?"

A *hatbox*?

"Where are we going? What about the hotel? My clothes?"

"All taken care of. No problem." He was still looking for a hatbox. Did his kind of woman *really* use hatboxes?

"I'm not going anywhere till I've talked to Garfield." She slipped off the bed to stage a protest, stood up, would have fallen if he hadn't caught her. She babbled defiantly, "I'm not moving a step out of here till—"

"Oh, I think we can leave Garfield till later, don't you?" He dumped her bodily in front of the wardrobe, and she found herself obediently opening the door and pulling out her Concorde bag. No will power. She folded in a light raincoat because it was the first thing that came to hand, and he inspected it over her shoulder. "You wouldn't care to swap that for something less— well, less *glaring*, would you?" he said. "Something darker? Blue, black, brown?"

She turned to give him an argument, but he was gone, across the room this time to strip off the bedspread, punch a deeper hole in the pillow, rumple the sheet. He stood back, chin in hand, to survey his work, then half filled a glass at the tap and set it down on the bedside table, spilling a few drops for verisimilitude. He set her alarm clock for six-thirty, then cut it off. "There we go," he murmured.

She changed the raincoat for a workmanlike three-quarter-length pea jacket in blue serge with too many buttons. Added a skirt, a sweater, a cream-colored blouse, underwear, a pair of flat-heeled shoes.

"Ready?" he sang out breezily. He was standing by the door, one hand poised on the light switch. He had on an oatmeal-colored British warm; a rolled umbrella was hooked rakishly on its pocket. "We'd best be running along."

"I haven't *started* yet," she protested. "What am I expected to—"

"Oh, I'm sure you've got tons," he said, and flicked off the light.

"I can't *see!*"

"Not to worry. Here." She felt something engage her arm above the elbow, encircle it, draw her across the room. The umbrella. The door opened ahead of her, and he urged her out, taking her Concorde bag as she passed him. "Here we go then." He locked the door. "Now we drop the keys off, I think . . . yes . . . here." He slipped them into the drawer of a table at the end of the corridor, then took her arm. "And we exit . . . that's it. . . ." He disappeared behind a drape of heavy maroon velvet in an alcove; a moment later his hand appeared and drew her in after him. A casement window opened onto a narrow balcony. "Nothing to it," he said comfortingly as C.J. looked down six stories to the courtyard. It lay in total darkness, at peace with its ghosts. She caught her breath and stepped back. "It's all in the mind, you know, vertigo," he said confidently. "Proven fact."

"So is suicide."

"Ha!" He chuckled, a nice rich nut brown sound. "Look, I'll go first, and you—"

She shook her head. "Not me. You're not getting me out there."

But he'd gone deaf. "Safe as houses. Hold your hand all the way, how's that?" He swung out, and as the balcony took his weight, it creaked. Her hand flew to her mouth.

"Now you," he whispered, out there.

"What's wrong with the front door?" she whispered back furiously.

"Nothing, except it's the *only* door. If they're watching, they'll be watching there."

"Who will?"

His gloved hand found hers and drew her toward him. "Left foot, right foot; keep your back to the courtyard; hold tight to the window frame. Got it? No jerky moves, all nice and easy. Relax. Ready?"

"I *can't.*"

"That's the style." He'd gone deaf again. "That's it, now, piece of cake"—and she was out there, clinging, eyes tight shut. "Good *girl*," he whispered about an inch from her ear, so close his breath torched her cheek. She felt an inane swell of pride, gratitude. Gratitude! I'm out of my mind, she thought. Done for. Her nose was pressed into a thick mat of ivy on the wall; she could hear spiders foraging in there, or ants, beetles, mice. . . .

"Here we go," he said cheerfully. "On my left there's a railing. You step over it—no trouble—and on the other side there's a stone ledge. Runs straight across the front of the hotel into a corner, say, ten or twelve yards. You can do it standing on your head—really. Child's play."

Child's play or not, he gave her no time to think about it. One hand in his, the other clutching at loops of creeper, she let him draw her sideways, back to the void, her mind blank. Then he vanished. His hand remained wrapped around hers like a poultice, but the rest of him had evaporated. "You there?" Her voice broke. "Dammit, I can't see you." You don't even know his name, she told herself practically and aloud, hoarsely: "Hey!" His hand squeezed hers firmly, and she pulled it into her throat so it wouldn't get away. "I don't even know your name."

"Thought I'd leave the introductions till later. But if you insist, name's Joss. Now, give me both your hands, there's a good girl. That's it. And relax. I'm going to pull you up. Nothing to worry about. Ready?"

She felt herself rise through space, felt a single tremor as his body swung out of the horizontal into a kneeling position above her, then another as he stood upright; then she was beside him, and he was dusting his coat and—for God's sake!—straightening his tie. They were on the lower sill of the roof, a high-pitched slope rising to a windy tasseled ridge; next stop the Milky Way. The wind sobbed and buffeted her clothes. C.J. made a despairing grab for him and hung on for dear life. With her face pressed into the dense weave of his coat, she had a sickening thought. It came out before she could stop it: "How do I know Garfield sent you? I mean, you could be anyone."

That rich nut brown chuckle of his swept off on the back of the breeze. "Bit late to worry about that, isn't it?" He patted her shoulder with his wraparound hand. She didn't answer.

"I think you'll find the footing's pretty firm from here on." He was pulling her forward again, along the sill toward a stepped gutter. "Up there, see, that chimney, from there across the roof ridge there's a steel fire escape—not bad actually. Quite solid. Just watch your step and do as I do."

"How'd you know the way?"

"How'd you think I came in?"

"Oh." He'd risked his neck to find a way in in the dark? Why?

"Do you know Larry?" she gasped, following him up to the ridge.

"Nearly there. Next part's the worst."

"Can I hold your hand again?"

"Rather." He made it two words, standard Ronald Colman.

She had no recollection afterward of distance or geography. Much of the time she seemed to be walking with her eyes closed. There were four roofs, linked by a series of rusting ladders bolted to the brickwork and falling in terraced steps from one to another, then a precipitous last lap she would remember for the rest of her life down a freestanding aluminum extension ladder. It shuddered when she stepped out onto it, bringing her as close to hysterics as she had been all night, but Joss appeared to have majored in female hysterics. He calmed her down and finally climbed with her, a couple of rungs below like a human safety net. That part she would never forget: the solidity of him and his croons of praise all the way down— "That's it, marvelous, terrific, first-class, fantastic!" Finally a bouquet of drains and decaying plaster rose to meet her, and they were in a tall, narrow alleyway between buildings. As she reached the bottom, strong hands caught her, though they turned out to be not his but the property of a mass in a peaked cap and no face who apologized for touching her—"Sorry, miss" —and, like some butler in a thirties comedy, announced, "If you'll excuse me, sir, I'll see to the ladder first." He disappeared briefly and manifested himself again when she was least expecting him.

"Any sightseers while I was away?" Joss demanded.

"No, sir, not a soul. Must be a good night on the telly."

"Heaven help them."

"Yes, sir. Would you step this way please, miss?"

"His name's Prebble," Joss explained, taking her arm.

"That's the idea," said Prebble.

The car was a monster from another age, taller than C.J. by a couple of inches and as long as a bus, dart-shaped at the back and all-over silver. Hemmed in behind tall railings in front of an apartment house by more modest Toyotas, Renaults, and Minis, it exuded the air of a grand duchess serving stout in a working-men's club. Prebble handed C.J. into the scented rear. "A Bentley, miss," Prebble whispered, watching her face. "Finest model ever built. All-round independent suspension, power steering, overhead—"

"I don't imagine the lady's in the market," Joss cut in, sliding in beside her. "Shove along, shall we? There's a good chap."

"Yes, sir," said the mass amiably. "Right away, sir."

He lived in a high-ceilinged apartment over the place Vendôme, though she was not to know the details until the next day. From three large windows giving onto the square he commanded a privileged view of a floodlit Napoleon in Roman drag on top of his column and at street level a rash of winking names that spell Paris to every woman who has never been there: Cartier, Caron, Schiaparelli, Boucheron, Van Cleef and Arpels. He made no attempt to switch on the lights when he let them in. "Show you your room," he said, and led her down an airy hall suffused with the afterglow of Napoleon's floodlighting. He pushed open a door and handed her the Concorde flight bag. "This all right for you?" The bed was a four-poster draped in something white and diaphanous. Not a man's room. Not a child's either. "Anything you need in the morning," he said, backing off, "just ring the bell. Mme. Félix will look after you. My housekeeper. Got that?"

Got that? Officer and gentleman.

She started to turn on the light, and he swung on his heel and walked away.

She stage whispered after him, "We haven't *talked* yet. About tomorrow. The rendezvous. How do I—"

"Oh, that." He stopped in shadow a good ten yards away, quite still. "Yes, I forgot to mention that. The rendezvous is off."

"Off?" She took a step into the hall, and he backed off a step to compensate. "But Garfield *agreed*," she protested. "Even dates, nine in the morning to—"

"Yes, so he said. He changed his mind. Says we'll hold off for a day, see what happens."

"But that's *ridiculous!*" She was more afraid than angry now; out of control.

"Garfield says you need the rest," he cut in flatly, no amusement in him this time. "Give you a full day off. Sleep. Catch up on the magazines. Anything you like so long as you don't go out. Mme. Félix—ring her for breakfast anytime you like. Bell's beside the bed."

He turned in under an open arch, leaving her flat, and in a flash of foreboding she called out, "Where will you be?"

He stopped again, no face to him. "Oh, I've got a couple of errands to run. Back before dinner tomorrow."

Panic rose in her, a nausea, the old dizziness. "You won't be here?"

"Here and there." His hand rose and fell.

"But—"

"Sleep well," he said sharply, and merged with the deeper shadow beyond the arch.

TWELVE

A silver Bentley of the 1956 marque, Paris license plates, two occupants, approached the French border post at Annemasse at 5:23 the next morning.

The young guard on duty, alert to the smuggling potential of exotic cars at such an hour, rousted his sergeant and the sleeping customs officer, and for twenty diverting minutes they searched the monster from stem to dagger stern. Nothing was found: no illicit banknotes; no hoarded gold or jewelry; not even drugs. The travelers proved to be Englishmen, expatriates: the owner a certain James Oliver Seaton Sullivan, a company director living at place Vendôme, Paris 1er; the chauffeur, Herbert George Prebble, of the same address. Both men were scrupulously polite and answered questions willingly. It was only at the very end that the sergeant took note of the tiny scrap of maroon silk in the angle of M. Sullivan's jacket lapel, and of course, he stopped the search at once. Apologized for the inconvenience. Cursed his luck, the condition of humankind, his young subordinate, the damned socialists.

And saluted the chevalier off the premises.

There were no delays on the Swiss side. A bearded trooper waved them through as if they were royalty—and perhaps by his standards they were; the *petit Suisse* have a primal respect for visible wealth and accord it the dignity it merits.

The car swept down the hill into Geneva and silently out the other side, then hugged the lakeside road through Nyon and Rolle and Morges and Vevey rather than take the faster highway running parallel with it a mile or so inland. A watery sun rose late from behind the mountains, fought a few brave skirmishes with the lake mist, and surrendered. Rain fell, light clean Swiss rain, house-trained. The Bentley purred on at a steady fifty and reached Montreux as the town was getting down to business. Herbert George Prebble parked in the lee of a small hotel and led his master inside. They emerged a little after nine o'clock, bathed and shaved and breakfasted, Sullivan now impeccable in a suit of dazzling silver gray. The Bentley turned east and ascended through little streets jammed with neat dull apartment buildings until it reached a white wedding cake of concrete facing out over the lake. Tiers of miniature balconies jutted out from its slab front like ice cube trays in a giant refrigerator. A few elderly couples sat on the balconies taking the air.

Sullivan paid great attention to the names listed in the lobby: a regular little United Nations. Mrs. Shakina Mahnaz lived on the sixth floor. The stenciled card framed under her bell said her name was Mena Sabbah, no clue to marital status; no mention, of course, of her good friend Larry Bartell. Sullivan took the service stairs and stood for a few minutes outside her door to make sure that she was not only up and about but alone. When he pressed the bell, a shocked silence greeted him from within, a tangible quality of electric terror, tactile. He rang again and won a squeak of distress, then a tentative "Who this is?" followed by a reprise in French and a clicking sound as the peephole cover was lifted inside. He stepped back a pace to give her an unobstructed view and held his passport open as a sign of good will. Putting his mouth to the door, he announced quietly that Larry had sent him. She gabbled something he couldn't understand—Iranian he guessed, and, from the tone, scornful. He assured her he was not a lackey of the ayatollah, or a policeman, or a snooper. He was Larry's friend, he said, and to prove it, recited word for word the contents of the unsigned letter Mena had received by hand two days before, the very same letter Larry had asked her to read to him over the phone. Sullivan told her from where Larry had called her that evening and roughly when. And in the uncertain silence that followed this revelation he whispered the first of many loving messages he had been commissioned by Larry to bring to her—*oral* messages, naturally, in the interests of security, though of a deeply private and emotional nature.

After the second message she couldn't get the door open fast enough.

Joss Sullivan called his American input number two hours later from a booth on the outskirts of Vevey. A taped voice told him he was being recorded and to be brief. He told the machine to call him back when he got home, gave his local time and his ETA, and hung up just short of fifteen seconds later. Then he called the apartment in the place Vendôme and told Mme. Félix he would be returning by plane. M. Félix should be at Orly to meet the Geneva flight arriving at 4:20 that afternoon. Prebble would follow at his own pace in the Bentley. Was all well at her end?

The girl was still fast asleep, Mme. Félix reported. Imagine. A good sign, no?

Yes, Sullivan agreed. Sleep was always a good sign.

BOOK TWO

Trust is good. Control is better.

LENIN

THIRTEEN

"Where are we going?" Polly Garfield asked her husband.

"Mmm? Oh, fine," he replied absently. He was sitting as far from her as possible in the back seat of the car, shoulders hunched, hands on his knees, like a small boy at an interview. There were coffee stains on his tie, and his shoes were badly scuffed. He needed a haircut.

"I said, where are we going?" she repeated, and saw Nick Montero's head lift speculatively behind his bulletproof screen. If Nick could breathe for him, he would, she thought irritably.

"Oh. Not far."

She knew perfectly well where they were going, of course, and the knowledge turned her cold inside, but that wasn't the point. *He* was the point. Twenty-four hours ago he'd called her in what for him had been a state of advanced agitation. Could she drop everything and fly down to Washington? "Come join the Case Control Board." Ha ha! Which could have meant anything: that he was ill, that he was lonely, tired, depressed, hungry, generally out of sorts, at a loss for someone to talk at, down to his last clean shirt. Anything. A little scared, and perhaps a little angry as a result, she'd put a lot of friends to a great deal of trouble and flown into National in the late afternoon—to find that whatever his emotional needs, they weren't sufficiently advanced to get him out to the airport to meet her. He'd sent Nick in the armored coffin instead. No messages.

She'd spent the night alone in a room at the Saint Clair, a small overstuffed hotel near Foggy Bottom that served as a kind of residential club for State Department mandarins. She waited up, but Luke didn't call, left no messages, sent no flowers. She fell asleep finally over the journals of André Gide at two-thirty in the morning, and at five-thirty, when one of the Saint Clair's aged matrons wheeled in a breakfast she hadn't ordered, she was still alone. But there was a card on her tray. A card and a single carnation. (Why a carnation? She hated carnations, he knew that.) The card read: "Nick will pick you up 7:00 A.M. Stay in your room till then. Nice to have you aboard, mate. L." Nautical chic.

She and Nick left the hotel through an underground parking lot, drove in a closed van to Nick's son's apartment in Georgetown, and there switched to a vast old funereal Buick with curtained windows—curtains *drawn*. They picked Luke up outside the Kennedy Center. He hopped off a tour bus and dived into the car like a rabbit down a hole. No explanations. "You got here all right then," he said, as if she'd just stepped off the plane, and pecked her nose, and that was that.

From Washington the road to Pennsylvania snakes through the lush Maryland countryside, and if you're so inclined, a ninety-degree turn of the wheel will take you through somnolent villages of nineteenth-century houses that seem to belong anywhere but in the America of moon shots, mass murder, and silicon miracles. A half hour later they were looking out over the field of Gettysburg, and Polly's heart was in suspension. They hadn't driven out this way since Craig was killed, May 1951, because for them it was that kind of place, an emotional watershed.

The first time Luke ever set his cap for her he'd brought her here; he was eighteen at the time and slated for West Point, a hero *manqué*. He'd driven her out after a dance, still in their finery, and fought Gettysburg for her all over again, from memory: the order of battle, state of readiness, attacks and counterattacks proposed and executed, Meade's ninety-seven thousand here, Lee's seventy-five thousand there, and Lincoln's words in memoriam. Oh, he'd impressed her all right, though not in any of the ways he'd planned. She hadn't fallen for the soldier boy bravado (or for the ignorance it exposed of real life and day-to-day values). No, she'd fallen for his gaucherie, for the embarrassed smile that lit up his blue eyes, for his total lack of conceit, for his stillness. She'd fallen for him because no man she'd met up to that point had been so obviously in need of her. A month later that need became acute when he failed the physical for West Point—an old back injury, long since forgotten—and went up to Yale instead to study ethics and Romance languages; after which, they'd taken him, too frail to be a soldier boy, into the diplomatic corps and made him a spy.

Polly had missed the logic of that.

Nick turned up toward Seminary Ridge and parked. Without a word he got out and strolled off, stiff-legged, into the grass. Polly watched him measure the distance between himself and the Buick until he was safely out of earshot, then drop into the grass and stare out along the valley to the monolithic statue of Lee.

" ' "Shoot, if you must, this old gray head, But spare your country's flag," she said,' " Polly intoned, trying to raise a smile, but Whittier's lines couldn't reach Luke Garfield today. He sat poker-faced and intent, the boy who well over half a century ago had proposed to her on this very ridge, the man who had told her in this place a young lifetime later of their son's death in another battle half a world away. For God's sake, tell me the worst, she prayed.

"Do they still teach kids that poem in school?" he rasped suddenly. He hadn't moved, wouldn't look at her.

"Whittier? I don't know. I doubt it. Bob Dylan's more in their line nowadays, isn't he?"

"Who?"

She smiled. "Never mind."

He took in a lot of breath. "I sent C.J. to Paris yesterday."

"And?" Her heart zoomed into her mouth.

"And what?"

"And is she all *right*, you fool? Is she hurt? Is she—"

"She's fine. Why?"

"*Why?*" Yesterday's anger rose in her like an expanding bubble. "You bring me out here, *here*, to this place, not a word the whole way. You lead me to expect the worst. You—"

"Sorry."

"Sorry, he says!" He had a knack for making her feel uncommonly foolish when she lost her temper. "And why C.J.?"

"Larry Bartell."

"Oh."

The "oh" must have had the wrong intonation because he pushed open the door and squeezed out, marched away. He came to a slight rise and stood there, a hand shielding his eyes against the sun. Sulking, she guessed. She followed, determined not to yield, a tall, willowy woman, once honeyed of hair and skin, a tennis player of no mean reputation in her day; a beauty, they said. Reduced by marriage to power play in small doses. But she knew better than to try to pacify him: silence was really the only language he understood.

"She wanted to go," he said at length. "She left me no choice."

"Well, she's a big girl. Knows her mind. What exactly have you asked her to do?"

He stuffed his hands deep in his coat pockets. "Bring Bartell home."

"You mean he doesn't know the way?"

"You know what I mean," he snapped, and though she didn't, she refrained from saying so. She glanced at him quickly, sideways. Part of his mind—the historian's eye—was on the battle below, replaying it. Pickett's charge, she guessed; he had a patriot's fascination for Pickett's charge. Ten thousand men killed or wounded in fifty minutes in a suicidal attempt to cross a mile of sweet grassland between this ridge and that. A casualty rate unequaled even on the first day of the Somme, he'd told her once in that tone of reverence young men reserve for gratuitous carnage. She waited for him to simmer down.

"I thought you might like to help me out," he said, still avoiding her eye.

"In what way?"

"Manning a phone. Acting as cutout between me and—well, C.J., other people."

"Lovely. What's a cutout?"

"They talk to you instead of me; then you tell me. It'll take up a few days of your time, maybe a week. If you think you can't—"

"I can," she said quickly.

"Fine," he said. His code word for "I'm very grateful." His attention strayed back to the battlefield.

"Is that all?" She sneaked a hand under his arm.

He nudged it away. "Isn't that enough?"

"I mean, is that all the explanation I'm entitled to?"

"For what?"

"For being dragged down here under false pretenses."

"Rubbish!"

"Rubbish yourself," she retorted equably. "I'm here because you want to keep an eye on me. You're worried about something —about me, too; I can see it in your face. Better to have me here under your feet than up there on the hill at home, that's what you're thinking, isn't it? Why?"

He let out a hollow groan, mock despair, and settled his chins on his chest. What had once been a phalanx of muscle from cheekbone to jaw was now a fleshy landslide of collapsed flesh that quivered under stress. In the end, Polly thought, watching it quiver, he'll revert to chubby babyhood: pink, white, and gurgling. And how far off was that at his age?

He said abruptly, "They shouldn't have called me back. I'm yesterday's man, discontinued stock, defunct. You were great, Luke, the greatest. Please don't come back. Now they want me back."

"You resigned," she said calmly, anger overlaying it. "The day the president took office you wrote telling him it was time, you'd had enough. You sent the letter by hand. He took you up on it, that's all, reluctantly, a year later."

163

"But why call me back? Why me?"

"I'm going to lose patience with you in a minute, Luke, see if I don't. Because Larry Bartell asked for you. By name."

"So they say," he growled.

"And what's that supposed to mean? That they're lying? You really believe Fred Goldman would lie to you?"

"If he could turn it to advantage, yes."

"Luke!"

"And so would I in his place. In certain situations—"

She hated this side of him, the conditioned insider, the moral juggler; it sickened her. "Don't say any more! I don't want to hear! One minute you tell me you've sent C.J. off into a void; the next, that lying and deviousness are perfectly acceptable. Well, I have news for you, Luke Garfield . . ."

He hmmmphed a couple of times and stared off into the long distance. "You know me better than that, woman. C.J.'s all right, don't worry about her. But—"

"No buts!"

Her voice must have carried a good deal farther than she had intended because along the ridge at that moment, Nick climbed painfully to his feet and shambled off another hundred feet or so. Nick the diplomat. Hear no evil.

She said very quietly, "Will you please tell me what's behind all this? If"—she couldn't resist it—"if it's the male menopause, I'd like to know now."

That reached him. He shook with silent laughter. "Could be. Now that could well be the answer."

"Tell me."

"Do I look stupid?" He glanced down at her, half-serious. "Do I strike you as senile? Mentally adrift?"

"You look tired."

"Worse still. Well, someone evidently agrees with you. Someone thinks I'm so tired I'll buy the Brooklyn Bridge ten times a day from any bum who happens along."

"I take it we're talking about Fred again."

"If the cap fits, eat it. Old Fred's the fellow with the stories, isn't he? The indispensable messenger boy? Employs bright young men who did their training at Langley. Who were at college with Larry Bartell. Who just happen to be hanging around in Frankfurt when Bartell decides he wants to come home."

"I don't see how you can blame Fred for that."

Or anything else, she thought, loyal to the last. Polly liked Fred a lot—currently against her better judgment, perhaps, and a lot less than when he'd been safely tethered to Marge and the children and a life of commendable stability—but unwaveringly. Admittedly she'd found his new bachelor image a little hard to take when he came up to the house in search of Luke the other night, but men like Fred didn't change inside. She wouldn't abandon him.

"I'm not blaming anyone . . . yet," her spouse snapped irritably. "I'm just taking stock. What they seem to expect me to believe, Fred included, is that this is all coincidence. Bartell's ex-wife just happens to find work in a corporation her father holds stock in. Less than a week after the *Washington Post* runs a story on her second marriage. It just happens that she's been missing since Christmas; husband number two hasn't seen hide nor hair of her. But—and this is really beautiful—the kids *have* seen her. Every weekend they see her, rain or shine. A nice man comes along in his car and drives them home to their mom. A nice ex-Langley field operator, would you believe, currently Lydia's private errand boy. However—"

"Luke, I don't—"

"—that's not the best of it. The best of it is the kids won't tell poor sap number two where Mama's hiding out. Can you imagine? Near-normal teen-age kids living with the same man week in, week out, subject to all kinds of subtle pressure, obligated to him for every little household service, yet somehow these bravos have the strength of character—the *motive*—to keep their mouths shut."

"You mean you don't believe him either."

"I mean, to put it mildly, he's lying through his teeth. Lying to order, which is a different thing entirely. Lying to conceal. Lying to persuade me to *believe* he's concealing."

A cloud momentarily crossed the sun, and in the brief eclipse Polly shuddered. "That's speculation."

"Not at all."

"What is it then?"

"Fact." He beamed without a trace of humor. "Young Sayer made a big production of this *Post* story. How the reporter and the photographer hounded them for a week or more; how the two of them were ambushed one Saturday; how Lydia left three, four days later. He painted this picture in my mind, very strong colors. So, in my place, what would have been your first response?"

"Oh, check it out, I suppose. Go along to the *Post*, ask to see the files, and—"

"And read the story. What else?"

"Talk to the reporter?"

"No need. How about look at the picture they printed with the story? Hmm? How about that?"

"All right. Look at the picture. So what?"

He jammed his pipe in his teeth for the pleasure of leering at her around it. "Picture shows Lydia and John Sayer with their mouths open. In flagrante delicto, so to speak. In a supermarket. A wall of Uncle Ben's rice boxes in the background, very tasteful."

"Is that all?"

"That's more than all."

"I don't get the point."

"The point"—he handed her his pipe-clad leer again—"is that the John Sayer I met yesterday and the John Sayer in the picture are two conspicuously different young men."

On the way back to town she remembered she had a revelation of her own. "I think they're tapping the phone at the house."

"Naturally." He was quite unmoved. "They'll be tapping Art's line anytime now. They'll tap yours, too, when I get you installed. Nick's fixing up a room for you over the garage: phones, recording equipment, a bed, somewhere to cook."

"But what's the point if you know they'll tap the line? Why can't I come stay with you at Art's?"

"Because the game has to be played out. Because I'm expected to respond in kind."

"I don't understand."

"You're not required to. Ask your friend Fred someday."

"But if they know where C.J. is and they listen in to what she's—"

"Exactly." He took her hand and wrapped it in his. "Can you think of a better way to keep them informed?"

FOURTEEN

"The Texas Arrangers?" Senator Donald Sherwood swung his stocking feet up onto the littered desk, dislodging half a dozen draft bills in the process and an avalanche of unrelated paper. It clattered to the floor and spread like foam. He ignored it. "Listen, I'm warning you, Luke, get me started on that bunch, and we'll be talking all night."

"Suits me," Garfield said equably, emptying a chair of stacked box files.

The private office of the Senate minority leader had a lot in common with C.J. Poole's: too much action chasing too little space. Half of one wall was covered with a corkboard on which official paper grew like fungus, much of it bleached with age. Mountains of discarded forms occupied the floor in every corner. Tapestries of old order papers and torn-out newspaper clippings festooned the wall behind the desk. From a place of honor over the mantel, Franklin Delano Roosevelt gazed down in gentle remonstrance, his face half-obscured by a Mondale campaign banner. Garfield glanced around critically. "You live like this all the time?"

"Is there some other way?" Sherwood growled.

He was physically a small man but one on whom nature had smiled expansively. He wore a giant's personality and a giant's nose, very little hair, a cigar of Churchillian hugeness, and bright red suspenders over a white shirt with wide black stripes. In another life Don Sherwood had run guns across the Mediterranean to Tito's guerillas in Yugoslavia, playing nip and tuck with German patrol boats along the way and working hard on his first ulcer. Later he'd joined forces with Garfield in Germany to interrogate Nazi war criminals in preparation for the Nuremberg trials. Over the years both men had traded shamelessly on their wartime relationship for mutual favors and acts of professional advantage. Neither had found cause to regret it, though as Garfield knew to his cost, with professional friendships there was always a first time.

"What do you want to know?" Sherwood asked.

"What *is* there to know?"

The cigar performed a fat arabesque from one side of his wide mouth to the other. "Well, now, suppose I ask *why* you want to know? You're out of it, aren't you? Checked in your dagger, hung up your cloak. Official. We drank to it, remember?"

"So we did."

Sherwood examined him fixedly, then cracked a slow grin. "Usual terms?"

"Terms?"

"If what you're working on throws up material I can use—political capital, working collateral, you know what I'm talking about—I get first refusal. Deal?"

"With the usual riders."

"National security interests are sacred; I play straight with you; your name never comes up. Okay, let's go."

"All right. How do you rate them? The Arrangers?"

Sherwood lit the dead stump of his cigar. "As players, out of sight. Brilliant. Professionally I can't fault them."

"And morally?"

"What's morals? I thought we were talking politics."

"Sorry. Slip of the tongue."

"Okay. Professionals. They run the White House. They run the president. They carry the cabinet. What else do they need?"

"How about credibility?"

"Don't make me laugh, please! Credibility? You sit in a poker game with four aces in your hand, that's credibility. They make their own credibility. Particularly up here on the Hill. They're the best damn consensus engineers I ever saw, and believe me, I've seen plenty. Come a key issue, and they have fixers swarming all over this joint. Armies of 'em. Once upon a time I coulda told you to the tenth decimal place how close I could shave the majority on a big one. Nowadays I stand listening to the roll call and *guess*. That's the Texas Arrangers for you; that's Stafford and Lang."

"They're buying votes, you mean?"

"Aw, come on, Luke, where've you been? This is Accommodation Hill, remember? It's *all* buy, buy and sell, tit for tat, a vote for a promise, a short-term investment for a long-term gain. Maybe you heard, we call it democracy."

Garfield was watching Sherwood's stocking feet, a far better guide to his emotional state than the expression on his face. They were scissoring very fast—in, out; in, out. Garfield said casually, "Have you ever caught them at anything unsavory? I mean, by conventional standards."

"Oh, *sure*."

"It's that run-of-the-mill?"

"By House standards, yes. By the standards of the people out there"—he nodded at the window—"I wouldn't know anymore."

"Care to quote an example?"

"Oh, domestic blackmail—that kind of stuff. Basic. A guy on a toot, member in good standing, respectable, gets a little horny one night, a little drunk, starts pawing a piece of flesh, gets hooked, gets in deep; usual story. Suddenly pretty pictures turn up, no accusations, nothing traceable, then a compromising letter possibly; then maybe he gets a call from Lang. They meet; a nice lunch, say. They trade possibilities. Then, hell, Luke, don't look at me like you never heard it before. Langley pulls that kinda stuff fifty times a day."

"And you consider it normal practice? Par for the course?"

"Don't put words in my mouth." Sherwood bit down hard on his cigar. "Let's say it's not unheard of. Let's say that under this administration it's not unheard of more than somewhat."

Garfield nodded. "All right. What's the general opinion of their intentions up here?"

"They're well poisoners."

"But their money's good."

"And their muscle. Listen, I don't know where you're going with this, Luke, but let me tell you something. Nobody up here's under any illusions about these guys. They are what they seem. They built their man. They bought him a set of political credits. They spent several undeclared fortunes putting him in office. Any one of the three of 'em could have had a prime cabinet seat—State, Defense, Treasury, whatever—but they didn't want that. They wanted de facto control. The reins, Luke. And short of changing the system or assassinating their boy, we're stuck with them. Tough shit. We've had worse. Davis Lang runs a tight White House, as you know. Nobody tells Ralph Kramer how to run Langley. And let's face it, Brock Stafford's probably the best national security adviser we've had in years. Yeah, I'm admitting it! He's tough; he hews a firm line; he takes no kind of shit from Moscow. He's done something else: He's kindled a new spirit up here on the Hill. He has balls, and he plays the Moscow game to perfection. If we don't like something *Pravda* prints, we call it a lie. No circumlocution, no heady intellectual finessing. We scream *lie!* We crack nuts with steam hammers."

"Sounds like you approve."

"My constituents approve. Where the hell do you think that leaves me?"

"Touché."

In an outer office telephones rang like muted campaniles. A girl laughed, a bright, sharp sound. Briefly a radio came on, a wail of anguished country-and-western, then instantly clicked off. Sherwood, they said, ran a loose ship but kept his crew. He tipped back his chair at an even more dangerous angle, smoke billowing around him.

"I was at his confirmation hearing, you know. Stafford's. Fantastic performance. Never raised his voice, never lost his temper —and that committee, I'm telling you, was after his ass. It had the right. Figured he had to be lying. Obvious. Day he was tapped for office *Fortune* put his industrial holdings at about one and a half billion bucks. Day of the hearing he was a pauper. Down to his last five homes and his last two yachts. Gave it all away, he told us. Gave away North American-Stafford, the conglomerate. Gave away Stafford Oil, the family heritage. Gave away global interests in steel, chemicals, electronics, mining, transportation, government-related defense industries. Gave away everything, for the privilege of a four-year crack at posterity." Sherwood spit a fragment of tobacco over the desk onto the carpet. "Posterity, my ass. 'Look,' the king says, 'I'm wearing no clothes,' and the suckers believed him. It had to be true because they were seeing it live on TV." He sent three perfect smoke rings spiraling up to the ceiling. "You know, Luke, someday I'm gonna write me a discussion paper for campaign managers. Subject: What do you have to give the American people, aside from a constitution, an education, a free press, a system of checks and balances, and the right to choose, to keep 'em from handing their birthright to the first huckster who comes along offering snake oil at fifty cents a quart?"

"Maybe a new system," Garfield murmured, playing into his hands.

"Horseshit! Systems create Staffords. No, the secret is to change the people, and we both know people can't be changed. QED. It's the one inalienable right they have left. Matter of fact, it's the only guarantee we have we'll ever beat communism. Moscow says people are changeable, perfectible, and we know they're not. We can't say so, this being a liberal democracy, but we *know* it. We know you can remodel the public appetite, or raise its awareness, or improve its literacy, and by God, you can sure as hell raise its expectations. But change human nature? Not in this life. Not for Jesus Christ or Muhammad or Buddha or Jimmy Carter. Two thousand years from now John Doe will still be selling out for snake oil at fifty cents a quart. Guaranteed." He contemplated the bulge of his stomach. A chuckle rose in his chest and shook his stumpy frame. "Here endeth the lesson," he wheezed.

"Maybe you'd think differently if you won a round or two now and then," Garfield said gently. He was still watching the scissoring feet. If anything, the tempo had risen in the last half minute or so. Don Sherwood was waiting for the pitch and with far more trepidation than the occasion deserved, in Garfield's view.

He lay back, eyes closed. "Ah, now, winning. That's always the problem for us minorities, Luke, winning a round or two now and then. Gets kinda monotonous being outvoted all the time. Here we are, ready to reshape the world if only dot dot dot."

"Like to make a start? A small start?"

The scissoring feet froze in mid-swipe. "What'll it cost?"

"A little information. A phone call."

"Who with?"

"Your friend Waldren in New York."

For an instant Sherwood's face registered bewilderment or a passable imitation of it. Then the name clicked. "Waldren! *Clayton* Waldren? You think Clayton Waldren's gonna win me a round against Brock Stafford?" He threw back his head and laughed harshly. "Luke, ol' buddy, take some friendly advice, will you? Forget it."

"Why?"

Sherwood swung his feet off the desk into a pair of judiciously placed loafers and bounded upright. "You seriously think I'd be sitting here pressing my ass if I thought Waldren had something to sell? You're crazy. Give me a million-to-one chance to fry Stafford in his own fat, and I'll grab it—none faster—but on the basis of evidence, sonny, not guesswork; fact, not fancy."

"Waldren tried to sell you fancy?"

"He kinda suggested we could bring down the administration together. Break Stafford; impeach the president; have Davis Lang shot at dawn."

"On what grounds?"

"On the grounds"—Sherwood settled his rear on the corner of the desk and leaned closer—"the impeccable grounds that the White House is setting up to blacken the good name of Larry Bartell."

"Oh."

"Oh is the word."

"*That* Larry Bartell?"

Sherwood's grin parted around his cigar. "The same."

"How'd Waldren approach you?"

"Phone call. About a month ago. Said he was a film editor, free-lances for the networks in New York. All true, incidentally. He'd been put to work on a big new documentary, very hush-hush, top secret State Department film. Why didn't I drop everything and rush right over, just the two of us, no microphones, no notes?"

Garfield was too tense to look at him; feigning amusement, he glanced up at the wall clock and automatically hauled out his pocket watch to check it.

"So you rushed right over."

"I told him 'yeah' and 'great' and 'maybe some other time.' "

"Never say no outright. Golden rule."

"Sure."

Garfield met his gaze. "But then you had second thoughts and checked him out. Sent someone to check him out."

Sherwood grinned sheepishly. "Maybe."

"And?"

"I sent my exec, Tom Babson." He shrugged. "Okay, Luke. There's a story, I admit it, but not the one Waldren's peddling. There's political mileage there; I can smell it, and I can build on it—for what it's worth. But the Bartell thing is strictly fringe, Luke, believe me. Jesus—Larry Bartell! You think anyone *cares*

173

about Larry Bartell? You know anyone who'd go out killing dragons for him?"

"But you won't tell me what you can smell."

Sherwood made a face. "He'll tell you. Let Waldren tell you. You'll see what I mean."

"You'll call him for me then?"

"Why not?" Sherwood swung away, taking his innocence with him, but Garfield mentally noted the balled fists, the stiffened angle of the head, the squared shoulders. Body talk. Don Sherwood was too old for play school and way out of practice.

"Do I swear an oath in blood?" Garfield asked impassively.

"Swear?"

"Not to compromise your . . . political mileage." He hesitated. "Whatever that might be."

"So I trust you." A spread of hands, a big smile.

"But I haven't told you yet why I want to meet him. Maybe I ought to."

"*Trust.*" Senator Donald Sherwood plucked the dead cigar from his mouth and jammed it behind his ear. "Goddamnit, Luke, if we can't trust each other, who can we trust?"

"Who indeed?" Lucas Garfield replied cordially.

He called Polly. "You getting settled back there?"

"Luke, this place is filthy! It's—"

He cut her off. "There wasn't time for housecleaning. Sorry. Does the equipment work?"

"Your little man says yes, fine. Who is he, by the way?"

"Oh, an old friend. Retired now."

"We're all retired now," she retorted sharply. "Who's Joss?"

"He came through?"

"On the answering machine. Eleven-thirty his time, he said. I take it you know where his time is."

"What did he say?"

"You want me to tell you over the phone?"

"Do you know a quicker way?"

She told him. A call-back request, no number given, no place, just times.

"Uh-huh."

"Is that all, uh-huh?"

"I'm going up to New York. Nick's taking me."

"Now?" He heard the swish of something satiny as she fished for her watch. "It's four-thirty. And why drive? You won't get there till—"

"Back in the morning," he said. "Sleep well. Better still, sleep light."

"Fat chance."

"Good name for a boat," he said vaguely, and signed off.

FIFTEEN

Garfield dozed and fitfully dreamed during the drive to New York and woke just as Nick turned off Fifth Avenue into the long dead past.

For a second or two—not more—it was 1953 again, Eisenhower in the White House and Lucas H. Garfield newly appointed to nurse the New York connection for Langley. Suborning UN delegates was the brief: road-testing potential cross-over Charlies, propositioning third world turncoats, juggling double agents moonlighting as triples, writing off the occasional cold war casualty. And this street had been one of his chosen battlegrounds, this anonymous canyon in the East Thirties where all the faceless hotels in Christendom come home to die. The Middle Kingdom. No man's land.

All changed now, of course. The hotels still awaiting the mortician, but harboring between them whole vistas of reeking burger joints and delis, massage parlors and photocopying shops.

There are moments in an old man's declining years when he can be forgiven for thinking the Reaper is auditioning him.

This is how it'll be, Garfield thought. A picaresque journey down a familiar street, a disembodied hand pointing: Remember that hotel? That face? That body? Recall the lie you told there? The deception it led to? The sellout? In your ear, a familiar voice singing the threnody. And wailing and clanking behind in the chains you bound them with, the corpses you sent out alive, the half men you sent out whole.

"This it?" Nick called over his shoulder, bringing him back, and there was argument for a while about whether Nick should go in with him as defensive tackle and wet nurse, but Garfield won and watched the Lincoln pull away into the traffic stream. For a while he lingered on the curb to light his pipe and give his tails time to decide their priorities, and if in that instant he cut the figure of a tired old spy dithering on the brink of his nemesis, well and good, because it was pure cover, because it was the role he was playing for all he was worth. Marking time, he looked up at the hotel. It really was as faceless as they come: a vertical neon sign the color of newly spilled blood on top, a sturdy young black in admiral's uniform out front—the Royal Aldebaran, if you please, cosmic majesty for fifty bucks a night. Pipe alight and drawing, Garfield nodded to the black admiral and took the alleyway to a paved yard at the back. The red-painted fire door was where he'd been told to look for it, and so was the business card taped under the bell: "Florian Grimaldi, Theatrical Wigmaker: Definitely no callers without appointment." He rang the bell. In the alley a trash can overturned, a cat yowled. From the hotel kitchens across the yard came a violent, eruptive hiss and the bouquet of old cooking oil.

From behind the red fire door, the scrape of feet on metal stairs and a voice, castrato quavery: "Mr. Goodrum?"

"Yes?"

"And, uh, there's a password, I believe? The, uh, *mot juste*, ha-ha?"

"Doomsday," Garfield told the woodwork, feeling ridiculous.

"Ah, good—yes, that's it."

An assortment of locks and bolts rattled: the door swung wide.

There is no pretending with freaks. You either accept their deformities as alternate expressions of the human condition or insult their intelligence, in which case revulsion is as plain to them if you conceal it as it is if you shriek it in their faces. The apparition discerned suppressed shock in Garfield and, out of habit, forgave. It smiled charitably.

"Waldren, sir. Clayton Holmes Waldren at your service."

Garfield shook the proffered hand with unnecessary warmth, for Clayton Waldren was less a midget than a cripple in miniature, a child bent at the waist like a half-open jackknife with a small hill on its back and a goblin's crooked face. As a consequence of the hunched back and the need to screw up his head to look the world in the eye, his cheek lay flat to his right shoulder, thus reducing the face to half a mask, the sort of Halloween mask an imaginative child might make out of papier-mâché, paint, and spit; punchinello's face more or less, framed in large gold eyeglasses of immense magnification. Below the hump, however, he was all business: gray pin stripe suit; white silk shirt; club tie. The creature of a shotgun marriage between Coney Island and Wall Street.

"My dear fellow, come in. Come in, do." He waved Garfield below. "And watch the stairs. Steep, you see. Old, like the rest of us." He laughed, a clear, braying sound like a trumpet note in a marble hall. Garfield marked it down as nervousness.

They descended to a basement room, unlit but for a pilot light on the projector set up just inside the door yet unmistakably—in an insidious sense—alive. Garfield had the irresistible sensation of being watched, of being on display. He turned to peer about him and, as his eyes became accustomed to the dark, picked out the faces. Hundreds of them. Unfaces. From floor to ceiling on three sides the room was lined with noseless, eyeless, mouthless wooden heads surmounted by exotically crafted wigs, a toy audience gazing blindly down from banked shelves.

177

Waldren smiled at his discomfort. "The atelier of Mme. Guillotine, I always think. Heads, you lose, yes?"

He made a little lurching jump from behind to relieve Garfield of his coat, then whirled it around him in matador fashion.

"Matter of fact, it's the atelier of Arthur Schwartz." He indicated a lurking beanpole in the shadows beyond the projector. "Allow me to present my good friend *Arthur*. Known in the profession as Florian Grimaldi. Artistic license, you see. Arthur, Mr. Goodrum from Washington."

Beckoned into the light, Mr. Schwartz advanced reluctantly. A white and silver man of middle age, skeletal, hollow-eyed, he stopped short by ten paces, glanced doubtfully at Waldren, opened his mouth, uttered the discordant honk of the clinically deaf, swallowed hard, and retreated.

Garfield summoned a courtly "Sir," and Waldren beamed with pleasure.

"More private here, you see. And Arthur can run the projector." He draped Garfield's coat over a chair. "Well, then." He rubbed his little hands together energetically. "Let's get started, shall we?"

The network had approached him a little more than five weeks ago, he began, settling himself on a stool at Garfield's feet. A very back-door type of arrangement; sledgehammer subtlety. He laughed his single trumpet note again at the memory. Hush-hush, they said. *Top secret*.

He was playing the words as Galway would play a flute lullaby, soft in the lower register, but for dramatic luster he had acquired a mid-Atlantic English accent and a Dickensian way with his hands. Garfield guessed he'd rehearsed the speech to his bathroom mirror every day for a month. His sensation of being "played to" in the theatrical sense was now acute.

He was a *free lance*, Waldren explained, giving the term weight—had Senator Sherwood mentioned that by any chance? —so Mayday calls and cries in the night were not foreign to him. "I *am* the best, you see," he said apologetically, as if fame were a communicable disease for which he couldn't be held responsible. "Unrivaled credentials in the field of documentaries—awards, medals, ask anyone." However, he'd had a backlog of work at the time and a *front*log, too, and it just wasn't in the cards. No way, he told the network. Impossible. No can do. "And I went on saying no until they forced me to say yes," he cried excitedly. "The fee is quite extraordinary, I assure you. Shocking, really." He gave in to a whoof of amusement, and as his body shook, he took his listing head in both hands and for a while supported it as if it were a heavily laden tray. 'Must have Waldren,' they said. No one else. Though when I say *they*, I mean *him*, of course. Mort Simon, senior vice-president, production. Mort came to me personally on this, you see. As a favor to him, he said."

"He's a friend of yours?"

"Friend?" Waldren relinquished his head for his knees. "My dear fellow, there are no friendships in television."

"But Simon's heading up the team working on the program?"

"*Team!*" Another braying trumpet solo. "The *team* is Mort and me, period. I deal exclusively with Mort—in the strictest confidence, I might add—and Mort deals exclusively with the State Department—in even stricter confidence. That's the arrangement."

"No producer? No director? Lighting, cameras, sound, all the—"

One much-magnified yellow-green eye fixed on Garfield. "Not a soul. Just Mort and me. Hush-hush. Top secret. 'But why *me*?' I said to Mort—because I have this reputation, you see; I can be difficult, a pest, and have been on numerous occasions. It's a question of standards, a question of honesty. I'm not afraid to speak out to the press, for instance; everyone knows it, Mort included. But he says *talent* is why he needs me—*dear* Mort—talent and integrity. 'Because this is historic material we're dealing with here, Clay,' he tells me. 'It deserves the best.

This is the H-bomb, the death ray, and the secret of the Incas rolled into one, *capisc'*? No talking out of school on this one, Clay. No leaks.' "

"Yet a few days later—a week? ten days?—you're leaking it to Senator Sherwood."

The little man squinted slit-eyed into Garfield's soul. "An investigator, the senator said. Exactly who do you investigate *for*, Mr. Goodrum? May one ask?"

"The Senate Foreign Relations Committee, as Sherwood told you on the phone."

"Ah, yes, so he did." A rampart of even teeth appeared. "Good to know. Good to know."

"So you broke a professional confidence. You mind telling me why?"

"That dull little word *integrity* Mort's so free with." A warning scowl. "No one holds a lien on my conscience, Mr. Goodrum. No one. Whatever the fee. That's the way I am. When I smell a rat, I yell *rat*! Good and loud. That's my reputation."

"As Mort Simon knew when he hired you," Garfield said dryly. "All right, can we start by getting down to what this program is all about?"

"Certainly. It's about Larry Bartell—at first sight. Scheduled to run an hour with breaks: all on film. One-third library footage: Larry the *Wunderkind*, Larry at chess, little Larry meets Ike, Larry for Kennedy, the freedom marches, baiting Nixon, the People Power conference, talk shows, news clips, so on. Another third is filmed comment. Talking heads. Brock Stafford, Davis Lang, a few of Larry's Harvard cronies from the sixties; the—"

"All highly complimentary, I take it."

"Oh, *ardent*." Waldren brandished a slim gold pencil. "They cut him off at the *knees*. And the final third is the famous State Department film, the material I'm going to run for you now. Film *provided* by State, I should say. In fact, according to the script, it's Soviet security film. Sixteen and a half minutes in all. Shot by the KGB. Five segments, five separate incidents."

"And they show?"

"Larry Bartell selling America down the river." He made Garfield the gift of a misshapen grin. "One segment shot in Kampuchea, one in New Zealand, another in Japan, one in Brussels, one in Thailand. The Kampuchean segment runs the longest—seven minutes twelve seconds. In the Brussels and New Zealand footage he's on screen for less than thirty seconds."

"And that's worth an hour of prime time?"

Waldren raised the gold pencil: Wait! "Alone and unsupported? Possibly, but probably not. However, we have a secret ingredient, you see. We have *news* value. The film shows Bartell playing undercover spy, agent, whatever they call them nowadays. But it also shows him playing character assassin, and that's the clincher. Shows him selling one particular American down the river, in living color, five times over. The human element, you see. One on one. Practically soap opera."

"And that's why you called Sherwood?"

"Partly."

"Who's the man he sells down the river?"

Waldren squinted ostentatiously at his watch. "Wouldn't you rather see that for yourself?"

"All right."

The little man rose briskly and flapped his arms at his helper in a wild semaphore. With great dexterity he added a flood of sign language. "Sequence one, Arthur, *if* you please," he shouted over it.

Theater, thought Garfield woodenly. Pure theater.

The opening shot was a mass of congealed color, and Waldren clicked his tongue mawkishly. "My God, I ask you, *look* at it. Sunset over the rainbow factory. Damn fool's shooting into the sun through laminated glass—idiot!"

But almost at once the colors fragmented, pooled, coalesced, and through a fog of insipid yellows and browns the outline of a square white single-story building emerged, the camera approaching it fast on a curving run.

"Phnom Penh Airport," Waldren said. "Know Kampuchea at all?"

Toward the end of the shot the smudged outline of a rear-view mirror intruded at top left, and below it, the driver's elbow. Cut. To an Air France Boeing 727, ghosting silently from right to left across a landscape of brown earth, glinting rice paddies, tarmac, feathery palms—all vastly overexposed.

"The Paris plane. Still only once a week."

The cameraman was settling to his task with more confidence now, but the picture quality was still soupy. The scene switched to a busy concourse, an exclusively Oriental crowd sequence, then panned across a wall of curved glass. It reached a sea of heads lapping around an open door and steadied. The heads grew arms and began to wave as a procession of figures appeared indistinctly through the dusty panes, descending from the Boeing. One by one they crossed the apron, passed through the door, and were engulfed by the crowd, each face registered momentarily in alarming close-up.

The seventh face was Larry Bartell's.

Garfield recognized him at once, though by no stretch of the imagination was he the Larry Bartell last seen walking into the Council for Ethnic Freedoms building in Geneva. Time and tide had whittled old Larry to the bone, ballooned him at the gut, bequeathed him an Adam's apple that rose and fell awkwardly in a skinny throat. He wore what in better days had been a safari suit, probably East German, a baggy comedy in mouse brown with a belt that hung embarrassingly near his crotch. He'd grown his hair, something on the lines of Fred Goldman's Afro, though cloudy gray-white rather than black, and Garfield wondered if it was some sort of prevailing fashion among the upwardly mobile and the downwardly radical alike. Under it the face was martyr thin and pale and, on this film, also that shade of metallic blue common to aging consumptives.

The camera homed in for the close-up; Bartell felt its eye on him, glanced up in fleeting distress, recovered, looked away, ducked, and set off at an angle. Comically the operator lost him, set the camera swinging left and right in a desperate bid to locate him, and ran out of film. Cut!

"Ah, the sheer professionalism," said Waldren.

The next shot had him shaking hands with three Chinese in the blue work suits and caps of the party hierarchy. Larry was a two-handed shaker, and you could see they didn't like it. A shot followed of all four of them getting into a dilapidated Ziv, then getting out again in a crowded street to enter a colonnaded French barracks of a building with Ho Chi Minh's likeness crowning the door arch. A gloomy interior, figures in a fog, then out again, all smiles and—this time—a wave for the camera. *Hi, gang!*

"Knows he's still being filmed," Garfield muttered, more for his own enlightenment than Waldren's.

"Knows? Course, he knows. What he's there for. Now look at his hair in this next shot, his clothes."

They'd cleaned him up, dressed him in tropical whites, cut his hair. It transformed him. He looked at least ten years younger, a filled-out, bouncy fashion plate. Garfield could almost feel his electricity. Astonishing. In the new scene he was lording it over a village of woven huts in a jungle clearing—Lord Jimming it, Garfield thought wryly—surrounded by naked toddlers and boys in loincloths. Larry ducking into the gloom of a headman's hut; Larry accepting flowers, flags, soundless hymns of praise. There were no armed sentries in the shot, but Garfield could feel their presence all the same, standing guard on the perimeter, AK-47s shoulder-slung at the hip. Larry had that air about him of being *contained.* Cut again—and he was now walking through a children's hospital, looking suitably stricken, the wards open to the sun, palm thatch flapping in the breeze, Uncle Ho's celestial likeness benignly ubiquitous. They made him bend over a cot and finger a baby's charred back, then again, with the child staring up at him over its shoulder, wide-eyed, black-eyed.

183

"Oh, yes," Waldren hissed again. *"Nice."* He tugged unconsciously at the leg of Garfield's pants. "Watch the color change here. Different film. Different cameraman."

Larry stepping out of a car—a Moscovich circa 1960 something. Still without a care in the world, still his younger self, full of life, full of the old Bartell cockiness; handsome, bright-eyed, laughing. How did he do it? A forest of hands reached out to him from a roped enclosure, and he danced toward them —danced, not walked—plucking at outstretched fingers the way kings and presidents do, barely touching, waving a small Vietnamese flag, ruffling a silky black head or two. In the next shot he'd lost the flag, and they'd given him a party cap; he wore it angled up on the back of his head, like Sterling Hayden at the wheel of a windjammer. Then he was off again, wading through a sea of children, applauding them as they applauded him, in the Russian manner, hands high over his head to urge them on.

Larry in love with life. In love with the whole third world.

"Remarkable man," Waldren said quietly. "Now watch this."

The quality of the light, or of the film, reverted briefly to the maelstrom effect of the opening shot, and when it cleared, Larry Bartell was an old man again. The smile had gone, the bounce; he moved slowly, painfully, the world on his back. Disconsolately he trudged along a street of fruit and vegetable stands. Gloomily he patted yet more child extras on the head. Grumpily he waved to a platoon of black-clad women in conical hats staring over the rim of a rice paddy. Desperately he scrambled up the slab side of a water buffalo while its diminutive minder hid his hilarity behind his hand. Starbursts of aggravated color flashed and swam throughout these maneuvers as the camera pursued him in and out of sunlight and shadow.

Waldren tugged once more at Garfield's pants. "Pay attention now."

Larry stood on a hill, on a small green hillock at the summit of a hill, the older, haggard Larry, swabbing his face with a large cotton square, his skin flushed to an alarming crimson glow, his eyes smudge brown.

"*Look* at the balance, I ask you." Waldren snickered. "The cameraman must have been metering the inside of his *crotch—* excuse my French."

The camera closed in tight on Bartell's face. Garfield could feel the weight of the heat bearing down on him, feel the fever burning inside the bony frame. Strangely moved, he felt an urge to reach out and touch the screen. *Don't worry, son. Nearly over. Nearly home.*

Larry turned and spoke to someone off camera, but they didn't love him anymore, and the response was negative. He scowled, threw out his arms, let them fall; an actor's actor.

"Now," Waldren whispered urgently.

The screen went blank, then filled with a long shot of a harbor seen from the same hillock. Brilliant, mottled; the images hazy. Far away, over a sweep of low hills, a concrete geometry of godowns and wharves lay pinioned under the sun. Cranes jutted, a dredger sat between the inner pierheads, a scattering of small coastal rust buckets rode at anchor, a few fishing boats beyond, a biggish tanker, and on the inner wall—*freeze—* moored alongside, a sleek modern ship, a liner perhaps, glowing indecently white against the slate of the sea. The camera zoomed in for a closer look and fondled the ship from stem to stern; picked out two men at the forward rail, three more in white boiler suits on the afterhatch; withdrew again into long shot.

"And two and three and"—Waldren sucked noisily at his teeth—"boom."

A balloon of oily black smoke inflated around the afterhatch and climbed lazily into the china blue sky. The camera zoomed in again, this time to run its hungry eye along the main deck, but it was already enveloped in smoke too thick to reveal the plight of the mortals lately at ease by the rail. Within seconds a black shroud had obliterated the superstructure, the funnels, the derricks.

"Note the flames," Waldren said mockingly. "Leaping, soaring, yes?"

"What flames?" Garfield grunted, too busy to note the sarcasm.

"Hear that, Arthur?" Waldren sang out gaily. "He sees no flames. Smoke without fire, he says."

The screen went blank a second time, and Waldren announced, "And so the consequences."

They were back again at Phnom Penh Airport, and the color was kinder to the eye, more subdued. First an establishing shot of the building, then a reprise of the concourse pan, then a cut to the arrival-departure area. A group of four Occidentals—from their dress, instantly and conspicuously American—stood in a doleful semicircle by the door. Off to one side six Kampucheans in the olive green and pith helmets of the People's Police were guarding a fifth—a tubby, mild-faced man of middle age in rimless glasses and a rumpled linen suit. The American's smile was parched but resolutely fixed, in the manner of a medieval saint awaiting the first stone. Moreover, it was a smile Garfield recognized.

"Hugh Douglas," he said mechanically.

"*Doomsday Douglas*—yes, indeed." Waldren fairly rocked with delight on his stool. "The president's *very* special envoy. And the incident?"

"The bombing of the Russian hostel ship at Kompong Som last winter. November, was it?"

"October. The sixteenth."

An element of gratuitous farce had now entered the proceedings on screen. Eight Kampucheans armed with long bamboo staves were herding the Americans like cattle across the transit apron toward a waiting U.S. Air Force jet swimming in heat waves. The Kampucheans had been chosen for local box-office appeal: They were very small—half the size of the Americans—painfully thin, and ragged to the point of nakedness. As an exercise in comic counterpoint it was almost Chaplinesque.

"Conclusions?" Waldren piped up.

"Breakdown of the U.S.-Kampuchean peace talks."

"For what they were ever worth," Waldren crowed. "Also the

beginning of the end for Hugh Douglas as a presidential insider."

"And Douglas is the man Bartell sells down the river?"

"The victim, yes." Waldren nodded at the screen. "Five times over, according to the script."

Larry Bartell was now waving himself out of the selfsame departure area, dull of eye and countenance, a posse of bureaucrats on hand to wave back. They'd taken away the tropical whites, and he was back in his own soiled, sweat-smudged buff safari suit. It fitted where it touched. It occurred to Garfield he might even have borrowed it.

"Mr. Laurens Bartell takes leave of beautiful Kampuchea." Waldren observed archly, "for the dubious pleasures of home. If he has one." He semaphored wildly to attract Mr. Schwartz's attention. "Thank you, Arthur. We'll hold it there for a moment, I think." He tracked around on his stool to face Garfield, amusement writ large on his clown's crooked face. "Questions, then, Mr. Goodrum. Or would you rather I dazzle you with my private insights?"

Garfield was still mesmerized by the blank screen, couldn't take his eyes off it, in fact. "You used the phrase *according to the script* several times. I assume with irony."

"You bet with irony."

"You don't believe the script?"

Waldren snorted derisively. "Believe! I don't *believe* any of it."

Garfield glanced cautiously down at him. "Who wrote it?"

"Now that's a very perceptive question, Mr. Goodrum. The short answer is 'Thomas W. Borrett wrote it.' The longer one is: Who's Thomas W. Borrett?"

"You don't know him?"

"Nobody knows him. I've asked around. Everywhere. Discreetly, of course."

"You ask Mort Simon?"

"Finally. A pseudonym, he says, top secret, hands off, all contact forbidden. Man of mystery."

"Is that usual?"

"A writer hiding his light under a bushel? No more unusual than sunspots on the moon, no."

"And that tells you?"

"That the writer's a State Department hack, what else? Probably several hacks; creative committee work. The whole thing's State Department committee work in my opinion, beginning to end. It's what I tried to tell Sherwood."

Garfield foxed up a look of senile bewilderment. "You mean you don't believe what's on the film either? That's creative committee work, too?"

The question momentarily stumped Waldren. "It is and it isn't. Depends what you mean. If you're asking me does the film *exist*, I'm forced to admit, yes, it does. If you ask does it show Larry Bartell flitting from flower to flower in Kampuchea, the answer's also yes. If you mean is it genuine Russian surveillance film—guaranteed, as per script—I have to tell you honestly, I don't know; I edited on copy, not on the original film. But *could* it be KGB film? Answer, who else gets to wander around Communist satellite countries making home movies?"

"Not the State Department," Garfield said politely.

"Very true."

"So?"

"So the best lies are based in fact."

Garfield felt for his pipe and matches in the bulging pocket of his tweed jacket. "Well, it *is* Bartell," he said thoughtfully, "no doubt about that. And I guess we have to assume it's also Kampuchea, though personally I wouldn't know. All right, how does the script make the film lie—if that's what it does?"

"Easiest thing in the world. And we don't have to say a word. Not one word. First you see Bartell standing on top of a hill, looking down at the port. Then you see the ship going up in smoke. From the same hill, same angle. Well, you're the average, semi-interested, semicomatose American sitting poleaxed in front of the TV late at night with a can of beer in your hand and your mind on bed. What do you think?"

"That Bartell blew the ship. Or had a hand in blowing it."

"Excellent! That's precisely what he's supposed to think. The editing instructions are quite clear on this point. I'm told to intercut Bartell and the smoke cloud three times—*three*, Mr. Goodrum—and that's as good as saying, 'Look what he did!'" He took a handful of Garfield's pants leg again. "Now I don't know what that conveys to you, my dear sir, but what it conveys to me is fake. F-A-K-E. Bartell was not on that hill when the ship went up, take it from me. If he had been, they'd have filmed him watching it, no need for intercuts."

"You take that one to Mort Simon, too?"

Clayton Waldren chuckled contemptuously. "There was no point in going to Mort Simon. I knew the choice I had to make: Either I turned the job in or I yelled rat. I decided to call Senator Sherwood. I felt obliged to. Morally obligated."

"But meantime, you followed instructions. You cut the film the way the script says."

"I had to." He shot a chill glare over his eyeglasses. "You people in Washington sure take your time coming up to the mark, I must say. Maybe you wouldn't come at all. How could I know? I had to consider that. I'm a professional, Mr. Goodrum. I have a reputation to think of."

"A reputation for speaking out," Garfield drawled placidly. "Yes, I know. Tell me, is this faking process repeated in the other four sequences?"

"To a lesser degree, yes. I—"

Waldren stopped, his eyes arrested by a flutter of movement beyond the projector. Under cover of the face-saving dark, Mr. Schwartz was swaying sinuously from foot to foot in hynotic slow motion, his eyes shut, face uplifted, hands clasped at his chin, lips moving in silent song or prayer. Waldren winced visibly as if he'd been caught in an improper act, but Garfield had his reflexes fully manned and shrugged tolerantly.

"He's a deaf-mute, you see—had you noticed?" Waldren snapped his fingers twice, very loudly, to illustrate; Mr. Schwartz neither heard nor sensed. For a while they watched his arcane gyrations in companionable wonder. Outside in the street, muffled by brick and distance, an irate driver thumbed his horn —bahnt, bahnt, baaaaahnt!—but that didn't do the trick either. Waldren sighed. "He's a genius with his hands, you know. A genius. Not that there's much call for genius nowadays."

Garfield said tentatively, "You were saying . . ."

"Hmm? Oh, yes. Where was I?" But at that moment Mr. Schwartz returned to the land of the living with jarring suddenness, and Waldren's depression fled at once. He awarded Garfield a particularly dazzling smile. "Yes, indeed, the script. Right. But may I suggest we take a little refreshment break first?" He rose and scuttled off across the room before Garfield could object. "Coffee?" he called back from a side table. "A cookie, perhaps? Chocolate chip? Ginger? Coconut?"

"Nothing."

"Well, I'm sure Arthur won't say no." He pivoted, a plate held out in front of him, his hump upstanding behind him like a dunce's cap. He pushed the plate under his friend's nose. "For Arthur, cupcakes!"

Mr. Schwartz saw and registered and hung his head in abject pleasure.

Garfield didn't know where to look.

"The fact is"—Waldren resumed, a handkerchief tucked in his collar to catch the crumbs—"the script's a joke. To anyone of average intelligence it's an insult. Listen. Consider what Hugh Douglas's mission to Kampuchea was *really all about*," he said, rolling the words around his tongue like old wine. "Forget the script for a moment. Just cast your mind back to last October, to what the papers said. The mission started out as a presidential initiative, no less, a personal and private crusade by the man in the White House, two hundred and some days after his inauguration, to—lovely phrase—*get the motor running*. Talks about talks. On his own admission he clinched the deal himself in a personal phone call to Heng Samrin in Phnom Penh.

"The president also claimed, you may remember, that only his kitchen cabinet buddies were in on it. Not State, not Defense —no one. Well, perhaps he was protecting their backs, who knows? But that's what he said. Top top secret—Douglas to fly to Phnom Penh in mid-October." Waldren shook out the handkerchief and began polishing his glasses with it, physical distraction for an unquiet heart. Satisfied, he thumbed the handkerchief back into his breast pocket. "Now this is where the script takes over. Slight detour around the known facts, so to speak. Two weeks *before* Douglas was due in Phnom Penh, the KGB turned up there. In the person of Larry Bartell."

Garfield nodded slowly, as if he believed it, too. "Any proof? A White House spokesman says . . . Usually reliable intelligence sources?"

"Nothing like that. *We* just say it, show the airport scene, period."

Garfield muttered something unintelligible but was otherwise unmoved.

Waldren's tiny paw descended on his arm, light as a moth, insistent. "What I mean is, how does that strike you as a practical proposition? Seven hundred thousand KGB minions around the globe, probably several dozen already on the spot, yet the finger falls on Larry Bartell. The future of Soviet expansionism in Southeast Asia at stake and Moscow pumps in a tricky Dick American? Come now—surely."

"Unlikely," Garfield agreed.

"Unlikely!"

"He was *there*. He's there on film, isn't he?"

Waldren smirked. "Yes, but *when* was he there? When? Moot point. But back to the script. Bartell flies in, we say, and does the rounds, as you've just seen: the schools, the hospitals, shaking hands, kissing babies—do they kiss babies in Kampuchea?—and all the time he's sniffing the air—yes?— testing the ground, working out how he'll torpedo the talks, ruin Douglas, smash any possibility of a U.S.-Kampuchean détente, presupposing we could ever agree on one." He tugged again at Garfield's pants leg. "You're with me, are you? All according to the script so far. The Gospel according to State."

"I'm with you."

"Good. So Larry finally hits on the answer. He'll blow up the Russian hostel ship at Kompong Som the day Douglas arrives. *Sensational!*" The superlative sprayed a rain of warm spittle across the back of Garfield's hand. "I don't have to tell you about Kompong Som, do I? Old fishing port on the west side, small coastal trade, now a naval base and growing. The Vietnamese use it to patrol the Gulf of Siam. The Russians use it to refuel and supply their Pacific fleet. And there were Russians actually working there last October, you see—hundreds—engineers, surveyors, naval architects, electricians, mechanics, redesigning the inner port, building new destroyer pens, submarine pens, bunkering facilities. And of course, they lived on the hostel ship; one shift working, one sleeping, always someone on board. So put a firecracker under that lot, Bartell says to himself, and—well, instant outcry: CIA-engineered terrorist plot! Universal outrage! Death to America! Trick was, it couldn't be a real bang; he knew that. Engineers don't grow on trees, even in Mother Russia. But fake bangs are easy and look just as good—sound without fury, smoke without fire. Ask Hollywood."

"A fake explosion? The script claims it was faked?"

"Certainly," Waldren said proudly. "Whole point of the operation. How else do you think they were all set up, ready and waiting to film it? Coincidence?"

"But we *know* it was real," Garfield protested. "My *God*, do we know it!"

Clayton Waldren played his first ace with excessive nonchalance. "There's a satellite picture—we carry it—taken seventy-two hours after the fire. Shows no visible damage to the dockyard, none to the hostel ship. Script says there's no room for doubt. None. The bombing was faked."

Garfield retreated once more behind the mask of senile perplexity. "You expect me to believe"—he began shakily, pretending a sudden shortness of breath—"that the State Department had a satellite picture available in seventy-two hours proving the explosion was a *fake*"—he snatched a gulp of air—"proving KGB culpability, proving American innocence, and we didn't use it? Didn't put it out on TV? On the wire services? Worldwide?" The enormity of it rendered him temporarily speechless, or so it seemed to Waldren, who smiled approvingly at his guest's distress and took a firmer grip of the pants leg.

"That's exactly what we say, yes."

"But why?" The question was very nearly soundless, more an invocation than an appeal.

"Is there ever an *obvious* reason for fooling most of the people most of the time?"

"But they do give a reason presumably. They have to."

"Stoicism." Waldren wrapped the word in an amused prehensile pout. "Do I have the right word? Pretending indifference to pain. Knowing something's bound to hurt but knowing you'll muddle through in the end."

"That's an *official* explanation? Stoicism?"

"It's what they mean, roughly translated."

"It's what *who* means?"

"Brock Stafford, our revered national security adviser. He makes a formal statement. On film, of course."

"What does he say?"

"Basically, that the whole thing was a KBG propaganda exercise and Washington lost—through no fault of its own. That Moscow created the advantage and played it very shrewdly. Quite complimentary, you see. It's a form of honesty, comes over well on television. He says the State Department put out an immediate denial of the Tass accusation, but Tass countered with a set of news pictures radioed direct from Kompong Som. Looked like the end of the world there—smoke, fire tenders, ambulances, bodies on stretchers, the works. According to Stafford, the media took care of the rest. They ran the pictures, quoted Tass ad nauseam, and pretty well agreed it could have been Langley-inspired. Most of the European papers actually said so the next day. Then came the riots outside our embassies, remember? The usual trouble spots at first—Beirut, Athens, Tokyo—then Rome, Paris, London, everywhere."

"But how does Stafford explain away not using a satellite picture that proves it was all a fake?"

"He says it turned up too late. Forty-eight hours too late, at least. 'Proof of innocence offered too late is proof of guilt'— quote unquote. Moscow would've claimed we'd taken the picture *before* the explosion, he says. So he sat on it knowing our turn would come someday. He half believed Bartell was mixed up in it even then."

Waldren paused for a reaction, but Garfield was in no hurry to oblige. "Shall I go on?" he demanded. Garfield allowed him a surly grunt.

Waldren eyed him speculatively—a glance that had great shrewdness in it—then cast an eye out for Mr. Schwartz; but Mr. Schwartz had temporarily suspended visual contact again and had his back to them, head cocked high, fingers weaving in an agony of frustration at his back. Waldren sighed, a large sound coming from such a small cavity.

"Well, you know how it ended, of course—the Douglas visit. News of the bombing reached Phnom Penh midmorning. Douglas was having a private audience with Heng Samrin at the time; just the two of them and a pot of green tea; bizarre, really. Russian ship ablaze down there on the coast, thirty-odd Soviet heroes sizzling nicely in their beds below—or they were according to Tass—who else but the bloody bloodthirsty CIA to blame, and here's this fat pig of a Yankee hypocrite calmly swilling tea with the head puppet. Well, in minutes the Russian ambassador was on the line—gross U.S. provocation, murder, arson, pimping without a license—and what's the head puppet planning to do about it? As it happened, before Heng could do anything about it, there were troops everywhere—thousands of 'em, Vietnamese, of course—whistles, sirens, tanks, half-tracks. state of emergency, martial law. And before the tea was cold in the pot, poor old Hugh Douglas and his team were on their way back to the airport, wondering what hit them. Never darken our doorstep again, talks off, finished, dead—*get out!*"

Garfield ran a comb of fingers through his stubbly white hair and tried hard not to smile. He tapped the pocket of his tweed jacket. Retrieved pipe and matches. Fired a match. Touched the tobacco. Puffed until the bowl flowered scarlet. All to gain time to smother a bounding sense of elation.

"And the moral?" he drawled carelessly. "There's bound to be a moral—according to the script."

Waldren had recovered his sense of theatre. "More morals than you can shake a stick at, Mr. Goodrum. Nothing too subtle, of course; this is television, after all. Good triumphs in the end. America bloody but unbowed. Truth will out. The tireless search for world peace goes on unabated."

"And Bartell?"

"Ah, well. We've proved he's more than just a paper traitor, haven't we? A full-blown KGB undercover agent, in fact. Rank of lieutenant colonel, high-executive clout. And we go on to prove that Kampuchea was just round one in a campaign to destroy Douglas's credibility as a negotiator."

"Does Douglas have anything to say about that?"

"On the program? No."

"Why not?"

"I couldn't say. Maybe he turned them down; people do that. And who can blame him? The president dropped him, remember. *Sacked* him. Knowing Douglas was in no way personally at fault. Knowing—actually having *proof*—that he was being manipulated. Still dropped him. I mean, that's not a gesture likely to win a man's dying gratitude, is it? Douglas leaves the groves of academe at a month's notice to front for a president he has no special liking for—no political stomach for, come to that—and his reward is purgatory. He does his damnedest, and he gets stuck with labels for his trouble: diplomatic Jonah, mobile disaster area, *Doomsday* Douglas. Everywhere he turns

195

another banana skin. And to top it all off, he's fired because it's easier to drop him than explain why he failed. Oh, no"—Waldren manhandled his sagging head up at a challenging angle—"in his place I don't think I'd care to sit in on the show either, thanks a lot. Who needs to be a spectator at his own autopsy?" In his heat he had lost the last vestiges of his mid-Atlantic Englishness.

Mr. Schwartz was fiddling hopefully with the projector, snapping some preparatory gadget or other off and on with irritating insistence. Waldren glanced at him, annoyed, then at Garfield.

"Perhaps we could run the next, uh?"

Garfield dosed the air with a stream of aromatic smoke. "Yes. See it through to the end, why not?"

And he coughed loudly to cover an involuntary chuckle, a deep-chested monosyllabic bark of relief as his freewheeling imagination ran headlong into a solid wall of comprehension. It was an agent's business to be used, he reminded himself again. To be played. To be led by the nose.

Had he been forty years younger, he might have let out a very undignified whoop.

SIXTEEN

"What other missions?" Polly yawned.

"You'd know if you read the papers." Garfield swung his feet up on the bed and trapped the phone under his chin.

"What's that you're eating?" she called down the line, suddenly very wide-awake.

"Relax. Ham on pumpernickel."

"Is that all?"

"It's all they had. That and coffee. Black."

"Black coffee at midnight?"

"I won't make a habit of it, I promise."

He heard the camp bed squeak as she sat up. "*What* would I know if I'd read the papers?" she demanded. "Hugh Douglas you said . . . wasn't he one of Sally Ann Cathcart's cap and bells brigade? Little fat fellow with glasses?"

"What do you mean, cap and bells?"

"A performer—someone you have on call for parties. Either very funny or very serious. He was the serious type. Intense. Blushed a lot, as I remember. Didn't he work for one of the foundations? Georgetown somewhere?"

"The Benjamin Foundation. He—"

"I remember! It *was* Sally Ann Cathcart. Henry met him through the Pentagon and signed him up for her hit list. He wrote long papers on defense policy; very yawny. Wasn't he a Red? I seem to recall something about his being tinged."

"Tinged? Who says?" Garfield inquired through a mouthful of black bread.

"Well, the Fret Set, I guess. The president's men."

"He isn't Red," Garfield said confidently, then paused to examine the statement for flaws. "Well, maybe a shade of Washington pink," he amended. "By the standards of the Hoover Institution or the Center for Strategic Studies, I suppose you'd say the Benjamin Foundation's a shade left of center. More rose-tinted."

She wasn't listening. "He's against the arms race. I heard him say so. Where did I meet him last? On his own now, I think, isn't he? Divorced. Sally Ann says he's really just anti-Washington—that's his value. Drop him into a Georgetown soiree, and he goes off like a bomb." She paused. "Am I warm?"

"White-hot. Go on."

"He seemed to me to be naturally anti. Is that his character, do you think? Anti missile screens, anti weapons in space, anti fifth-generation computers, television, acid rain, nuclear power, jogging, health foods, space research, you name it." She hummed her thinking hum, a diapason he'd learned to recognize as a prelude to insight. "That's kind of funny, don't you think?"

"Funny?"

"A man like the president choosing a man like Hugh Douglas for a personal envoy."

"Why? Envoys aren't clones. Diplomacy is the art of sending honest men abroad to lie for their *country*, not for the party in power. When you accept envoy status, you take an unspoken oath against political bias."

"But Douglas is—well, at least halfway to being a socialist, isn't he?"

"Which can be an advantage when you're dealing with the other side. Maybe not much of an advantage, but better than none. Doesn't matter how far apart national positions are, if two men sitting down at a table share a community of interest, they'll spark. That's worth a lot of talk."

"Oh, Luke, come on, who do you think you're kidding? That kind of diplomacy went out with your father, and you know it. Douglas didn't get a *chance* to spark. He probably wasn't meant to."

"Oh? Really, now. Do tell."

"He was sent out to *fail*. I mean, it's logical, isn't it? Failure *was* his mission, whether he knew it or not—and on balance I'd think *not*. I mean, it's so *obvious*. You pick a political situation you can't possibly change and send in someone you can afford to throw to the wolves. You sacrifice a member of the vocal opposition to gain a tactical advantage."

"Honey, what are you talking about—advantage? Who gained? Not Douglas. Not the president. Not Langley. No one on this side of the Atlantic."

"Then someone somewhere else who *matters* on this side of the Atlantic," she retorted triumphantly.

In the dead silence that followed Garfield became aware of a faint mechanical sighing on the line, the soft, rhythmic lisp a recording device makes as it steals the thoughts out of your mouth. Go to it, boys, he urged silently. Go run that little gem up the pole and see who salutes. Oh, Susanna! Out of the mouths of babes . . .

"Hmm," he said noncommittally. "Well, maybe. Maybe."

"Not maybe. Plain as your nose. So tell me what else our Larry's supposed to have gotten up to. Those other missions."

Our Larry, possessive, he noted.

He played it to her in footnote form, much as Clayton Waldren had recited it to him, though it had sounded a lot more melodramatic in Waldren's version.

Item: November 12, four weeks after the Kompong Som incident Hugh Douglas was dispatched in secret to Auckland, New Zealand, to engage in talks over New Zealand's long-standing refusal to permit missile-carrying U.S. warships in its territorial waters. On day three of his visit Tass released pictures showing two U.S. nuclear submarines cruising at operational depth fifteen miles southeast of the Cook Strait. Satellite pictures, of course.

"And that was enough?" Polly was incredulous. "They took Moscow's word? How can anyone prove that submarines photographed from two hundred miles up were cruising fifteen miles from anywhere?"

"Science can, apparently. And a little unscheduled honesty from the right quarter helped. The Tass story was released early enough to give the New York networks time to tackle Washington before the evening news bulletins went out. And at the Pentagon someone blundered. A nice fresh-faced young ensign—name quoted in the film, since resigned the service—told the truth: admitted there'd been a breach of territorial etiquette on the part of two U.S. submarines but only—and essentially—in New Zealand's interests. They'd been shadowing three *Russian* subs halfway across the Pacific."

"And?"

"And they lost them. In the Cook Strait."

"Oh, my," declared Polly.

Item: December 18 Hugh Douglas made a pre-Christmas run to meet NATO chiefs of staff in Brussels to discuss the installation of a new generation of Tomahawk missiles in Europe. On the day he flew in, an English political weekly (much pinker than Douglas) ran three pages on precisely where and when the missiles were to be sited.

"Every last mouth-watering detail." Garfield droned on. "Maps, technical data on storage and triggering, control codes, preferred flight paths, plus a lot of Madison Avenue-type hype on how to soften up public opinion ahead of installation."

"And Larry Bartell passed the information?"

"So the film says."

"Poor Douglas."

"Won him his spurs," Garfield said, "and his nickname—Doomsday Douglas. Courtesy of one of the syndicated cartoonists. Oliphant, I think. Anyway, the president refused to give up on him. Common loyalty, he said. 'What specifically is Hugh Douglas guilty of? What in all conscience can he be accused of?' "

"How about being the wrong man in the wrong place at the wrong time?"

"Apply that as a standard of political substance, and there'd be no one to vote for."

Item: January 28 Douglas flew to Tokyo to gauge Japanese government opinion on the setting up of a comprehensive new missile defense system. This time the press was on his tail in brigade strength—secrecy or no secrecy—and he didn't disappoint them. His arrival coincided with publication of a special edition of *Shinbun*, virtually a reprise of the Brussels experience: all the sordid technical details spelled out in riveting color. The Japanese antinuclear lobby blew up all over him: fistfights at the airport, water cannon, police charges, marches, demonstrations. In Hiroshima they burned Old Glory. In Tokyo they got to the air force jet that had brought him in and rechristened it. Painted 'Enola Gay' the length of the fuselage. Couldn't clean it off. Had to fly it home like that."

"Is that all?"

Garfield swallowed the last shred of dried-out ham. "One more. Thailand was a farce. Mid-February, six days before the president dropped him. Douglas was supposed to sit in on an ASEAN conference in Bangkok—a defense subcommittee setup —no particulars given but the usual 'secrecy' observed. About five hundred journalists trailing him. A circus! Well, nothing happened for four days; washout. The media were even reduced to reporting the conference. Then—"

"This is crazy," Polly whispered from her camp bed in Washington.

"Crazy is as crazy does. A fire started in a Bangkok night club—a clip joint, pushers' paradise, basement club. It was around midnight, and the place was packed. The whole block went up—the club, shops, warehouses, apartments. Burned all night. They were digging out bodies for days."

"And Douglas was accused of starting the fire? My God, Luke, how—"

"He wasn't accused. Story next day was that the fire started when some drunk tossed a lighted match in a bathroom trash can. An American drunk. Everyone said for sure he was American, swore to it, though he was never found."

"But that had nothing to do with—"

"Didn't stop a few thousand Thais from swarming around the embassy that night. Didn't stop them from smashing windows, burning cars. Trouble was—"

"And Douglas?"

"Was in the embassy at the time. Tried to drive out; he had a dinner date at the foreign minister's house. The crowd practically lynched him. From there on his Jonah tag took over. Nothing he could do about it. The Thai government went very cold on him. Suggested he take the high road home, forget he ever came."

From her end, pensive silence.

"Not so funny," he said, finishing the coffee.

She didn't answer. Outside his window, across the cluttered, rain-black desolation of what had once been Gimbels's roof, the Empire State Building loomed frosty white. Garfield eyed it with a sadness born of nostalgia.

"Where are you staying?" she asked suddenly, reading his mind.

For answer he whistled a tune they'd danced to there before the war; 1941, late summer. He'd been on a forty-eight-hour turnaround from Bern, and there'd been time the second night for dinner before his plane. Dinner and . . .

"Pennsylvania six-five-thousand!" she laughed, coming in on the final phrase. "You're at the old Penn!"

"They changed the name a couple of times since we were here."

"Glenn Miller," she said wistfully with a sigh.

"At the Café Rouge," he agreed. "Damn near fifty years ago. Think of it."

"No, don't!"

"No, well, maybe not."

Her silences were getting longer. This one she followed with a fretful hiss of frustration. "What do you think, Luke?"

"About what?"

"Did Larry make those things happen? Does it sound credible?"

"Credible!" he snapped, forgetting himself, forgetting the place, the dolorous hour. "Good God, woman, what do you mean, credible? Was the Bay of Pigs credible? Was Kennedy's assassination credible? Do you imagine Langley stopped to consider the credibility of overthrowing Allende, bombing Libya? If it's expedient, it's credible." He was talking for the record, now, to that ugly, rhythmic lisp on the line that devoured private thoughts. Stupid of him.

"But do you believe it?"

He caught a yawn and tried to suppress it, felt his ears close with the effort. "They've got him on film," he said irritably, wanting her off the line now, checking his watch. "He's on film in every one of those places—Phnom Penh, Auckland, Brussels,

Tokyo, Bangkok—and they can't all be coincidental. First you see Larry; then the sky falls in; then Douglas rides out of town on a rail. Same sequence, different variations, five times over."

"And you're saying Larry managed to do all that without help? You're trying to tell me he's Superman?"

He sighed. "No, not without help."

"Help from *this* side of the Atlantic," she persisted. "How could he have done any of it without knowing in advance where Douglas was going and when and why? Without somebody here tipping him off. Somebody very—"

"I have to go out," he said abruptly to cut her off. "Now."

"But you agree with me? Douglas was meant to fail. It was in somebody's interest he should fail." Like a good motor, warmed to perfection, she was now running in overdrive. "And if you accept that, you have to accept that what we're talking about now is a conspiracy of—"

"I agree with Oliver Wendell Holmes," Garfield interrupted her portentously, swinging his feet to the floor. "For most men, the truth is what they can't help thinking must be true. Hugh Douglas was a victim of what people couldn't help thinking."

"And Larry?"

"Him, too, I guess. I don't know."

She let her breath go in another short, sharp gust of irritation. "Oh, I wish *I* knew what to think, Luke."

"You and the rest of us upright bipeds." He yawned and told her to go back to sleep.

She said she would but characteristically got in the last word. Fred Goldman had called. Three times. Yes, on the cutout number—at 7:30, 9:25, and a little less than an hour ago. Urgent, he said. Would Luke please call him back the moment he checked in from New York?

"He said that? About my checking in from New York?"

"He said it."

"And you said?"

"That I'd pass on the message."

"You didn't ask how he happened to come by your number?"

"Of course not. What do you think I am?"

"Or how he knew I was in New York?"

"Don't be ridiculous."

"And you said?"

"I asked how Marge was, and the children, and when he last looked in on them, and where I could call her."

"And what did he say to that?"

"He hung up."

SEVENTEEN

The way they had him hogtied, Garfield reasoned, he might just as well have made the Paris call from right there in the room, but somehow the idea jarred with his notion of how things should be done, and he dismissed it out of hand. So, taking coat and hat against the rain still hammering away at Gimbels's roof, he slipped out by the Thirty-third Street entrance and crossed Seventh Avenue to Penn Station. Not the Penn Station of old, of course: Time's wing'd chariot again, everything changed. This Penn Station was a glass palace of space age kitsch, black and silver, momentarily silent, vast and exhausted, a revelation to him, though there was nothing new about the lost souls haunting it at that hour, nothing new in that department whatever. He felt their eyes burning his neck as he marched to a rank of unoccupied phones and wished he hadn't been in such an all-fired hurry to play things by the book. There's such a thing as discretion, he reminded himself. Even when you're only playing games.

The first four phones he tried were dead. The fifth had been neatly beheaded, the sixth was coated in chocolate fudge (at least he hoped it was chocolate fudge). The seventh, praise be, gave him Paris and Joss telling the overseas operator he'd be glad to accept the call. They'd just finished breakfast, he reported, all quiet on the western front and Condition Green for Go. The girl a little overwound this close to the firing line and not too sure who her friends were, but no problem, he'd talk her down. Great weather for ducks in Paris that morning but otherwise looking goodish. As always, Garfield found the sheer pitch and languor of Sullivan's voice restful.

He went to the heart of the matter.

"Will she do it?"

"Oh, I think so."

"No last-minute doubts?"

"If there are, she's keeping them to herself."

"That's what I'm afraid of."

"She'll go. She'll let him find her. I'll take it from there. It's running, Luke. Give it a chance."

Joss, he remembered too late, had no nervous system in the accepted sense. He could not be hurried, worried, threatened, chivvied, angered, depressed, scared, or otherwise moved. If he experienced everyday feelings occasionally he was careful never to let them show.

Garfield said, "Those questions, did you run through them with her?"

"A to Z, can't fault her."

"You can add a couple more." He dictated, and Sullivan read them back. "And tell her I expect answers," he added irritably, mentally arming himself against future shock. "I want information I can check. Not promises, not lectures, not flights of philosophical fantasy—*answers*. And if Bartell won't talk, fine, we drop him. Wherever he is, whatever his condition. Cooperation, or there's no ticket home. That's the deal."

"I rather think she's *au fait* with all that." Joss censured him gently. In the background a voice intruded, a woman's voice, hoarse, not C.J.'s. Joss said calmly, "*Merci, non, madame. Et s'il vous plaît, fermez la porte.*"

"She'd better be *au fait*." Garfield went on. "Tell her that from me. And what about you? You're—"

"Champing at the bit, old boy. All set."

"All right." Garfield squared his shoulders and prepared for a tale at least as tangled as Clayton Waldren's. "The woman in Montreux. Who is she? What does she know?"

Afterward he remembered it physically as a sensation of being burned inside; inside each and every vein and artery and cell, a slow burning erupting finally in a massive cardiac arrest, but pleasurable. "Oh, *yes!*" he murmured at one point in Sullivan's report, and later, in a kind of ecstasy, "Well, I'll be damned!," and when Sullivan reached the point where Mena Sabbah had delivered up her soul and her conscience to Larry's "closest, dearest friend Jems Soolivahn" and in total confidence revealed the name Larry had shared with her—may Allah strike her down if Jems should dishonor her by repeating it—the name of Larry's *other* friend, you understand, Larry's friend and patron and protector in Geneva, though also the devil on his back, at mention of this name Luke Garfield so entirely forgot himself as to sigh like a lover requited and grin like a fool.

Full credit to Sullivan, who must have realized at this point that he'd touched an open nerve, that he kept his curiosity to himself, for Garfield was in no mood to enlighten him. On the contrary. First, he made him repeat the name and its context; then, to ease his mind, he demanded confirmation that no one —specifically C.J. Poole—was within earshot at the time, nor could she, by whatever miracle of artifice or accident, have acquired knowledge of the name since Sullivan's return to Paris yesterday. Then he questioned Joss closely on his drive to Montreux, on the condition of his tail throughout the journey, on his flight back to Paris, on the loyalty of his household. Finally, reassured on all points, he turned to check his rear and roll with this heaven-sent punch and, in doing so, observed a rangy young fellow with cropped hair and a ten-yard muffler lounge into a cubicle three down from his own and initiate a loud and suggestive call to a girl in Newark, New Jersey, on an instrument Garfield knew to be mechanically deceased.

With a ghost of a grin he turned back to the receiver. "Look, Fred, be reasonable, will you?" he said loudly, and was deeply gratified to hear the boy break off his passion in mid-sentence to catch the next line.

From Paris, Joss said lazily, "Feel the heat from here, old boy. Company?" and Garfield told him yes, it was unseasonably warm. On a firmer note he asked if Joss had heard from his father recently.

"Called him soon as I got back last night." A faintly mocking note entered Sullivan's voice. "Your friend Larry turned up after all, surprise, surprise. At the hospice. Clocked in around five-thirty. A.M., that is. Morning."

"Late."

"Very. Said he'd been sidetracked. Father John thought he was lying, but there you are—they all lie, don't they?"

"How did he introduce himself?"

"Luke Garfield called him from Washington; go see Father John Lattimore, rue Saint-Auban, somewhere to sleep if only the floor. Pretty much word for word what you told him to say."

"Was he alone? On foot? Cab?"

"Don't know. Lattimore wasn't there, didn't see him till after breakfast. By then the nuns had made him take a bath and logged him in."

"Under what name?"

"Laurens Tadeuz Eisenstern. Address Kiefernweg, Kronberg, West Germany. Born Hamburg May 26, 1932, Jewish. Trade, baker and pâtissier."

"Passport?"

"None offered."

"How'd he look?"

"Physical description fits, Lattimore says. Like a glove. Five-nine; eyes brown; hair curly gray; skin and bone. Speech style flip; manner nervous and probably neurotic; spoke perfect French. Educated but doesn't want you to think so." Joss paused. "I'd say he's trying to tell us something, wouldn't you?"

207

"Tell us what?"

"He went there, Luke. He clocked in, bedded down, chanced his neck. You said he wouldn't. You said he had no reason to trust you, so why should he go?"

"Exactly."

"So he's ready to play. He's saying there's nothing up his sleeve."

"Is he?" Ripples on a pool, wider still and wider, lapping and overlapping. Larry the chess master and his friend Miko from Geneva. A partnership? How long had it been going on? How many years? "When did he leave the hospice?"

"About midday."

"Alone?"

"As far as *he* knew, yes. One of Lattimore's hounds tailed him. A social worker, lady of a certain age, not Larry's type at all: head scarf, curlers, shopping bag, flat heels, the lot. But good. Thought she was minding a psycho. Capital liar, your Father John. Target took the metro, changed a couple of times, then cut into a house in the rue Galande, Left Bank. Stayed awhile, trickled round the corner to the quai Saint-Michel, house on the river—remember that old terrace across from Notre-Dame? traffic goes past there nowadays nonstop—went in there, top floor. About thirty seconds later—no exaggeration—he came pelting down again, bat out of hell, shot out onto the quay and —zoom!—gone."

"And?" Garfield was gripping the phone for dear life. He ran under a bus. Threw himself into the Seine and sank like a stone. Met his other friend from Geneva—

Sullivan coughed diplomatically. "All a bit too hairy for a lady of sensibility, I'm afraid, Luke. Target damned near landed in the poor woman's lap. She was halfway up the second flight, couldn't duck him, nowhere to run. Came very close to having a nasty accident. He must have seen her."

"So she quit."

"Withdrew," Joss amended, gallant in adversity.

"What did she do?"

"Went back to the hospice and briefed Lattimore. Time I got in from Orly and talked to Lattimore we'd lost three hours."

"What did you do?"

"I put a pair of eyes out front and one on the Boul-Mich in case there's a back way. They've been on site ever since. No movement in or out all night, nothing so far this morning, but there are lights on in there. Someone's up and about."

"Who owns the apartment?"

"No one I can put a finger on. Managed by a property agency in the boulevard de Courcelles, but they're only sub-agents for an agency in Ghent. Behind Ghent there's a Belgian holding company. But this is all hearsay, Luke, nothing firm yet. I thought it better not to pry till we'd had a chance to talk."

"No!" Garfield bit off the word, released his stranglehold on the receiver. "No, don't pry. Leave it be. Leave all of it." He glanced sideways at the muffler three cubicles down, and the boy, sensing a sea change, renewed his monologue *con gusto*. Under cover of it, Garfield said softly, swiftly, "Get your men off the quay. Now. Right away."

"Whatever you say, old boy. Your chukka."

"Just fixed points around the rendezvous, exactly as I told you. No loose tails, no idlers. None of that. Keep it all out in the open, and give him rein, plenty of loose rein."

"Roger."

"You're happy technically? No problems there, no hitches?"

"All done," Joss said.

"Good. Good." A dozen new worries now obsessed Garfield—new worries, ramifications of old ones, fears, doubts. Then it was over, and he said calmly, "Must be nearly time."

"Eight-fifteen here."

"Soon as you have anything. The moment she makes contact."

"Will do."

Garfield couldn't account for the walk back. One minute he was replacing the receiver, the next he was standing at the corner of Thirty-fourth Street with a hot dog in his hand, a soft white bun as long as a train and a million calories of phallic sausage leaking pork fat. A sign blinked at him from across the street, "Don't Walk," but in his head everyone was walking, a big parade, Larry Bartell in the lead in crisp tropical whites, then C.J. in a blouse of virginal lace, then Lydia and the wrong John Sayer, and Roy McKinnon shooing the kids ahead of him, and Mena Sabbah, and in an untidy wedge behind them, like mourners trailing a hearse, Fred Goldman, Don Sherwood, Brock Stafford, Tyler Bloomfield, Davis Lang, Ralph Kramer, and the crumpled, crippled, jackknifed caricature of Clayton Holmes Waldren, the sorcerer's apprentice. At the very, very end a short, stocky, prissily dressed figure strutted in their wake, maintaining a hunter's distance—Larry's other friend, you understand, his friend and patron and protector from Geneva. The devil on his back.

Miko Schellenberg, by all the saints.

Garfield turned for home, still in his trance, still parading dramatis personae, when without warning his left foot skidded from under him shockingly fast, outward and upward. His right foot took off in pursuit, and the world tipped crazily. In free fall he felt the earth rise to meet him and shrank from the blow. Oh, my God, Polly! And out of nowhere two powerful hands locked on his arm, and a great force swung him out and around and superhumanly up. All over in a fraction of a fraction of a second. No harm done. Breathless, numb, but no harm. Could have been your last moment on earth, he heard Polly cry out in anger. Cracked skull, brain damage, coma, death—happens to doddering old fools every day! Is that any way to go? Turning, dumbstruck, half expecting to find the muffler at his elbow or some other muscular hero of Langley's mobile army, he found himself staring instead into a black face as terrified as his own. Round, flat, grizzled, ruffed with curls the color of smoke; the body below it thick and work-hard straining out of a uniform of some kind—postman, guard, janitor, porter.

The face opened to gulp air. "Damn near bought it that time, mister!" Relief and anger mixed. "You damn near dead!"

"I wasn't looking. I slipped. I—" The words froze on Garfield's tongue. His heart was close to breaking through his ribs.

"People moochin' around this time a night! What for?" The black man's anger really ignited now. He swept a hand across the night, across the rain and the bog of pulped litter at their feet. "Ain't fittin', man your age. Ain't fittin', ain't healthy. What you lookin' for—a hot time? Well, I tell you—one a these nights this town's gonna sneak right up and break your ass, you hear me? *Break* it! More shit on these streets than sidewalk"—he turned to go—"and you better believe it, old man."

He was too proud to wait for apologies, gratitude, promises. He plowed off southward, head down, butting into the rain; deed done, mind spoken, soul saved. Seventy-five if he was a day.

Back inside, Garfield roused Nick Montero. Change of plans, he told him gruffly. They were going back to Washington. Tonight. Now.

He didn't say why, and Nick, of course, didn't ask.

EIGHTEEN

Joss wrenched the old Peugeot across three lanes of traffic and skidded into a gap at the lights.

"Oh, my God." C.J. opened her eyes. "Will you please—"

"Not to worry," he said breezily.

The rain was coming at them like black darts, dancing in fountains off the rusted hood, penetrating every torn seam and ligature of the rotten frame, hammering the roof like death's drummer.

"You nearly killed us!" she shouted over the racket.

"Oh, d'you think so?"

"*Think* so!"

"Relax. It's just nerves. Nothing to be ashamed of."

"Ashamed!" She put everything she felt into that word— pique, rejection, infatuated rage, terror—but it came out about

as forcefully as an old maid's premenstrual sob. "I . . . am . . .
not . . . ashamed!"

"Course not," he said, eyes on the lights. "Good girl."

"And will you, for the love of Christ, stop patronizing me!"

The love of Christ would have shaken him to his puritanical
core if he'd heard it, but he didn't. The lights changed, and he
roared away. They went like a bullet for a blind corner, cut in on
a mountainous truck, outmaneuvered a madman in a Lam-
borghini, and beat a second set of lights by a whisker.

"What are you doing?" she wailed, and he said something
soothing, but she missed it. They were now racing back the way
they'd come, weaving, swaying, occasionally skidding sideways,
the engine laboring frantically, tall, narrow housefronts to the
right, the Seine to their left. Then, without signaling a turn, he
swung off into a wide boulevard and—clatter, screech, bang—
went into a whining four-wheel glide across the sodden pavement of the place de la Bastille. She clung to the dashboard,
the seat, him, and when she dared look again, the rue de Rivoli
was unraveling ahead of them like a frayed nerve.

"What *for*?" she raged over the boiling engine and the thwap
of rubber and the keening bodywork. "What are you *doing*?"

"Just making sure we're alone."

She ducked as a bus loomed massively over them. "You don't
think it's going to work, do you? You think he won't come."

"Nonsense. Course he'll come. And I'll be with you all the
way. Guaranteed."

"Personal guarantee?"

But he didn't hear personal questions. Congenital deafness.

"How can you guarantee—" She began again, needle stuck in
the groove, but he'd given her up for Lent or something.

He wore a thin cotton shirt, a night-black short-sleeved show-
us-your-muscles sport shirt that clung to every hill and hollow
of him as if it had grown there. It was sodden from the walk to
the garage, but he didn't seem to mind. Rain doesn't register
with him, she thought. Rain or cold or traffic or me. Especially
me.

But that was no more than she'd expected. Everything about him was what she'd expected. Uncanny. Point for point, he was in every way what her overstretched imagination had made of him in the dark the night before last at the hotel. His shape and texture, his coloring, his look, manner, gestures. In repose, in thought, smiling, scowling, she knew him as if she'd designed him. Officer and gentleman. My friend Mr. Nobody. The dark side of the moon. Joss.

Wasn't Joss a Chinese idol? Or was it incense? Or luck? She ought to look it up, might be a clue there. Fourteen across: girl's last hope. Four letters.

More likely, though, it was a random code name. Garfield had simply warned him off, warned them all off. No names, no explanations; she's Larry Bartell's girl, his lifeline, his unbuttoned lip, not to be trusted. Not to be feared either, apparently, if her experience of yesterday was any guide.

Left alone with Mme. Félix and her butterball of a husband, she'd been given virtually proprietorial rights to the apartment. The *patron's* wish: Go anywhere, look at anything, Liberty Hall. So she'd taken full advantage, and it had gotten her nowhere. Of several thousand books in his library, not one she pulled bore an inscription. The study next door could have been a museum setting: Sheraton, Hepplewhite, Cheriton long case clock three years older than America, crystal tantalus, Jacobean goblets, woven silk rugs, nothing personal. The desk was barren of bills, billets-doux, invitations, checkbooks, diaries, notepads, mail of any sort. There were no photographs anywhere, no portraits in oil young enough to be recent kin; of family not an inkling; of wives or chatelaines not a clue. His bedroom—well, now, she'd reasoned, why not? Open house is open house, right? Look in, look around, just don't touch, that's all—and having searched it methodically, she emerged none the wiser. At that stage she'd begun to get distinctly paranoid. They'd locked his identity away, that was the answer—books, letters, signed pictures: "To darling Joss from Deirdre"—and yes, mam'selle, no, mam'selle, *invited* her to roam to her heart's content. Why not? Nothing to find. Trouble was, anger got you nowhere with a man whose responses were geared to questions you hadn't asked. Joss short for Josiah? Joseph? (No, not Joseph; whatever else he was, he wasn't a Joe.) Joshua then; Josh shortchanged to Joss. "You do *have* a name, I hope?" she'd demanded tartly over dinner, eye to eye across the silverware—quail, lobster thermidor, salad, cheese, fruit; M. Félix to serve at table, Haydn on the Bang and Olufsen, fresh flowers floating in a silver bowl; Hollywood gothic—but his reply was could she stand another glass of the Sancerre, and she hadn't had the courage to make an issue of it.

Hopeless.

At some point during the meal she may have given five seconds of her time to Larry Bartell, to Larry lying out there, dying out there for all she knew, waiting for morning, waiting for her; but as swiftly as she'd switched him on she switched him off again. Some other time, Larry, I'm busy right now. God, she'd thought, this is crazy, it doesn't happen like this. The paradox, of course, being that no one would have understood better than Larry that it always happened like this.

Joss cut in on her thoughts, unnaturally sharp. "Listening?"

"Listening," she snapped back.

They had crossed the river, and if anything, the rain was worse. To her right, the slim blade on the dome of Sainte-Chapelle glowed briefly in a vagrant sunbeam and went out again. The drenched bulk of Notre-Dame dripped into the Seine. On the quai Saint-Michel Joss hugged the river side of the freeway and at one point ducked his head and glanced up, but when C.J. looked, there was nothing to see, just rain pelting the dirt gray of an endless terrace and the braying traffic and raincoats wedged by the dozen in doorways. Farther on fountains of white water soared up from the river in a network of triumphal arches as a trio of *bateaux pompes* doused imaginary fires by the quai de Conti.

"I'm dropping you off at the Mabillon metro station, corner of rue du Four and Saint-Germain," Joss said. "Not far now."

"Oh!" She felt sick again.

"You follow the sign that says, 'Direction Gare d'Orléans Austerlitz.' Travel two stations. The first is Odéon. You get off at the second, Maubert Mutualité. Get up to the street, turn left, and cross the rue de Beauvais. Walk three blocks on the boulevard Saint-Germain. Rue Saint-Jacques runs across it. Did he say what corner?"

"What *corner*?"

"There are four."

They were passing gray blocks of learning. Young people of indeterminate sex, buglike in transparent ponchos and third-generation greatcoats, sprinted for the cover of doorways.

"He didn't say." She was having trouble with her air supply. "What do I—"

"You play it safe. You stick to one corner, the corner you reach by walking the route I've just told you. Don't stop when you get there; turn left and walk around the block. And remember, this is a funny neighborhood. All types: students, tourists, junkies, thieves, tarts, and a few plainclothes *flics* on the lookout for easy pinches. Pace yourself to reach the corner at twelve minutes past; that's all that matters. Then once around the block and walk away, any way you like but away, and walk as if you knew where you were going."

"Walk where? *Where* do I go for the next hour? Where—"

"Relax." His hand covered hers, barely touched it but left a mark deeper than a branding iron. "Go sit in a café. Inside, not outside. And never the same café twice."

"But what if—"

"I said I'd be right behind you. I will."

"Oh."

At the Mabillon metro station he leaned across her to open the door, and for a millisecond their faces touched; brushed anyway. Fractionally. "Now remember." He handed her out to the pelting rain. "You make three circuits and no more. Twelve minutes past ten, past eleven, past noon. If he's not there by

twelve-twelve, he's not coming, so walk west on Saint-Germain
—that's against the traffic flow, you follow me? I'll pick you up.
And don't worry, I'll find you."

Don't bother finding me. Just don't leave me.

He'd set her down on the wrong side of a pedestrian barrier,
in the street, in the slashing rain, the traffic roar intolerable,
blind panic advancing on her out of the midmorning twilight.
Her face said it all: This is mad! I'm not up to it! I can't do it!
And glory be, for once he got the message, took note. "Wait,"
he said, and for a moment she thought he was about to get out
and come to her, but he didn't do that. He ferreted for something behind his seat, drew it out, poked it through the open
door. A rolled umbrella. "Here," he said, "mustn't forget your
brolly. Catch your death in this weather."

Her fury sustained her all the way to Maubert.

Coming up into the light again, into the rain, opening his
damned umbrella against the black sky, breathing deeply to
calm herself, she remembered the last time, the last rendezvous
she'd kept in a cause briefly dear to Larry Bartell's heart.

New York, the fetid summer of '72, Columbus Circle, late
afternoon. She was to have made a pass to a Students Against
the War fugitive, a boy. "It's nothing, C.J., honest. Just one of
the brethren on his way south, nobody you know, needs bread,
a change of clothes, something to eat." Larry calling her from
Boston. "Favor, kid, personal to me. Just an itsy-bitsy little
valise, okay?" Con Ed had been warning all day that if people
kept their air conditioning running full blast, they'd blow the
city power supply. It was that kind of summer afternoon. Broadway stank, exhaust fumes crawled over the street like ground
mist; it was hard to breathe.

She'd never come so close to a disaster before. Heard about
them, read about them, but never had the experience. She'd
made four or five circuits of Columbus Circle and was trying to
look nonchalant when the world kind of stood still. It actually
seemed to stop. The traffic, the noise, the people; everything

froze except the principal actors. From down Broadway came shouting, then whistles, and a clapping sound she assumed later must have been shooting. Then several people were running, apparently toward the park. The one in the lead darted out onto Central Park South, a skinny kid in a plaid shirt and jeans. He made a very odd noise as he ran, a terrified bawling that looked and sounded like laughter. Twenty yards short of C.J. he got suddenly tired and knelt and folded. At that point he was swallowed up in the crowd. C.J. had dropped the valise where she stood and bolted, caught the next train back to Washington. When she asked Larry on the phone the next day, he said it hadn't been their man at all, probably some petty crook, but she couldn't believe that. He never asked her to make a rendezvous again.

At the end he hardly ever called her at all.

On the first circuit she timed it badly and reached the corner of the rue Saint-Jacques at 10:05. About-turning smartly, she took cover under a handy awning and made a show of brushing herself down, shaking the umbrella, but watching, all the while watching. Then she went back and mistimed it again: 10:14. A brisk walk around the block, and she was on the boulevard again, heading east. Bad move. She crossed the street and walked into the first café she came to: vast fake Lalique mirrors, booths with wooden seats, scrubbed tables deeply gouged with initials. She took out an aerogramme and began to write, Joss's idea— "It's what Americans do in Paris." Except she found herself writing to her dead mother, which was creepy. "Do you remember how you always promised we'd go to Paris someday? Well . . ."

On the second circuit the rain stopped and the sun came out. For ten whole minutes it was a different day and a different city. She no longer felt strange, knew where she wanted to go, the time it took to window-shop from here to there. Experience. An old man in a beret bowed to her comically from his newsstand—second time of seeing, she guessed—so she went over and tried out her high school French and bought a copy of *Life*. It gave her a tremendous lift, this simple act of commerce, so she did it again: Buying was a marvelous way of squandering time. Moving up on the Saint-Jacques corner by stages, she bought a box of genuine Montélimar nougat, a purse-size dispenser of Givenchy III toilet water, a pack of three incredibly expensive lace handkerchiefs, a pair of navy blue kid gloves, and volume one of *Les Thibaults* by Roger Martin du Gard—all from the roll of notes Joss had given her for pin money. At 11:12 exactly by her watch she turned the corner again and found she was still on her own: no touch on the arm; no whistles; no high signs. So back around the block again, and this time she did something quite daring: She turned the corner yet again and marched up the hill, keeping well clear of the gushing gutters, and took a stroll through the narrow streets around the Sorbonne. She found another café, well crowded, a student hangout, ordered coffee and a croissant, and stayed for half an hour. She was beginning to feel tired, a lot more tired than she had a right to be, but she put that down to tension. Hypertension. Larry.

He's not coming. He's *not* coming. Don't *let* him come.

Third circuit. The cafés of Saint-Germain were filling up, though not with the likes of Sartre and Simone de Beauvoir and the intellectual left of *The Mandarins*. The majority were tourists, nonentities looking for celebrities and finding only each other. How would she know him? she wondered, scanning faces at sidewalk tables. How would he know *her*? What would he say? At twelve minutes past midday she reached the corner for the last time, felt her heart stuttering as she pushed through a torrent of hurrying bodies, felt relief as she broke clear. Wow! All over. Thank God. Another day then. Tomorrow. Maybe she could persuade Joss to take her to the Louvre this afternoon. Maybe—

I could walk this route blindfolded, she thought gaily. Draw a map in my head. Left off Saint-Jacques into the rue du Sommerard; left again into the rue Thenard and down toward Saint-Germain. On her right, unless her French was totally cockeyed, the Special School of Public Works, and more kids in plastic ponchos, and a bell jangling inside, sounding the end of a work period. Tomorrow, when she did this part again, she would—

She felt eyes on her. For the first time that morning, eyes on her. Not just curious but intent. There was a difference. She glanced nervously over her shoulder—thieves, junkies, tarts, *flics* —but the street behind was clear, and she decided she'd imagined it. Imagination, woman! Eyes! But the stare drew her again, forced her to meet it, forced her to look up at a second-floor window of the École Spéciale des Travaux Publics into the eyes of a man in a brown raincoat. It was a big window, but he filled it, high and wide; a window traced with vague patterns where idle hands had doodled delicately in the dirt. A strong man, hard—she could tell that at a glance, even at that distance, instinctively—a strong, hard man in a brown raincoat, flat face, square jaw.

And then he was gone. Half a second? Less. Gone. Might never have been there. So fast she hadn't even stopped walking.

Oh, wow! Joss, you promised, you promised! Where *are* you?

She hurried on toward the boulevard Saint-Germain, but the street was suddenly overflowing with people, lots of people, tribes of workers swarming out of the hive, swarming home for the sacred ritual of lunch. Twenty yards on, and she was surrounded by them, their umbrellas crowding her umbrella, the gamey smell of their bodies crude and alien and animallike. She had to run to keep up with them now, to avoid being shoved from behind, tripped, toppled, pulled down, trampled on. Oh, Joss, please! *Please*? Then the bodies in front stopped dead and pooled out from the sidewalk into the street, into the narrow gully between the cars parked on either side, and she was swept out with them. A closed van pulled out from a parking space, a smooth, wristy swerve, tires screeching in the wet, and she thought, Thank God, it's Joss. But it wasn't Joss, it was a much smaller man, cap, dark glasses, raised collar. The van slowed, the door swung wide, and she felt hands on her, one at her waist, one high on her back, cutting off her line of retreat. "Wait!" she wailed, but someone pushed hard from behind, and she pitched into the seat. Behind her, other hands grabbed her feet and folded them in. The door slammed. The van spurted away.

She felt an arm reach over her and bang the door lock. Then they were turning this way, that way, and she was flung with the turns into the door, into his arm. She came upright at last, and he said, "Cool it, baby, dig? Don't bug me while I'm driving."

He was smoking a joint, a needle-thin joint, the tang of it sweet and heady, and for a moment he reminded her of Larry. But only for a moment. Then she began to shake, and there was nothing to do but sit there and let it happen.

NINETEEN

It was well after six when Happiboy led her down the path between the stones. The night was black as pitch outside the circle of candlelight and perfectly still except for the plop of rain in the puddles and the slow drip-drip of trees on the dead. Hearing them come, Larry took a long, strengthening slug from the plump bottle at his feet and turned again to his audience, his voice raised so Happiboy would know they had company.

"There are poets and poets," he said. "This one, my friends, was a poet. Listen." And he quoted the bit of the lyric he remembered.

If he'd recited in Swahili, he couldn't have made a more profound impression. They stared at him in awe, open-mouthed, or at that part of him they could see through the tent of blankets, for Larry was wrapped up like an old squaw, cocooned from head to toe, hands inside to conserve the heat. They sat, Larry and the four kids, on the low marble parapet of a grave, facing inward like friends cozy around a fire, their faces washed by the coppery sway of candle flames, their feet on the mortal remains of an American rock luminary long dead. The name on the stone was JIM MORRISON, cut in plain Tempo, no seraphs, and for eternity's sake some genius had fashioned the two O's into nuclear disarmament logos. Others had smothered the stone with initials.

"He wasn't no *poet*. He was a singer," protested the thin one from Roanoke, name of Poke, a man of several summers. "He had this group, The Doors. He was the king, bigger than Presley, bigger than anybody. I read about it in *Rolling Stone*."

"He was a dope," Larry said flatly, staring them down in turn, their covetous children's eyes, their unformed faces. "A dope and a dope for *this*." He uncovered his bottle and shook it at them. "He wrote lines, sang songs, bugged off, checked out, died in his bath right here in Paris. How big does that make him?"

"You knew him?" The boy in black leather goggled.

"I knew 'em all," Larry said.

The kids turned to the headstone. It was decked out like an altar with two fluttering candles in wine bottles and a cracked urn of rust brown roses and the dead man's marble bust with a joint in its mouth. The flat of the grave was a tangle of candy wrappers, bottles, and cigarette butts left by earlier worshipers; the upright writhed with graffiti and lipstick kisses. "My spy is in California and He knows," someone had written. Another disciple had carved a couplet from one of Morrison's songs.

"Scream of the butterfly, wow!" whispered Poke's sidekick, a green-eyed gnome from New Mexico made flame-haired by the candlelight. "That's almost kinda, you know, like—holy."

"That's almost kinda, you know, like—crap!" Larry lisped cruelly. "Butterflies only scream for junkies, girlie—and junkies are too numb to care."

"What are you then?" drawled the saggy blonde from Detroit on Larry's right. "Some kinda fucken social worker? Is that what you are?"

"No, baby." Larry patted her hand through the blanket. "What I am is some kinda fucken survivor from Suicideville, which is more than I can say for this guy." His heels played a sharp ratatat on Morrison's marble slab. "What I am is a guy who outlived all the poets with grit in their eyes and shit in their veins. I was there when the circus left town, honey. I saw the clowns with their faces off. Am I getting through to you?"

"You should live so long," said the blonde without a flicker of feeling. The ends of her fingers were toasted brown to the knuckles. The boy in black leather had a hand wedged in the open zip of her jeans.

A little way off, in the shelter of the trees, Larry heard Happi-boy cough. His what-the-fuck-is-it-now cough. His who-are-these-imbeciles cough. These imbeciles were, in fact, the Apostles of Total Innocence, a random selection of wide-eyed kids from all over the cretinous record-playing world for whom Jim Morrison was a saint and his grave a shrine. They had been streaming in since Happiboy dropped Larry at the graveside around ten o'clock that morning. (After all, Larry had argued, what better cover could a running man have than kids in search of a drugged dream?) They had come singly at first, then in groups—Americans, English, Irish, French, Italians, Scandi-navians, Japanese, Poles, Vietnamese; punks and straights and mods and rockers, some bearing flowers, some bearing cameras, most come to scrawl eighth-grade platitudes on Morrison's marble or other headstones within easy reach, all come to talk and stare. Great cover, innocence. Off and on an elderly keeper tried to shoo them away and sweep up the garbage they left all over the graves, but he hadn't bothered Larry much, in spite of the blanket, in spite of the occasional unaccountable outbursts of sobbing, because Larry in his lucid moments had talked of Chopin and Balzac and Bizet, whose bones also lay at rest here in Père Lachaise, and his talk had been scholarly, the un-mistakable voice of the academy. A mad scholar, *alors*, but indisputably *bien cultivé*.

"Hey, you know?" The boy Poke strained at Larry over his granny glasses. "They say he's alive still, old Jim Morrison— you hear that story, did you? They say he faked his dying and there's nothing under here but an empty coffin. Jim's off somewhere living free. It was his way of dropping out—right, Buzz?" He turned for confirmation to his green-eyed friend, who nodded gravely. "To escape the publicity machine is why he did it— and the media and the business freaks and the pigs and all that. And now he's living free." He repeated the phrase, moved by the sound of it. "Living free, yeah. Completely. Like, you know—free." He blushed under the concentrated power of their stares and raised a hand to his jaw to hide a mass of disfiguring acne.

Out of the dark, from a neighboring grave, a girl's voice sighed dreamily. "Yeah, yeah."

Larry sighed, too. "That's right, kid, he's living free. Rent free, right under your feet. Tell me something, is the whole of your generation this dumb or are you the pick of the litter? Listen to me. Life is a one-way street, lovers. You don't get to ride there and back just because you happen to play guitar and jerk off in public!"

"You're a foul-mouthed heap of shit!" hissed a southern puritan from the outer ring of darkness.

"Damn right, sugar!" Larry roared over his shoulder. "And I got that way keeping company with dead losers!" Except that it came out more like a hiss of escaping steam than a roar. The effort sapped him of every last ounce of strength. He convulsed. The kids watched, entranced at first, then with less enthusiasm. One by one they stood up.

"I think he's some kinda, like, you know—wino," said the boy Poke doubtfully, backing off. "Buzz, you wanna leave now?"

"He could check out, the way he's hackin'," said the boy in black leather. "I seen drunks hack up their guts that way."

The blonde from Detroit slipped a hand between his thighs. "Know of a better place to split the mortal coil, sugar bun? Come on, leave him. Let's go."

"Get outa here!" Larry croaked, going down for the third time. "Get . . . out . . . of . . . here! Ba-ha-ha-ha-hastards!"

They laughed—scared laughter, uncertain—and, having laughed, were obliged to retreat or face the consequences of squaring up to a bum in a blanket who drank schnapps straight from the bottle.

The schnapps!

Wallowing in agony, Larry bowed over his pit of pain and, head down, out of Happiboy's line of sight, whipped the bottle from under his blanket and jammed it in his mouth. He gulped giant mouthfuls, quickly, greedily, spilling the stuff down his chin onto his shirt, not caring. He heard a low growl burst from Happiboy, heard his feet thudding over the soaked gravel toward him. "You dumb shithead! You crazy goddamn lunatic bum!" But Larry only gulped faster, lights going on all over the bleak, unpromising world, and gagged as it blew back on him, and sucked one last glorious, throat-searing swallow before Happiboy vaulted the headstone and snatched the bottle and sent it spinning through the dark to smash on some other mortal resting place. "You dumbhead! You chiseling, thieving, double-crossing little—I'll *kill* you! Hear what I say? I'll—" But then C.J. came into the sway of candlelight, and he turned and chucked his arms in the air and said, "He's all yours. All yours. Just get him outa my life, will you?"

At that moment—Meaningful Moments in a Charmed Life: Final Episode—Larry Bartell sideslipped off the parapet onto the flat of the slab. Legless. No feeling. His head cocked up on the headstone; his arms fell anywhere. He was much shorter than Jim Morrison, he noticed: he'd need a smaller grave all around. He saw C.J.'s face swim over the headstone, and then the tears got in the way.

"Larry?" she said.

He had nothing to say. Nothing to say it with. No voice, no strength.

"He's crying," she said.

"Get the chair over here," Happiboy ordered, no-time-for-tears. "And keep an eye out for those fu—for the kids."

"Why does he need a wheelchair?" She sounded like someone in a dream. A bad dream.

"Because he's a growing boy who needs his rest," Happiboy snarled, and bent his wiry whip of a body and heaved Larry up, rag doll floppy, and rolled him over his shoulder and stood up. Powerful little bastard, Happiboy. Pride of the 101st Airborne.

"Here, get the damn chair straight, will you?" he ordered. "Right. That's better. Now hold it."

Larry felt himself dumped, though minus the sensation commonly associated with being physically handled. He watched C.J.'s left hand float through space, hesitate within an inch of him, then touch his cheek, as an unwary child might stick its hand in a flame or touch a leprous clubfoot. It withdrew sharply.

"He's cold," she whispered. "He's . . . deathly cold."

"Belongs in a fu—in the morgue," Happiboy said brutally. "What I've been telling you." He threw the wet blanket over Larry's knees and tucked it in. "Where'd you get the fucken booze from, you little crap artist?" he hissed in Larry's face, right in under his nose. Larry smiled. What he could do, if nothing else, was smile. Beatitude. State of grace. Happiboy pulled back and got the chair rolling—bumpety-bump. "He stinks of booze. You'll have to watch the bastard like a hawk. Christ knows where he gets it from."

Something in his tone alarmed C.J. very badly indeed. Larry heard the tremor in her voice; knew it of old. Oh, C.J., oh, girl, panic now and you're dead. We're all dead.

"Aren't you coming with us?" she stammered.

Oh, boy, thought Larry; surely to God you know the answer to that one? Old Happiboy's fixing to bail out, baby. Lotsa deals cooking, would you believe? Pots to mend and junk to push. Like, friendship is sweet, but business is forever.

"Am I coming with—look, I'm sorry. Okay? He's not my problem anymore."

"You think he can take care of himself?"

225

"He's got you to take care of him. You just got through telling me—"

"I'm *alone!*"

Oh, C.J., oh, girl. Don't say that. Don't even think it.

But Happiboy didn't believe her either. "Sure. You're all alone. Anything you say. Come on—this way."

"I mean it! There isn't anybody else. I thought—we thought he was—well, mobile. On the phone he was fine; he sounded fine. He didn't say—" She was having difficulty keeping up. Happiboy was almost running with the wheelchair now, running away, Larry thought, running out of time, patience, moral justification. "*Please?* I can't do it alone. I thought he'd be—"

"I'm *finished!*" Happiboy stopped so fast she ran into him. "I wash my fu—my—" His forbearance in the presence of a lady finally deserted him. "I wash my fucken hands of the crazy little shitball, hear me? Period. End. Final. You dig? I picked him up; I risked my neck for him; I gave him a place to hang out. I cleaned him, fed him, checked in at that fucken junkie palace for him. I brought him here this morning. I checked you out, I picked you up, I spent four hours loopin' the loop around this godforsaken shithole of a town making sure the two of you had a clean pair of heels, nothing to worry about. And what's he do to me, the prize fuck? How does he thank me? He gets stoned! All over again he gets stoned." He shoved off again, moving fast toward the green, blurry glow of the streetlamps. "No thanks, sugar. No more. Not for him. Not for you. Not for the fairy on the Christmas tree. You're on your own. And believe me, before you know it, you will be. He'll die on you before you can make it home. And fucken good riddance," he bawled in Larry's ear. "Little runt!"

Larry smiled. Larry gave him—gave them both—the benison of his full and frank and fruitful smile. And closed his eyes wearily on the draggy tears. And let the pain take him on another long ride down to the cool, cool dark.

TWENTY

"Shall I play it over?" asked Polly.

"Might as well." Garfield turned the chair so he was facing the window of Don Sherwood's private office: Washington sunlight outside, April showers, a rainbow, creeping tentacles of midday smog. All things to all men, this damned town, he thought, and barked fretfully down the line, "What's keeping you, woman?"

"I'm rewinding the tape. For heaven's sake, Luke!"

"Oh." He stuck the pipe in his mouth and clamped down on it hard. He had been up since eight-thirty, barely two hours' sleep after the drive down from New York, but nothing short of Pentothal could have kept him in bed this morning—and probably not even that. In Paris it was raining. He'd called the hospice from a public phone. John Lattimore had been out making his rounds of the local sinbins, but a nun had told him it was raining. Heavily. "I guess the Lord has His reasons," she'd said in a soft Kentucky burr. Garfield had no answer to that.

"Ready?" Polly called down the line.

"When you are."

He heard the hiss and crackle of a long-distance line, then Polly's opening, "This is Montero Cars, good morning," and Joss's urbane "This is Joss." A pause. "We have a connection. Time here, eighteen-oh-four. She's alongside. I have to be quick. There are three of 'em: target, a cutout, and Orange Four." Orange Four was C.J. "The cutout is male; I can't identify. He's using a closed van, unmarked. He made the pickup at twelve-fifteen, been shaking his tail ever since. They made touchdown four minutes ago. That's all."

"Wait! Where are they? Is she all right?" came Polly's voice urgently, and Garfield rolled his eyes at the ceiling.

"That's all," Joss repeated politely. "I'll be in touch." The line went dead.

"Sorry about that," Polly said, coming back on.

"No comment. Anything else?"

"Fred Goldman called again, every hour on the hour since eight o'clock. Making seven calls in all since last night. Call him urgentest."

"Must be getting damn near critical by now, whatever it is," Garfield said comfortably.

"Then try calling him back, why don't you?"

"Oh, he'll find me when he really needs to. You bearing up over there?"

"Thrill a minute."

"Thought you'd like it. I'm at Don Sherwood's office. Call you later."

"Lunch would be nice," she said archly. "For a change."

"Yes, wouldn't it? Pity you can't spare the time."

Donald Sherwood tossed his briefcase into a corner, his hat at a peg and his coat at the floor. He glanced at Garfield, perched feet up in his chair, and frowned. "You still here?" Disappointment. "Sorry. Had to step out."

"Urgently," Garfield murmured noncommittally.

"What?"

"Your secretary said it was urgent. Said you wouldn't be back before lunch. I said I'd wait anyway."

"Oh. Yeah."

Resentment poured off Don Sherwood like steam off a lathered horse. He glared again at Garfield's scuffed brogues canted up on his desk and started to say something, then thought better of it and turned his back on him, stripped off his jacket and flung it violently at a chair, bit off the end of a javelin-length Havana and spit it into a wastebasket, kicked off his loafers, loosened his tie, stomped down the room from door to window and back again, testing for evidence of disturbance, not once looking his visitor in the face. Finally he planted himself at the window, looking out.

228

"You stuck to that chair, or is this gonna be a stand-up fight?"

"Fight?" Garfield was at his most saintly. "We have something to fight about?"

"Okay, so I'll take the couch. See if I care." The humor was labored, and so was the act of retreat. He swung his feet onto the chesterfield with exaggerated comedy, and the performance was so out of character it hurt. His socks today were bright scarlet, to match the bright scarlet of his shirt. "What am I supposed to do now?" he demanded.

"I just thought we might talk about Waldren, Don," Garfield said mildly. "That's all."

"So tell me about Waldren." The scarlet socks began metronoming very fast, flick-flick, flick-flick: anxiety, tension, frustration, all there.

"You mean he hasn't called you?"

Sherwood sighed. "You know you're one hell of a pill to take sometimes, Luke, anybody ever tell you? Okay, so I talked to Waldren this morning. So what?"

"Not last night? I was sure he'd call you last night. Minute I left him, in fact."

The senator teetered on the brink of denial but pulled back in the nick of time. "All right! It was last night. So make a liar out of me for twelve hours."

Garfield eyed him with a professional executioner's detachment. "Who said anything about lying, Don? You have a right to protect your sources, a fundamental right; we all have. And I've no doubt there are situations where your moral responsibility to Congress obliges you now and then to economize with the facts." It was about as far as he was prepared to go to give Sherwood a way out. There was always a first time with professional friendships. "But why should we lie to each other? Doesn't make sense. Implies a lack of trust. And I'd be the last man to accuse you of that."

"Luke, listen to me, will you?" The feet momentarily froze in mid-swipe, then started again; the cigar gushed smoke. "Sometimes the ice is just too thin—understand what I'm saying? Sometimes it won't take the weight of more than one man at a time."

"You mean you're worried about getting your feet wet."

"*Our* feet wet. Everybody's."

"Ah, so we're *all* out there on the ice, are we?" Garfield struck a match and set it to the blackened tobacco. The fog from his pipe and from Sherwood's cigar joined forces in the middle of the room and made a mushroom cloud. "Well, well. So who's *everybody*? I wonder. Your constituents, whom God preserve? The population of Washington, D.C.? The United States? Civilization as we know it? Or aren't you at liberty to say?"

"Luke, will you drop it? Please?"

"Political mileage, you said." He mimicked. "I can smell it, and I can build on it. But not what Waldren's peddling, you said. Larry Bartell is strictly fringe."

Sherwood groaned. A pantomime groan. "You were always a shitty loser. Always!"

"Then tell me who or what you're trying to protect, Don." He blew out the match. "What's at stake? Your image in Congress? Your reputation back home?"

"Neither. Both."

Garfield allowed a stretched pause, then said softly, "The Texas Arrangers got you over a barrel by any chance?"

"No! Goddamnit, Luke, will you knock it off!"

"Hmm." Garfield puffed contentedly. On the wall behind the desk, Mondale's campaign grin cut maniacally across Roosevelt's paternalism. In the outer office there was laughter, the incessant tintinnabulation of telephones, the pecking of typewriters. Garfield opened his feet to get an unobscured view across the desk of Sherwood's flushed and scowling face.

"You know, Don," he said evenly, "we can sit here sparring all day, if that's the way you want it. But it won't change a thing, and you know it. You know me. In the long run I'll worm it out of you, fair means or foul. In the end you'll talk."

"I'm not your man, dammit! Wrong man, wrong time, wrong place. Believe me, Luke, I'm a branch line."

"All branch lines lead to Rome. In time."

"Not this one. Not me. Believe me, will you? Just take my word for it?"

"Oh, but I do, Don. I do take your word. I believe you. I believe in you. But you see, I'm under an obligation here, a moral obligation. What are you under?"

"A fucken *steam* press!" Sherwood roared, and outside, everything stopped at once. He leveled his cigar, arm out and shaking. "Now get outa here, Luke, will you? And wait. That's all you have to do now, understand? *Wait*."

Garfield stared at him for a long time, then lowered his feet slowly to the floor and stood up. "Well, I guess that's it for the time being then." He picked up his coat and shrugged it on. "Pity, though. Seems to me you have more to learn about what's going on here than I do. Still, as you say, wrong man, wrong time, wrong place." He had talked himself to the door, and as he opened it, he looked back at his perspiring opponent. The senator seemed smaller somehow, reduced. "Never was much point in beating a dead horse, Don," he said sadly.

Sherwood came up off the chesterfield very fast. "What do you mean by that? Dead horse?"

Garfield grimaced as if in pain. "Just take care of yourself, Don, you hear? And love to Julia when you see her."

"Look, wait a minute, will you, Luke? I—"

'And tell Fred Goldman you did him proud,' Garfield said through the closing door. "Tell him I said so."

It was a good deal harder to get out of the Capitol building that year than in, a tedious and irksome chore debatably worth the wear and tear it cost on nerves and temper. Shorn of his White House pass of passes, Garfield was denied the privilege of floating above the herd, and the experience came as a shock.

Marine guards manned barriers on every staircase, reminders of the high profile now granted the antiterrorist movement.

More marines patrolled offices, committee rooms, lavatories, maintenance areas, and boiler rooms, and not neat, white-capped, blue-jacketed marines either, but young thugs in combat camouflage and flak vests who impaled you on arrogant stares from the moment you entered until the moment you left. And if, God forbid, you should have the bad luck to trigger one of their metal detectors, they'd strip you naked without a thought. To get in, Garfield had been obliged to acquire three separate passes, color-coded to mark the hour of the day, the day of the week, and the status of the barrier of issue. To get out, he had to return them, duly stamped and signed. "Failure to produce your pass of origin may cost you the rest of your day," warned the notices malevolently. Outside—when he finally got outside—a marine checkpoint blocked the top of the steps, and a second lay in wait at the bottom, just inside the labyrinth of concrete antiterrorist fortifications that now flanked the Hill on three sides. Heaven help the man who raised his voice or in any way spoke out of turn at this point, for good old American courtesy and humor were constitutionally out of fashion hereabouts, and the snap judgments of soldiers living by the book were inclined to be harsh. "A difficult person is a dangerous person," read an Orwellian note to the wise on the back of the main entry permit. It was not intended as a joke.

Garfield fell into line at the top of the steps, a long line at that stage of the lunch-hour exodus, and began to fill his pipe. He applied the lighter and was raising smoke when a firm hand nudged his elbow and a flak-jacketed marine not long out of diapers snapped, "Sir, no smoking this side of the lower checkpoint, sir!" and slapped the butt of his ugly machine pistol for greater emphasis. He was carrying one of the new Ingrams, Garfield noted, a design cousin of the ray gun Flash Gordon toted in the comic strips.

"Whatever you say, son," Garfield mumbled, swallowing his pride. The boy stepped back a pace but continued to watch him.

Fretfully Garfield stuffed the pipe into his pocket and wondered, not for the first time, how in God's name things had gotten this far.

Like most Washingtonians, he'd been too busy to arch more than an amused eyebrow when the initial program of anti-terrorist construction got under way in the early eighties. This won't last, he could remember thinking, eyeing the grotesque concrete structures going up in the glorious approaches to the White House; this has to be temporary, a fad. But fads had a way of developing their own momentum, and this one proved to be a runaway success; a lot of very patriotic people were soon making fortunes out of it. So the concrete grew and multiplied, and not long after the first wave of anti-American bombings and shootings in Europe a few years later, it actually quadrupled its area. Great barriers took root around Capitol Hill, sprang up in defense of the State Department, the Pentagon, the FBI, the Department of Justice, Embassy Row, the World Bank, Blair House.

As a longtime student of national psychoses Garfield had guessed what might follow and had duly issued warnings in the highest places—to no effect. His minutes were ignored, along with his trite observation that if you create a mountain, someone somewhere will feel compelled to climb it. In due course someone did.

The first positive response was a wave of telephone bomb threats, all hoaxes and mostly teen-age in origin; then, fed and watered by lavish media coverage, hundreds more. Harmless, as a columnist put it, if you didn't count the police time.

Later on the more ingenious hoaxers eschewed the telephone and took to issuing their warnings through the computer networks. Several pirate messages came up on the White House-Pentagon link, and one fourteen-year-old genius actually sneaked his "Pay up or die" gag onto NORAD's early-warning console. Meanwhile, the fortifications became a natural canvas for a *nouvelle vague* of aerosol artists, a breed much given to candid graffiti on a bold scale, and the public cleaning bill soared. In the end, of course, as Garfield had forecast, the challenge of the mountain itself became too compelling. Somebody simply had to take on all that concrete.

It happened one weekend in late August. A "commando" of four well-dressed boys and a comely girl took a train to Washington and attempted to blow up the recently armored National Gallery of Art, a target of almost inexhaustible publicity value. It was a failure, luckily. The bang fizzled, and the kids were caught red-handed, though being well-brought-up middle-class radicals with caring parents and excellent lawyers, they were out on bail in less than thirty-six hours. Their "cause" was acid rain; they were against it, though the girl insisted the "commando" was also at least technically in favor of new equal rights legislation.

After that bomb threats fell away to two or three a month, the only disturbing new element being that half of them were genuine, small but real. Random attacks on public buildings for purposes other than burglary—i.e., vandalism, arson, "strategic burglary"—rose alarmingly, and assaults on local and national politicians in the course of speaking engagements doubled and tripled, particularly in cities with university campuses. The "freedom to act" developed an endemic currency among the young and wishfully young, and leaks of classified material to the media by morally indignant administration officials became so commonplace that the Texas Arrangers reduced the number of presidential press conferences to fewer than one a month.

There were times, Garfield recalled, when he had to pinch himself to believe that it was really happening in his America. Times when Larry Bartell might never have left.

But the Great Plus, as the man in the Oval Office described it without a trace of sarcasm, was that weighed in the scale of world terrorism, America's domestic brand was "pretty small potatoes." Better still, American soil was still providentially free of the taint of imported terror, "because the odds are too high

for those people to try it over here." And something else he'd
said in that broadcast; what was it? Oh, yes. "What we should
all be more concerned with is the safety of American citizens
abroad. Because the real dilemma for a democracy in the new
age of vandalism is how to protect our people overseas and
cling, at the same time, to some remnant of civilized conduct."

"Sir, your pass, please, sir!"

Garfield had reached the head of the line. A marine sergeant
barred his way.

"Sir, you have some kind of personal identification, sir?
Driver's license, personal correspondence? No, sir, we don't
take credit cards."

Garfield produced his wallet and tried in vain to unstick the
lunatic grin irresistibly gummed across his face; he could feel
it there, fixed and ineradicable. Dear God, that was *it!* Part of
it anyway. A large part. The dilemma for democracy. How to
protect our people overseas and still retain some remnant of
civilized conduct. My God! A phone. He had to get to a phone.
Brad Cotten; before he slipped out for lunch.

"Sir, thank you, sir. Sir, you hand your pass to the man on
duty at the lower checkpoint, sir, with this exit clearance, sir."
He stamped it hard. "Sir, have a good day, sir."

Garfield practically Fred Astaired down the steps. Scale, he
thought, plunging downward much too fast. Reduce it to manageable scale. Sift the pieces; toss out the conflicting ones; make
a cohesive whole of the rest.

They'd been brandishing the truth in his face all along. "This
is a farce," they'd been bellowing in his ear nonstop since the
night Fred Goldman rowed out to *The Duchess*. "We're sub-
jecting you to intensive farce in the interests of—"

Of what? Was it really all for the purpose of returning Larry
Bartell to the country of his benighted birth?

He reached the lower checkpoint and handed his papers to
another marine sergeant. He was given a pink card in return.
"Sir, use this next time you're over. Keeps the traffic moving,
sir."

Garfield pocketed the card. "Thank you, Sergeant." He released another lunatic grin. "Thanks for everything."

He caught Brad Cotten at Rudi's, a chophouse newly ascendant among Washington's nudge-and-whisper brotherhood. The tables were equipped with phones for the benefit of tyros who needed to be seen talking out of school.

"I'm with a friend here, you know?" Cotten's natural cynicism had no overlay of subtlety.

"All right. If he asks, we're talking appointments. Government service, local service, that area."

"Shoot."

Garfield had settled for a phone in a bar currently filling up with the lunchtime crowd. He glanced quickly at the faces immediately in range. How would I know, he thought irritably, if they *were* heel tappers?

"Brad, listen. You talked about two thousand friends of ours, remember?"

"Sure, I remember."

"And the people out on the Beltway said they had turned up working for agencies in the Brooke-Davis group. Ex-CIA—"

"First-class brains with first-class frames," Brad Cotten said down the line, and Garfield guessed he was trying to impress his tablemate.

"Right. So you said. But was there anything else? Anything special your contacts mentioned?"

"Such as?"

"Brad, I don't want to lead you. This is important."

"Ah, wait a minute. You mean about their being, uh, ethnic Americans? Is that the polite term these days?"

Garfield had to delay his reply for a second or two; his mouth had gone dry. "How ethnic, Brad?"

"Blacks, Arabs, Asians, Eskimos for all I know. But Italians, too, and Hispanics, Germans, French—I don't know."

"All racial backgrounds."

"The whole teeming world, Brother Luke. Far as I know."

"Anything else about them stand out?"

"Their skills, you mean? Yeah, they all had second strings to their bows. Engineers, doctors, pilots, all kinds."

"Anything else?"

Cotten barked his impatience down the line. "What do you want for your money, Brother Luke? Total recall?"

"Preferably. What was the feeling about them out there on the Beltway?"

"They were all really gifted guys, Luke, and that was the rub. Kinda made people wonder why they were fired in the first place. All that talent, tough, clean-living, topnotch degrees, languages—"

"Their own languages? The languages of origin, I mean?"

"Sure. The Chinese talk Chinese, the Italians Italian, the Arabs—"

"I'll get back to you later," Garfield interrupted, and hung up quickly.

When he was outside again and padding aimlessly in the bright sunshine, the realization surfaced with scarcely a ripple of surprise: Brad Cotten was part of the playlet; of course, he had to be. A key element even. Cotten, after all, had had the job of pointing the patsy at Sherwood, of coming up with all those fascinating data on the Beltway Bandits. As an outsider he couldn't be trusted to keep a story like that to himself. But as an insider, as the beneficiary of some future favorite son treatment? Oh, yes.

Scale, again. Reduce the imponderables to manageable scale.

He came to a halt at the curb. The towers of the Senate Office Buildings were at that moment somewhere to the rear, if he remembered correctly, and over there, yes, the Plaza; that had to be the statue of the immortal Taft. But the elderly blue Plymouth that pulled up between him and the view was entirely strange to him, and so, in the visual sense at least, was the man who slid out from behind the wheel, a stocky, unspectacular man wide as a barn door, big feet planted squarely to distribute the load. His glasses were the reflecting kind and showed

Garfield twin images of himself, whale-shaped hulks with pin-heads and flyaway, spiky hair.

"Hi, Mr. Garfield." He had that facility which comes with long practice of speaking without actually appearing to move his lips. "Name's McKinnon, Mr. Garfield." A slight frisson of activity rucked the corners of his mouth. "Maybe John Sayer mentioned me."

TWENTY-ONE

"Mr. McKinnon."

Garfield subconsciously noted the physical manifestations of Mr. McKinnon's professional status. The car was younger than it was made to look and equipped for high-speed pursuit: sculpted wheel arches; wide support tires; fishtail exhausts. It carried three aerials—flyback, coil, and ring—and a magic coating on the windows that turned the outer surfaces to mirrors. Also, the summer-weight hound's-tooth Mr. McKinnon wore so tightly across his built-up torso was too snug to conceal the holster. A left-handed shooter, too, Garfield noted, a breed much prized over in Fairfax County as princes of the short-range art.

"Maybe you'd like to get in the car," McKinnon said politely.

Garfield shook his head. "No, I don't think so, thanks. Not just now."

Which would have been the moment to start running, if running had been an option, had the door not swung wide and a voice appealed snappily from inside, "Please, Garfield, a few minutes of your time. I give you my word there's nothing to fear."

Analyzing his motives later, Garfield reached the conclusion that he complied for no better reason than that the voice seemed to him to belong to an honorable man (whatever that meant in the contemporary scheme of things). He climbed in, and they shook hands across the armrest, no introductions necessary.

McKinnon slid into the driver's seat and without looking around asked, "Where to, Mr. Bloomfield?"

"Garfield?" Tyler Bloomfield's response was nicely deferential.

"You tell me," Garfield said.

"You're still using Dr. Mickelson's apartment at the Watergate, I guess. We can go anywhere you wish."

"The Watergate'll do."

"Hear that, McKinnon?"

"Yes, sir."

"Go there."

Crisp, decisive, unambiguous, it fitted his personality perfectly. Impatient with fools, Garfield recalled, mentally pulling the file. A hacker out of deadwood, a leader from the front (unlike Larry Bartell), a follower of his own advice. All the virtues, they said. And handsome, no denying that. Square-jawed, work-pale, silver-haired, with just the right amount of patrician remoteness. A touch of the heretic hunter in the line of the mouth, though Garfield took leave to doubt that he was much of a hypocrite. Paradoxically there was something of the fallen angel in him, too, the well-meaning angel fallen on stressful times. Twenty cents in every dollar to charity. Church on Sunday. Polly would approve. Definitely approve. So what was he? A saint? A zealot? A Holy Joe? A crank?

A Christian idealist who made guidance systems for space missiles, that's what he was. A devoted father who raised private armies to combat future shock.

Bloomfield settled his back poker-straight in the far corner. "I guess I could say I was just passing. Happy coincidence." He took hold of the wide platinum wedding band on his left hand and began turning it around and around. "A lot of people involved in this mess"—he shot a hard look at Garfield to make sure he'd registered the word—"regard lying as mandatory. *De rigueur.* They see it as a kind of strategy."

239

"So I hear."

"Well, I don't happen to have that kind of mentality, and from what little I know of you, you don't either. Is that a fair assessment?"

Garfield raged inwardly at the man's patronizing tone but bit back a tart rejoinder. "I'd like to think so," he managed, and reached for pipe and lighter to give his hands something to do.

"Then let's settle for the fact that we know who we are and why we're here, shall we? No game playing."

"Suits me."

"Good."

Bloomfield's steady, tiger-bright stare took him in from head to toe, chestnut-bronze irises flecked with black and gold. If he recognized an equal, he made no attempt to show it.

He said slowly, "I have two functions here. The first is to assess what you know and what you don't. The second is to fill in any obvious gaps." He paused. "There was a third—to make a value judgment on your integrity as a public servant—but I don't think we need concern ourselves with that."

"My integrity is in doubt, is it?"

"Not with me." Bloomfield gave him a twist-of-lemon smile and tapped a matte black grille over his head. "I had the advantage of listening in to your meeting with Sherwood just now. I'd say your integrity's intact."

"Thank you. And does Sherwood know you have his office bugged?"

"Sorry. Not my province."

"No, I guess not."

They were passing the White House, and Somebody was just in from the airport, a VIP Somebody worthy of a helicopter and a full military turnout. Crowds gaped at the railing. On the Ellipse, flags fluttered bravely over a marine band. The sun drew flashes of white fire from the silver instruments. Martial sweetness and light.

Bloomfield watched the tableau slide by. "It's been a long

road. I'd like you to know it wasn't my idea to make you walk it."

"If that makes you feel better, fine by me." Garfield raised smoke clouds. "So what am I supposed to say next?"

"That's up to you. What you've learned. What you've guessed. Anything relevant."

Garfield nodded as if he found this eminently reasonable, but he continued to puff away for a good half minute more, part of his mind in Paris. At length he said in a rush, "Yes, well, I suppose someone had the 'great idea,' didn't they? Someone usually does. Brock Stafford most likely, knowing him. It sounds like him: big risk; big budget; big dividends. If it works."

"Won't it work?"

But Garfield hadn't heard him. "An American Foreign Legion, kind of, that was the idea. An antiterrorist strike force, low-profile, high-voltage. An underground, clandestine force made up of ethnic Americans functioning on what maybe three or four generations back had been their home soil." He took a look at his companion's face, but it was entirely without expression. "Asian-Americans, Italian-Americans, Dutch, German, Hispanic, Belgian, Arab, whatever you needed. Deep penetration was the objective, wherever the terrorists were most active or hardest to dig out."

"As you say, ambitious," Bloomfield said, apparently to the back of McKinnon's head.

"And dangerous. Dangerous tactically, but a damn sight more dangerous politically. American agents fighting without invitation on foreign ground? Or did you expect to be invited?"

"Your story, Garfield. Your privilege."

"I see. Uninvited, then. More usually a wartime assignment. But then I'm sure someone has already pointed out this *is* war. Americans dying all over the world—the bomb, the gun, the knife, torture, kidnap. Innocent people, businessmen, tourists, priests, the sitting ducks of terrorism. How many dead since the Libyan bombing? Two hundred? Three? Five? A thousand?

Davis Lang would know. A great man with figures, old Davis. But statistics are only relative, Brock would have said; what counts is the principle, and the principle here is to hit back. Scream foul. Crack nuts with steam hammers."

"You make your point," Blloomfield said heavily. "What next?"

"Recruitment. CIA personnel were obviously ideal. They had the required cultural input and a multi-ethnic range of choice. Of course, there was a big problem there, too. The men you were looking for were the best of the breed—five- to ten-year men, proven material, mentally sound, morally committed, nothing off the peg. But once you'd found them, you had to cut them out from the herd, and the only way you could decently do that without signaling your punch was to fire them. Cut out the fat, as we say in the bureaucracy." He chuckled. "Two thousand top Company men fired overnight! The fat!"

"President's campaign pledge," Bloomfield said in a bored monotone. "Policy, everyone knew it. Next?"

"Next was distribution. Feeding the men out to where they were needed: half the countries in Europe, I suppose, and all the others we know about—Africa, Asia, the Mideast. Couldn't just send them out with a loaded suitcase and a tube of suntan lotion. There had to be a whole bag of logistical checks and balances and a mountain of justification. And this is where the Beltway Bandits came in: Brooke-Davis and all those fat new government contracts—desalination experiments in the gulf; nutrition schemes in the Horn of Africa; computer technology in Europe. Whole slew of opportunities there for seeding bright young agents in the right places. And when that option ran out, there was always Stellatronics and the Bartell Corporation, multinationals with tentacles in every kind of little pie and hard-working young men doing their bidding. No trouble at all to slip a few of your new legionnaires into the commercial ranks."

"None at all."

Garfield squinted through the pipe smoke. "How am I doing?"

"Surprisingly well."

"Good. Timewise, my guess is you had the distribution stage under way toward the end of last year, just before Christmas. Everything under control, matters proceeding smoothly, the men moving out in groups, settling in. Then Larry Bartell hit you."

Bloomfield's tiger stare turned Garfield's composure inside out. "Hit us with what?"

"Ah, now that I couldn't tell you. Whatever it was that threw you into a panic over Lydia." He sucked noisily on the dead pipe. "Whatever it was that made you take her out of that apartment, out of circulation. And that newspaper ploy, my God!"

"You think that was our doing, do you?" Bloomfield half smiled and shook his head. "The newspaper ploy was Larry Bartell's idea, his and his alone. It was his way of applying pressure."

"On whom?"

"On Lydia, who else? He had the idea she could pursue Washington to buy him his ticket home. Through her father, of course. When it didn't work out, he tried a little blackmail."

Garfield held up a hand. "Wait a minute. You're way ahead of me. How did this all start?"

"Larry wrote her a letter, at the beginning of last November. Pleaded with her to use her father's influence, get him a presidential dispensation. He was ill, he said, dying. Naturally Lydia showed it to Thurlan and—"

"Naturally Thurlan showed it to his six best friends. You, I take it. McKinnon here. The Texas Arrangers. And who—the president?"

"The president has no access to this situation."

"Of course not," Garfield said dryly. "What then?"

"We advised Lydia to ignore it, but then Bartell wrote a

second letter and, in mid-December, a third. The last one was hysterical; he said he'd plaster her name across every front page in the world."

"Starting with the *Washington Post*?"

"That's right. Our mistake; we didn't think he'd have the nerve to go through with it. He did."

Garfield contemplated this for a while. He looked up. "Any particular reason why I wasn't allowed to meet the real John Sayer?"

Bloomfield shook his head. "He's been with Lydia since this started, since before Christmas. She needs him; you didn't."

"Very chivalrous, I'm sure. So Larry—I'm thinking out loud here—Larry just drifted into this coincidentally, did he?"

"Not entirely."

"Not entirely." Garfield pumped air into the tobacco, but it remained dead. "How about Mr. Clayton Waldren's television documentary? That a coincidence entirely? Or did Larry just happen to wander into camera range to order?"

Bloomfield put his head on one side. "Now that's an interesting question. How do you see his part in the Hugh Douglas affair?"

"You want to know? Or want to know if I know?"

"Either. Both."

They were skirting the Potomac. In the navy yard across the river, cranes stood black against a suddenly pink-tinged sky. Garfield watched the angles change, the kick of startled light on water. If McKinnon was aiming for the Watergate, he was taking the leisurely route, he thought.

"All right," he said briskly. "Hugh Douglas was a diplomatic patsy. That was his role. He was programmed to fail, sent out to fail. Washington set him up, hit him from behind, and buried him five times over. You can take Washington to mean whatever you want it to mean, but we both know who I have in mind. Just what Larry Bartell's part in it was is anybody's guess, but mine isn't very original: I think he was a patsy, too. I think he had nothing whatever to do with pulling Douglas down, but someone somewhere sure as hell wants the world to think so. Someone American, that is, someone who has an in with the networks. The only value Mr. Waldren's so-called documentary has is to prove that Larry destroyed Hugh Douglas. Why?"

"Sorry, that's not in my brief."

"All right, then why show me the film?" Garfield felt a lick of sweat trail down his back with exquisite slowness and wished he'd had the sense to take his coat off before getting in. "What help is it to you that I saw something I didn't believe?"

"Oh, precisely that. You placed certain constructions on matters of fact. You mentally rejected what you considered to be matters of fancy. That's progress." He had the good grace to look away. "I'm sorry, Garfield. I'm not doing this out of choice."

There was probably a very nice fellow lurking under that veneer of patrician arrogance and coldness, Garfield thought fleetingly. Pity he would never meet him. He said, "But did I have to go through that charade? Was Waldren the only man you could find for the job?"

"Yes, I thought of that at the time." Bloomfield was speaking directly to the far window. "But I was overruled. The consensus was that you had to be, well, pushed. Nudged. You had a lot of ground to cover, and there wasn't much time. You had to be goaded, made angry. The idea was that if you felt you were being made a fool of, you'd jump to conclusions pretty quickly. Anger is an efficient catalyst in some cases."

"And in my case?"

"Very effective." The troubled mouth parted briefly in a brilliant smile, as if it had broken through a layer of ice, then faded as the inner ice closed over it again. "You saw through the Douglas operation right away. Do you follow the reasoning?"

Garfield indulged the dramatic pause as the beads of sweat on his back conjoined to form small rivers. "I think so. Yes, I see the reasoning. Douglas had to be seen to be his own executioner. That was the trick."

"And?"

"And—" He stopped, stared sightlessly into the middle dis-

245

tance, shook his head impatiently, scowled. "Imagery." Giving in to necessity, he snapped the lighter to his pipe bowl. "Here's a project that calls for imagery, planting an indelible image in the public mind, an image that has to be planted quickly because in a very short time—months—it has to become a weapon capable of destroying itself. Yes." He let it stew awhile. "Self-destruction. How to do it. Big question. And the answer came back: Let the media do it. Harness the media—without letting them know they've been harnessed, of course, or it all falls down. Big trouble. But harness them *how*? Answer this time: by extrapolating a series of incidents in which the things you can't see become more relevant than the things you can. Sleight-of-hand stuff, major league. And the secret, your planner decides, lies in turning news into gossip, because what sells newspapers and hogs air time is not events but *people*. Events are boring unless they have a gossip factor, so—next question— what could make a tedious, boring presidential mission newsworthy? Why, the man you choose to send on it, what else? So pick your man carefully. Pick an opponent. A critic. A liberal. A holy cow!"

Bloomfield had found something to interest him outside.

Garfield went on. "So the planner, a worldly man, experienced, feeds the media their first piece of good red meat. Observable reality. The Kompong Som incident."

"How?" Bloomfield interjected. "Kompong Som was a Russian propaganda exercise. You heard what Waldren said. You saw the film, the script."

"Yes, I heard, I saw," Garfield agreed. "But I don't believe any of it. That explosion was part of the plan to discredit Hugh Douglas. No, don't ask me how it was done—I'm not that far down the road—but I'll stake my life on the fact that it *was* done, that somehow someone managed to pull two halves of the same plan together, here in Washington, over there in Kompong Som."

"Big magic."

"It was all big magic." Garfield caught another glimpse of

246

the navy yard: masts and cranes and fading light. "So after the hostel ship we have nuclear submarines in New Zealand waters: classic confrontational politics. Then missile leaks in Brussels and Tokyo: all great copy in themselves but pure gold with Douglas as pig in the middle. By the third incident he's stuck with that image: a perambulating, star-crossed, world-girdling disaster. Nothing can happen within a thousand miles of him without his being to blame. The Bangkok fire was a case in point. I accept that no planner is going to put a hundred-odd lives to the torch to satisfy an appetite for theater, so the fire itself was an accident. But what a bonus! It had to be used. So maybe the planner worked up that demonstration around the American Embassy, who knows? Maybe he didn't. Either way it proves my point. He didn't have to. The story came out the same way. The *effect* was the same. *Doomsday* Douglas strikes again! Oh, yes. Once a premise is laid in the public mind, it sticks, becomes a self-perpetuating, self-serving reality. It's the basis for all advertising, after all, all pulp publicity, all propaganda."

"All politics," Bloomfield murmured. "And the truth?"

"The truth is that Douglas was innocent of everything but being there. But that's not what we'll remember, if we remember him at all. All we'll remember is that he was a Jonah."

Bloomfield eased back on the cushions, a hand to the small of his back, a faint grimace of pain momentarily twisting his mouth. "Does that explain why he was sacrificed? What he was sacrificed for?"

"What anyone's sacrificed for. Advantage. Long-range, deep-laid, undetectable advantage. And the power that goes with it."

"Can you put a name to the advantage?"

"Not yet."

"But perhaps?"

"Yes, perhaps." His brain was a canvas; his imagination, brush and palette both. Fact is what you make it, he thought, careering off on false scents; facts are the broadest strokes, the brightest colors, the boldest slash of naked pigment, the explosive image that lodges deepest, works way, way down into the fissure of memory, and finally enters the brain's blood. Fact is a parasite that feeds on human credulity (like Larry's other friend, you understand, his friend Miko in Geneva, his friend but also the devil on his back).

Bloomfield said hesitantly. "We haven't discussed Sherwood."

Another primary color! "Sherwood? No, I can't fix Sherwood. Temperamentally, politically, I can't see what the hell he's doing in bed with Brock Stafford and Davis Lang; all I can say is I trust him—totally—so there has to be some compelling reason. The kind you commit political suicide for."

"Has he done that?"

"Remains to be seen." Garfield sucked air and flame into the black stud of tobacco in the bowl. "But he's a pivot in this; he has to be."

"Voluntary?"

"He couldn't be dragged into it. He couldn't be bought, I'll say that for him. And I'll tell you something else: If he'd known about your plans for Hugh Douglas, he'd have blasted you to smithereens right there on the Senate floor." He trod water for a moment in the hope that conviction might overtake him before he had to go on. It didn't. "He's pure politics, from the feet up. That's his bag, the stuff in his bones. Instinctive political confrontation. He can't help himself. He may not be a hundred percent wise or a hundred percent honest or a hundred percent clever or talented; but he's fifty percent shrewd and fifty percent competitive, and that's what gives him his edge. If you'd gone to him with the straight proposition for either the Hugh Douglas scam or your undercover army strategy, he'd have blown you sky-high."

"But he hasn't, has he? He's defended himself and, by extension, us. His political enemies." He grimaced. "Stupid word."

Garfield ignored the gibe and found himself staring at the back of Roy McKinnon's crew-cut cannonball of a head. He noted in passing—a scrap of behavioral lore to be stored away for another time—how intently a man listens with the back of his neck when a conversation is officially closed to his ears. Or should be. McKinnon, he decided, must be high on the ladder to merit this degree of trust. So who was watching Lydia while he eavesdropped on prohibited conversations? Or was Lydia part of the lie, too?

Bloomfield said smoothly, "Why should you feel that Sherwood is doing wrong by collaborating with his president?"

"Ask me another," Garfield growled acidly.

"A moral man's lies count for something, don't they? I mean, they *can* occasionally. If he's protecting something vitally important to him, perhaps it's also vitally important to us."

"Define *us*."

"You, me, the president, the country. If you like, Stafford, Lang, Kramer." The tiger eyes burned like blowtorches.

"What do you want from me, Bloomfield—a blank check?"

"Not at all. Just an admission that there may be an underlying moral justification for all this. That if Sherwood is party to a conspiracy, it's at least a conspiracy of—"

"Angels?"

"I was going to say 'of honor,' but you're choosing the words here. *Angels* is fine with me."

Garfield hacked out a cough and was carried off by its reverberating thunder. At the end he was breathless and there were tears in his eyes. "Bloomfield"—more tears, dammit!—"what's all this moral justification stuff about, you want to tell me that? You need my seal of approval on your actions, is that it? Brock Stafford holds his breath while Luke Garfield makes a judgment? What's your assignment? To persuade me to bless the cup? All right, no problem. I bless it. Sherwood's lies are moral lies. The Foreign Legion ploy is an act of Christian charity. Destroying Hugh Douglas was honorable in the sight of God. As honorable as bringing Larry Bartell home to the bosom of the great American family."

He was boiling over, his radiator dry, transmission gone, engine dead, tires flat. He flung out the hand with the pipe in it—a gesture of resignation—and saw McKinnon's muscles bulge in expectation of a blow. Yet even at this low point he was aware of acting a part, acting out a muddled old man's decline into distress, choreographing each special effect. He pulled himself together abruptly. "Sherwood came into this in good faith," he said hoarsely. "That's my opinion for what it's worth. He got involved because someone came knocking at his door. He stayed involved probably out of a sense of duty. That's the kind of man he is."

The stillness in the car was suddenly electric. Bloomfield went rigid, the wedding band once again clear of his finger, his eyes lit with fire. For a moment he seemed incapable of speech. Then he said softly, "*Who* came knocking?" And when Garfield failed to respond: "Who, Garfield? You said, *someone* came knocking. You know, don't you?"

"Maybe."

Bloomfield had lost all sense of occasion now. "Then who is it, Garfield? Tell me. The name. Someone you knew a long time ago, yes? Out of your past, Sherwood's past, the two of you. You were in Europe together at the end of the war, you and he, Germany. Nineteen forty-five. And you had a common denominator, a human common denominator. You used him; he used you. His name, Garfield; what's the name of the common denominator who came knocking at Sherwood's door? *Tell me.*"

They were passing the White House again, for the third or was it the fourth time? The crowds had gone, and the marine band. Shadows were lengthening in black bars across the barbered turf of the Ellipse, and the rain held off by a miracle. Upriver, over toward Langley, the sun was spilling cinnamon gold down the sky from cloud banks the color of blueberry fool, a lurid effect, Wagnerian. On the next circuit, Garfield thought vaguely, it'll be raining.

"Who, Garfield?" Bloomfield's hand touched his arm. "What do you gain by withholding? You know it. We both know you know it."

What we know, Bloomfield, is conditional intelligence, he

thought, pulling his arm free. Everything is conditional. Christ was born on Christmas Day; He died on the conveniently movable feast of Easter. He said with great emphasis, "I have a couple of questions of my own first."

"Go ahead. I'll tell you what I can."

"I want no half answers. A straight yes or no."

"And if I give you what you want?"

"I'll say what you want to hear."

"Ask."

Garfield paused for a moment, anxious to get the sequence right, the pace, no mistakes. "All right, first question, yes or no. Does Langley maintain the link with Prisoners of Conscience?"

Hesitation. "Yes."

"It's still used to monitor the underground movements?"

"Some."

"To infiltrate them?"

"You mind telling me where this is leading?"

"Yes or no?"

"Yes, it's infiltrated."

"Good. Now, this Foreign Legion project. Does it have any connection, directly or indirectly, with the watch on Prisoners of Conscience?"

"You know the answer to that. Yes. And let me remind you, incidentally, that Prisoners of Conscience was your idea, subborning it was your pet project. Another route into the radical undergrowth, you said; I've read your position paper, November 1973. Well, if it's any consolation to you, it works, so don't preach to me, Garfield. Let he who is without sin—"

"Does the general watch on POC include C.J. Poole? Personally?"

Bloomfield's jaw jutted challengingly. "This is ridiculous. Of course it does. She *is* Prisoners of Conscience."

"You tap her phone at home? Open her mail? Run random checks on her movements, her friends, her contacts? All that?"

"You know we do."

251

"Langley does or you do? Which? And by you, I guess I mean whatever marriage of convenience you happen to be party to."

"We do." Cold anger, allowed to build inside but not to show.

"*We* being who?"

"I can't answer that."

"Well, I think I can. The umbrella organization is industrial, so naturally the president has no access to it. But that's its strength. Stellatronics Industries, North American-Stafford, the Bartell Corporation: three multinational giants carrying on the business of business worldwide. Three self-supporting, interlocking structures, and behind them, out of sight, a global anti-terrorist apparatus. The ultimate extension, you could say, of the American Dream. Corporate justice. No overt connection with Langley—arguably none, anyway—and none with formal government. Which leaves your foreign legionnaires free to act with the rights and freedoms of patriotic Americans. Fine. And the Beltway Bandits, I assume, provide the necessary entrée to the more sensitive theaters of radical action." He paused reflectively. "I seem to remember a clause in the Neutrality Act somewhere about U.S. citizens' being forbidden to fight in foreign wars, don't I? Yes, I'm sure I do, but I guess you have that covered, too. International terrorism is not, in the de facto sense, war—is that the argument?—and anyway, how many times has Langley slipped around that one? All those undeclared hostilities south of the border. So bad for the image." He laid a sardonic eye on Bloomfield. "But I'm preaching again, aren't I? I don't expect you to answer that."

"Don't worry, I won't. Have you finished?"

"I'm just getting warmed up. So you knew all there was to know about C.J. and Larry Bartell, past and present."

"We've been reading Bartell's letters to her since 1980, and hers to him."

Garfield sighed, more in pique than anger. "You've had the Montreux address staked out then. The Iranian woman."

"Mena Sabbah. There's a general surveillance running on her, yes."

"Long?"

"Since Bartell first used her: spring 1980."

"Phone taps, mail intercepts, all the rest?"

"If you mean, did we intercept the letter you had sent from the bank in Lugano, the answer's no. We taped the call Bartell made from Paris when she read it over to him." Bloomfield couldn't resist the temptation. "And in case you're wondering; yes, we also taped the chat she had with your man Sullivan."

Garfield gamely held on to his temper. "And followed him home to Paris, naturally," he said with the utmost tolerance.

"Naturally."

"So it would be a little stupid of me to ask if you're running cover on Larry Bartell as of right now."

"On Bartell, Miss Poole, and Straker; yes, it would be."

"Straker?"

"American. The man John Lattimore mistook for Bartell at the hostel yesterday. One-time addict, down and out. Bartell found him in Paris three years ago, put him back on his feet. He's grateful."

"He looks like Bartell?"

"There's a slight resemblance. Enough to confuse anyone with only a verbal description to go on."

Garfield paused, knowing he was about to give away a point but unable to choke down the question. "You seem to be telling me I've been totally superfluous in this operation?"

"Have you? I wouldn't say that." Bloomfield studied his nails. "You were the essential link, I'd have said. Miss Poole wrote pretty glowingly about her State Department friend Lucas Garfield. And Larry was impressed. Hardly surprising he asked for you when the chips were down."

"But you'd already slammed the door on him! You had the chance to say yes—three times!—when he wrote to Lydia last November. Why was it no then and yes now?"

253

"Sorry, not in—"

"My brief," Garfield finished for him harshly. "Is he coming back? I mean, isn't that the central question here?"

"You'll understand. In time."

"But you're not saying?"

"Can't say."

"So what was my part in this?" Garfield felt the sweat on his body go ice cold in anticipation. "What have I actually done, Bloomfield?"

"You've given him hope." Bloomfield glanced down at his watch, a Patek Philippe, the kind that is carved from a knob of solid gold. "That's a hundred percent more than he ever gave anyone else."

"You mean *false* hope."

Bloomfield flicked dismissively at the air. "If we're talking semantics, no hope is entirely false, is it? Contradiction in terms."

"There's nothing semantic about wasting him. Is that what you have in mind? And who gets to do the dirty work? Langley? Some bright young man with a Brooke-Davis sinecure? Your friendly neighborhood Stellatronics salesman?"

"I don't know." The patrician mouth stretched tight. "Nor should you. And that's the last question I'm prepared to answer. You promised me a name."

"When I'm satisfied!"

"Now!"

Garfield spotted the State Department building off to their left and called out to McKinnon, "Pull in at the next corner."

The crew cut went up. "Mr. Bloomfield?"

"Do as he says." And to Garfield: "The name. Please."

Garfield made a production of gathering his coat around him, of stuffing pipe and lighters into inner pockets. "The name is Schellenberg," he said finally, and watched the bolt strike home. "Miko, short for Miroslav, Schellenberg."

Bloomfield breathed out, breathed free, grinned almost boyishly. "Thank you. Miko Schellenberg, good. Why couldn't you say so?"

"Why couldn't you?"

He got out at the curb, and the air fell on him like balm. But there were no farewells. Garfield had a brief shaving mirror image of himself in the reflecting surface of the window. Then the Plymouth gave out a chthonian snarl and a shriek of rubber and left him standing.

TWENTY-TWO

Strictly speaking, Garfield should have made a beeline for the nearest phone and called Polly. To establish a current state of option, as the textbooks have it. To assess damage, the chances of limiting it; to count the cost, make hasty revisions in his game plan.

To check—perhaps most important of all—the condition of his agent (C.J. Poole), her case officer (Joss Sullivan), and the goods in transit (Larry Bartell). At the very least, according to the book, he should have started from the premise that the operation was blown as far as he was concerned and dropped the whole ungodly mess in Bloomfield's lap. *Somebody's* lap. For as any Company intern cutting his teeth on exfiltration theory could have told him, when a controller is blown, everything is blown. And Garfield was the ultimate blown controller. His agent lines were tapped and useless. His strategy was a joke, being a strategy not of his own choosing but one wished on him by the same planner who had led him by the nose from the outset. Tactically he was a pawn like all the other pawns, and pawns have a constitutional right to lie down and die when the going is intolerable (correct, Larry?).

Tactically, therefore, he should have thrown in the towel, called his wife, folded the support resources, and gone home.

In fact, he did none of these things. In practice, he conned himself into the fiction that he still had options and could, with a little luck, use them. It's debatable that he gave very much thought to what might happen if he actually realized those options, brought Larry out, saved the day, but then it was probable that at the time he was hardly functioning intellectually at all. Perhaps his determination to go on sprang from a blind faith in himself, the old soldier's blind faith in action for its own sake: Keep marching till they tell you you're dead.

His starting point was logical: Operationally he was too far from the action to influence events; therefore, don't try. Secondly, Sullivan was far better equipped anyway to deal with blunt contingencies, and nothing would shake him off C.J.'s trail once he was on it. As for Larry Bartell, well, here Garfield permitted himself a shade of professional double-talk. Bartell had brought it all down on himself, and to take that line of reasoning a stage farther, so had C.J. She had engineered a route back into this pariah's life, and he into hers. Ergo, they accepted liability for each other's errors and shortcomings. A straightforward question of choices.

Advantages? There was one at least. The play was on and well into its intermediate stage, and while there's life, there's hope. Garfield's faith in his own planning was unshaken, though he went over it again for the umpteenth time searching for weaknesses.

Joss had booked two tickets on the midevening bus from Paris to the Mediterranean coast, one for C.J., the other for Bartell. Joss was to follow by car. C.J.'s orders were to ride through to Béziers, the pretty little cathedral town in the Languedoc, where, at eight-fifteen the next morning, on a bench opposite the statue of Victor Hugo in the Parc des Poètes, Sullivan would pick them up and drive them to the marina at Cap d'Agde. There they were to board Sullivan's forty-foot sloop *Verdunce* and prepare for sea. In the course of the next day Sullivan was to have passports cleared and collect the ship's papers from the customs house at Agde, all aboveboard, no backdoor shenanigans.

At this stage Garfield was confidently expecting somewhere in the area of seventy thousand beach bodies and yachtsmen to descend on the marina for the long May Day weekend. By Saturday, when *Verdunce* was due to sail, weather permitting, the Gulf of Lions would be peppered with thousands of small craft all the way down to Cap Creux and the Spanish border. *Verdunce*, by all the laws of mathematics, was bound to get lost in the crowd—if anyone knew where to look for her. Sullivan's schedule was to slip at three in the morning, clear French territorial waters by four, and lay a course for the Balearics. Garfield was allowing him three full days to Palma and from there on it was fairly painless: Palma to Málaga; Málaga to Tangier to confuse the issue; Tangier to Madrid; Madrid to Mexico City. Precisely what he was going to do then was hazy and dependent on a whole heap of as yet unworked arithmetic, but with Larry Bartell alive and vocal in Mexico City, Garfield reckoned his bargaining power would quadruple overnight.

So, coat over his shoulder, tie askew, jacket open to reveal a deplorable shirt, Lucas Garfield stubbornly put all thoughts of imminent defeat behind him and took himself for a walk. As it happened, he walked for several hours, till well after dark, till the lights came on like sprinklers in the towers and the rain turned his clothes to pulp. But he didn't walk alone. At his heels, discreet as recalcitrant pilotfish, walked his tails. And at his elbow, also invisible, walked a diminutive man with bootblack hair and a cast to the eyes that embarrassed to hell anyone who tried to look him in the face.

In fact, it was impossible much of the time for him to shake off the illusion that Miko Schellenberg was really there, taking three strides to Garfield's one, arms going like pistons, neat as a pin, announcing all over again how they'd glue the world together someday if they ever got the chance, absolutely. Just the three of them: Miko and Luke and Robin Sherwood Hood.

257

TWENTY-THREE

Some you lose.

That winter of 1945—the most terrible, the most pestilential, killing winter since the Hundred Years War—Garfield and Sherwood had crossed and crisscrossed Allied-occupied Germany twenty, thirty, maybe forty times. By air when they were lucky, by truck when not. By jeep, by troop carrier, by tank, by motorbike and sidecar, on bicycles. On hands and knees and bleeding feet, Don Sherwood swore, for Sherwood was a martyr to his extremities and that winter suffered the agonies of the damned. All in the cause of duty.

Some duty. An essay in Kafkaesque fantasy, more like it. As one of a dozen teams of principal investigating officers, they were honoring a pledge, Eisenhower's pledge that the taskmasters of Nazi Germany would not only pay for their crimes but be seen to pay—in open court, before the assembled justices of liberated Europe and America, before God and a jury of world opinion, di-da-di-da. But pious sentiments take no account of sore feet and even less of human nature, and it was human nature that had tied their frustration in knots. Their job was to assemble evidence of material value to the interrogation of war criminals the following spring, and by late December they had compiled a hundred files thicker than phone directories, an avalanche of evidence sufficient to hang every minister, bureaucrat, general, cop, gauleiter, and black marketeer in the Third Reich—so long as the sole criterion was word of mouth. Two factors militated against them: a dearth of documentary evidence (mountains of it had been burned, of course, during the Allied advance) and the statutory imbursement system, which permitted small cash payments to individuals volunteering information. In a country where even the rats were starving, bread was life, and if information was currency, and currency bread, then talk, for God's sake, tell them anything. The philosophy was painfully realistic. The evidence by and large was not. Mention any name, and people would hand out a tale to break your heart: the man across the street, the woman on the corner, the black-market butcher across town, the priest suspected of breaking the seal of the confessional. And yes, if you pressed them, Hitler, too, Goebbels, Ribbentrop, Himmler, the pope, yes, we saw with our own eyes, personally heard every word. Well, almost every word . . .

When it got so bad the investigations were actually going backward, they ran into Miko. Then the sun came out.

They'd spent Christmas Day at an air force tactical reconnaissance wing in Wiesbaden, seeking, if you please, through the medium of aerial photography to prove that the existence of concentration and forced labor camps in certain areas could not have been unapparent to civilians living in their immediate neighborhoods. The farcical nature of this exercise, not to mention its dubious value as legal tender, finally got through to them, and in a belated release of Christian spirit they cracked a bottle of ten-year-old Haig confiscated from a Washington desk general the week before and got down to some serious drinking. They were hampered in this by somewhat Spartan living conditions. For security purposes they had been quarantined in the end section of an isolated Quonset hut—green-painted brick, tin roof, tin walls, two tin beds, a table, a blackboard, two water glasses, no heat—so they celebrated the army way, flat out on their beds, the bottle passing companionably back and forth, their voices lifting occasionally in cracked tribute to little towns of Bethlehem and silent nights, their humor regressing slowly but inexorably into adolescence. And on the stroke of midnight Miko stuck his patent head around the door and in a loud whisper asked would it disturb them if he swept up in there.

Don Sherwood actually fell off his bed laughing. He was always Miko's biggest fan, but that first time he really flipped. The cheek! The face! The brassbound, bloody, bullshitting audacity of the bastard! Sweep up? At midnight? On Christmas Day? Jesus, what are you selling, mister? Because, of course, it had to be something. Always was.

While they were busily hooting themselves into a state of asphyxiation at this supreme act of conmanship, Miko deftly sideslipped in and closed the door. He set down his props—broom, bucket, dusters, and so on—and, when they got hold of themselves, was in position at the foot of their beds, waiting to make his pitch, a fat, sleek puppet well under five feet tall in a faded gray boiler suit that had to be the best-pressed boiler suit in the world. Then he began talking, and that's how nobody got any sleep that night.

What Miko did, without a preliminary drumroll to cushion the shock, was to break into his life story. And when Sherwood, already a goner, had hysterics halfway through and collapsed on the floor again and called him a holy son-of-a-bitching liar, Miko agreed, yes, he was, and promptly broke into quite a different life story in the hope they'd like it better. They were drunk by this time, of course, or they wouldn't have stood for it, and maybe they were also in psychological retreat from the cold, from their aching eyes and backs and feet, from the pervasive air of degradation that hung over their work and the mounting pressure, yet Miko in part forced that retreat on them and in the final stages deflected their sarcasm by sheer force of personality. How can anyone be fat and not a Nazi? Sherwood howled at one point in choking raptures, and Miko laughed and agreed it was quite impossible and stood there grinning, all dapper and dainty and skippety-hip on his polished little feet till Sherwood hung his head in apology. And Miko thanked him, his mat of patent hair sleek as glass, his flyaway eyes goggling everywhere but where you could meet them head-on. The plain fact was, they surrendered. Miko overwhelmed them with blatant hypocrisy and high good humor and guile, and then he dictated the peace treaty.

At first they took him to be a Pole—because of the "Miko" and the general look of him and the way he acted and got under their skin—but around four in the morning, his pump nicely primed with ten-year-old Haig, he confessed to having a German soul. No denying it. A Polish heart, yes; a Czech accent, unfortunately; a Hungarian excess in his gestures; a Prussian dash with the saber (oh, yes); a Frenchman's sly wit; a secret passion for the English aristocracy—but undeniably a German soul. Also—and here he approached the nub with great delicacy—a German identity actually. And currently the status of German prisoner of war.

At this Sherwood collapsed once more and applauded from the floor: Encore! Encore! Miko bowed. If it crossed his mind he was being ridiculed, he took pains not to show it, though as Garfield came to realize later, Miko had no sense of the absurd in relation to himself. In his own mind he was neither abasing himself nor selling out; he simply traded human responses on the open market and paid the going price. (He was still plain Miko at this stage—as in Fido or Pluto or Here, boy!—and like a good dog, he was happy to perform for as long as it took to win the masters' confidence. How young they were, the two of them, and how naïve, to think he could ever have taken them seriously.)

Having advanced on the real object of the floor show, Miko now showed great restraint and withdrew from it. Instead, he encouraged Garfield and Sherwood to take the spotlight and tell him their life stories (which amused him greatly.) At five o'clock and still as fresh as paint, he absented himself "for momens only" and returned with a wheeled cart bearing three folding chairs, a paraffin heater, a Primus stove, ham, eggs, bread, butter, coffee, cigarettes, chinaware, cutlery, and a frying pan. By six o' clock they were seated at the table, wading through a gourmet breakfast and debating the relative merits of Puvis de Chavannes and Picasso in his Blue Period. At seven the debris cleared, their bedding shaken out and squared away, the floor swept, Miko finally put to them the small matter of his immediate future.

He had been much abused. Yes, of course, the fortunes of war and so on, but still, they should judge for themselves.

The English had made him a prisoner at Flensburg, he explained. Flensburg being that final jumping-off point in the Baltic for rats intent on leaving the sinking Third Reich, the English, not unreasonably, had formed the impression that he, too, had been trying to escape the conqueror's wrath. Of course, nothing could have been farther from his mind. In fact, at the very instant of his arrest he had actually been on his way to volunteer such humble talents as he possessed: his impeccable German, for instance; his French, Italian, Serbo-Croat, Czech, Polish, Russian, English; his unrivaled knowledge of German government affairs; his commercial, military, and spiritual contacts throughout Europe; his intimate experience of Soviet methods in the public sector. Not to mention the small fact that he had been a noncombatant throughout the war and was therefore blameless, or that as a devout Catholic he was therefore trustworthy before God. The English, in reply, put him behind barbed wire and later shuttled him here and there: down to Aachen; up to Cologne; back to Flensburg, where he considered escape but recanted on grounds of honor; then to Koblenz, where he was made to work in the fields like a common peasant; then Saarbrücken; then Frankfurt; and finally Wiesbaden. By the time the English had loaded him onto the Americans and the Americans had transported him to Wiesbaden, Miko said, he had formed grave doubts that anyone remembered any longer why he was being held. Dozens of POWs had slipped away since he left Flensburg—from the camps en route—and nobody seemed any the wiser or in the slightest way concerned. And at Wiesbaden he had been given so much freedom—the privileged rank of cleaner and trusty, thirty-six-hour passes—he could have walked away anytime he chose. He hadn't, of course, on another point of honor; also because the food was good. As a civilian he couldn't hope to find work half so agreeable or a millionth part as rich in free vitamins. However—and here he sat himself, greatly daring, on the end of Sherwood's bed, as if to give this part of the speech greater significance—he was now prepared to consider alternative employment, a more challenging role in the nation's affairs, and in that sense the arrival of Colonel Garfield and Major Sherwood at TacRec 3 could be seen—forgive him the expression—as an act of God. He had been privileged to overhear that they had come to study aerial pictures of concentration camps, and it crossed his mind they might therefore have a vocational interest in certain associated matters, such as, say, atrocities carried out by the SS in the name of national socialism. In which case—

What it boiled down to was that Miko had friends. Names, places, connections, or should he say, rather, access to numerous avenues of historical research? Given time and persuasive resources—he meant money, food, whiskey, cigarettes, perhaps the odd vial of penicillin for the more intractable cases—he felt sure he could lead Colonel Garfield and Major Sherwood to many items of sociological interest. In trifling return for these services he would be officially seconded to them as a special assistant—he had the terminology at his fingertips and several precedents to quote them—and for greater security of tenure, a new, more authoritative identity. An English identity ideally, perhaps American, but certainly not Polish or Czech, and under no circumstances German. French, he conceded grudgingly, might strike a happy medium. Should such an arrangement appeal to them, he could guarantee almost immediate results; in fact, he saw no reason why he shouldn't begin his inquiries right away. Say, tomorrow.

It was Sherwood who went for it. Garfield was all for laughing it off and getting back to the salt mines, but Sherwood said wait; Sherwood said let's think about it. Okay, he's a con man. Okay, he's on the make. Okay, he's shifty and smooth and a twenty-four-carat liar, and we know it; but maybe that's what we need right now. He had this hunch, he said, and the hunch said let's wait and see. So they waited a week, and at the end of it God took a hand (as Miko claimed forever afterward, a clear act of God). Sherwood had flown to Berlin to check out a case history at the American military hospital, and while he was there, a Dutch captain of signals died on the operating table: traffic case, his jeep took a Dodge truck head-on, and minced him. The officer's name was Schellenberg, Jan Schellenberg, and from his picture he was chubby and vacant-looking. More to the point, there were his papers lying in a wire tray not three feet from where Sherwood sat in the superintendent's outer office. It may not have been an act of God, but it was pretty close. Sherwood pocketed the papers and left. Thus was Miko Schellenberg born. Thus his work for Garfield and Sherwood began.

He performed for them brilliantly, though not quite in the passive role of a dog performing tricks. He asked to be taken to Berlin, in the first instance, and there arranged to visit numerous persons of his acquaintance whose anonymity he found it essential to guarantee in advance. He would visit them alone, he said, his gargoyle eyes everywhere but on theirs. Complete discretion, absolute trust; it was the only way, yes? Yes, they said, and followed him not openly, but not so invisibly that he was left in any doubt. But pursuit was a joke, and the joke was on them, for Miko was as skillful as a fox at laying cold trails, and no one could deny Berlin was an ideal ruin in which to lay them. After three disastrous attempts at tailing him they gave up. And after the first few days it didn't seem to matter. Miko came through. In spades.

In the first few weeks he produced wads of internal memorandums between Himmler and his minions, between Hitler and Mussolini, between Hitler and his generals. He unearthed blacklists—effectively death lists, Jews and others; whole boxes of contract bids for the design and construction of death camps. He even "recovered" one day, out of the blue, the notes Hitler had prepared for his speech to the new German Labor party in

264

February 1920. They listed the twenty-five points of his program for national recovery, including the pivotal Point IV: "Only a member of the race can be a citizen. A member of the race can only be one who is of German blood without consideration of creed. Consequently, no Jew can be a member of the race." Miko himself considered this of only marginal interest.

Within a month he was coming and going at all hours, more often at night than during the day, blithely disregarding the curfew regulations and constantly running afoul of Allied patrols. He also began making regular crossings by God knew what routes into the Russian zone, his old brown attaché case bulging on these journeys with edible bribes, drugs, medical supplies, coffee, and cigarettes. When Garfield demanded to know why they were necessary, whom he was meeting, in what conditions, to what end, Miko would smile and shake his patent head, and when Garfield lost his temper—as he did on more than one occasion when bailing Miko out of close arrest—Miko would stand and stare in complete wonder, as if he were a spectator at a boxing match in which someone else was on the receiving end. Similarly, when they pestered him over a drink now and then to come clean with his real name, his real story, his real home, his real anything, Miko would pretend they were joking and tell them yet another life story, and once, when Garfield could have sworn on his mother's life that he was running some kind of tit-for-tat deal with the Russians to facilitate his crossings, Miko subdued him with the look of a wounded puppy. Even if such things were possible—this look implied—how in the name of reason could Garfield believe Miko capable of dishonoring a friendship? Garfield, nonetheless, continued to suffer the odd twinge of uneasiness, and the feeling intensified. Miko was too good, too effective, too altogether unnervingly prescient. Challenge the credibility of any scrap of information he produced, and within days he would cover your challenge with precise and indisputable proof. For no apparent reason he would urge a course correction in the conduct of an interrogation days before it became obvious a correction was necessary, and when you asked him why, ah, it was just a suspicion he had, a lucky suspicion. What Miko could see with both eyes closed was otherwise invisible to anybody else. But unease is an itch, it can be scratched; and since by mid-March both Garfield and Sherwood were totally immersed in pretrial interrogations and as mentally devastated by the process as any of their victims, what the hell, it was easier all around to let Miko ride, let him go off and root and snuffle on his own. After all, he never gave them cause to regret it. Why would he?

Captain Miko Schellenberg, ladies and gentlemen, Dutch captain of signals (deceased), nice fellow, accommodating. Get you anything you want from a pound of butter to a conviction.

Garfield lost sight of him quite suddenly at the end of July. Sherwood was ordered to fly to Bonn to hear some highly privileged submissions *in camera* from members of the then embryonic Gehlen Organization, and he took Miko along as interpreter and general gofer. Miko never returned. One day, it appeared, he slipped through the defensive ring around Hitler's former secret service chieftain and spent a full hour with Gehlen in deep and fruitful conclave. "They sang a couple of mantras together and found nirvana," Sherwood said disgustedly when he got back. On the last day Gehlen formally requested that Captain Schellenberg be assigned to his staff. Temporarily. As a gesture of American-German détente. "What could I say?" Sherwood asked. "And maybe it was time."

It *was* time. Though they never discussed it, it was forever after accepted between them that Miko had probably bought in with dud checks, which would at any minute start bouncing. But as it turned out, Nuremberg proved to be less a series of trials based on evidence than a laboratory for the study of individual responsibility in the chain of command, and if Miko's evidence was manufactured, it didn't matter because in the end it killed no one.

It wasn't quite the end of the story, though. Miko wrote Sherwood a letter a week before he left for the States in August 1948, a personal letter, no address given but postmarked Berlin.

Miko had been privileged to overhear, he wrote, that Sherwood was due for release and felt he couldn't let him go without expressing, in the warmest and most cordial terms, his regard for Don as a fellow professional (his actual phrase) and his profound appreciation for all that Sherwood had done for him. Garfield's name was not mentioned.

How long Miko had clung to Gehlen's coattails after that, and to what effect, was anybody's guess except perhaps for Bonn's—and Bonn wasn't saying—for when the first tidal wave of press vilification swamped the West German security services in the early fifties, Captain Schellenberg was found to have slipped his mooring. No doubt exercising his celebrated gift for anticipation, he faded silently into the long night of his middle years. What became of him nobody could say—least of all the West Germans, who were feverishly bent on finding him for reasons they preferred not to discuss with friends—and though Garfield, back at Langley again in 1955, filed at least three general search requests a year to the European counter-intelligence network, nothing surfaced until 1959. It was January and freezing. At a matinee concert by the Red Army Choir in Prague, Miko or his living, breathing double was photographed entering the theater with two rock-hewn anthropoids later identified as members of the Czech Interior Ministry's special security cadre. A name was pinned to him: Signor Ugo Cuardi of Milan. Verdict: perhaps. The second sighting, in May 1963, was even less satisfactory. A French agent making a monthly drop in the Polish capital claimed to have seen Miko entering a shop in the middle of Warsaw—no picture this time and no name either. Miko had his watch cleaned, browsed while he waited, and left by a side exit, thereby evading more precise identification. Verdict: unsubstantiated. The Austrian service tabbed him next, in Prague again, 1968, a month after Alexander Dubček's vision of communism with a human face collapsed under the massed weight of several hundred Russian tanks, though as the NATO central registry delicately pointed out, everyone in the world suspected of sleeping with the Soviets was being seen in Prague that summer. So, verdict: peripheral/probably inaccurate. Garfield nevertheless pressed the Austrian source pretty hard on that occasion, so hard and so persistently in fact that his masters finally ordered him to lay off.

And that was pretty well it.

Occasional faint scratchings emerged from the undergrowth in the course of the seventies that could have been Miko and just as easily could not, but by then the existence of a recycled, possibly reborn Captain Schellenberg was very old hat indeed. Besides, Garfield had other things to worry about, specifically his chairmanship of the Cleaners, the watchdog committee on American intelligence affairs that overnight raised him far above the day-to-day pursuit of Soviet agents. Like it or not, he allowed Miko, in fact and fancy, to fade from his immediate concern. As far as itches ever entirely fade, that is.

And sure enough, here he was back again. Miko Schellenberg, still clinging to the name that first gave him substance, Larry's other friend, you understand, his friend from Geneva, but also the devil on his back. The connection was irresistible: Larry Bartell was *in loco parentis* with the radical underground in Europe—up to his hairline as lecturer, messenger boy, and pamphleteer, if circumstantial evidence was anything to go by. Therefore, Miko was probably his arm's-length controller. Therefore, Miko was also—

He had been walking with no sense of direction and little expectation of arriving anywhere and was now mildly surprised to find himself approaching the Watergate. He crossed the street, and there, at the end of the driveway, staring keenly into every passing face but Garfield's, was the same young black cop in the same night cape and cap guard, beating nervous time in the palm of his hand with the same nightstick.

"Evening, son," Garfield said loudly as he passed, and the kid nearly had a fit.

In the elevator Garfield became oppressively aware of the

stares of two painted Washington widows and guessed he must cut a pretty wild figure, what with his sodden clothes and his flyaway hair and the scowl of concentration on his bristled face; but in trying to mitigate this deshabille, he made the mistake of cracking a twisted grin and growling some fool's reference to the state of the weather, and they nearly fainted, both of them, at his feet. It wasn't his day for chivalry.

Light showed under the door of Art Mickelson's apartment, and for a moment Garfield contemplated it, absolutely still. Fleetingly he ran the old mental video of violent death he had lived with since adolescence—the burning sensation, the exploding out of vital parts, the terrible impact of ragged metal on shattered bone—and he wished he'd talked to Polly before coming back, wished he had the comfort of knowing he'd spoken to her one last time, because that was the only fear death held for him any longer, the prospect of leaving her without a word. Then it was over, and he let himself in.

Fred Goldman was already on his feet. He had a glass in his hand and a welcoming grin on his face to soften the blow, and he advanced with the assurance of a man who knows his terrain, him and all his glistering gold.

"Hey, Luke, you're soaked."

Garfield didn't check his stride. He kicked the door shut behind him with a violence people normally surrender to only in films, and strode to within six inches of Goldman's deeply fanged mustache.

Goldman did not budge, but then Garfield didn't expect him to.

"You set me up for Bloomfield this afternoon?" he demanded, hands on hips.

"Yes, Luke."

"You the planner?"

"Here." Goldman pushed the glass at him.

"Me, Bartell, Douglas, Sherwood? One package?"

"Why don't you sit down, Luke?"

269

"Grief and goddamn," Garfield muttered, and against his own best interests as injured party collapsed into a chair and drained the glass.

He took a shower to gain time and raise his flagging performance curve; but the hot water had a narcotic effect on him, and he emerged feeling steam-dried and sedated. He also emerged wearing a Chinese dragon bathrobe of Art Mickelson's, and this he realized too late was a major tactical error, though he would have lost even more face by going back to change it.

He dumped himself in the leather throne behind the desk, swung the chair to face the window, and took up his refilled glass. "The whole story, now," he growled. "No blanks."

"No blanks," Goldman chanted amiably, and raised his glass in salute. He lit another of his black cigarillos, a performance with a lot of gold in it: signet ring, watch, Dupont lighter. "Maybe I should apologize first for the treatment, Luke." He spoke without looking Garfield's way. "It wasn't out of choice, I hope you realize that."

"Everyone is so concerned about how little choice he had in this. You and Bloomfield both. Didn't it occur to you just to lay it out for me, step by step, the night you came out to the boat? Here's the problem, Luke, you mind helping out?"

"Yup. It occurred to me." There was a deceptive laziness about the voice that Garfield recognized immediately as a touch of the old steel. Notably absent at their last meeting, now magically restored. "It occurred to me, but I ruled it out."

"Why?"

"Question of time. You don't persuade easy, Luke, maybe you noticed that." Goldman flashed him a wide, insincere Tatar grin. "And that's not a criticism in the normal run of things. Your greatest virtue, in fact. But I had a crisis on my hands, assets to protect, the roof falling in. I needed people to *act*, Luke—move, move, move—and that included you. Two years of hard work in the balance, Luke—you can understand that—millions of dollars, a whole structure, and here's a fink like Larry Bartell about to blow the whole thing to kingdom come. Christ, Luke, what was I supposed to do? I needed the Poole girl in Paris to hold Bartell's hand if necessary. I needed you to move on down the line, so I could feed you what you ought to know, piece by piece, but not all of a piece or I'd have you blowing the whistle on me, too. Sayer, Cotten, Sherwood, Waldren—I figured the simplest way to move you on was to provoke you, get you really steamed up. If you thought there was even a hint of a cover-up, you'd hang in there till doomsday." He drew deeply on the cigarillo. "Also, it kept you out of my hair."

"Glory be." Garfield fell silent. "And I came through for you. Proved you right."

"I'm not crowing."

"You have every right to. But tell me, why would I have found the straight version so hard to take?"

He watched Goldman's reflection in the glass, noted the way he repositioned his long body in the chair, how his jaw rode up over his tie as if the collar of his shirt were suddenly too tight.

"It's your attitude." Goldman waved vaguely, trailing smoke. "I mean, damn it, Luke, you know the way you are. Never accept anything till it's proved ten times over: rule of life. And your temperament. It has to be done your way, or it doesn't get done. Nothing runs smoothly unless it runs on the Garfield Principle." He was floundering, but Garfield wouldn't throw him a line. "Well, I didn't have time for any of that. At least give me credit for leveling with you along the way. I've shown you everything. Cards face up. I wanted you to see the whole issue clearly, know it was right."

"Why? Who cares how I see it?"

"I care! I wanted you to understand that some solutions were unavoidable. That in the final analysis they were—"

"Don't tell me. Morally justifiable." Garfield addressed the tableau of crystallized light spread out six stories below. "Morally and/or politically justifiable. Well, my God, Fred, what've you done that I wouldn't? Is that the problem? Incompatible definitions of morality? You worried I won't accept your definition? That I'll walk straight out of here and sell your soul to the *Washington Post?*"

Goldman's head came around so fast it was almost comic. Their eyes met in the window glass.

"Luke, that's not funny," he said with massive restraint. "That's not at all funny. Think what the hell you like, but don't run away with the idea that there's any choice for you in this, either, because there isn't. Never was. You walk the same line I walk. You accept my definitions or you don't walk out of this room."

About four seconds later he laughed, very loudly, very abruptly, like a small bomb going off in a well. Carrying it through like the good pro he was, he slapped his thigh and threw back his bush of black curls and laughed till the walls shook.

But for Garfield the laughter came too late. About a million years too late.

"I'm listening," Garfield said at length when the laughter subsided, and waited patiently while Fred sucked life into a fourth cigarillo from the lighted end of his third.

"Okay, Luke, let's get down to cases," he said, and stretched out deep in the client chair, throwing one long leg over the other.

"The whole thing started a couple of years ago, mid-September, six weeks before the election. Don Sherwood's at home alone in Georgetown one night, just wound up a committee meeting, and it's late; his wife's away in Connecticut, his exec, Tom Babson, just left in a cab, the TV's on to catch the late-night news, no one else in the house."

Garfield made a noise to convey that he followed the scenario thus far.

"Suddenly—no warning—there's a voice over his shoulder. Very relaxed, very gentle. Says please to sit tight, Senator, and don't be alarmed. Then the voice comes around in front, and it's a nice-looking young guy, clean, well dressed, no thug. Unarmed. Turns out to be a Russian hood name of Aleks Rostov, worked at that time out of Aeroflot in New York, not that Sherwood knows this till later. Meantime, he's delivering a message, he says, from the senator's old, old friend and protégé, a friend who continues to hold him in very high regard. Read it. And he hands over a letter, and it's handwritten, signed 'Miko.' Just Miko. Well, Sherwood goes into his outraged legislator act while he figures out whether to scream or faint, but Rostov has all the time in the world, and in the end Sherwood reads the letter. It was Miko to a tee, he said, never any doubt about that: the writing, the style, the bent English, a kind of Polish Uriah Heep tone to it—good as having him right there in the room."

"And what was Miko selling?" Garfield asked the window.

"He was making an offer of service." Goldman waited hopefully, but Garfield apparently had nothing to add. "Man-to-man offer of service from Miko to his old, true, valued friend and supporter Major Sherwood. And through Sherwood to the glorious U.S. of A. Miko's first and only abiding love—or words to that effect." Goldman's black eyes glinted wickedly in the window glass. "The letter says he wants to meet and talk, that's the bottom line. Has a proposition. Naturally he can appreciate how the senator might be a bit wary of a reunion in the prevailing circumstances, but Miko advises courage and sober reflection because this could just be the single most important contribution Sherwood will ever make to the well-being of his country, the West, and the entire free world."

"Miko was always a fine salesman," Garfield murmured, meaning it.

Goldman flapped a hand. "To make a long story short, Don Sherwood tells Rostov he'll think it over, come back in a week, which is fine with Rostov because that's what he was told to expect. Then Sherwood came to see me." Garfield wheeled around in the chair in surprise. "He came to me because he couldn't go to you."

"Is that so. Why?"

"Because you had a direct commitment to the president, just then. You'd have been honor-bound to report anything Sherwood told you, and he didn't want that. He wanted the White House kept out of it till after the election."

"Because he was pretty sure it wouldn't go in the president's favor."

"Right. Look, he's a politician, Luke, not the Archangel Gabriel. Okay, the second strike against you was personal: Sherwood said you didn't like Miko and wouldn't trust him. More to the point, Miko wouldn't trust you."

"Never a truer word spoken," Garfield said.

"So there's your answer. Sherwood came to me because I was your boy once, the old imprimatur. Also, I had no official ties but all the right connections."

"And even better, you were in the security business," Garfield observed to no one in particular. "A big inducement. Extensive foreign commitments, obviously knew your way around, a large field force of ex-Langley officers like Master Todd Hales to play with."

Goldman shrugged off the innuendo. "Exactly. So Sherwood asked my advice, and I told him go ahead, say yes. For old times' sake, no strings attached. No guarantees in advance, but he should at least sit and listen. What could he lose? Anyway, Rostov came back as agreed, and he brought Miko's next suggestion, which was that Sherwood map out an informal fact-finding tour of the NATO bloc countries for after the election—early December—any itinerary that appealed to him but keep two days free, one in Paris, one in Bonn. Miko would fix times, places, and pickups—the first meet to put his offer in detail; the second for Sherwood to raise questions, doubts, and, he hoped, go along with the idea."

"And Sherwood went?"

"With a dozen of my people on his tail and twice that number in Paris and Bonn. Went like a dream." Goldman rubbed his big hands. "In Paris, when Miko laid out the proposition, we got every damn word, Luke, start to finish. We got pictures, we got voiceprints, we—"

"You mean Sherwood went in wired for sound? Miko didn't search him, didn't sweep him?"

Goldman enjoyed a moment's technical supremacy. "Luke, the kind of materials we're using nowadays"—it was the tone he might have used to a retarded child—"carbon fibers, high-density plastics, that kind of stuff, a sweep is a waste of time. And as for body searches, hell, these gadgets are so small you could lose a transmitting bug on a pinhead. Miko knew that."

"Very encouraging," Garfield managed to say in return. "So what was Miko's proposition?"

Here Goldman went suddenly coy. He had a tale to tell, and he was going to tell it his way come hell or high water—a beginning, a middle, and a clear-cut cliff-hanging end that would win him ten curtain calls and a vote of confidence. So he neatly sidestepped the question and answered quite another. "Oh there was a proposition, sure," he said languidly. "First the mating dance, then the proposition, just like you'd expect."

Garfield decided to give him rein. "I see. He explained his sudden switch in loyalties, did he? I would love Moscow unto death did I not love Washington more."

"Right." Goldman chuckled, shook his head in admiration. "You know, I actually like him? Miko? He's incredible, Luke. Brilliant. He can get Sherwood running so hot and cold the guy doesn't know whether he's coming or going. Emotional blackmail. Sherwood falls for it every time, fantastic finesse to it. And that's how the first meet started in Paris, Miko making Sherwood feel morally responsible for everything bad that ever happened to him and everything good that didn't. He took the wrong road back there in 'forty-six, Miko said, knew it then, knew it better now, but at the time couldn't do a damn thing about it. It was his fate, his evil star. For a time, he said, he'd held the world in his hands that year: a job he loved, people around him he admired and respected—he meant Sherwood, not you—a chance to serve, maybe make a good career, all the things people in his position never dared dream of—you could practically hear the violins at this point, Sherwood sitting there with his jaw trembling—and then, says Miko, it's all gone; puff of smoke, and his whole world disintegrates. And he reminds Sherwood how when they flew to Berlin that day, Sherwood told him the job wouldn't last out the year and Miko would have to go. And that explains why he did what he did, he says. He panicked and grabbed for the first meal ticket that came along. He didn't want it, hated doing it, but he'd lost hope, lost faith."

"Gehlen," Garfield murmured, and fancied for a moment that he saw Miko's image reflected in the glass alongside Goldman's, an aging yet ageless Miko, creased yet creaseless, standing cap in hand for heaven's reward. In a pig's eye! "He didn't have long to wait for the next meal ticket, did he?" he remarked. "Miko never went hungry for long."

"But he was good with Gehlen," Goldman protested as if that were the issue. "He says so, and it happens to be true; we checked the record. He was brilliant. Also pretty fair at the refined double cross, of course, because that's his fate, like he says, his evil star. Finished him with Gehlen, as you know. He'd made a bunch of useful contacts on the East German side while he was working for you—he admitted this, incidentally, the first meeting—and when he moved in with Gehlen, he kind of kept these contacts oiled. Never knew your luck in those days, he said; contacts were gold. So after a while he was trading back and forth across the wall—merchandise, medical supplies, a lot of information, running both ways, being Miko—and no trouble, no problems, till one week the traffic got a little heavy and the West German counterespionage boys tumbled him, practically caught him with the jam on his fingers. He had to get over the wall fast—spring 1953 as far as I can fix it; he's not too good on dates, Miko, hates to be pinned down. Anyway, he made a bee-line for his friends on the other side, and they handed him over to the Russians. The Russians sweated him good for six months. At the end of that time they discovered he was Bulgarian—"

"He says that?" Garfield interrupted.

"He says it."

"Where in Bulgaria? When?"

"Ah, he's a little vague on that, too. Just Bulgaria. Pick a town, any year between 1930 and 50,000 B.C. He says the Russians liked the Bulgarian part. Gave him a job building domestic personality files on the West German cabinet, and from there on he never looked back."

"Miko never looked anywhere but back," Garfield said tartly. "That's how he stayed in business so long. One eye over his shoulder, one in front. How else d'you think he got to look like that?"

It didn't occur to him he'd made a joke till Goldman roared with laughter.

"After that"—Goldman was enjoying his narrative, becoming more assured as he went on—"after that he just naturally rose. Soviet citizenship—"

"When?"

"Ah. Say around 1968. Good year for being Russian, 'sixty-eight, the Prague Spring. Then, sometime around the early seventies, he had a long spell in Moscow—six months, a lot of briefing in depth, met Andropov, liked him, made his mark with Brezhnev and got marked in return. Then they sent him out to bring the European destabilization machine up-to-date. Miko says it hadn't been the same since the days of the Comintern in Paris between the wars: too much fragmentation; too many fractious groups fighting each other instead of the class war. And no real support from Moscow aside from the old revolutionary brotherhood malarkey—sheets of Leninist dialectic, lectures, rah-rah for the people, but no money. The machinery was rusty, the philosophy was out of date, and the people running it were out of control. Miko changed all that. First he took the major terrorist groups in hand, the way Moscow had with the Vietnamese and the Palestinians. He penetrated *Action Directe*, the Red Army Faction, the Red Brigades—put in his own boys, good, tough, bright young guys, trained to work on the inside. Then he poured in support finance, which gave his people status within the groups and a lot of operational edge. All strictly hush-hush. After that he began working up a system of cross-pollination between the different groups in Europe. Then he extended the cooperation to the Mideast and Africa. From there he went one better and instituted the system of what he called *Action Indirecte*, where the Italians would make a hit for the Palestinians, say, or the Basques for the IRA, and tit for tat as and when required. What he was working up to was what he got finally in 'eighty-four: the Red Army Faction in Germany joined up with *Action Directe* in France. The next natural step was a European union, and Miko had that under way, too. He had a mind to call it the International Brigade—claims he was in the Spanish Civil War for a time—but the kids got there first and called it the International Proletarian Combat Organization. Within a couple of months they had a Belgian wing, the Fighting Communist Cells. Good things catch on fast, Miko says; they develop a speed and scale you'd never believe if you hadn't been in at the birth. There's one golden rule, though: Keep power politics out of it. I know, sounds weird, but what Miko says is they're crazy, these kids, off the wall; once they smell interference from outside—like manipulation from our side, or Moscow's side, the Mideast governments, anyone, any hint somebody up there is pulling strings, *finito*! The Marxists feel that way about Moscow, the Maoists about Peking, the anarchists about everyone. So Miko played it close to the doublet, never showed so much as an ankle. Naturally things got out of hand from time to time, he says. The attacks on NATO installations, then anything that looked vaguely capitalist or vaguely profitable or vaguely NATO-symbolic. And in the end it came down to an all-out campaign against anyone and anything American. A lot of the groups went Muslim, Miko says, especially after the Libyan thing."

"And you believed all this?"

"He supplied proof, Luke. Names, places, connections."

"I bet he did. If things were going so badly wrong—all this

anti-Americanism he finds so offensive—what made him hang in there? His sense of duty?"

Goldman eyed him coolly. "He says man is the prisoner of his fixations. Can't see the forest for the trees. Gets stuck on the theory, ducks the practical." And hotly: "Goddamnit, Luke, he got sick of it. I don't give a shit for the guy, but the voiceprint says it and my gut feeling says it: He got sick of playing god-father to a plague of fucking locusts, and one day he said, 'Right, enough, that's it.' I believe him. I believe it happens that way."

"All right, you believe it." Garfield sighed. "So what did he want, Fred? What, after all this, did he really want?"

"Luke—" The tower with curls coiled itself first one way, then another in the client chair, much squeaking of expensive leather, much crossing of long legs, much flashing of glitzy gold. "Let me just cover the ground I have to cover, okay? My own way. I'm not holding back on anything, I swear. I just want you to get this in the right sequence, the right way—"

"Your way. Bloomfield's way. The Texas Arrangers' way."

"In perspective, Luke." Goldman cocked his head winningly, and when Garfield waved a tired dismissal, he grinned hugely and chain lit his fifth cigarillo. He smoked them only halfway down, Garfield noted. Scared of cancer but not scared enough to give up more than halfway. A twentieth-century phenom-enon, he thought. Like freedom.

"Miko comes to the second meet in Bonn loaded with micro-film. I mean the works, Luke. His files, his game plans, his chain-of-command structures, his fallback positions, operational projections into the twenty-first century, his pay sheets. And a scad of material on people he has running back room links with the main European movements: the Greens in Germany; the antinuke people; the CND campaigners; Basque separatism; the foreign workers' lobby in France and Germany. There's no end to it, Luke. It's a crock of gold, I'm not kidding. But that was problem number one. The product was too wide-ranging to handle in the conventional way. Langley couldn't handle it. They don't have the charter, and they don't have the scope.

Under current defense policy nobody could handle it exclusively, and this had to be a one-time exclusive arrangement."

"So the Stellatronics operation came into being."

"Stellatronics, North American-Stafford, the Bartell Corporation, a commercial octopus, Luke, big enough and powerful enough to put out tentacles anywhere in the world—legitimately —and pump down those tentacles the best antiterrorist fighting men we could lay hands on. Resources, tactical support, finance—"

Garfield half closed his eyes and fashioned a vision of Sodom and Gomorrah out of Washington's flash and dazzle. He said softly, "You imagine for a second that Congress will stand for it? Europe? Opinion in the third world? Good God, Fred, don't you realize the moment this gets out—"

"We'll be in place and ready!" Goldman snapped back, teeth bright, eyes bright. "You think we see this as a long-term play? Jesus, Luke, we know it can't be that. We're planning on a six-month exercise if we're lucky. Three if we're not. But the fact is we're on schedule, Luke. We're getting men in place, thousands of men and more coming. We have Miko's blueprint. The man who put this nightmare together, Luke, he's pointing us where to hit. And when we have every inch of ground covered, every—"

"What's the proposition, Fred?" Garfield was at his most silky smooth. "Kill every environmentalist? Every man, woman, and child who carries a banner against the bomb? Do we send the foreign workers' lobby to the gas ovens? Is that what you have in mind?"

But Goldman merely grinned down at him and shook his mop of curls. "You never give up, do you? The Garfield Way or no way. Well, if you really expect an answer to that, Luke, the answer is no. What we intend to hit are the bombers and the gunmen, the main attack groups, the operational cells, the controllers, the support operations. And when we have them on that little old spot, Luke, and we aim to"—Goldman had too much air in his lungs for comfort and expelled it in a whoosh through the famous Tatar grin—"we'll take 'em. One sweep. Once and for all. The big net."

"And that's the end of radical opposition forever, is it?" In spite of himself, Garfield felt the heat of inner conflict: the old warrior's bloodlust; the old philosopher's weariness.

"No, Luke," Goldman said soberly, "that's not the end, and we don't expect it to be. It's a gesture, that's all. One gesture. It's a single, simple word said loud and clear so everyone everywhere can hear: *Stop!* It's our way of saying we've had it, of saying, 'Look to us for help, sympathy, support, but don't come blowing up our wives and kids, or we'll destroy you all over again.' "

He fell silent and moved a significant step or two away to distance himself. Garfield had no stomach for laughter, but it came unbidden.

"You know, Fred"—he shook his head—"that must be the most facile, futile, naïve reading of the balance of human affairs I've heard in twenty years. Longer. It makes McCarthy sound like Martin Luther King. I bow to you, I really do. And if that's the shared opinion of your friends the Arrangers, and the president, and your gallant band of freedom fighters, then I bow to them, too, because—God help you all—you're a hundred years too late, man, can't you see that? Two centuries of social engineering, a war of independence, a civil war, two world wars, Korea, and Vietnam—and you're still preaching an eye for an eye? Congratulations, Fred. Really. You take the prize."

Goldman nodded as if they had reached some agreement. "Exactly what I said awhile back, Luke. It's your temperament every time. The Garfield Way or no way. And you wonder why I didn't fill you in right away?" He blew more smoke rings. "You want me to go on? Or shall we leave it at that?"

"Please yourself."

Goldman spread his hands. "Okay, I'll please myself. One other interesting detail came out of the Bonn meet. Miko said he had Larry Bartell under discipline. He said he liked Larry, and someday, if we played it straight and all his dreams came true, he'd hand us Larry on a plate. Just name a place and he'd deliver—but not just yet, he said, because he had plans for Larry; he was central to a very particular play, something Miko'd talk about when the time came."

"And Washington accepted all this naturally. I repeat, what did he really want? What was he after?"

Once more Goldman went very quiet, though not on this occasion to hold down an uneven temper or even to nurse his resentment. Tension; he's building his own tension as he goes along, Garfield thought. Actor. Actor's actor. Like Larry Bartell.

"He wanted what Moscow wouldn't give him," Goldman said. "The status he deserved, the position, the trust."

"You're joking."

"I don't expect you to understand, Luke, but at least do me the courtesy of listening." He paused. "Miko's a psychopath. I don't think there's much doubt about that. He sees nothing irrational in selling out one side of the house to gain an advantage with the other. Nothing wrong. Okay, back in 'sixty-eight he went the Kremlin route, and he made friends, and they love him dearly; but that isn't enough, not for Miko. Any other line of business, and he'd be a candidate member of the Politburo— this is Miko talking, by the way, not me. He'd have everything, a house in the Moscow hills, a dacha on the Black Sea, cars, all that shit—about fifty percent less than he's already got, but that's not the point. Okay. When Andropov became president, Viktor Chebrikov took over as head of the KGB. Andropov's deputy. Worked with him thirteen years, natural successor. He was sixty then—you know all about him, Luke—a timeserver, slightly more enlightened than Genghis Khan, but only just. Standard Kremlinite and no chicken; had a mild kidney condition but otherwise healthy in all departments." The tension in him was now discernible, a growing rigidity of body and voice. "Well, Luke, Comrade Chebrikov faded from the scene a month ago." The sound of the words so charmed him for a moment that he had to stop and listen to their echo in his head. "He collapsed at home. Been in intensive care ever since, kidney

dialysis, the whole bit. He'll never go back; he's finished professionally." Goldman rocked with pleasure, side to side. "His
deputy is standing in for him, and there's a quorum of party
hacks waiting in line for the call, but nobody wants the deputy
as chief, and the Politburo's split three ways on the second-
echelon men. So they, uh, compromised, Luke. They're giving
it to Miko." He waited. "Understand what I'm telling you?
They've appointed Miko caretaker head of the KGB. From May
first, four days away. In four days Miko's going to be up there
on Lenin's Tomb, Luke, watching the big parade. Our Miko."

He couldn't sit still after that. He leaped to his feet and
poured them each another large scotch, then walked a few circuits of the room to get his pulse down and came to the window
to take in the view. Garfield placidly sipped his whiskey.

"And he foresaw all this, did he? Miko the seer. Two years
ago he saw Chebrikov's retirement, the Politburo divided, the
world at his feet?"

"He saw every damned last detail." Goldman enclosed the
universe in one round-arm embrace, spilling a little whiskey in
the process on his black silk suit. "He wrote Sherwood that
letter the day he first figured how it might all work out. If he's
lucky—very lucky—he'll have two or three years in Dzerzhinsky
Square, but the odds are against that, I'd say. It'll be a year.
But he doesn't care about that. People will know. People will
point: There goes Miko Whatever-he-calls-himself. A man. He'll
have it."

"And what was the clincher?" Garfield asked in as bored a
tone as he could muster. "He didn't buy into that race by selling
out his own people. How did he buy in?"

Another world-girdling sweep of the arms, but this time
Goldman was stretching. He squared his shoulders, let them
go loose, in-out, back-forward. He reached for his glass.

"He bought in with Hugh Douglas, Luke." He said it with
pride. "That was the price. In essence that was the whole deal.
Miko gave us something we wanted very badly—a way to the

terrorist center—and we gave him what he wanted most. He needed one big dramatic boost to get the top job, and for that he needed a patsy. We gave him one. Simple exploitation of assets. He waited till Chebrikov was on the brink—that was last October—then he called in the Douglas option. We'd discussed it for months, so Miko just had to give the word. When it happened, it happened quickly, all in three days: Chebrikov had a fall getting out of his car one morning, the next day the Politburo discussed his health, and the day after that they began looking around for a successor. That's when we hit. Miko told Moscow that Hugh Douglas had been appointed a special envoy and was off to Phnom Penh. He said he had a play in mind to sabotage the visit, and he'd like to go ahead with it. They said go. You know the rest."

Garfield raised an objection. "But the film, the film with Bartell in it. Kampuchea, those other places. Why that?"

"Miko's idea. He had no intention of letting anyone claim his laurels after the event. He'd been saving Larry for this one operation—the perfect poetic irony if the story ever got out, an American destroying an American dream. Had the thing filmed for the benefit of the Politburo, hell of a performance. They give Oscars for less."

"And Larry went along with it."

"Larry didn't know half the time what year it was. He did what he was told. It's been that way with Larry and Miko for a long time, Luke. We wouldn't have taken a chance on him otherwise."

"And what about the chance you took with me?" Garfield asked after an age, diffidently, as if the last thing he wanted were an honest answer. "Why come to me to bring Bartell out? I thought I was *persona non grata* with Miko."

Goldman was still standing, still gazing down at the rain-smeared lights of the capital. He seemed not to have heard at first and brushed away an overhanging fringe of curls with a fretful flick of the hand, his face impassive. Then he said slowly, "You might say we were getting a little desperate.

Miko was." He took a long pull at his whiskey and leaned his weight back on the desktop. "You were the lesser of two evils, Luke, put it that way. Bartell had to go; there was a direct link between Bartell, the Poole girl, and you."

"And Miko, of course, wanted no hand in Larry's going."

"He'd outstayed his welcome."

"Outlived his usefulness, you mean. Come on, Fred, admit it. The Douglas play was finished, happily concluded. Bartell was on film in case of accidents. Miko had his moment of glory and more to come, his cup running over. I'd say Bartell was lucky Miko let him go at all." He looked up sharply. "Or has he?"

Goldman was gnawing delicately at his upper lip, all the way up to the bridge of his perfect mustache. "What is it with you, Luke?" he asked conversationally. "A point of honor to make me eat shit?"

"Eat what you like, Fred," Garfield said imperturbably. "Just answer the question."

But Goldman preferred to answer his own questions and had one ready on the tip of his tongue. "You want to know the truth? Bartell could have stayed put, no problem, every luxury. Miko even thought of taking him to Moscow, getting him treatment there, proper care, anything. He likes him, genuinely, he said so a million times. But Bartell? Oh, no—Bartell wants out, Bartell wants to come home; wants what he doesn't have; wants America, Lydia, the kids, everything he threw away. A couple of months after the specialist gave him the verdict—early November this is—he wrote home. Home to Lydia. And not once but three times. 'Take me back, honey, what do you say? Get your old man to use his influence!' "

"Miko didn't care for it."

"Miko was on the razor's edge."

"So let me guess." Garfield shoveled more tobacco into his pipe. "You and Miko put your heads together and set up the Frankfurt meeting. Nice piece of chess play: the coincidence gambit. Miko sends Larry to Frankfurt; you send Todd Hales. Miko tells Larry to position himself out front of the Inter-

Continental, knowing he won't be able to miss seeing Hales, who is, incidentally, an old Harvard buddy and a Company man, the ideal conduit to the inside world. Naturally Bartell falls for it. Sets up that meet by the skating rink, buys the whole package, hook, line, and sinker. But then—and my God, this must've floored you, Fred—Bartell asks for *me*, of all people, Luke Garfield, big man at the State Department, C.J.'s friend, ask him."

"Small price to pay, Luke."

"Yes. Small price. And meanwhile, everyone is proved right. You and Miko particularly. Here's Larry promising to do what Miko always feared he would, spill the beans, get the world talking: names, places, connections. And we all know about Larry, don't we? He's the worst kind of blabbermouth. Larry needs glory, the world at his feet, the VIP treatment. He wouldn't be content with whispering in Langley's ear. He'd want front-page headlines, TV exposure, the lecture circuit— if he lived that long. And we know whose name he'd whisper first: Miko Schellenberg's. Larry, the snake in the grass, selling out his friends for the fiftieth and last time. That must have made you feel a whole lot better."

Goldman didn't like the implication. "It worked out, didn't it?"

"Did it?"

But he'd become immersed again in the ragged prickle of light through the rain.

"I'll ask you again, Fred." Garfield felt his pulse rate rise, its beat pounding in his thigh, his chest, his throat, his head. "Simple question. Does Larry come home or doesn't he?"

Goldman raised his glass and sipped a little whiskey. When he spoke, it was with a wounded innocence that reminded Garfield of the expression on Bloomfield's Christian face just before he pulled the car door shut on him that afternoon.

"Luke, what can I say to make a touchdown with you? Anything? The ten-times-proven truth? Look, without Miko we have nothing. That's a fact. I mean that, no exaggeration:

Without him it's a big fat zero. We need Miko. Do I really have to spell this out to you? He's indispensable, first known case in recorded history. He's everything we've worked for in the past two years and everything we're working for now. It all hangs on Miko, on his sitting down behind that desk in Dzerzhinsky Square next Monday morning. Expose him now, let one breath of any of this get out, the faintest hint of his involvement, on our side of the blanket or his—and he's through, Luke; it's over. The whole deal: the men, the resources, the money, the effort, the time, the planning. And for what? I mean, what are you actually asking me to weigh in the balance against Miko Schellenberg and what he represents? Jesus Christ, you're asking me to weigh the skin and bone of Larry Bartell. A thief. A huckster. A media jackass. A terrorist. Political jackal. Coward. Pimp. Sometime corrupter of young persons. Jailbird. Drunk—currently four fingers short of slugging himself to death with a gin bottle. You want me to go on? He's a criminal, a traitor, a liar and a cheat, a bum and a con man."

"And what the hell do you think Miko Schellenberg is?" Garfield roared.

Goldman had let his cigarillo go out. He tossed it aside and lit another with his fine gold Dupont. "Miko's a winner," he said quietly, taking his time. "You know that better than I do. He's a gambler playing one spin ahead of the odds. He runs the bank. He's got every door and window covered, and they've just given him the roulette wheel. The croupier works for him, and the pit boss is his big brother. What do you want me to say, Luke? That there's a place at every table for losers, too? Every dog should have his day?"

Garfield nodded vaguely, not at Goldman's metaphors, or in any implicit acceptance of his argument, but at some ineffable truth on his mental horizon.

"I want her safe and sound," he said slowly, working hard to keep his voice level. "I want your personal guarantee no harm will come to her."

"You've got it."

287

"I hope so." He rammed his thumb down hard on the packed tobacco and, ignoring the offer of Goldman's Dupont, struck a match and raised smoke for all he was worth. "I urge you— really, Fred—very earnestly, not to let me down. Very earnestly."

He glanced up in time to see Goldman's momentary flight into panic.

"Because I'm something of a gambler, too, if you remember. Old, old hand at playing the percentages. I don't own the house, but I can cheat with the best of them, my friend. Cheat up front, and cheat out of sight. Cheat Miko." He blew out the match with passionate force. "Cheat you, if necessary, without turning a hair."

TWENTY-FOUR

In Lyons they hit the dog.

An omen. For C.J. it was the beginning of the end. All their ends. She gazed on death and, gazing on it, saw clean through the frail tissue of her own mortality and knew she could never be fully alive again.

And things had been going so *well* up to then. So smooth, so fast, so safe, so locked-in secure as the car purred through the night. Larry flat out on the back seat, Happiboy relaxed behind the wheel, relaxed because they'd made Lyons and it was still only 2:00 A.M. He'd come out of his shell just a half hour before, when they swept in under the city lights and the route signs showing Vienne, Marseilles, and Nîmes. "Hey, so far so good," he'd said, and to celebrate: "You can call me H, okay?" Ten minutes later, blasting through the industrial garbage of the south side, he changed his mind: big decision. "If you like, you can call me Al."

He'd been driving for six hours straight—twelve if you counted the time they'd spent switchbacking around Paris on the way to pick up Larry—but he wasn't tired, and he hadn't lost concentration for a minute. It wasn't his fault. It wasn't anybody's fault. It was everybody's.

The car was a big Citroën, the biggest, the kind that looks from the outside like an unidentified flying chafing dish: big, deep seats, whore's bedroom carpeting, quadraphonic sound and cassettes of string orchestras playing a type of wall-to-wall music Larry used to call Mantovarnish. Happiboy had picked up the car in a courtyard garage off the avenue d'Italie, having taken it in exchange apparently for the old van, a handshake, and a half kilo of flour in a plastic bag. A three-minute transaction, no bother. Happiboy later refused to discuss the details, refused to discuss anything, in fact, till they were well past the Auxerre turn, when he finally gave in to her nagging and explained why he'd decided against the express bus to Béziers. The explanation was that he didn't much dig the notion of riding shotgun on a semicorpse in full view of the traveling babbling public, and when she protested that he hadn't been invited to ride anyway, only as far as the bus station in Paris, he went dumb on her. Numb on her. And drove. Fast. The Autoroute du Soleil.

About a dozen times a minute—or so it seemed when she thought about it—she fingered the locket at her throat, a hinged heart in gold enshrining two faces she didn't know from Adam—one man, one woman, midwestern parental—and a nugget of plastic with perforations which Joss called a homer. "It sends out a signal, a sort of constant dial tone. I pick it up and the beat frequency tells me where you are. Roughly." He'd told her not to draw attention to it by touching it, just wear it around her neck, forget it was there, but it had the irresistibility of a sore tooth. In the first two hours she convinced herself it wasn't working. Then, somewhere on the stretch between Beaune and Tournus, the Bentley surged by them like the ghost of Christmas Past. Happiboy promptly overtook it because he was at that stage of the adolescent menopause where practically everything was a challenge to his virility; then, fifty miles or so farther on, it pulled into a Total service station at Dracé Le

Sarron just as they were pulling out, Herbert George Prebble definitely at the wheel; she saw him. But there is a curious sort of camaraderie abroad at night on French highways and a dozen other cars of distinctive marque appeared and disappeared regularly all the way to Lyons. Happiboy didn't seem to be unduly worried by any of it.

Larry made several brief personal appearances during the night, never the same man twice. The first time, not long out of Paris, his face rose up without warning at C.J.'s shoulder, a fearful skeletal death mask made green by the instrumentation lights; C.J. shrieked with fright, and Happiboy sent the car careening wildly across three lanes in sympathetic shock. From there on he dreamed lavishly, occasionally treating them to the sound tracks of some of his more potent nightmares. Once he began singing in a cracked light tenor a song which in its day had carried C.J. heart and soul, "I Don't Wanna Play in Your Yard," and perhaps he imagined he was really singing to her, the long-ago her, for tears started down his face and filtered through the gray stubble to his mouth and bubbled there. The effect was so acutely that of age pining for youth that C.J. had to stop up her ears or scream. But she couldn't cry for Larry Bartell anymore, or with him, or at him. "It's no use," she wanted to shout. "You've finally drained me; you've dried me up; it doesn't work anymore." Later on, with perfect lucidity, he taught a class in the social history of literature at Harvard—flat on his back under a French heaven, two generations out of date, half a world out of place—and finished on a favorite quote, Hemingway's epitaph to Scott Fitzgerald: "It was a terrible thing for him to love youth so much that he jumped straight from youth to senility without going through manhood." Then he broke down and sobbed as children do, as if the world had ended.

On the long approach to Lyons—a ferocious glow in the sky marking the place where it straddled the Rhône—he began an incantation against the powers of darkness, half a speech and half a prayer, delivered perhaps to a very large assembly because at times his voice rose to a shout. Floodgates came into it early on, and Lydia and the children, and the stimulation of the young for profit, and Prohibition and the spread of organized crime, and rock-and-roll and the rape of art, and propaganda politics and the death of truth. Happiboy chuckled deep in his throat as if he'd heard it all before. Then the night lit up, and they ran in under the city limit markers. Larry went instantly to sleep, and C.J. settled back to navigate because Happiboy had told her there was no more badly signposted route in the world than the one that took you south through Lyons. Oh, yes, things were going very well.

They were almost out the other side when it happened, funneling through a wasteland of industrial development where the highway suddenly becomes three highways side by side, overhead indicators pointing every which way, confusing . . .

And at the height of the confusion they hit the dog.

Or the dog hit them.

It must have leaped at least two crash barriers to reach them, and it came too fast for evasive action. Happiboy was looking left. C.J. was looking up, watching for the Marseilles indicator. The dog was looking nowhere. Happiboy saw a blur out of the corner of his eye, no shape to it, just tawny speed, and hit the brakes and swung the wheel. A monstrous bang stove in the door on C.J.'s side and jarred up her arm. Happiboy told her later she screamed so loud he thought she'd been hit; for a split second there it was war, but C.J. heard only the heart-rending yelp from outside, the awful winding ululation, and the crunch of steel on bone.

Then she went to pieces.

There is no stopping on a highway, but Happiboy stopped. He had to because C.J. had flung her door wide open and was on the point of throwing herself out. They ran back together in the scudding rain, but ten yards from the heap C.J. stopped short, and Happiboy went on alone. It was a German shepherd, young, beautiful; he guessed its back was broken, and certainly its legs, but when he hunkered down beside it, the first bite nearly took his hand off. "What are you doing?" C.J. shrieked furiously. "Don't hurt it!"

"There's nothing to do!" he yelled back. Two cars swept by, hooting, flashing their headlights, then a truck thundered past so close Happiboy felt the heat of its exhaust. "We can't stay here!" he bellowed. "There's nothing we can—" But she was standing smack in the center lane, flagging down a truck. "Help me! Help me, oh, please stop!"

That was where it began, she decided later, where the beginning became the end. All their ends. But she couldn't help herself.

The first truck sailed by, then a second, and a third, all in jolly headlight-winking convoy; then Happiboy was beside her, dragging her back to the barrier. "Are you out of your mind?" His face in the streetlighting was a paler shade of green. "You want the whole fucken world to know who you are? What you're doing here? What *he's* doing?" He flung out an arm at the Citroën, then followed it with his eye and saw Larry sitting motionless in the road beside the car. "Oh, for Christ's *sake!*" He turned to run back, but C.J. dragged down on his arm.

"You can't leave it! I won't let you leave it like that!"

He shook her off. "I told you—there's nothing we can do! And we can't stay here!"

She felt the lights on her before she heard the engine: up-down, up-down. What's wrong? they said. What is this? She dropped Happiboy's arm and ran out into the center lane to meet it, flagging it down. Happiboy came after her, then stopped because it was too late; the Bentley was pulling in. Herbert George Prebble leaned out and touched his cap. "*Est-ce que vous avez besoin d'assistance, madame?*" The English way with French.

Happiboy shouted, "We hit a dog. Ran right under the damn wheels." But up close C.J. was whispering, "Oh, please, Prebble, please!" so close she could have thrown her arms around his neck. "Please go look. I'm sorry, I'm sorry, but do something, please?" And she looked in vain through the dark glass for Joss and prayed he'd get out and magic it all away and take her home to the place Vendôme. But of course, he didn't budge. Nothing personal.

Prebble shut her up before she could say another word with a look he reserved for stunning elephants. He called out, "Hold on a tick, sir. I'll give you a hand," and slipped out into the rain and marched quickly down to where Happiboy was waiting. "Morning, sir." He saluted; then they shook hands like Frenchmen. He touched Happiboy lightly on the shoulder and steered him away from the Bentley. "Hurt bad, is it?"

"Nothing you can do," Happiboy said flatly, and waited for the Englishman to look up and see Larry stretched out in the goddamned road, but his attention was fixed firmly on the dog.

"Now then—" Prebble squatted. "What we got here then, my lad, eh?" He placed his hand on a spot over the dog's eyes and the eyes closed at once in gratitude. "That's the style." With the other hand he explored its back and legs; it seemed a miracle to Happiboy the dog didn't take his hand off at the elbow. "Poor young squirt," Prebble murmured and sucked his teeth. "Done for, all right. Shame. Better put him out of his misery."

"You mean?"

"Short and sharp's the word. Find the right spot. Same with men, eh? Kill or cure." He stared up at Happiboy. "Old soldier yourself, sir, I bet." His hands were massaging the dog's neck, deep into the tawny ruff, reaching and feeling, talking all the time, talking Happiboy down, talking the dog down.

"How can you tell?"

"Soldier myself once, sir. Always tell." Reaching, feeling for the spot, kneading, anesthetizing. "Coldstreams. Twenty-two years. Regimental sergeant major."

"Pfc," Happiboy said, watching the hands mesmerically. "Hundred and First Airborne. Vietnam," he added, as if that explained everything.

"That's the way." Prebble agreed and then very quietly: "Just move around a bit, sir, stand between me and the car. No need to upset the little woman, is there? Short and sharp. No messing."

Happiboy moved to oblige and, glancing quickly along the road, saw that C.J. was now talking to someone sitting in the rear of the Bentley. Christ, he thought, you stupid goddamn crazy bitch! Why not broadcast your life story over the Voice of America?

"That's the style," said Prebble. "Now he'll probably kick a bit, but that'll soon be—" He did it before either Happiboy or the dog could second-guess him. A quick lift and a twist, the tiniest click of bone detaching from bone, a high-pitched yelp, and it was over. For a moment the body kicked in a paroxysm of nervous reflex, then lay still. "There now." Prebble dragged the body under the crash barrier. "Leave him be. Out of sight, out of mind." He straightened up, dusted off his hands, pulled on his gloves. "Hope your little lady's not too upset, sir. But if I don't get back to him, it's a cert my governor will be. Late already." He held out his killing hand, and Happiboy shook it.

It was at this point they realized they were no longer alone.

When they turned, the young man smiled, a very nice engaging smile. He touched the roll of newspapers he was carrying to his yellow forelock. "Didn't like to interrupt, gentlemen. You seemed to have the situation well in hand." He stood like a boxer, Happiboy thought, slightly forward on the balls of his feet. The belted raincoat gave him a dashing look. What part of America the accent came out of, though, he couldn't guess, and what the hell were the newspapers for?

Prebble recovered first. "No problem, sir, thanks all the same. Little accident, all over." He turned to Happiboy. "Well, we'd best be getting along, sir. Drive carefully now." And with a finger to the peak of his cap he marched back to the Bentley, smart as a parade horse. Happiboy noticed he didn't shake hands with C.J. when he got there and wondered briefly if it was because she was a woman or because he placed civilians in a class above himself; then he looked back anxiously at Larry and, too late, remembered the boxer.

"Thanks," Happiboy said flatly.

"Your friend okay?" The man idly flicked his newspaper baton in Larry's direction.

"Had a couple too many, you know how it is. Taking him home."

"Going far?" The grin was friendlier still, but Happiboy was getting vibes about the accent that made the old wound in his gut come on like napalm burn.

"No, not far. Thanks anyway." To ring the curtain down, he shouted to the girl, who was still standing by the Bentley. "Hey, sweetheart, come on, will you? It's late."

When he glanced around, the young man was still grinning. He touched the rolled newspapers to his forelock again in sardonic salute. "Well, as long as you're okay," he said, and strolled back to a car parked just ahead of the Citroën, a dark Mercedes, one of the stretch limousines they use for funerals and state occasions. He climbed in and the car pulled smoothly away.

"I'm sorry," C.J. said when she caught up with him.

"Just don't talk to me," Happiboy said, peeling Larry off the tarmac. "Just fucken forget it, will you?" He fed Larry into the back seat. "I must be crazy. I could be home now. I could be asleep."

Larry cried out, "Where is he? Where is he?" But they had no answer to that and locked him in and got back in the car.

Happiboy took off like a hare, his anger feeding off his troubled vibes; but the Bentley made a somewhat more dignified start, and they soon lost it. By the time they crossed the bridge at Solaize they'd left its headlights several miles behind.

"What were you talking about?" Happiboy demanded twenty minutes later, one eye on the rear mirror.

"I wasn't talking. I was . . . apologizing." She was too angry to feel shame.

"Who was he?"

"Oh, some old man. He was tired."

"Where's he going?"

"He didn't say."

"I bet. And what did you say?"

"I said we were on vacation. Touring."

"And that was it?"

She had a tremendous yearning to paint prophetic pictures of an elderly Joss running down the Autoroute du Soleil to join his not-yet-elderly wife and lover C.J. at their villa in Nice (no, not Nice, too built up, somewhere old and romantic, maybe Beaulieu), but she pulled back from the temptation.

"Don't do this again," he'd told her, opening the Bentley's rear door far enough for her to see his face, the ice forming on it. "Go back there, and do as you were told." It's all changed, she tried to tell him, his name's Happiboy, and he won't leave us alone, but Joss seemed to know all about Happiboy and was in no mood for semantics. Why? she thought, listening to him, watching his long brown face harden. Why don't you like me? Where does the chemistry go wrong? What do I have to *do*? "I want to talk to Garfield," she'd blurted, interrupting him, and he said he'd just talked to Garfield and his instructions were to carry on, swim with the stream. "I can't swim," she'd joked, but he hadn't found it at all funny, and at that moment she heard the dog yelp and guessed what Prebble had done.

The end began.

The end began around 3:00 A.M. on the escarpment above Vienne, where the highway runs below a palisade of exotic villas built to command the lake view. Happiboy had had his foot down hard for the climb and at the top eased off to meet the speed limit.

"I can't," Larry groaned from the back seat.

They ignored him.

"H, goddamnit," he called out again.

"You talking to me, Larry, or is this more fucken stream-of-consciousness crap?"

"H, listen—I have to!"

"You talk to him," Happiboy ordered C.J. brusquely. He

still hadn't forgiven her, and she was too proud to plead, so they just sat there hating each other.

"What do you have to do, Larry?" She turned to look at him over the seat. He was flat on his back again, rocking with the pitch and roll of the car.

"I have to go to the can."

"Well, now, isn't that just peachy!" Happiboy exploded. "Listen, you miserable bastard, if you think—"

"You'd better stop somewhere," C.J. said tartly. "I won't be held responsible if he—"

"Jesus Christadelphia! That's all I need! All right, then, check the Michelin. See if there's a stop coming up."

"There is. It was on the sign down the road just now—some-place called Saint Rambert-d'Albon."

"Okay, we'll go there."

"It's twenty kilometers."

"Tough!"

The place was closed. *Fermé*, said the circular sign as they came in off the approach road, and Happiboy thumped the wheel in frustration because it was too late to pull back. "He'll have to go in back somewhere," he raged. "Goddamn asshole!" The road fed into a wide service area with seven separate islands side by side under a single winglike roof, twin gasoline pumps and a glassed-in cash booth at each island. Off to one side lay a repair bay, and right ahead a café-restaurant and a small glass-fronted specialty shop. All closed.

Swearing under his breath, Happiboy pulled up on the central island and lugged Larry out of the car. Half walking him, half dragging, he set off for the café, then stopped and waved back at her. She rolled down the window. "What?"

"Switch the damn lights off, and get in the driver's seat. When I give you the high sign, come on over. You think I'm gonna drag this bum an inch farther than I have to, you're crazy."

She watched him try the door of the café, the door of the shop. Then he slung Larry under his arm and hauled him down

a concrete path to the back of the development. They disappeared, and C.J. slipped across behind the wheel. Cautiously
she drove across the area and pulled up outside the café; then
her puritan instincts took over, and she pulled the car around
till the café was behind her. Privacy; they deserved privacy, at
least. She doused the lights, and the night closed in on her
like a blanket. It unsettled her, the sudden silence, and in self-
defense she switched on the radio. An announcer for France
Inter came on, reading the news at thirty thousand words a
minute. Still, he was company. A voice. A person. Oh, Joss,
wherefore art thou? She fingered the locket. From me to you,
mister: blee-bleep, blee-bleep, I need you. Do . . . you . . .
read . . . me . . . buster? Sorry I fouled up, but I'm not a moun-
taineer like you or an old soldier like Happiboy. I'm adrift, like
Larry. I'm a—

Without knowing why, she glanced across at the passenger
window: a magnetic tug, nothing scary. And a face rose in it like
a rising sun. First a cap, a flat cap with a peak, then a wide,
square brow, then a pair of round, lunatic eyes, then a flattened
nose and a jaw with a yellow Vandyke beard. Except the beard
was all one with the hanks of yellow hair that fell to his
shoulders, and he was grinning so hard it must have hurt. Why
can I see him? she thought faster than thought. Why? Then
two explanations tied for first place: One, he was holding a
flashlight under his chin to frighten her, and two, when she
wound down the window to talk to Happiboy just now, she'd
forgotten to wind it . . . UP.

He lunged in the same split second she pulled the shaft into
drive, but he was still fast enough to get his hands on her. Huge
hands, terrible gross, rubbery hands with—

She nearly blew the engine trying to run with the brake on;
then she connected and released it and blasted off, straight at
the service islands. What made it worse was the noise, the
terrible keening, blaring storm in her head, which she later
identified as her own screaming, and, behind it, the mechanical
hur-hur-hur of his laughter and the grating sound his boots

made as she dragged him along, half in, half out of the window. He was still grinning—God, she couldn't stand it!—and she knew he'd grin if you hit him and grin if you killed him and grin when he killed you. The service islands whirled up out of the dark—God help me, where are the lights? the car has no lights!—and she swept through a gap somehow, and pulled the wheel hard over, and the centrifugal force threw his body out and up high and wide, and he cackled, screeched with pleasure. Back again—oh, you bastard! oh, my God!—back through the service islands and—

Suddenly he disappeared. A thump as something fell. A crash, and he was gone. She switched on the lights and wheeled around again, pumping the horn: Happiboy! Happiboy! For God's sake!

But if Happiboy was around, she couldn't hear him, and she couldn't see him, because in all this darkness she was the sole source of light in the world. No light existed anywhere except where she shed it, and for the moment she was shedding it on the madman. He was picking himself out of an avalanche of empty oil cans, and she registered him whole. Flat cap, red checked shirt, denim work jacket and jeans, boots, work gloves. He was still grinning and went on grinning when she drove at him full tilt to kill; then he hurled himself aside with ludicrous ease, grinning still. She was turning again, turning, turning, when a pair of headlights struck her sideways. Swinging to meet them she saw a tanklike truck lurch out of a belt of trees— a Toyota Land Cruiser—then the madman running for it, leaping up onto the running board as the truck came for her. Foot flat to the floor, she sent the Citroën screaming between two service islands, then hard around again, and the storm in her ears was worse than ever—her screaming, higher and higher. Once she thought she saw Happiboy—a racing shadow—but there was nothing he could do if it was him and nothing she could do if it wasn't. Live alone, die alone, Larry always said. Damn you, Larry. Go to hell.

It had become a game: The first one to run for the highway

was it. This can't go on, she thought frantically. It has to stop; somebody'll come; I'm tired. But nobody came, and it didn't stop, and her throat ached. On one circuit, the Toyota's reinforced grill caught the Citroën high on the rear window arch, and C.J. felt cold air and shards of something sharp peppering her hair. The second time they hit her on the turn, and the impact almost rolled her over. Recovering, she swung and swung again, doubling and redoubling in and out of the concrete islands, and for a moment she felt she was winning, they didn't have her maneuverability, she could stay ahead—just. They switched tactics. She was sideslipping, rubber screaming, out of one bay into the next, when the Toyota came at her from the side, at an oblique angle from way out in the parking area. At forty miles an hour it plowed through a glass cash booth, flattened both pumps, leaped the service island, and hammered the Citroën's tail as it squeaked through. In her rage C.J. screamed and swung the car completely around; but they had her number now, knew her weaknesses, and there they were again, smashing through another pay booth to cut her off.

The truck missed her by the skin of her life, and the momentum carried it way out. It turned in a long, shuddering arc, and C.J. thought—or persuaded herself long afterward that she'd thought—okay, that's it, I give up. She made an aimless run for the repair bay, was actually contemplating what she'd say to them, when the Toyota suddenly bucked left-right-left like an unbroken pony and swerved away from her. Almost at once its windshield shattered, went magically white from the center outward as though a sheet had been thrown over it. Then it hit a service island head-on and rammed its way through. Halfway along, its belly grazed the island's raised curb and set up a spiral of sparks that rose into the night like a flock of fireflies. Then the whole car seemed to shudder once, a giant coughing, and a thin blue flame rocketed out of the ground to a height of twenty feet or so, and expanded, and burned bronze, gold, white in swift succession, and finally grew a mantle of smoke that climbed and climbed into the night-made-day.

C.J. narrowly missed the repair bay door as she turned in a long, wide, screeching circle around the flames and at last saw Happiboy. She drove over to him, she didn't know how, and just sat there, shuddering, while he shoved her out from under the wheel and dumped Larry, sacklike, in the back.

All she remembered for a long time after that was Happiboy saying, "What did you do, for Christ's sake? What in hell did you *do* to those dinks?"

But she was out of range before an answer occurred to her. Out of range and out of reach.

The middle of the end was a narrow street in a town of narrow streets that could have been a film set for *Grimm's Fairy Tales*.

But she didn't see the streets yet. Waking, she saw white-washed walls of stuccoed plaster and a white-painted low-beamed ceiling, and a set of *Elle* covers from the fifties framed in split cane. The window—a poky little casement window—was open, and a curtain of Italian voile swayed in the breeze. Down below she knew there was a walking street because there were no cars, no mopeds, and she guessed it was night because the blocks of light spilling from the window onto the bed lay perfectly still, the color of cream.

Later she learned that the town was Montpellier and not an hour away from their exit point at Cap d'Agde down the coast. Home, Happiboy told her, bringing her orange juice and coffee and promises of food, rest, and long life. She'd slept the day through. It was nine in the evening, and the plan was to leave at three in the morning, hit the boat by four-fifteen at the latest, bed down again, and put to sea at three the following morning. "No jet lag," Happiboy said. And the miracle was complete, he said—come on, move it, chop-chop—for Father Larry was downstairs playing Queen of the May, regaling the family circle with his bon mots. The last of which had been—and Happiboy was quoting—"Where's my girl?"

Where's his girl? She bathed and dressed and did her hair

and wasted a lot of time sitting in the window seat, looking down on the people and trying hard not to think of last night. She had an idea Happiboy had made the same decision himself. We should quit now while we're ahead, she thought. We're mad.

The family circle proved to be a professor of economics at the university, his German wife, and their three children. He was a long, thin Hamlet with a Solzhenitsyn beard, no mustache; she was Gretel in braids and flounces. Gilles and Helga, friends of Larry's, pleased to meet you, and who remembers surnames, yes? But Happiboy had lied about Larry. Larry was out. Larry was drugged or dead or dreaming in a folding wheelchair at the table, a bubble of froth in one corner of his mouth and a look in his eyes that C.J. had seen before in paintings of dying saints. She might have taken this in her stride at any other time, but for Gilles and Helga. For some reason they didn't seem to have noticed their friend was all but unconscious.

Over supper, all their conversation was directed at Larry. "Isn't that so, Larry?" And "You knew her, didn't you, Larry?" And "Come, Larry, another glass," when the glass in front of him remained untouched, the food uneaten, the questions unanswered. In the yawning silences between, Gilles and Helga apparently heard unspoken responses because they prattled on without a break, while Larry's hands hung in his lap like claws and his shoulders fell over his chest like folded wings. "More cheese, Larry?" "Coffee, yes?"

C.J. held on to her sanity by considering a more practical line: How many people knew Larry Bartell by his real name? What kind of professor do you have to be to have Larry for an intimate? She tried to signal these questions to Happiboy, but Happiboy wasn't playing.

Over the runny Brie Gilles confided his small problem. A nuisance, he said—and reached out to lay a knob-knuckled hand across Larry's shoulders—but there was actually a small demonstration planned for tonight, you see, a *petit boum*, so to speak, organized by the student body and a few committed members of the faculty—Youth Against the Bomb. The children would be marching, too. A torchlight procession, speeches, banners, and later, on the Esplanade, jazz and bonfires and a promenade. A fine night and a full moon, great good luck. But unfortunately he was duty-bound to lock the house before leaving—a precaution necessary these days—so perhaps Larry and his friends would care to sit out in the place de la Comédie and watch the proceedings. Yes, starting at midnight.

For the first time Gilles directed his question at Happiboy, who shrugged noncommittally and nodded and stared down again at his plate. C.J. fingered the locket at her throat and thought of the dead Alsatian on the highway at Lyons. The dog had marked the end, she knew it, the beginning of the end; the rest was a death rattle, and nothing anyone could do would change it. But she said nothing either.

Gilles brought out a map and with a red ball-point pen traced the route to Cap d'Agde. To begin with, he said—addressing Larry again—the highway was out; God forbid they should try to use the Languedocienne after their experience of the night before! Nor for that matter could he recommend the coast road between Sète and Agde; it was too open, too obvious; all that open beachfront and nowhere to turn. No, the best route was the most roundabout one. He sketched it in with his red ballpoint: the D986 to Ganges; yes, indeed, a long way but safer. *Safer.* Then, from Ganges, this narrow little byway wandering up into the mountains along the Hérault gorge. Then through Saint Guilhem-le-Désert to Gignac, and on to Pézenas and Florensac and Agde. With the full moon, beautiful! Quiet. Pass one *voiture* in twenty kilometers, and it's a miracle. A full three hours to do it in. Leisurely.

Yes, nodded Happiboy, still dumb, and Gilles took him through the whole thing again.

Watching him, watching his ugly white hands and his fat red ball-point, his braided wife, and his attentive flaxen-haired children, C.J. felt the sickness growing in her, a sickness unto death, inexplicable. "And here, and here, and here," he chimed, in his absurd Charles Boyer accent. But the long face under the Hamlet hair and the silly beard had nothing to declare on the subject of life, death, and loyalties, and C.J. ended by praying the same old prayer: Oh, God, send Joss a fast blee-bleep.

The streets were built for Grimm, and the tone was melo-dramatic. To give effect to the hundreds of hand-held torches, the town streetlighting had been dimmed. Walls and lampposts were plastered with dire warnings of nuclear hell on earth, and from overhead wires across the cobbled walkways, life-size figures swung from hangmen's nooses. Farther on, in a tiny square, medieval mourners stood in silent communion around the coffined body of a beautifully dressed, very much alive little boy.

They walked in a bunch around Larry's wheelchair, Gilles pushing, Helga and the kids behind, and as they walked, bands of grotesque mutes raced by, young men and women in the torn habits of pacifism and the black/white painted faces of protest. A few raised clenched-fist salutes when they recognized Gilles, but he ignored them.

Gilles left them at a sidewalk café in the place de la Comédie; handshakes all around and "I pick you up twelve-thirty, yes?" C.J. gave him a thirty-yard start, then told Happiboy why she thought he was lying. "Sure he's lying." Happiboy was rolling a slim joint.

"Well, what are you going to do about it?"

Happiboy lit his joint. "Give him another fifty yards, then get the hell out of here." He glanced across at Larry. "I knew it was a mistake to listen to this bum. You hear me, *bum?* When he came around last night—after the fun and games at the service station—and said to come to Montpellier, to his god-damn buddy in Montpellier, I thought: Ignore the bastard, say nothing, just go where you're supposed to go. And—"

"And you didn't."

"No."

"Why?"

Happiboy glowered at her over the table. "Because I'm stupid. Because I think with my brain instead of the seat of my pants."

"You also think he knows best. You said so. Last night."

"I say a lot of things I don't mean."

"Say something you do."

Happiboy got up. "Let's go."

They talked it over, logically and rationally, and then they drove the route Gilles had suggested. The logic of the booby hatch, the rationality of the blackjack table. They were driving it three hours ahead of schedule, they reasoned; they were a whole day late, and Joss was bound to be waiting at the boat, the natural fallback, and C.J. couldn't face another night on an open highway, it was totally out of the question, sorry.

What she didn't tell him was that it wouldn't matter in the end what route they took, though after the first hour this premonition lost some of its sting, for the road was as empty as Gilles had said it would be, and the hills as lonely as polar icefields. In the moonlight everything was white. The green of forest and fern gave way to chalk and limestone, cols and towers marched out of the night like hooded monks, and beyond Ganges, as they climbed higher still, the gorge of the Hérault opened up like a sword slash in the earth, and on the bends they could see the river rushing and spuming eighty feet farther down through centuries of worn rock. In flashes, through gaps in the hills, they saw the pinpoint lights of Saint Guilhem-le-Désert perched on its mountain, and the abbey of yellow stone floodlit on its precipice. Then the road swung down and began to wind with the river.

C.J. knew it was coming, as surely as if a voice were chanting it in her ear. Here, she thought, now! They were taking a long left-hand curve littered with minor rockfalls from the spring rains, and as the road bent back on itself to become a tight right-hander, powerful headlights jumped to full around the bend ahead of them. Happiboy had dropped his speed to twenty and now reduced that to a crawl; then the full force of the lights caught him, and he lost vision. C.J. screamed, "No, don't stop!" as he stamped on the brake; then the engine stalled, and the door was plucked open from outside.

"Out, please." The voice was pleasant, relaxed, even kindly. "Switch off, Mr. Straker. That's it, thanks."

Happiboy had put a face to the voice before he squeezed out into the road. "Well now." The young man still wore his raincoat and his smile, still carried his roll of newspapers. Behind him stood a broad, short anvil of flesh in a homburg, but it was the youngster's party, no question about that. He opened the rear door. "Miss Poole, you mind getting Mr. Bartell's chair out the trunk?" And one-handed he dragged Larry feetfirst into the road. Without a word of protest, C.J. did as she was told. Watching her, Happiboy was reminded of dinks he'd known who had walked patrols three clear feet above the ground on dreamdust. "Thank you." He was so polite, this guy. "There you go, Mr. Bartell. That comfortable?" He fussed over Larry's lifeless limbs, arranging hands and feet this way, that way. "Now, if you'd go stand over there by Mr. Stegelmann, Miss Poole? Obliged."

He turned to Happiboy. "Just check you out, you don't mind, Mr. Straker." He came forward, already bending, to frisk Happiboy from the ground up, and that was when Happiboy made his mistake. He made no conscious decision to do it; it was a slow and witless, half-hearted move that started out a whole second too late to be effective. But it taught him something, something that had been bothering him since the night before on the road in Lyons. He made his lunge, outward and downward, going for the throat, fingers stiff in the killing mode: the roll of newspapers came up from below, end on, and struck him under the heart. It dropped him where he stood. For a moment he lost vision, breath, all consciousness. Then he heard the voice above him, still pleasant, not in the slightest way put out. "You'll be fine, Mr. Straker. Just let me help you up, that's great, that's fine, and sit quiet in the car, okay? Okay."

Happiboy was vaguely aware of C.J. slipping into the seat beside him, and when he found the strength to look up, Larry was disappearing into a cloud of all-enveloping light, pushed this time by the helpful Mr. Stegelmann.

"You mustn't let them take him," he heard C.J. hiss in his ear, but he couldn't think of a sensible answer to that.

"Do you hear what I say!"

But only the pleasant young man heard what she said, and he leaned in at the door and smiled his detachable smile. "I heard what you said, Miss Poole, and you're wasting your breath. Just sit tight. We won't keep you long."

The cloud of light dipped suddenly, then came on full again, and the young man nudged Happiboy into position behind the wheel. He shut the door. "You listening, Mr. Straker?"

Happiboy mumbled.

"Then listen carefully. You, too, Miss Poole. You make a three-point turn and drive back the way you came. Drive nice and slow, you get me? One hour to Ganges, turn right, and another hour at least to Montpellier. Okay, go."

"Wait a minute," C.J. began, "what happens to Larry? What are you—"

The young man touched the end of his newspaper baton to the skin of Happiboy's throat. "You'll be met in Montpellier, Mr. Straker. Go back to the café in the place de la Comédie, and there'll be someone waiting. Miss Poole knows the party. Friend of Miss Poole's. Right, Miss Poole?" He banged hard on the roof twice. "Now go, Mr. Straker. Go."

Larry heard them pull away, saw the flash and blip of stoplights as Happiboy shunted the Citroën around, heard the final hiss of power as they left him alone. He heard Miko shout something—in what language? Miko had so many—then Rostov strolled over in his Saks Fifth Avenue Humphrey Bogart raincoat and switched off the lights.

Miko bent solicitously over Larry's shoulder. "Is better now, Lerry, the dark? Sure. Remember I tell you before? Strong light, strong language, strong drink: all no good. Aaah, Lerry, why you make so hard on Miko?"

Rostov came to stand behind him and Miko had one of his turns. "No! No!" He fluttered his little hands like a bird in the rain. "Go away! I talk first. With my fren Lerry. Alone!"

"Yes, sir. But we need to be out of here in five minutes, no more."

"Five minutes." Miko chortled. "Hey, Lerry, you hear this boy? Whole lifes is five minutes. We know, huh? you and me. When you born, five minutes is hunred years. When you dying, is nothing. Sure. You tell this boy, Lerry."

Larry assumed he was required to deliver a nugget of wisdom at this point, but he'd lost the gift of speech. Hey, Miko, why are we talking dead? Who's dead, Miko?

Miko sat himself on a low wall. Somewhere below, wild water sang hymns to the rock.

"You know how many years, Lerry? You and me, how many years we go? Is too many, that's how. Too many for frens not trusting each other. Your trouble, Lerry, is you don' ever grow up, absolutely. You don' get unnerstanding. You see; you hear; you never learn. But, hey, listen, I forgive you, I completely forgive you." He had arranged himself at Larry's side and now suddenly reached for Larry's hand. "I don' feel pain no more, Lerry, you know that? I get hurt so many times, I don' feel pain no more. Always I want people be happy; I want make peace; I want everybody loyal. So what happens? They walk on my head. I give my life twenny, thirty times over to different peoples and finish up always the same: They walk on my head, Lerry. I give loyalty. I give you personally loyalty, more than anybody. I give you presens. I give you girls. Wine I give you, and frenship. You get sick, I give you doctors. What more to give, Lerry? You want the blood in my veins?" He got up, his little hands flying in high emotion. "Why the first time I take anything from you has to be your life, Lerry?" he shouted. "Explain me why!"

But the only explanation he got was the echo of his own words, volleying back from the mountainsides.

Miko sighed and took hold of the chair. He turned it with difficulty, away from the car, away from Rostov and Stegelmann. The low stone wall curved off the road and became a bridge wide enough for a truck to cross. On the far side the mountain rose steeply. To the left a mud track cut through a stand of young trees to a clapboard inn. To the right another track climbed up and around a shoulder of rock. Below the bridge the river bawled and rioted in its rocky bed.

Footsteps sounded behind them, someone coming up fast to help—Stegelmann? Rostov?—but Miko would have none of it. "No!" he shouted. "Go! Go back! Is my fren Lerry, okay? You think I don' have no feelings?"

Miko got his friend Larry's chair rolling again, and they moved onto the bridge. A stone bridge, Larry noted, built to last five minutes or a hundred years, depending on whether you were coming into the world or leaving it. Personally, he had no feelings either way. No feelings at all, in fact. None in his legs, none in his gut or chest or arms or neck or—well, maybe a little in the head, the odd pulse here and there of divine electricity. How are you on divine electricity, Miko?

"Is sad for me, Lerry. You unnerstand what I'm telling you? Is very, very sad. You think I get satisfaction losing a fren? Is that what you think? Well, listen, I tell you a good secret, Larry: Real frens is gold. I know. You would stay my fren, Lerry, and I give you everything because I so close now, Lerry. Close to the biggest time in my life. I go to Moscow, Lerry, you hearing me? I have the top of all there. I wanted take you with me. The top, Lerry. Moscow!"

From the dark Rostov called out, "Time's up."

Miko bent over him. Larry could feel Miko's nearness, Miko's fatness, Miko's violet-flavored breath on his cheek.

"Lerry, you stand up for Miko now, hey? Jus' once."

Larry wanted to laugh. Wanted to shout. Wanted to hear the

mad cadences of his laughter crash down from the rockface. Just once more, Larry. Help the man one more time.

"Sir?" Rostov, anxiously from the car.

"So wait! You damn wait!"

And he bent to Larry again and took a forearm in each daintily gloved hand. What are you wearing tonight, Miko? The royal blue? The equerry's gray? The brown? My eyes are dim; I cannot see.

"Here, Lerry. Now. Jus' once. Come, Lerry, come."

He did it for Miko. For you, Miko, he said with his eyes, and willed heat and life and the breath of passion down into the blocked-off arteries and felt a surge of tension fill him, starting from the feet up. He rose painfully on Miko's arms and heard Rostov shout quite urgently, "Just a minute, sir! Wait!" and start forward at a run, three paces, four. And Larry set both feet on solid earth and looked down from a misted heaven on his friend Miko.

"Lerry, good. Now you jus' stand there for Miko and—"

But Larry Bartell had lost all need to stand right there for Miko. He gathered his last spark of will, his last failing breath of energy, and fell into Miko's arms and, in falling, hurled his bagged bones at Miko's chest and felt him stumble, felt him check and stumble again, and turn, and waver, and overbalance.

And fall.

Then the pain took him for a long, long ride into the creepy, painless dark, and soon he felt nothing at all but free.

Cool, loose, and free.

TWENTY-FIVE

They parked the car under an acacia swarming with butterflies and took lunch in the restaurant overlooking the ravine, a great, airy, clattering barn of a place full of children and loud French weekenders. The tablecloths were paper, and you kept the same plate for all three courses—fish, meat, and salad—but the food was a delight and the wine plentiful. Too plentiful. Polly steered clear of it on principle, but Luke drank close to a liter of the local paint stripper.

Afterward they climbed the hill because he insisted, though he was in no shape for it by then. They sat down halfway up to the old town, and Polly took a picture of him sitting on the wall, the abbey above and behind him and the crumbling little houses and the waterfall plunging down to a fetid pool.

"It belongs in a picture," she said, going back to him. "One of those old paintings—what kind do I mean? Sort of religious."

"Pre-Raphaelite." He grunted with effort as he got back to his feet. He knew she was playing her ignorant-me game, and he knew why—he always knew why—but today he didn't want it. Today was different. She took his arm. "I wish we'd brought the car. I'm beat. Shall we go back and get it?"

"No!"

They walked on, and Polly returned to a conversation they'd abandoned in the plane on the way down from Paris. "I wish you'd try again with C.J. Honestly, Luke, she's—"

"We've been through this. She's a big girl—said so yourself, several times."

"Sometimes even big girls need help. Big boys, too."

He glared at her. "Is that meant to include Joss?"

A car pulling a trailer drove by, and they had to cling to the low wall to give it room. Polly remembered the bridge and the river crashing eighty feet below, and the whitewash marks the police had splashed on the stonework to show where Larry had gone over. She clung to Luke unnecessarily hard.

"Yes," she said with spirit, "it does. Look, he's a pleasant enough boy, I'll give you that. But he doesn't *need* her. He doesn't love her either. I doubt he even *likes* her. He's seeing her because of you. Because of Larry, what happened here. And it'll break her heart when she finds out."

"She's better off in Paris for the time being."

"I don't argue with that. Professionally."

311

"Professionally is all she's got," he snapped grumpily, blowing now like an old whale. "Prisoners of Conscience is made for Paris. It wouldn't stand a chance in Washington. Not anymore."

"I want her to be happy! Is that too much to ask?"

"It's too much to ask for yourself, let alone for somebody else. Give her time. Give them both time."

"Yes." She sighed. "Well, at least they have time." A thought that effectively killed further conversation until they reached the top of the hill.

The village had been built by one of Charlemagne's generals and for longer than anyone could remember had lain deserted. In the sixties, though, the flower children had found it and come to live, and paint, and sculpt, and make music in the broken dwellings, and now it was verging on the chic. The parking lot was full of tour buses and the little square a mesh of holiday color.

But the cemetery was deserted. It lay under the yellow stones of the abbey between vegetable gardens and the town hall. It was very small, and evidence of recent burials was hard to find. Larry's grave was small and neat and well cared for, but modest. Luke pointed it out when they were still some yards away. "There, that one."

"With the gray marble?"

"That's right."

"But isn't this a Catholic cemetery? Shouldn't he—"

"He said he didn't care. Any ground would do."

"He *said*!"

"In his will. Oh, he left a will, all right. He was pretty conservative in the end, old Larry. Left a will, a little money, his books, records, a couple of chess sets—good ones—and instructions for his burial. If he had one."

"Who had the will?"

"Oh, some woman he met in Switzerland: Iranian woman. She saw to the details. The grave, everything."

They reached the plot. Garfield walked around the headstone to the foot of the grave. "You know something else? He even wrote his own epitaph. It was right there in the will. How he wanted everything done. Type of marble, everything."

"Oh?" She saw the twinkle in his eye and felt a momentary unease. "What does it say?"

"Come and see."

"No. You . . . just read it to me."

"Come and *see*." He held out a hand to her, and very reluctantly she went to him.

The laughter shocked her—because of its loudness, because of the place, because it was hers. "Oh, my God." She clapped a hand to her breast.

"A local mason did it," Garfield said, grinning at her. "I shouldn't think he knew what it meant."

And they stood hand in hand and read it again:

Here lies
LAURENS TADEUZ EISENSTERN
Chess player

COME BACK, LARRY—
ALL IS FORGIVEN

FRANK ROSS is the pseudonym of an English writer and journalist who has spent the past ten years living and working in Europe and Africa.

A *Conspiracy of Angels*, his fifth suspense novel, results from many months of personal research among what he describes as "radical elements" in France, West Germany, Italy, and Spain.